Tony Warren is a former actor who turned into Britain's youngest scriptwriter. In 1960 he created *Coronation Street* and wrote all the early episodes. He has written three previous novels, *Foot of the Rainbow*, *The Lights of Manchester* and *Behind Closed Doors*. Tony Warren lives in Manchester and continues to be a consultant to *Coronation Street*.

Also by Tony Warren

Foot of the Rainbow
The Lights of Manchester
Behind Closed Doors

FULL STEAM AHEAD

Tony Warren

ARROW

Published by Arrow Books in 1998

1 3 5 7 9 10 8 6 4 2

Copyright © Tony Warren 1998

Tony Warren has asserted his right under the Copyright,
Designs and Patents Act, 1988 to be identified as the author of
this work

First published in the United Kingdom in 1998 by Century
Arrow Books Limited
20 Vauxhall Bridge Road, London SW1V 2SA

Random House Australia (Pty) Limited
20 Alfred Street, Milsons Point, Sydney,
New South Wales 2061, Australia

Random House New Zealand Limited
18 Poland Road, Glenfield
Auckland 10, New Zealand

Random House South Africa (Pty) Limited
Endulini, 5a Jubilee Road, Parktown 2193, South Africa

Random House UK Limited Reg. No. 954009

A CIP catalogue record for this book is available
from the British Library

Papers used by Random House UK Limited
are natural, recyclable products made from wood grown in
sustainable forests. The manufacturing processes conform to
the environmental regulations of the country of origin

ISBN 0 09 925181 7

Typeset by Palimpsest Book Production Limited,
Polmont, Stirlingshire
Printed and bound in Great Britain by
Cox & Wyman Ltd, Reading, Berks

For Gordon and Marguerite McWilliams
with love

Lines from 'Sea-Fever' by John Masefield are reprinted by kind permission of The Society of Authors as the Literary Representative of the Estate of John Masefield.

Lines from 'Lord Finchley' by Hilaire Belloc are reprinted by kind permission of the Peters Fraser & Dunlop Group Ltd.

Lines from 'Lover Come Back To Me' by Sigmund Romberg & Oscar Hammerstein, © 1928 Harms Inc, USA and Warner/Chappell Music Publishing Ltd, London W1Y 3FA, are reprinted by kind permission of International Music Publications Ltd.

1

Sorrel Starkey and Mickey Grimshaw had come a long way from Irlams o' th' Height. That was the village where they'd both grown up, four miles to the north of Manchester. And here they were, swanning around Belgrave Square, in the back of a navy-blue limousine provided by Mickey's London publishers. These days Mickey wrote novels. But it was *Angel Dwellings* he was thinking about, 'Britain's Classic Soap Opera', that's what it always said on the souvenir mugs and the jigsaw puzzles. How many years was it since he'd invented the thing: thirty-three, thirty-four?

Sorrel must have been thinking something similar, their thought patterns often coincided. 'If you hadn't written a show about a Salford tenement, we wouldn't be sitting here dressed up like two ham bones.'

'Do I smell of dry cleaning?' His morning coat and striped trousers had been hired especially for the occasion.

Sorrel leant over and sniffed, 'No. Well only a bit. It surprises me you haven't got your own.'

'I've not got my own because I don't go to weddings.' Though he had his mock-lofty voice on, he was only partially joking. 'As I'm not a breeder, I don't find it necessary to attend their tribal rites.'

'Oh shut up,' she said easily. 'Anyway, you came to my wedding. You even gave me away.' And then she wished she hadn't mentioned that because it had brought dear dead Barney to mind. And this morning she was trying not to be the grieving widow; this was Mickey's big day and she was there as a leading lady accompanying the man who'd made her famous.

Their limo had been forced to slow down in the heavy traffic but Mickey was more interested in an imposingly porticoed house in the middle of a long cream Belgravia terrace. 'Isn't that the spiritualists' headquarters?' he asked Sorrel. Though they came from the North they both knew London well. In fact, in their youth, they'd once shared a mews flat just around the corner from here. 'Wasn't your friend June drummed out of the spiritualists' union?'

Just as he'd meant her to do, Sorrel rose to the bait. 'She wasn't my friend at all, it was my mother who called her that.' Friend? In her time June had managed to seduce Sorrel's first husband and steal her dog. Actress and author had both known the gaudy psychic since all three of them were eight years old. Known her and loathed her.

The car began to move forward again as Mickey said, 'This waistcoat they've sent me has no back to it – just a strip of very cutting-in elastic. I feel as though I'm held together with paperclips. Isn't it funny how June's vanished from the headlines? At the time of the scandal she was never out of the papers, and now you don't see her name from one year's end to the next.' Without pausing he added, 'You look very nice Sorrel.'

Mickey's compliments always flew in as importantly as something arriving by private aeroplane, but they didn't come often so Sorrel decided to savour this one. She'd gone to a lot of trouble to look good for him; she was wearing a slate-coloured silk coat and white gloves, and a wide white hat – with the brim turned back just far enough to please the press photographers.

'Of course I was the one who taught you how to dress,' he continued blithely. And for the first time that morning she felt like smacking him. Not bad going when you considered that it was already ten o'clock. The man with the odd eyes – one blue and one green – was dearer to her than any brother and every bit as maddening!

As the navy-blue motor car edged its way towards Buckingham Palace, watery spring sunlight reflected off the lake in St James's Park.

'Just look at all those daffodils,' said Sorrel.

Nature was always wasted on Mickey. 'Never mind

them; just look at all those people gawping at us.' He said it in tones of deepest satisfaction. There was no false modesty to Mickey Grimshaw. As a small boy his ambitions had always been full of the expectation of moments like this one. 'Would you be startled if I wept?' he asked.

'If you wept I'd send a hundred pounds to Comic Relief! My God, some of the fans have even come down from Manchester. Look, there's that pair who always hang around outside the studio gates.'

One woman detached herself from the crowd gathered at the top end of the Mall and tapped urgently on Sorrel's window. The chauffeur, more used to the style of literary luncheons than to the ways of fans of *Angel Dwellings*, pressed the button which lowered the glass pane.

'Hiya, Lettie.' Sorrel's public always referred to her by the name of the character she played in the soap – Lettie Bly. 'We're ever so glad you've dyed your hair back to red again.' Other sightseers were joining in. 'It is.' 'It's her from the *Dwellings*.' 'Why hasn't she got the new dog with her?' By now the ringleader had her head right through the window. 'Congratulations, Mickey,' she shouted toothlessly. 'You've brought pleasure to millions.'

That's my *real* reward, he thought. That beats any medal from the Queen. But Sorrel removed all tender sentiment from the moment by bawling, 'Watch your head, Missus – the window's electric!'

'The window's electric,' Mickey mocked, as they began to move forward again. 'You can take the actress out of the *Dwellings* but you can't take the *Dwellings* out of the actress.'

'Yes and just look where it's got her!' retorted Sorrel, happily. They were already sailing through the opened gates of Buckingham Palace. And now the car had been flagged to a halt by a policeman. 'And look at those sweet dogs.' Springer spaniels were leaping around the Rolls Royce in front of them.

'They're sniffing for Semtex,' explained the chauffeur.

'I'm so glad we left our bomb at the Savoy.' Mickey shifted his top hat from one knee to the other.

'Behave, Mick,' hissed Sorrel.

'Why? It's precisely *not* behaving that's got me here. If I'd done all the dull safe things my father had in mind, I'd never have landed up on the New Year's Honours List.'

'Well at least be a bit impressed.'

'I'll be impressed when we get to see something you can't see through the railings.' The car swept beneath an arch and into a gravelled courtyard. A liveried official was standing on the steps of the palace with a long list in his hand – just like the Lord Chamberlain in a pantomime. 'I'm impressed now,' said Mickey. But she had already taken to worrying whether all the sitting had creased the back of her new silk coat.

'Who is the recipient?' intoned the official.

'I am.' Mickey helped his star down from the car. 'Is there a Ladies inside? Excitement always goes to Miss Starkey's bladder.'

'Up the stairs and on the right. You are to proceed up the other staircase, Sir.'

Sorrel felt herself seized by mild and unexpected panic. She didn't quite know what she'd been expecting but it hadn't included being parted from Mickey this early on in the proceedings. This entrance hall was so *grand*. Why, the crystal chandelier over her head was bigger than the house she'd been born in. And then the flunkey cut everything down to size by murmuring, 'I shouldn't really ask this but would it be all right to have your autograph?'

The picture gallery was on the first floor of the palace. Mickey felt as though he had walked into the head-quarters of Raphael Tuck, the quality greetings card manufacturers, because almost every picture on the walls was already familiar. Charles the First and his horse were magnified to such a size that they reared right up to the lofty ceiling. But the original of a world-famous Venus proved to be no bigger than the top hat which Mickey had been obliged to leave in the cloakroom.

The writer eyed the assembled crowd. He had often read about 'the great and the good' and if these were they, they were a distinctly nervous-looking lot. The Edwardian smell of mothballs hung in the air. Mothballs and dry cleaning. Most of the men in morning suits looked like civic dignitaries. The only good-looking ones seemed to be in naval and military uniform.

The city aldermen were making the kind of conversation that Mickey supposed strangers in a golf club might attempt. They were noticeably not talking to him. This reminded Mick of his schooldays, when he'd always been the last boy to be picked for any all-male team. Not that it had ever depressed him much because, when girls were doing the choosing, he was generally snapped up quite quickly. This had led the other boys at his mixed junior school to assume that he was going to grow up to be a big hit with women.

Since then the world had become more sophisticated. Many of the men here would have seen Mickey interviewed on television, heard him say that his early open homosexuality was the driving force behind his whole career – the thing which had caused him to have to try harder than his straight rivals. Bold statements of that kind came at a price: the most social intercourse being offered to him in the royal picture gallery was nervous sideways glances.

Mickey was unconcerned, he was quite used to it. Had the same men been accompanied by their wives, he knew that most of them would have been perfectly well-disposed towards him. As it was, they were wary of striking up a casual conversation, in case other men mistook them for gay.

'It's not often you see Jesus in his hat, is it?' Looking like somebody's well-loved cleaner who'd been dressed up for a wedding, the woman who had addressed him was pointing towards a Rembrandt of the Garden of Gethsemane. 'My feet are killing me.' The tones were purest Liverpudlian. 'I wanted to wear my comfy shopping shoes so I could really enjoy myself. But my daughter-in-law insisted on dragging me into Dolcis.'

Mickey allowed that, yes, he was 'him who wrote it' and thanked God for women.

Another woman, one who seemed to be dressed as a General in the Red Cross, seized the opportunity of joining in. 'Has anything been said about curtsying?' She had popping-out eyes, like a bulldog.

'Not yet.' The little Liverpudlian started to laugh. 'Curtsying? That's the last thing I thought I'd end up doing when I volunteered for Meals on Wheels!'

The bulldog General had moved right in on Mickey. 'I know you.' She said it almost accusingly. Here we go, he thought. She wants a bit of gossip about the show.

'I once met you with June Gee, in Birmingham.'

Birmingham, with terrible old June? He supposed it was possible. Yes, he'd been doing something for ATV and she had dragged him off to one of her demonstrations of clairvoyance – in a hall at the Botanical Gardens.

'She was a very wicked woman.' The popping eyes looked ready to burst with indignation.

'She *did* go to jug,' protested Mickey, mildly. And then he wondered what on earth he was doing defending June. 'I hadn't thought about her in years, and that's the second time she's been mentioned today.' In Mickey's experience, this generally led to the person turning up.

From the far end of the gallery a voice called out, 'If I could just have your attention for a moment please . . .' The man addressing them was as gracious and as stately as his frogged uniform – the perfect person to be standing in the middle of a room that boasted a white marble fireplace on every wall. He was there to make sure that everybody was properly instructed in how to behave in the royal presence. Mickey found the phrase 'You will know when the Queen has finished speaking with you' slightly ominous.

Those due to receive knighthoods would please gather at the top end of the room. Mention was then made of the Royal Victorian Order. Companions of the British Empire were put on stand-by. It seemed that the OBEs and the MBEs were still free to play amongst themselves.

Left to their own devices the crowd relaxed a little. But the courtier's speech had inspired class-consciousness and Mickey Grimshaw MBE finally understood the true meaning of the phrase 'the lesser orders'.

'Aren't you the man who invented *Angel Dwellings*?' Would people still be asking this in the queue on Judgment Day?

'I am.' Not that he'd mind answering any questions put by such a traditionally tall dark and handsome naval officer. In fact there were two of them, and both were beaming at him.

'Thought it was you. You won't remember us but we once had a drink together, in Aunt Charlie's, on Turk Street in San Francisco.'

Well, well, well, thought Mickey. We *are* everywhere! Aloud he said, 'We're putting out to sea ourselves this afternoon. Sorrel Starkey and I are sailing for New York on the *QE2*.'

Trust that Mickey to have gone and asked for her to be given directions to the loo, thought Sorrel. By now she was seated on a spindly little cream and gilt chair, one of the hundreds arranged like theatre seats in the palace ballroom. At the other end was a raised dais, but Sorrel automatically thought of it as 'the stage'. Red velvet drapes hung down from a huge canopy, decorated with painted medallion portraits of Victoria and Albert. Of their great-great-granddaughter there was, as yet, no sign. Punctuality might generally be held to be the courtesy of kings but the Queen was running late.

Still, there was plenty to look at: Yeomen of the Guard, and Gurkhas in green uniforms with black patent leather pillbox hats on the sides of their heads, lined the back of the rostrum. And a royal stage manager had already bounded on to tell everyone that they should be ready to get to their feet when the royal party eventually entered.

The music changed to 'I'm Going to Buy a Paper Doll That I Can Call My Own' and Sorrel remembered a tenor in white tie and tails singing the song, in a pink spotlight, in a show called *Look Who's Here*, at the Blackpool Opera House. That was the year she first met Mickey – on holiday. And they'd been startled to discover that they came from within half a mile of one another.

'I'm going on the stage.' He'd said it with absolute certainty, even then. And she, who had always shone in Sunday School concerts, had finally learned that it was possible to do this for a living. It was Mickey who'd pushed the pair of them into radio *Children's Hour*. He who'd found the flat they lived in when they were first trying to make it onto the stage in London. And when he turned into a writer, ignoring the fact that they were no longer supposed to be on speaking terms, he had coached her himself for the audition for the part of Lettie Bly. Quite simply, Mick had always been there. Why, he'd even introduced her to Barney.

I mustn't cry, she thought, as she remembered her lovely dead husband. Not here. But pushing one thought aside had caused Sorrel's mind to lurch into another – the thought which had never been far from the forefront since . . . I'm not going to think about it, she told herself. There's nothing I can do for at least a week. I'm going to put the whole problem out of my mind.

This might have been easier said than done had the music not changed to the National Anthem. The Queen and her party finally took their places on the dais. She was wearing what looked like a very ordinary but serviceable woollen jersey dress from Marks & Spencer. But the blaze of diamonds on one lapel shrivelled any criticism to ashes. Take it or leave it, she wasn't just a queen, she was an empress.

Not for nothing had Sorrel once appeared in a production of *The Sleeping Prince*. Extending her arms and turning her hands into something that would have done credit to Anna Pavlova, she sank into a deep court curtsy. And that was the moment the actress knew – with absolute certainty – that her knicker elastic had just snapped.

'Your turn next,' said the official. And Mickey began a final rehearsal inside his head: out to the dais, four steps forward, bow . . . Why was the music changing to that tune? If there was anything guaranteed to wreck him, it was 'I Dreamed a Dream'. The song reminded Mickey of his miserable childhood, of planning to escape by going on the stage, of promising to turn Sorrel into a star. It also brought to mind a recent and disastrous stab at romance. Christ, he thought, I feel like Judy Garland near the end!

'Mr Mickey Grimshaw: MBE for services to television drama.' He'd made them change the citation from 'Michael'. Mickey was the name of the person he'd invented for himself.

The walk to the dais took longer than he'd been expecting. Then came the four steps forward. Wasn't she tiny? My goodness, *Spitting Image* had been good at their job. But the eyes that were looking straight into his own were as canny as any he had ever encountered. Quick at summing people up himself, Mickey had finally encountered somebody who was even quicker.

The Queen had a handbag over one arm, an attendant held the medal at the ready. 'So pleased you could have it,' she said. The words sounded like a recorded message. And then she enquired, 'Do you write *Angel Dwellings*?'

'I don't write episodes any more, Your Majesty, but I did invent it.' She seemed to be expecting him to say more. Searching wildly through his mind he came up with, 'Your Majesty will remember that she once paid us an official visit.' Was that even grammatical?

'Oh I remember that, I remember it very clearly.' The Queen sounded almost indignant, as though he'd been testing her suitability for a place in a retirement home.

In one deft movement she hung the medal on the

specially provided hook in his lapel. In the next, she took his hand, shook it, and gave him a little push which sent him on his way. He was so startled by this shove ('*You will know when the Queen has finished speaking with you*') that he quite forgot his final bow. As he marched towards the archway on the opposite side, he told himself that he must remember to teach Sorrel that tiny dismissive movement – she could use it on over-lingering autograph hunters.

And now he was out of the ballroom and a man was removing his medal and clapping it into a leather-covered box. 'Congratulations, Sir. Perhaps you would like to sit at the back until the investiture is over.'

In next to no time the National Anthem was being played again, the Queen had nodded and smiled her way off the stage, and Sorrel was heading towards him with a guilty look on her face. He knew that look of old; it generally meant she'd blown a scene in the show. And instinct told him that she was being hotly pursued by a reporter. The newspapers in here?

'It's a man from the Press Association,' she hissed. 'It seems they're allowed. Darling Mick,' she added in happier tones, 'I wept buckets.'

He quickly checked for mascara streaks. No, she was too professional for that; she must have thought to use waterproof, 'We have to look lovely for the photographers.'

'We have to get rid of this man.' She said it out of the side of her mouth.

'Sorrel, what have you done?'

Standing on tiptoe and putting her mouth to his ear, she whispered, 'I lost my knickers.'

The man from the Press Association was right up to them by now. 'Could I just have a word, Miss Starkey?'

'I'm afraid she's lost her voice,' decreed Mickey.

'She hadn't a minute ago.' He sounded very accusing.

'It comes and goes,' pronounced Mickey, airily. And for perhaps the ten thousandth time, Sorrel understood why she'd always let him boss her around. 'I'm doing the talking for her today,' he said firmly. And with that he manoeuvred Sorrel and himself into the crowd heading for the exit.

'He'll definitely turn up again outside,' she warned him. 'And you know what they're like these days, they'll print anything.'

'It's not as though your mother's still alive,' Mickey paused to sign an autograph. 'I presume you want Miss Starkey's too?' As the actress scribbled her signature on the back of somebody's official invitation, he said to her, 'Anyway, today's the day we run away to sea. And they don't have tabloids on the briny!' That was the moment he suddenly found himself struck by an enormous thought. 'Autographs, Buckingham Palace, the QE2, Sorrel, do you know what we've done? We've made it happen. We've turned into the people we thought we wanted to be when we were little.'

'What did she say to you?' And where were they going for their celebration lunch? That's what the other reporters, the ones who'd been kept waiting outside in the quadrangle, wanted to ask Mickey, when he and Sorrel finally emerged into daylight and exploding flashbulbs.

'We're going somewhere we haven't been for thirty-five years.'

Sorrel had been curious enough to join in the questioning herself. 'Where?'

'If I told you, it wouldn't be a surprise.' He had already instructed the chauffeur to be ready to take them to St Martin's Lane. As the car began to round Trafalgar Square, the new MBE said to the woman he'd made famous, 'We're going to Olmi's.'

'Olmi's? But it's just an old Italian caff.'

'Think back to our youth, Sorrel. Think back to the days when we could only afford their spaghetti and their ravioli.' In the 1950s, Olmi Brothers' San Carlo Restaurant had been the haunt of every out-of-work performer in the West End. 'Remember how our envious little eyes would stray to the bottom of the menu.' Mickey had assumed the tones of an old-fashioned port wine and plush velvet actor. 'Chops,' he proclaimed. 'Succulent lamb chops. And steaks, yum-yum. Today, Sorrel, you may have anything you want. Today I'm giving you the freedom of Olmi's menu.'

But when they got there the cafe had gone. And in the back of the car they went straight into a big argument as to where it had originally stood. 'See that bar over there,' said Sorrel, 'the one called Brief Encounter. It was there.'

'Wrong. It was further up.'

She had been too excited to eat breakfast so she was ready to grab at any straw. 'Perhaps Brief Encounter do refreshments.'

'It's a gay bar.' Mickey's tones were scathing. 'If we went in there dressed like this we'd be sent up rotten. They'd probably ask us to sing a selection from *My Fair Lady*.'

'I don't mind gay bars.' Gnawing hunger was uppermost in her mind. 'And, God knows, you could do with a new boyfriend. We might just manage to kill two birds with one stone.'

Mickey immediately went steely on her: 'You don't think I'm aware that you've been keeping a major secret from me . . .'

'Olmi's was always veal,' said Sorrel quickly. 'And I don't eat veal. You should have remembered that.'

She was definitely prevaricating. And cars behind them were sounding a blast of protesting horns. 'I can't stay here much longer, Sir,' said the chauffeur.

'Then take us back to the Savoy. And whilst we're there we can change into something a bit more suitable for a life on the ocean wave!' Mickey's moods had always been changeable as quicksilver and now he was suddenly gleeful. 'I've got a brand-new blazer. I'm going to look a bugger in it – like an old chorus boy from *No, No, Nanette*. What do you propose travelling down in?'

In the end she settled for a scarlet jacket and cream tweed slacks. The Savoy furnished them with a packed luncheon, the chauffeur stowed their luggage in the boot, and the dark blue Jaguar began to make its way towards Southampton.

'Aren't we lucky?' said Mick. 'If we hadn't starved when we were young, we wouldn't be able to appreciate all of this.'

Sorrel was having a second go at the Savoy's smoked salmon sandwiches. She was also being stabbed by a fit of conscience, 'Mick . . .'

'What?'

'I shouldn't have joked about finding you a new boyfriend. Not so soon.'

He sang a melancholy snatch of 'I Dreamed a Dream', and then he said, 'It's okay. There's no fool like an old fool. But I always knew what I was getting myself into. The one thing that really annoyed me was that he chose to sleep with somebody else, behind my back, on my own good bed.'

Though Mickey still had an apartment in San Francisco, he was talking about the unhappy events which had spoiled any affection he might once have felt for his little house outside Manchester. 'Joe and I had five good years, but they're over. And I'm not going to try again. Star's mate, it's an impossible role to cast!'

He didn't need to explain any further, Sorrel knew all about the difficulties of celebrity and personal relationships. Knew that the people who came running were often the wrong ones, that those who held back because you *were* famous would probably have been the most likely candidates for anything lasting.

Not that she was looking for anybody herself. Barney had been enough and more. But the idea of Mick going through the rest of his life on his own did not appeal to her. 'You'll find somebody,' she said. 'Why, you might even have a little shipboard romance.'

'Did you mean to sound just like an old black-and-white Jessie Matthews musical? Screw romance! In the future, I'll have a happy social life with my friends. And if I want sex, there'll always be willing hustlers. Stop looking so shocked, Sorrel, I've never pretended to live in any kind of imitation of heterosexual life.'

She licked her fingers and said, 'I just hope you don't go round telling other people this.'

'I wouldn't have told *you* if you hadn't dug.'

'Hustlers!' The way she pronounced the word brought the late Edith Evans to mind.

Mickey's rocket went straight up. 'I'm not talking about unhappy little rent boys on the corner of Bloom Street in Manchester. Proper hustlers have always held a respected place in gay society.' He hadn't intended it to sound as pompous as it did.

He's unhappy, she thought. I should just sink back into all this dove-grey upholstery and leave the whole subject alone. Instead she said, 'Fancy even thinking of paying for it!'

That did it. 'Tell me your precious secret, Sorrel.'

'No.'

Her tone was, for once, enough to warn him off. This really did have to be something serious. Surely she couldn't have started drinking again, on the sly?

Sorrel pushed aside all thoughts of her own problems. It had been a mistake to show she had been shocked. But even after all these years, whenever Mickey Grimshaw lifted the veil off his private life, she was startled by the differences between the gay world and her own. And he wouldn't have revealed anything at all if she hadn't gone and poked her nose in! Conversations of this kind generally ended with Mickey saying, 'You haven't got a dick, Sorrel, so you wouldn't understand.'

Today he said, 'I'm getting too old.'

Filled with contrition she asked, 'You mean you can't do it any more?'

'Of course I can do it!' Mickey was almost shouting. And then he put a finger to his lips and pointed to the back of the chauffeur's head.

'He's probably got the phone number for the *Sun* in his top pocket,' murmured Sorrel, who'd been caught that way before.

14

'No I haven't,' said the driver, calmly.

That's going to have to be a big tip, thought Mickey as the actress began to burble a little speech of apology. And I'll make her pay her half of it! The car, which had been travelling along a road between upland meadows, turned a corner and began to descend.

'Ships!' cried Mickey joyfully. 'Beautiful magical ships.' And in exultant tones he began to quote John Masefield,

> '*I must go down to the seas again, to the vagrant gypsy life,*
> *To the gull's way and the whales way where the wind's like a whetted knife . . .*

'And look! See that red funnel? That one's ours.' He sounded as uninhibited as the day she first met him. 'I love the *QE2*,' he enthused. 'Love her. She's my grown-up Blackpool.'

The porters, who whisked their luggage from the boot of the car, looked like ferocious brigands. 'They're your last glimpse of brutal reality,' said Mickey, as they stepped into a reception area which resembled an aircraft hangar with carpets. 'From here on it's *de luxe* all the way. Unless you're seasick,' he added cheerfully. 'Not that queue, Sorrel. Not unless you want to exchange our cabin for something in the bowels of the ship. We have to check in at the desk marked Grill Rooms.'

This was a queue which was distinctly shorter. 'I'm not sure I'm up to this much privilege,' said Sorrel. 'I've only ever been on one other ship. It was called the *St Tudno*. We spent the morning going round the bay at Llandudno.'

The woman ahead of her was dressed in black from head to foot. Slightly dusty black, Sorrel was surprised to note. She only had a rear-view of the dumpy passenger: gaberdine suiting and scuffed black patent leather high heels, and a curiously strong and sweet aroma which

Sorrel hadn't smelt for years – a perfume called 'Joy' by Jean Patou.

'I'm afraid you're at the wrong desk, Madam,' the Cunard clerk was saying. 'This ticket is for a Mauretania Restaurant cabin.'

'Not so grand as us, two sittings,' Mickey murmured in explanation to Sorrel. Had he been a paying passenger himself, he would have given the Mauretania very serious consideration – Mickey had always been fond of a bargain.

'Nice to see you again Mr Grimshaw.' The man behind the desk detached the top layer of their tickets. 'And good afternoon to you, Mrs Shapiro. Perhaps you'd both like to go upstairs and register your credit cards.'

'I thought you were supposed to have got it all for free,' said Sorrel, as they moved towards an escalator.

'Not drinks on board. Not things you buy in the shops. Cunard aren't *that* generous.'

'But he called me Mrs Shapiro and my credit card's in the name of Starkey.'

'I already faxed them to explain about stage names. Let's get some newspapers. The *Evening Standard* might just have us at the Palace.'

But it didn't. And when they got into the credit card queue, they were assailed by another blast of 'Joy'. This time the perspiring woman was in the next line-up, and once again she was encountering a problem. 'Stella Artemis,' she was saying to a uniformed official. 'I'm known as Stella Artemis.'

'But that name isn't on the passenger list. May I see your passport?' The pair of them went into a confidential huddle.

What a mess of an inside of a handbag, thought Sorrel. Mickey was thinking that the woman looked like a Pekinese with high blood pressure. By now both his own credit rating and Sorrel's had been checked out, and they had been supplied with Cunard's own platinum cards – valid for the duration of the trip. Having been told to take a seat, they moved to try to find some and Mickey said, 'That very scented woman had the worst face-lift I've ever seen.'

'It was a lift and collagen injections.' Sorrel turned round cautiously to get another look. Seen as whole, in long shot, there was something familiar about the figure. It was as though somebody Sorrel had once known had been set upon with a bicycle pump. The height was unchanged but the rest was cruelly bloated. And the curls, escaping from beneath the draped black jersey turban, looked as though they'd been dyed with Zebo grate polish.

'My God,' breathed Mickey. 'It is. It's terrible old June Gee.'

'And it's not five minutes since you said that we were bidding good-bye to brutal reality! No, it can't be her. She would have said something.'

'Just like we did? No, June didn't say anything because last time she billowed into my life I threatened her with New Scotland Yard.'

Sorrel was still watching the dyed brunette pick her way towards the tweed sofas in the glass bay of this upper waiting room. The ship was moored just the other side of the windows. You could see uniformed stewards leaning over the rail, and individual lifeboats hanging above the windows of staterooms. 'You're right. It is June and she's certainly not lost her radar equipment. Look how she's settling herself next to the best-looking man in the place.'

Mickey took in the situation at a glance: 'June Gee meets Jack Lawless!'

'Who's he?'

'One of the most massive porno stars of all time.'

If this was the case, Sorrel thought she'd better stop staring. 'Gay or straight?'

'That's always been the million-dollar question. He's made both kinds of films, but those guys are in it strictly for the money.' Mickey was suddenly sparkling with a wicked brand of anticipation that she hadn't seen in him since his love affair fell to bits.

17

'Mickey, you wouldn't be so stupid! The tabloids are bound to have spies on a ship this size. You're really much too famous . . .'

'And much too old.'

'I didn't say that.'

'No, but you thought it. And quite right too.' Then he began to twinkle again. 'Some of those porn stars are the most tremendous hustlers.'

She knew he only said these things to get her going. At least she *hoped* she knew it. Sorrel risked stealing another glance at the man on the sofa. Jack Lawless was presently refusing a cigarette from June's squashed packet. He looked like a whole load of American film stars rolled into one: a hint of Elvis, a bit of Tom Cruise . . . 'The person he's most like is the young Tony Curtis in *The Sweet Smell of Success*.'

'See how June quivers in the waves of testosterone!'

A Tannoy pinged and then a disembodied voice said: 'Passengers holding embarkation cards numbered two hundred to three hundred and fifty may now board the ship.'

Sorrel had worn flat heels in the expectation of a wooden gangplank with rope handrails. The reality proved to be much more like getting on an aeroplane. You went down a carpeted tunnel where passengers were obliged to pose – momentarily – for the official photographer.

And then: 'Is this it, are we actually on board now?' Sorrel asked Mickey. But he was already embracing a dark-haired woman whose badge proclaimed her to be the Social Secretary. Surrounded by red-jacketed stewards who were also wearing white minstrel gloves, she was reminding Mickey of some escapade from a previous voyage – when they'd gone looking for flamingos in Namibia.

'And all we found were sand flies,' laughed the woman. Sorrel made a show of joining in the general hilarity, but she couldn't shake off the feeling that everybody must be able to spot her as someone who'd only ever sailed round the bay at Llandudno. Of course I've been to a lot of other places by plane, she told herself. But somehow that didn't seem Admiral Benbow enough for round here.

Now the social secretary registered a portly married couple, resplendent in 'his and hers' blazers and white drill trousers. The woman even sported a neck-scarf decorated with ships' ropes and anchors. 'Welcome back to the QE2, Mr and Mrs Hodgkins.' She beckoned the most mature-looking steward and said, almost reverently, 'Take this lady and gentleman to the Queen Mary Suite.'

Sorrel and Mickey were left to find their own cabins. 'It has to be admitted,' he said, 'that there is a lot of subtle class-consciousness on board.'

She wasn't at all sure that she was going to be good at this. But it must have been catching because Sorrel found herself saying, 'We're on Two Deck, aren't we? Is that meant to be okay?'

'Bang in the middle of first class, not *too* posh, but it still gets us a table in the Britannia Grill. And all I have to do in return is two lectures. Come on, we take this staircase.'

It led them up to a spectacularly long corridor where Filipino deckhands, in very clean red boiler suits, were man-handling luggage into the little hallways between pairs of cabins. Sorrel could feel a gentle thrumming under her feet, and disorientated passengers were milling around, peering at numbers on doors.

'2124 we're looking for,' said Mickey. 'It must come in the next gap.' It did.

'We've no keys.'

'They'll be on the dressing table. They always are.' The idea filled him with simple pleasure. Pushing open the cabin door, he crossed the threshold, looked around and said, 'Haven't we done well for ourselves? It's true the decor's a little butch for you, Sorrel, but that comes of the deal having been done in my name.'

The sizeable double cabin was panelled in walnut. Two portholes cast light onto a writing desk, and there was a fitted dressing table, opposite the wide twin beds.

'Where do we hang things?'

'There should be a big walk-in wardrobe, next to the bathroom. Oh look, somebody's already sent us invitations.' The envelopes were on top of a folder marked *Information for Guest Lecturers*.

Outside on the corridor, a public address system quacked: 'Would Mrs June Gee please report to the purser's office. Mrs June Gee to the purser's office immediately.'

'What was that other name she was using?' Mickey was already running a finger down the list of lecturers.

'Stella something.'

'Stella Artemis, here she is. A lecture every day and *not* in the theatre. She's tucked away in the Golden Lion pub. How are the mighty fallen! "Your Stars and the Sea",' he read out. '"Love Secrets of the Great Pyramid." Think back to the days when she was doing her so-called clairvoyance. This is the same woman who once persuaded an archbishop to stand up on the platform with her at the Royal Albert Hall. Is that somebody at the door? Come in,' he called out.

The young man who entered was blond and handsome, and wearing a black jacket, striped trousers and a follow-the-sun tan.

'David!' shouted Mickey, happily. 'Now I do feel I'm back on board. David's one of the restaurant managers,' he explained to Sorrel. 'We once got hijacked together. It was by an Arab taxi driver in Agadir.'

Before Sorrel could start feeling too out of things again, David was properly introduced. He quickly pronounced himself a massive fan of hers. 'In fact I grew up with a photo of you and Spud the dog over my bed.' This was said with a marked Scots accent. Sorrel was fascinated by the way he called Mickey 'Sir' in one breath and 'Hen' the next. It showed superb professional understanding of the personality of the guest lecturer.

David, it transpired, was here on official business. 'The captain's wife presents her compliments, and would you care to join them at their table.'

'I'll ring her,' said Mickey.

'You'd better.' His tone confirmed that he was a friend.

'I did like him,' said Sorrel, after he'd gone.

Mickey was already busy with the telephone, asking to be connected with Mrs Burton-Hall. And then, after a pause: 'Rosemary? It's me. Hot passion has come back into your life! Listen, thanks for the invitation but if you don't mind I'm going to say no. The thing is, if we sit with you and John we'll be obliged to behave beautifully. Sorrel's very good at that sort of thing but I was hoping to be a little bit wicked this voyage.'

An amused voice breathed into his ear, 'Not *too* wicked Mick, please.' Mickey was left listening to the dialling tone as he reflected that Rosemary Burton-Hall, who had once been an actress, still knew the strength of a good exit line.

But his own leading lady had taken umbrage. 'I know I'm only an also-ran on this trip, but you might at least have asked what I'd like.'

'I've saved you from what you wouldn't like. They're smashing, but they have to be polite to everybody who chooses to come up to their table. You'd lay yourself wide open to grabbing fans.'

Even as Sorrel was inwardly acknowledging the sense of this, Mickey attempted to take further control of her life by saying, 'Listen, Sorrel, I want to rehearse you again in the Queen's most useful little shove . . .' But he didn't get chance because somebody else was knocking on the cabin door.

'Come,' yelled Sorrel who had lived in too many dressing rooms to waste words.

Nobody entered. It was Mickey who flung open the door to reveal a little woman who . . . he put a brake on a snobbish thought. But it had been there and he was ashamed of it: the diminutive figure on the threshold of the cabin did *not* look a *QE2* passenger.

She had an obviously new perm and twinkling National Health glasses – the old-fashioned kind with clear pink plastic frames. 'I thought I'd just come and see who me neighbours was.' The voice was purest *Angel Dwellings*. But she didn't look the sort who'd come on the borrow;

more the kind of neighbour who'd tell you to knock if you were in need of anything.

'It's *you* isn't it?' she beamed at Mickey. 'You was on the one o'clock news at Buckingham Palace. Congratulations, lad, bloody well done!' For a moment she looked around almost guiltily. 'Can you say bloody here? At these prices I should think I can say what I damned well like!' Happiness shone out of her face as she looked up at Sorrel in wonderment. 'Eeh,' she cried, 'it's worth it already. But I mustn't intrude . . .'

'No, do intrude,' said Sorrel. Thirty years of stardom had taught her when it was safe to say that.

'Have some of this complimentary champagne,' suggested Mickey.

'No thank you. I don't want to spoil me tea . . . dinner,' she corrected herself. The guilty expression was back. 'I'm not sure I'll ever learn all this.'

'None of it matters.' Sorrel was resisting an insane urge to put her arms around the little woman in the royal-blue jacquard-weave frock that shouted 'catalogue'.

Their visitor must have noticed where Sorrel's eyes had landed. 'Could you tell me something. What's a "regular" dress?'

'Come again?'

But Mickey was ahead of her. 'You've been looking in the Daily Programme, haven't you?' Previous voyages had familiarised him with the style and wording of this publication. 'Tonight's listed as informal, and if you check at the front . . .'

'It says that it means "cocktail or regular frock".'

'It's a bit bossy,' said Sorrel.

'It's a lot bossy.' She certainly didn't lack spirit. 'I'm Mrs Fiddler.'

Handshakes were exchanged all round and their new neighbour came to a decision. 'I'll just have to wear me best black.'

'And I'll do the same,' said Sorrel firmly.

'Then I'll see you at the feeding trough. Will you be sporting your new medal?' she asked Mickey.

22

'Not tonight.' Instinct told him that she was dying to see it but that she wasn't pushy enough to ask. He pulled the flat black box, marked MBE, from where he had stowed it, in an inside blazer pocket. 'There.'

'Ooh!' Mrs Fiddler hadn't even taken hold of the silver-gilt star on its deep pink ribbon, but she was suddenly behaving as though somebody had pricked her with a pin.

'Are you all right?' asked Sorrel, anxiously.

'Never better. It's his hand,' she was nodding towards Mickey. 'How many people have you shook hands with between the Queen and me?'

'Nobody,' lied Mickey. And Sorrel instantly forgave him a lot of his trespasses.

'Well this *is* a different world! I'd better go and take a stiff brush to that frock. Black's always awkward when you've a dog in the house. I'll just have to do me best,' she was already heading for the door, 'and angels can't do more.' She was gone.

'Mick, how on earth is Mrs Fiddler affording all of this?'

' "Win the Holiday of Your Dreams", that's what I've got her down as.' He was already opening his invitations.

'And she's not my *size*.' Sorrel had sounded almost angry with herself. 'She's obviously not going to have the right clothes and there's nothing I can do to help out.'

'As Queen of the North of England that is, of course, your job.'

'So who got his medal out for her!'

This time the public address system actually sounded within the cabin. 'Will all persons not sailing for New York please make their way ashore: the gangways will be raised in twenty minutes. I repeat, the gangways will be raised in twenty minutes.'

Two bands in one day: this one was silent for the moment. Mickey and Sorrel and hundreds of other passengers were gazing over the ship's rail at the group of white-jacketed musicians, their silver instruments lowered, down on the concrete quayside.

Just don't let them play 'I Dreamed a Dream', thought Mickey.

'Shouldn't we have paper streamers to throw, or confetti or something?' asked Sorrel.

'They don't let you do it any more. They don't want to pollute the oceans.'

Oceans, she thought. Tonight I shall be on an ocean. A stiff breeze was already threatening her hair, and she drew a cream cashmere shawl around her shoulders. It had once belonged to Ruby Shapiro, her late mother-in-law. Wonderful Ruby, who had been Sorrel's own personal finishing school. Ruby would have been one jump ahead of every social nuance of a cruise. The shawl was comforting but it brought to mind the warmth of the Jewish family Sorrel had married into. She mourned Barney, mourned Ruby, saw gravestones in her mind's eye . . . It took a blast on the ship's whistle to bring her mind back to where it had started. Oceans: tonight she would be sailing on top of the Atlantic.

I was going to give Joe a ticket for India, thought Mickey. I was going to hand it to him inside a sealed envelope and watch his face when he opened it – Joe had always wanted to go to India. The present had been going to be his lover's reward for staying behind to mind the animals: Mick had been away for weeks on end, promoting his latest novel. But Joe, it seemed, had been claiming rewards of his own in the author's absence.

It's a good bed but I'll have to burn it, decided Mickey. And now that's settled, it's about time I got on with my life.

Down on the quay, the conductor must have received some secret signal because he lifted his baton, the musicians raised their instruments, the evening air was filled with the strains of 'Love Changes Everything' and the ship began to move away from the dock.

As the cheering rose to its height, Mickey suddenly noticed a silent figure in a white raincoat. A bit older and a lot more vulnerable than he'd ever seemed in his movies, Jack Lawless also looked like somebody who was feeling very much alone.

'Is that rain in the air?' Sorrel asked Mickey.

'Yes and we've got a party to go to.'

'Can we explore the boat on the way there?'

'Ship,' he corrected her. 'You can put a boat on a ship, you can't put a ship on a boat.'

'I bet I'm overdressed, underneath this shawl.'

'No, you're not.' He had already seen her black silk suit with the little Cartier skyscraper of diamonds on one lapel. 'This is the Social Director's cocktail party. It'll be full of cabaret artistes and guest lecturers and June.'

But when they got there she was only noticeable by her absence. It was a rival psychic, Helene Kramer the American medium, who was the first to mention this.

'Stella Artemis! Cunard can't have known who they were booking.' Mrs Kramer was all of seventy and neat as a French marquise. And Sorrel was relieved to note that the white-haired woman with the all-seeing eyes had also chosen to wear black with a jewelled clip. 'I'm not here in my own right,' she was explaining to Mickey. 'I'm just here to straighten Art's necktie.'

'Art Kramer, the man who wrote all the books about positive attitudes,' Mickey explained to Sorrel. With his bald head and his heavy gold cufflinks and his aura of good eau de Cologne, Art Kramer had already reminded her of Barney's father.

'She can't be doing mediumship.' Mrs Kramer was still talking about June. 'They don't allow it on board. I expect I'm being watched closely, at this very moment, to make sure I don't go into a cold reading.'

'Which would cost a fortune.' Mickey was murmuring at Sorrel again in cocktail party undertones. 'It used to be said that there was a time when Truman Capote wouldn't get out of bed before he'd called Mrs Kramer.'

Paul Daniels was the next guest to walk into the large

but curiously anonymous cabin, and he winked at Sorrel from a distance. She'd met him before, at Variety Club of Great Britain events in Manchester. Now he was talking to another entertainer, one who was a night ahead of himself – he was already wearing a white tuxedo.

'Not champagne for me,' said Sorrel to the waiter. 'Could you find me some Perrier water?' Nowadays it was so easy to say this. Yet all those years ago, when she'd first stopped drinking, she had always felt that the request for something non-alcoholic would cause everybody to remember the awful things that drink had done to her.

More and more people crowded into the Social Director's quarters. Those have to be the dancers, thought Mickey. At one time all of the boys would have been gay. Not any more; Sorrel was already getting appreciative glances from a muscle hunk who couldn't have been a day over twenty-six. So there *is* hope for the older generation, Mickey thought. And he brushed aside a bit of madness which had started to insinuate itself inside his brain, listening instead to the general babble of conversation going on in the low-roofed cabin.

'And there I stood, in the middle of that stage, in a force seven gale, in brand-new stiletto heels.'

'I kid you not, Jilly, I signed four miserable copies and that terrible Jeffrey had them queuing, four-deep, as far as the Lido.'

'. . . June Gee but she's dyed her hair black.'

'Who is she?' Art Kramer, the kind of man who could use one expansive arm movement to gather a little group of people around himself, had drawn together Sorrel, Mickey and his wife. 'Who is this Gee woman that everybody's talking about?'

'He takes no interest in what's going on in my field,' said his wife proudly. 'That's why I love him. June Gee is a disgrace to parapsychology. Far be it from me to use the word bogus . . .'

'But you're going to anyway,' said Art Kramer happily.

'She may have had gifts once . . .'

Sorrel wondered whether to pipe up and tell them about her own childhood experiences of June: the way the girl had been exploited by her own family, used as a juvenile medium. No, better to stay quiet and learn.

It was Mickey who said, 'She ended up running a phoney healing sanctuary. June took hundreds of thousands off people. At one time there was even an 0898 number where she was supposed to cure you by phone. Nobody got through to June herself, she just hired some girls who normally manned the sex lines.'

At that moment Paul Daniels came over and asked Sorrel whether she'd mind being introduced to some fans.

Finding himself left alone with Helene Kramer, Mickey said, 'Have you ever noticed that celebrities are always more star-struck than anybody else?' Her husband had taken empty glasses over to the waiter's tray. 'Helene, do you believe in the theory of synchronicity?'

'Most definitely. There are no coincidences.'

'Last time I was on this ship, I found that I had connections with ten different people. Three I knew already, and the others were linked to people from my past.'

'It happens to me every time. I don't want another drink, Art,' she called out. 'Just get your own.'

'I knew I was going to see June again today, knew it,' said Mickey. 'Out of the blue she was mentioned twice, so I just sat back and waited for her to turn up.'

'Your actress friend, of course, knows much more about her than she was telling me. June is bad news. Have you heard about the drinking?'

So that was the explanation of the changed appearance, he should have guessed. 'No.'

'Mickey, I've known you a long time.' It was a *good* hand that she rested on his arm. 'You first came to see me when I used to do my five days at the Fairmont Hotel in San Francisco. All those boys,' she sighed, 'most of them dead now. But whatever ails you will heal.' Suddenly her voice changed. 'Well, well, well,' she said. And in that moment she sounded almost eerily like Mickey Grimshaw did himself; it was a tone he saved for moments when sexual possibility began to loom up on the horizon. 'Oh my God,' cried Mrs Kramer, horrified. 'Art,' she called out, 'come and take me away. I almost did a freebie!'

Mickey didn't want her to go. Not yet. 'There's something else I've got to tell you, about me and June.'

'I know it already, and you are quite right.'

Mickey had the feeling that this was a conversational device that the psychic employed daily – somewhat akin to the way that he and Sorrel could deflect too many questions about *Angel Dwellings*. And Mickey had acquired other celebrity ruses along the way: he always left a party at its height, and he always went quietly so as not to get entrapped in further invitations.

'They wouldn't want me if I didn't write,' he said to Sorrel as he eventually steered her towards the door. 'And authors who live at parties don't get anything done.'

'But you're not going to write on the ship?' she protested.

'Just a bit, every day. Let's go and look for somewhere for me to do it.' They had reached a lift, he stood aside to let her enter. 'U for Upper Deck,' he said, pressing a button on a panel on the wall.

A middle-aged and married-looking couple were already taking up half the space in the compartment. As the lift began to rise the woman observed, 'I liked the ship better before the refit.'

'I liked you better with curly hair,' said her husband, reasonably.

'This one's us.' As Mickey and Sorrel stepped out he took her by the hand and led her round a corner.

'Fruit machines!' she cried out in disbelief.

'The *QE2* is a cross between the Savoy and an amusement arcade.'

'Well we're definitely in the pinball alley, here!'

'No, this is the Casino. Only it's not allowed to come into its own until we're outside British waters.'

Sorrel was already finding that the gentle roll of the ship was causing her to have to put her feet down in a different way. Looking beyond the fruit machines she saw green baize-covered gambling tables and roulette wheels. And somewhere in the distance a dance band was playing 'Putting On The Ritz' in strict fox-trot tempo.

'So is it all beginning to be Fred and Ginger enough for you?' enquired Mickey. 'And this is just the setting. Wait until you see it in full swing, with all the characters.'

Two of the characters were in place already: a tall slim man of about Mickey's age, and a woman with dark hair with a white streak at the front. Sorrel had particularly noticed them because she had once tried on the same white linen dress that the woman was wearing – tried it on and handed it back to the shop assistant as being too expensive.

As he leant against a gambler's high stool, the man looked darkly haunted. And the woman was gazing up at a security monitor, set high up on a wall, as though she was hoping that the blank television screen might suddenly spring into life and answer all of her problems.

'That pair look as though they could do with reading one of Art Kramer's positivity books,' muttered Mickey.

'But I know her face.'

'They can't be famous. Nobody with that amount of negativity around them could have got to be famous.' In the woman's expression Mickey had already read despair.

'Who is she?' It was driving Sorrel mad.

'Somebody who wishes she was anywhere but here. Let's go and see what kind of table they've got for us in the Britannia Grill.'

As they strolled through the ship, Sorrel said, 'I'd expected it all to be much more elderly than this.' Most of the other passengers bore the relaxed air of people who were living for pleasure. Who *could* that woman with the white streak in her hair have been?

'Some of the cruises are a bit Saga Holidays,' admitted Mickey. 'But the Transatlantic run is altogether more dashing. There's nowhere like a ship for scandal, and the sea is an amazing aphrodisiac.'

They had to descend a spiral staircase to get into the

grill. The manager wasn't David but he was every bit as friendly. 'Would you like to be a two or shall I put you with somebody else?'

'A two,' said Mickey, as the man consulted his table plan. 'Even if it means I can't smoke, still a two.'

'If you would care to follow me . . .'

The Britannia Grill could have been a West End restaurant. Except, the sun's going down into the sea, through the picture windows, and that bobbing flashing light must be some kind of buoy, thought Sorrel excitedly. And here in the restaurant, all the touches of pink and mauve and silver are a bit like an old-fashioned musical comedy.

But the tablecloth was purest white damask. And amidst all the chinking crystal and the bone china edged with silver ropes, right next to an arrangement of roses and freesias, sat an ashtray.

'Perfect,' said Mickey.

That was when Sorrel noticed where he was looking. Already seated at an adjacent table was little Mrs Fiddler. She had obviously been paired off with a dining companion. And that dining companion was Jack Lawless.

This sight so startled Sorrel that it acted on her mind like mild shock treatment – releasing the very thought she'd been seeking. 'I know where I saw that woman in the casino before,' she said. 'Only we knew her as young. Both of us. It's not somebody we ever knew properly. Last time I saw her was in Scholes's bacon queue. And you know where Scholes's was?'

'Irlams o' th' Height.'

2

Labour were in power in 1947. The war was over, rationing was still on, and the National Health Service had just come into being. As a result, in Irlams o' th' Height, it was generally prophesied that the Irish would flood into England by the boatload – to pick up false teeth and free wigs.

'Not that we need them to arrive in Saracen Street,' said Dinah Nelson's mother. 'We've got enough here already.' Her mother was a scurrying woman who worked in a shoe shop by day, and kept the house Protestant-tidy by night. 'And now there's this new child allowance.'

She was celebrating Wednesday half-day closing by black-leading the front room fireplace. 'But have one child and you get nothing. Nothing!' She rose to her feet and glared through the lace curtains at the Brogans' house. It was bang opposite to their own, in the middle of a terraced row, on the other side of the Street. 'Their priests force them to have babies,' she said darkly. 'If they have enough, they think they can get England back for the Pope.'

Not that Dinah's mother went to church herself. But religious differences still ran very deep. 'It's a rule of fear.' By now she was already gathering her black-leading implements into an old strawberry basket. 'They're so busy making babies they've no time to donkey-stone their front steps.' She removed some dried bulrushes from a copper jug and began to attack it with Duraglit wadding. 'I got mistaken for an Irishwoman once. By a priest, all in black, right down to the ground. "Are you Theresa Scullion?" he asked. "Do I *look* like a Theresa Scullion?" I said back to him. I wouldn't call 'im Father, it's what they want.'

In fact, with her black hair with the white streak in

front, Dinah's mother could easily have passed for Irish. People said that the streak must have come early because Eva Nelson was always on the dash – going at double speed. But Dinah knew that the distinctive streak ran in the family, that by the time she was in her teens she would probably have one in her own dark hair.

In most houses on Saracen Street the front room was regarded as sacred, kept only for courting and company. But Eva Nelson had been born ambitious: left to herself, she would have ripped up the rent book years ago and taken out a mortgage on one of the semi-detached houses on Ravensdale Estate. To have achieved that, she would have needed to have been married to a different husband. Dinah's father's attitude was: 'Why beggar yourself for bricks and mortar?' He liked a pint and a flutter on the dogs, and *Reynold's News* on a Saturday night, and two other papers on a Sunday. Tommy Nelson was also fond of bringing fish and chips home unexpectedly. And Dinah didn't just get presents on Christmas and birthdays. Her father was a man who could play the front room piano – self-taught. 'Sleepy Lagoon', 'The Lost Chord', anything. Dinah loved her dad, she thought he was smashing.

It was her mother who was the problem. Eva, who despised Saracen Street, idolised James Mason the film star, and loathed the Irish.

'But James Mason's Irish,' Dinah would protest.

'Yes but he comes from the better end, you can tell that. James Mason's mother wouldn't wait a week and then put all her milk bottles out together.' This was another dig at the Brogans, opposite. 'Look, they've wheeled Macushla out.' She was talking about her hated neighbours' youngest daughter. All criticism was automatically suspended in the case of Macushla Brogan because the child lived in a home-made wheelchair. 'It's October, there's no warmth left in that sun. She ought to have more on than a thin cardigan.'

'Can I go and talk to her?'

'Talk to her, yes. But you're not to so much as set foot over their doorstep.' Dinah waited for the final bit, her mother always said the same thing. 'And if you do go in, I'll know. God'll whisper it in my ear hole.'

Saracen Street boasted its fair share of interesting invalids: there was breathless Mr Parker who'd been gassed in the trenches in the First World War, and Mrs-Jepson-with-the-blue-lips, whose relatives sometimes pushed her bed under the front window so she could look out. But the most familiar sight of all was Macushla Brogan, spindle-limbed in her wheelchair, with Sid the lurcher in attendance.

Macushla was ten. She had very sparse, straight, blonde hair and a witchy nose and a thin mouth. But she also had the most beautiful eyes in the whole of the Height. Bright blue, like wet ultramarine in a paint box. Sometimes she could get restless and snappy, and that's when Sid would put a reassuring paw on her knee to calm her down. Macushla was Sid's queen.

There was greyhound in him. That accounted for the tin ribs. But where had those anxious eyes of palest green come from? A true lurcher needs the blood of an Irish wolfhound but Macushla always claimed that Sid was 'part kangaroo'. So there they sat, she in the ramshackle invalid carriage with the old bicycle wheels, he on a flagstone. A seagull was also hopping around on the pavement at a safe distance.

'They started flying inland this morning,' said Macushla to Dinah. 'It must be going to get colder.' If she sounded more Irish than her brothers and sisters did, this was due to the amount of time she spent with her mother. Though Macushla didn't go to school she was hungry for education. 'Have you got our French homework there?' she asked.

'We've got to write an essay on a visit to the market.'

'Dead easy. We'll put in lots of *choux-fleurs* and *framboises*.'

'I've not learned those,' protested Dinah.

'They're words from two lessons ahead of where you lot are at,' admitted Macushla, who already knew the textbook from cover to cover. 'Tell us what you did in Latin today,' she said hungrily. 'Give us a bit of the old *Fabulae Faciles*.'

'We just did some more of *Jason and the Golden Fleece*.'

'I'm batty about that Latin word you taught me yesterday,' cried Macushla. 'Bloody batty about it! *Amaveramus*: what a beautiful way of saying "we were loving".'

There were occasions when the cripple's wild enthusiasms almost embarrassed Dinah. 'Who were you loving?'

'Nobody. I'm just enchanted with the word.'

Enchanted? People just didn't say that in the Height. Macushla's body might be all tied up but her mind seemed free to yell at the top of its voice. And it makes me feel tongue-tied, thought Dinah. I feel things, oh how I feel things! It's just that I can't blab them out like Macushla can.

'Shall I bring you up to date with the latest?' asked the Irish girl. She could recount the adventures of the Brogans like a serial on the wireless.

Sid let out a warning growl, pulled back his upper lip, and revealed a yellow fang. It was an awesome sight. Quite enough to cause a little girl with a skipping rope to move further down the pavement.

'She once accidentally winged me one with that bloody rope,' explained Macushla. 'And he's never forgot it. Now then, let me remember what happened today.'

'Did they get the last coping stone on?' Dinah was already privy to many episodes of the saga. By occupation, Macushla's father was what was known as 'in the building'.

'They did. And then strong drink was taken to celebrate so no work was done this afternoon. Daddy came bowling home at closing time, gave us the lecture about eleven hundred years of English oppression, sang one chorus of "The Wild Rover", and passed out, bless him.'

'Did the postman bring anything?' This often took the story in another direction.

'Just a letter from the seminary. Paddy wanted a new

34

rubber inner tube for his fountain pen, and there was the usual plea for more Woodbines.'

Ambrose Patrick John Fisher Brogan was going to be a priest. He'd been away for years now, ever since he was thirteen. All the Brogans had long strings of names. The one that Dinah really wanted to hear about was commonly known as Rory. Oh, Rory Brogan! She only had to think about him to get the same funny feeling between her legs that you got when you stood on the top of Blackpool Tower and looked down. Rory Brogan . . . there it came again! She just hoped it didn't show on her face. It was all being kept very secret.

'Cissie and Josephine are going to give one another Twink perms.' The girl in the wheelchair was talking about her older sisters, who went all the way across town to special match-making dances at a church called the Holy Name. 'The man from Scholes's took the top of his finger off on the bacon slicer. And the babby's little motions are bright green.' Macushla always saved the most dramatic bit for the end.

But suddenly it wasn't like being told what somebody else had seen at the pictures, it was like having your own seat in the stalls. No, it was even better than that, it was for all the world like being in the film itself because Rory Brogan had just marched round the corner of Saracen Street.

Tall for fourteen, with the shoulders of a man, he also had the face of a Spanish saint who had somehow been handed the wrong set of eyes. They were merry and twinkling and ready for devilment.

'You're a bad bugger,' called out Macushla affectionately.

'I know,' he sang back joyously. And then, grabbing hold of their neighbour's child's rope, which was really too long for her, he began to skip. Most boys would have been scared to do it, scared of being thought girlish. But Rory skipped like Freddie Mills, like Randolph Turpin, like a champion.

'He'd look grand in the Lonsdale Belt,' said his sister.

'But he might get hurt,' cried Dinah, who didn't like the idea of his boxing at all. And then she worried that the depth of her own feelings might be on public view. These were something that were better saved for her diary.

Dinah Nelson didn't write a diary, she drew it instead. It is true that there were sometimes a few words inscribed on the page, but for the most part they were just covered in lightning-fast drawings of people and places and dreams. She began in pencil and then brightened everything up with Windsor and Newton's watercolours. And lately she'd started working round the outlines of the drawings in Indian ink. Black for anything *definite*, Dinah was a very truthful child; sepia ink was for . . . well a lot of sepia had been expended on Rory Brogan.

The diaries seemed to have evolved of their own accord. During the war her mother was forever saying, 'Now you must write a letter to your daddy.' And then Eva would sit down and print out a whole lot of words that her daughter was meant to copy. '*Me and Mummy miss you very much* . . .' It gave Dinah the shudders. Okay she did miss him, but she didn't want to do it in other people's words.

So one morning she didn't copy, she drew instead. And then she wrote underneath the picture. 'God bless Monty and the boys', which was just something she'd seen printed round the band of a cardboard cowboy hat – on Blackpool promenade. 'Monty' was General Montgomery. And as the Eighth Army pushed their way across the Middle East, Lance Corporal Tommy Nelson had received a whole stack of illustrated aerograms from Irlams o' th' Height.

He still had these letters but he wouldn't let Dinah touch them. She wanted to rip them up because they were childish and a bit too revealing. And anyway she'd got better at it since then.

Nowadays she did the improved versions into proper blank pads with *Drawing Book* printed on the front. You got them from the bottom newsagent's, the one down by the big advertising hoardings. They cost fourpence and she kept them hidden in the gas meter cupboard, at the side of the fireplace in the front parlour.

The painted diaries had their own Huntley and Palmer's biscuit tin with a view of Windsor Castle on its embossed tin lid. And in Dinah's mind, that meant that the drawing books lived in the castle itself, inside a special dungeon which happened to be circular and made of shining tin.

You could do wonderful things with your own mind, she'd learned that very early on. In your imagination you could go anywhere and meet anyone; and that would set the itchy yearning feeling going in her fingers – the urge to *make* something. It was a marvellously hungry feeling too, and the only way to satisfy it was by reaching for her drawing pencils.

Today she began to depict the outline of Rory Brogan with the borrowed skipping rope. Her pencil moved confidently and she didn't just draw one rope, she sketched in three – to give some indication of the speed with which it was meant to be turning.

But she couldn't fake Rory Brogan's eyes. She couldn't make them look at her because they never did. Dinah didn't like to take an indiarubber to Rory (in case it made something awful happen to him in real life) so she just outlined him again whilst she thought the matter over. She could, of course, have *forced* the eyes to look into hers. But that wasn't what she wanted: she needed them to gaze of their own accord.

The pencil had a life of its own and if she forced bits they never looked right. Somehow those faked corners of the overall design always lacked substance, looked like lies. But I will make it happen, she thought. I'll sell my soul to the Pope and Rory Brogan will look at me.

The personal column of the *Manchester Evening News* was full of advertisements thanking St Jude 'for favours received'. Beneath these, there were other adverts which told you how to get special prayers answered: it seemed you had to light a candle to St Martha, say seven Hail Marys and seven Our Fathers on seven consecutive days, and 'promise publication' on the eighth. Dinah had worked out that an announcement in the personal column would cost four shillings and eightpence. But nearly all her ready money had gone on Indian ink and drawing pads so she drew a lighted candle whilst wondering what she could get for thrupence ha'penny.

And she wasn't even supposed to know the words of Hail Mary. Eva would have a fit if she found out. And I know them in Latin too, thought Dinah, proudly. *Ave Maria plena gracias*. Oh yes! And if it was true that you had to kiss the Pope's toe to get what you wanted, then she'd bloody well kiss it. In private, in her heart, Dinah Nelson was the most passionate child in the whole of Saracen Street.

But life was lived in public. And people watched. Especially her mother. 'Outsiders are always telling me that they've seen you on Swinton Park Road,' she would say to Dinah. 'What's the big attraction?'

'I'm drawing Teapot Hall.' That was certainly true enough. She had made many drawings of the dilapidated sandstone mansion. It had a golden teapot, instead of a weather vane, on the top of its square tower. But on the way back from this local landmark, after looking carefully to both left and right to be sure that she was unobserved, Dinah would push open the door of St Luke's church, slide the tip of her nose around the edge, and *inhale*.

Incense: the odour of Catholicism was the scent of her love for Rory Brogan. It seemed to draw him closer to her. Not that he was particularly religious, but Catholicism was in his family's blood and in their bones. It was central to their being. To Dinah this meant that Rory himself was locked inside that sweet and mysterious smell which always reminded her of lilies, and of scenes with kissing in them, at the pictures.

Even thinking about all of this made Dinah long to go out into the lobby and take her school raincoat down from the peg. The thought led to the deed and soon her feet were speeding towards the highly forbidden church.

Set inside a garden, which had its own concrete Lourdes grotto and a life-size Jesus on the cross (with dripping blood and everything), the church looked like a single-storeyed, black and white cricket pavilion. But the garden gate marked *Portae Caelli* indicated that she was on the very threshold of Heaven. Dinah had not failed to look up the words in her Latin dictionary.

Here came the smell! There were no two ways about it, it was downright Parisian. 'Bring me your sins' it seemed to say. 'You may have noticed that I'm pretty wicked myself!'

It got stronger inside the porch: that was where all the holy publications and the saintly medals were kept in a wooden tract case. *A Penny Catechism* and *The Sacred Heart Messenger* were right next to the miraculous medal of St Joseph – in both a fourpenny size and a sixpenny one. Blue-enamelled medallions for the Virgin Mary and red ones for St Agnes. And enough rosary beads to make a handrail from St Luke's to the Vatican.

But the most interesting thing of all was a stack of little envelopes marked 'The Green Scapular' in smudged purple rubber-stamping.

Other children might be curious about the contents of Durex and Tampax packets, Dinah just wanted to see inside a scapular envelope. She already had some faint idea of what it would contain. Macushla Brogan had once undone a couple of the buttons on the front of her shabby frock to show Dinah a strange arrangement of green tape, hidden underneath. Tape which ended in a bottle-green felt tab, with sacred pictures stitched to it.

'I can't let you sneak more than a peep,' Macushla had explained. 'It's for getting a miracle. I don't want to risk weakening its strength by showing it to a Proddy-dog.'

In the church porch, the gum on one of the scapular envelopes was not fastened down properly. In fact . . . now it wasn't fastened down at all. Dinah's trembling fingers went under the flap and pulled out something that was a bit like a cloth necklace. The material was a cross between green bias-binding and shoelaces. And the pictures, of the Virgin Mary and of a flaming heart with

39

a dagger through it, were made of glazed cloth stitched onto the heavier felt.

She also pulled out a leaflet that described previous miracles, and even gave an address where you were meant to send details of your own – when you eventually got it. To Dinah's eyes, it all looked as solid as a Hoover guarantee. They couldn't be selling tarradiddles in a church porch. Fourpence to get anything you wanted: nobody could sniff at that. The only trouble was she only had thrupence ha'penny. And I've gone and undone their gum, she thought.

That was when she noticed that a bit of the stitching was also coming undone. 'Could you knock off a small consideration for that?' she asked the incense-laden air. Taking silence for acceptance she added, 'Thank you, Virgin Mary, that's most accommodating of you.' It was something her mother might have said in the Beehive Wool Shop. But Dinah was talking to Heaven. 'The miracle I want is that Rory Brogan's got to look at me.'

On the way home, Dinah passed the special area she thought of as The Place. But she didn't want to think about The Place today because she was already wearing the green scapular and . . . No, today was not the day for her special place. 'But I've not given you up!' The deeply superstitious child actually called the words out loud and disturbed some more of the seagulls.

This was the winter when the gulls stayed inland; 1947 was one of the coldest years ever recorded. Food was even more difficult to get hold of than it had been at the height of the war. But the Nelsons managed a black market chicken for Christmas. Dinah's dad pulled a pheasant's feather off an old hat of her mother's and stuck it up the chicken's bum before he carried it to the table. Laughter helped keep you warm in the fuel crisis. It was the same winter that people were reduced to chopping up unwanted furniture, the winter that stank of burning coke.

And when the spring came, the only way you could get an Easter egg was by taking your chocolate ration to Ashworth's shop; they were bakers and confectioners who still had their pre-war tin moulds. Dinah had a four-ounce bar of Bournville cast into a small egg with a skimpy marzipan chicken astride the top of it.

'And God alone knows how long Mrs Ashworth's had that marzipan under the counter,' observed Eva Nelson. These days the expression 'under the counter' had a whole new significance. The very dress material that Eva was urging under the bobbing needle of the sewing machine was also of the 'ask me no questions and I'll tell you no lies' variety.

They were in the front parlour. And the rhythmic rattle of the black and gold Singer was in direct competition with 'Twelfth Street Rag' because Tommy was playing the piano. Whenever he did this he always whistled under his breath. And Eva sewed with gritted teeth because that's where she kept the pins when she was dressmaking. Their daughter had only come in from the kitchen to say, 'I've done my biology homework, I'm going out for a bit.'

'No you're not,' snapped Eva. 'I want you to slip this bodice on for size.'

'One day you'll swallow one of those pins,' said her husband.

'One day you'll give up brilliantine. Just look at that chair-back cover. No prizes offered for where you've been sitting.'

Dinah wouldn't have liked her father to give up hair cream. A glistening head went with his twinkling eyes and his musical fingers. The tune changed to 'The Fleet's in Port Again' as Dinah took hold of the half-finished bodice and made to pull it over her head.

'Not over your blouse,' protested her mother.

Dinah panicked. 'I'll go upstairs,' she cried.

'You'll do it here. I've not got all night. Your father can close his eyes.'

Her budding bust was not the problem. Well not the

main problem. That was hidden under her blouse. It was the green scapular.

'I've not got all night,' repeated Eva.

'It'll fit,' said Dinah desperately. 'Your things always do. Don't they, Dad? Don't they always fit?'

'I'm not getting involved.' He played a couple of bars of 'If You Want to Know the Time Ask a Policeman'. He was wonderful at 'musical switches'.

But Eva was getting impatient. 'Dinah Nelson, take your blouse off.'

'No.'

'Yes. And don't you dare defy me.'

'Do as your mother says,' put in Tommy. He didn't often lay down the law, but when he did you just obeyed and that was that.

Eva chose this moment to get sarcastic. 'All you have to do is put your fingers to the buttons and start undoing . . . Oh my God, whatever's that?'

'What?'

'What? That snaky green thing. Dear God in Heaven, it's got a holy dangler! She's been got at by Catholics, Tommy. No, don't look, you'll see her front. Who hung this on you, Dinah Nelson? I want his name.'

'Nobody hung it on me. I got it in a packet.'

'Where?' The fires of Smithfield burned again in Eva's voice. 'Where did you get it?'

'St Luke's porch.'

'And what was you doing there?'

'I liked the smell.'

'She liked the smell! They'll go to any lengths to lure people in. Any lengths at all. You take that off and give it to me, it goes on the back of the fire.'

'You can't throw things on a gas fire.'

'Down the lavvy then. And don't try and be clever with me, Miss. Come on, hand it over.'

Things had got so serious that Tommy had stopped playing. 'I don't want any arguing with your mother. Just give it her and let that be an end to it.'

It was the fact that he'd sided against her which reduced

42

Dinah to sudden tears and downright defiance. 'No. She's not having it.' And buttoning up her blouse she ran out into the lobby.

'Just you come back this instant,' yelled her mother.

But Dinah was already at the front door. And now she was outside, and slamming the door behind her.

It didn't stay shut for long. 'Dinah Nelson . . .' The way her mother's head popped out brought Punch and Judy shows to mind. And so quickly did Dinah flee that the crocodile could have been snapping his jaws after her. But where was she running? She didn't know. And then she did know: she would go to The Place.

It didn't *look* anything extraordinary – just a piece of open land between the gents' public toilets and a fake Tudor pub called the Pack Horse. The kind of dirt patch that's known in Lancashire as a croft. A place where purple bomb weed blossomed, and people discarded fish and chip wrappings and bus tickets and toffee papers.

Golden rod had also managed to seed itself in one corner. And now it grew in majestic spikes around one great big stone. This didn't look like a stone in real-life at all, more like a boulder in a pantomime. Not of a size that would block the door of Aladdin's cave, but big enough for Dick Whittington to sit upon. And rumour had run through generations of local children that the boulder had a dramatic history of its own, that it had been hurled down from the sky in the middle of a thunder storm.

Could this have affected the atmosphere around it? Dinah didn't know. But she wasn't alone in thinking that the place was in a 'different style of drawing' from the rest of the Height. One day she had come across a rather cissified boy, just standing looking at the stone. He went to the same Sunday School as she did so she knew his name was Peter Bird. 'Does the stone make you feel funny too?' she asked him.

'It makes me want to kneel down and pray,' he said. And then he just walked off. That was the kind of boy he was. It had been years ago. They couldn't have been more than eight at the time. You came right out and said things at that age, things you would have thought twice about saying later.

But the odd atmosphere had continued to shimmer around the croft. And in the painted diaries she never drew The Place in hard lines; instead, she had evolved a technique which used a lot of little dots so that the finished effect was of dreams flitting into the bold outlines of reality.

What *was* it about The Place? Dinah could be riding on top of a bus, could be turning the corner for Broughs the Cleaners, could just be crossing the road to look at the poster for the Olympia Super-Cinema De Luxe when . . . the only way to describe it, was to say that her spirits would unaccountably lighten. She would feel that life was good, that everything was meant and okay. And always when this happened – always – she would realise that she was within sight of that special place.

And now she was standing on the croft, by the big stone, wondering what to do with the green scapular. I'll just have to stick it down my knickers, she thought. Elastic would stop it falling out at the knee. You had to be very careful with holy things, Macushla Brogan had taught her that. According to Macushla, the Brogans had whole teapots full of broken rosaries in their house because it was bad luck to throw them away.

There was nobody around except for the old man who always leant against the wall of the public convenience, smoking a pipe. He only ever watched to see who was going in so he certainly wouldn't notice that she was hitching up her skirt at one side, and stuffing the green tape necklace down the waistband of her navy-blue school drawers.

And that was how it started.

That was the beginning of years of hiding places. Down her knickers, in her schoolbag, under the lid of her roll-top pencil box. Under the mattress, but that was risky because Eva was very keen on shaking up flock mattresses; inside

44

the biscuit tin, with the painted diaries, was a good place. Nowhere was ever used for too long. Eventually, the green scapular even came to rest at the bottom of her first packet of Doctor White's.

All this furtiveness made Dinah very conscious of the fact that, all around her, Irlams o' th' Height was continuing with its own subdued holy war. It was as though something inside people like her mother and Mrs Brogan had to have something to hate. And I just want something to love, she thought. Correction: I want somebody. I want Rory Brogan. And in the hope that he would one day look at her, Dinah Nelson evolved a religion of her own. The atmosphere of The Place came into it, and a special prayer off the instructions inside the scapular envelope: '*Immaculate Heart of Mary, pray for us now and at the hour of our death, amen.*' And terrible fear came into it too because, on the day she'd founded her own religion, she'd told a black lie.

'I dropped the scapular down a fever grid.' She'd said it to her mother. And to make up for shouting at Dinah, Eva had given her sevenpence to go and see *The Dolly Sisters* at the Olympia. Dinah could never suppress the feeling that God would get her for that.

And there was certainly no sign of Rory Brogan looking at her. If anything, as she bloomed and matured and got a proper bust and a mass of shining black hair, he looked even more determinedly away.

Please just let him look at me, God, she would pray. Once I've caught his eye, you can leave the rest to me. Ta for making me into a woman but it's either beautiful Rory or I'm not interested.

Having your own sect makes you very conscious of other people's, and of their festivals and their feasts. At Whitsuntide, each district had a day when the children of the Sunday schools processed behind brass bands and church banners. In the Height it always happened on the Sunday itself. But this little local procession around the parish – in the brand-new clothes that were so much a part of Whitsun – was totally eclipsed by the spectacular demonstrations of faith which took place in Manchester city centre.

There, parishioners from up to three miles around would begin to converge on Albert Square from first thing in the morning. Church of England on Whit Monday, Roman Catholics on the Friday. Their bishops always stood on a temporary platform, in front of the great mock-renaissance town hall, to bless them. And then thousands upon tens of thousands of the faithful would process along the city streets, bringing traffic to a standstill until well after lunchtime.

You could position yourself on one spot and the procession would continue to pass you for two and a half hours. 'Good weather for the banners' was a familiar Whitsun greeting.

There was something almost medieval about the sight of these church banners, painted and embroidered, towering up, over Deansgate – their brass-mounted poles bobbing past soot-blackened buildings for as far as the eye could see. *St Anthony Pray For Us ... St Mary Magdalene Pray For Us ... Blessed John Fisher Pray For Us ...* And between the banners came the bands: brass bands, silver bands, Irish pipers in ginger tweed kilts. Between the bands, the children. New communicants, all in white with veils and rosaries clasped between gloved fingers, the boys in white satin knee-breeches and ruffled shirts, with little white skull-caps on the back of their heads.

Dinah had, of course, chosen the Friday to get the bus into town because the Catholic procession had a lot of 'Hail Mary' banners so she felt a bit of belonging. And behind these banners walked the Children of Mary (who were often old women) in white dresses and blue cloaks. The Agnesians' cloaks were red, and some of their marchers were also given to false teeth and bunions. But they all carried bouquets and they all smiled.

On they marched and on and on. Up into the air went a piper's twinkling caber and the crowd cheered. It flew higher again and they roared some more. Priests doffed shining black top hats and beamed towards the watching crowds, packed behind the barricades, as though the English Reformation had never happened.

But woe betide anybody who tried to cross the road. 'You don't do that on a Monday, do you?' The shout echoed between the buildings of Deansgate as clearly as any chant at a football match. And Dinah could see Ireland in the faces of all the men with pint pots in their hands, who were leaning against the tiled frontage of the Sawyer's Arms.

The climax of the procession was always deeply and irrevocably Italian. This was the part that she intended to draw in her diary when she got home. Though the march had already been dotted with contingents in the national costumes and red leather boots of displaced Ukrainians and Poles, none of them could ever have hoped to rival the splendours of the Manchester Italian Society. They always came last, they were always the best.

Suddenly Dinah felt she wasn't in Manchester at all. She would have to use black ink to capture the women's lace. And her brightest primary colours for the satins underneath. Their children were a flock of dark-eyed Michelangelo cherubim. They were so small they had to clutch onto white satin ribbons to keep themselves in line. One tiny hand for the ribbon, the other for their flowers – both boys and girls carried huge bouquets.

And with their arrival, the music became infinitely slower and sadder. It took the whole thing back to what the day was really about. But even an enamelled Christ, hanging from a gilded cross, could not suppress the whispers of 'Here she comes', 'Here she comes'. And some people went down on their knees, right there on the pavement. Borne aloft, on the shoulders of six wickedly handsome men, the Madonna of a thousand nodding lilies brought her own exotic scent to the end of the proceedings. All this Italian fervour had also sent Dinah to her knees and to her prayers. '*Immaculate Heart of Mary, pray for us now and at the hour of our death, amen.*' Her mother would have had a fit!

And as she was thinking this, and getting back to her

feet, all that there was left to see was a line of policemen and an anxious green and yellow double-decker bus that must have been trapped behind the procession since breakfast time.

> *'And it's no, nay, never,*
> *No nay never no more,*
> *Will I play the wild rover . . .'*

Outside the Sawyer's Arms, glasses raised like rebels, the gang of Irishmen were singing in a ragged semblance of unison, and stamping their feet in accompaniment. They were in 'best suits', and a couple of them sported trilby hats. And two more boasted gleaming gold collar studs at their neck bands, though they hadn't got round to wearing the actual collars.

'No, nay, never,' stamp, stamp. Up rose the song again. And Dinah decided that, if she ever drew these kerbside revellers, she would colour them to look like sides of beef. But they weren't really interesting enough to draw . . . Except, suddenly, they were.

Oh how they were. Oh how they very, very, very were! Three were younger than the rest. Though they too had glasses in their hands, alcohol had yet to leave its bloating mark upon them. One glance at this trio was enough to make you understand why Hollywood has often looked to Ireland for its leading men. And of the three, one shone the brightest: those shoulders, that thick dark hair, those impish blue eyes . . . It was Rory Brogan. And Dinah Nelson had finally got her miracle: he was looking straight at her. Well, as straight as eyes that dance with secret amusement *can* look. Oh God but he was bloody lovely!

'Hello,' he said.

The voice was so deep that it instantly gave her that 'top of Blackpool Tower and looking over the edge' feeling. And instead of replying sensibly she blurted out, 'You never looked at me before.'

'Well, you see, a man called Thomas Toolan bought

me this pint of beer and it's given me a drop of confidence.'

Immaculate Heart of Mary bless Thomas Toolan, she thought. Bless him for changing everything.

'What's a Proddy-dog doing in town on a Whit Friday?' The religious barriers weren't really back in place because the voice was gently teasing.

'Oh I get about.' She said it airily.

'I've noticed. I've been noticing you for years. You've got lovely.'

The very word she'd just mentally applied to him! Only, now, she couldn't think of anything to say back.

It seemed it wasn't necessary. 'Would you ever think of coming out with me?' He only sounded a little bit Irish.

'Yes I would do that.' She'd said it so earnestly that she was left wondering whether she had sounded dippy.

Suddenly he turned cautious and started to look around to see whether the other men were listening. In that moment Dinah could see what Rory's father must have looked like when he was young. 'We'd have to meet away from Saracen Street,' he said. 'You know what they're like.'

'Oh I do,' she assured him earnestly.

'The beer's loosened me tongue.' He said it gleefully. 'I'm not much of a boozer.'

'Me neither.' In her whole life she had only ever tasted two glasses of Christmas sherry and one sip of somebody else's port wine.

Rory had obviously been doing some quick thinking. 'We could go to town pictures, tomorrow night.' As if to explain why they couldn't go immediately, he said, 'I'm with the lads just now.'

One of them chose this precise moment to try to move in on their conversation. He even had the nerve to put his arm around Dinah's waist. 'So who's this?' he asked.

'I'll give you one second to take your hand off her. Thanks.'

This other man now had both of his hands raised like a surrendering cowboy. 'No offence, mate.'

'We're busy talking.' The authority in Rory's tone dismissed the man back into the crowd of revellers who had struck up a cheerful chorus of 'The Wearing of the Green'.

'I can't afford the best seats,' said Rory. 'But I could meet you outside the Gaiety Picture House on Peter Street at seven o'clock tomorrow night.'

'What's on?' she asked, anxious to prolong the conversation.

'No idea. Er . . .' The way he'd cleared his throat made it sound as though something awkward was coming next. It came. 'You won't say anything to our Macushla, will you?'

'No.'

'It's just that me mother's so set against Protestants.'

'Mine's the same the other way round.'

An old man in a bulky brown suit pushed his way through the crowd and handed Rory a brimming pint pot. 'Get that down you,' he said. 'We need to put some lard on your belly.'

'Ta, Mr Toolan. See you tomorrow night then, Dinah.'

He'd said her name. And all she wanted to do was go away and savour the way it had sounded. 'See you at seven.'

As she darted, happily, between the holiday crowds on Deansgate, the whole town seemed to belong to Dinah Nelson. And if it was really meant to be a Catholic day, so what? She'd got an ongoing Catholic of her own. It was odd that she'd never noticed, before, how much Rory resembled his father.

Some child, one who'd obviously had too much of brass bands and banners, started to howl. And that was the moment when Dinah remembered something that Macushla Brogan had once said: 'When Daddy's taken a drink he never remembers a thing about anything, the next day.' And Dinah was suddenly filled with terrible visions of herself, in her best two-piece, forlorn and forsaken, outside the Gaiety Picture House.

3

When Sorrel Starkey opened her eyes she had no doubts as to where she was. Though the bed was wonderfully comfortable, she was at sea. On dry land, looking through the QE2 brochure, she had anticipated that there might be a certain choppiness; Mickey had assuaged her fears of being seasick with much experienced talk of the ship having stabilisers – whatever they were. Still only half-awake, she felt as though her body was skimming through swishing noises, to an accompanying throb of distant ship's engines. And it was doing . . . she sought for the right words.

It was doing 'funny things' to her. Oh God! Now she felt as though there were strands of weirdly loopy elastic connecting her diaphragm to her brain.

Was Mickey feeling similarly nauseous? She looked towards his bed, which was nearer the portholes, but the covers were thrown back and it was empty. Some of the swishing noises stopped. These were the ones that had come from the bathroom. He must have just got out of the shower.

And now he padded into the cabin, dripping wet with a towel round his middle. 'Oh good, you're awake.' Off came the towel as he dried his cropped head. 'We never used to worry about being naked when we were young. So we can't start dodging behind doors at this late date.'

'I think I might.' She said it ruefully. 'Men's bodies last longer, it isn't fair.'

'I've got too much weight round the middle.' He was looking at himself critically in the dressing-table mirror. At a deeper level he was imagining what a stranger would make of the remains of a body which had once driven strong men mad. This self-examination was something of an insurance policy – against stupidity. And especially today.

Exercising caution, Sorrel had propped herself up on one elbow. The ship wasn't just going up and down, it also seemed to be swaying from side to side. 'What does seasick feel like?'

'Wouldn't know,' he said complacently. 'I'm a wonderful sailor. It's the only butch thing about me.'

No it's not, thought Sorrel, your ego's intensely masculine, and so are your legs, to say nothing of . . . It was no use, thinking only made the disorientated swimming sensation worse. 'And I'm suffering from the "Poor Me's" too!' Her mind had already started to take out her problems and to arrange them like haddock and plaice on a fishmonger's slab. The big problem – the one that nothing would get her to talk about – put her in mind of a nasty grey crayfish. And she said aloud that even the thought of food was making her stomach heave.

'You don't look good,' admitted Mickey. 'Why don't we get the steward to bring you a pot of weak China tea and some dry toast? I already had breakfast in the Lido. I was just sluicing down before lifeboat drill.'

'Don't say they lower us into the sea,' she moaned, sinking back onto the pile of pillows.

'Only for a few minutes. Just long enough to bob about a bit. Of *course* they don't lower us into the sea!' She really did look awful. 'Go and see the doctor. He's only on this deck. You can either have the tablets or the injection.'

'I think I'm going to die.'

'They all say that.' He was pulling shirts out of the wooden drawers in the wardrobe. It was more like a dressing room really, you could step inside and stand in the middle. White button-down shirt, navy cable-knit sweater, fawn chinos; people who've been on the stage can always get dressed in under twenty seconds. Tucking in a stray shirt tail, and backing out into the cabin again, he said, 'Have the injection. It costs a bomb, it puts you right out for six hours, but they always seem to wake up ready for anything.'

'What about lifeboat drill?'

'I'll go for both of us.' This reminded him to dive

52

back into the dressing room for his life jacket. 'I've no mechanical aptitudes whatsoever,' he grumbled. 'Can you help me get into this?'

'No. The colours hurt my eyes.' The life jacket was a complicated arrangement of webbing and moulded blocks, like bricks covered in fluorescent orange canvas.

'Oh look, I've got a whistle! And a little light. Sorrel, did you know that you were pale green? See if you can stand up.'

'I don't want to stand up,' she groaned. And suddenly the pillows were *too* soft, they only added to the gooey feeling.

Mickey telephoned the doctor. And then, carrying his life jacket instead of wearing it like everybody else, he climbed the stairs to the Steiner Hairdressing Salon where he took it upon himself to book Sorrel in for a five o'clock appointment.

'Edward will want to do Miss Starkey,' said the girl behind the desk. 'He's her biggest fan. He always has tapes of *Angel Dwellings* sent on to wait for him in port.'

This Edward now appeared in person, giving Mickey a look which said I-admire-your-show-but-you-are-far-too-old-for-me-to-be-interested-in-the-idea-of-anything-else. Gay men can get a whole scenario out of one exchanged glance.

The public address system was urging all passengers and crew to make their way to their appointed lifeboat stations. Mickey already knew that occupants of Cabin 2142 were meant to follow the signs marked CQ. The only trouble was that he couldn't find them. Making the appointment had obviously taken him up the wrong staircase, and in an attempt to retrace his steps he found himself heading towards the miniature shipboard branch of Harrods. That was where he saw a sight which caused him to dodge back into the milling crowd of orange Michelin Men.

Against the bow-windowed shop frontage a woman in a pink nylon tracksuit – fluorescent as the life jacket which sat on top of it – was examining a white court shoe with a broken heel. It was June Gee, looking, if anything, more puffed up than the day before. Podges of fat even rose up around the rainbow-shaded acupressure bands at her wrists – a new fashion in seasickness preventatives.

The crowd pressing behind Mickey obliged him to move nearer and he caught a distinct whiff of fierce brandy. CQ, yes that notice definitely said CQ. He had finally found the right route. And following all the rest of the signs he eventually came to the port side of the Lido – a self-service fast food area which brought good department stores to mind. Last time he'd been on the ship this life drill had taken place on the open deck. One thing remained exactly the same: he still couldn't manage the complicated fastenings of his life jacket.

'Having problems?'

Mickey had to turn around to see who was speaking to him in these deep and amused hillbilly tones. And when he did, he was treated to a look which was of a similar variety to the one that Edward, the hairdresser, had thrown at him. Similar but more flattering, more intriguing, and infinitely more experienced. It seemed to be saying 'Isn't-it-about-time-you-and-I-decided-what-happens-next?' Only it couldn't be saying that because the person who was smiling at him was somebody who had haunted the dreams of millions of gay men from Amsterdam to San Francisco. And expertly, and without any fuss, Jack Lawless was already fastening the fluorescent tapes around Mickey Grimshaw's body.

By the time Sorrel woke up again, it was the middle of the afternoon. Sparkling sunlight was reflecting into the cabin from the surface of an altogether smoother sea, and the world seemed a better place. The doctor's injection had left her feeling as though she'd had just half of one of the slimming tablets she used to take, the kind that filled her with energy and were always supposed to be on the verge of being banned.

54

But I didn't know the jab was going to do this to me, she told herself – ever conscious of her own addictive nature. Anyway, I can't get my hands on another one because the ship's doctor said the effects would see me through to New York.

There was a note from Mickey on the dressing table: 'Provisional hair appointment – uppity number called Edward – 5 p.m. Raving fan of yours! I will be having tea with Mrs Fiddler, from next door, in the Queen's Room at four.'

Sorrel might have been feeling better, but she wasn't ready to lay herself open to a chattering hairdresser with a tail comb in one hand and a can of lacquer in the other. He can do me tomorrow, she thought. By then I should be properly back inside my own skin. I'll call the salon now and attack my hair with the blow-dryer after I get out of the shower.

Three-quarters of an hour later, the Sorrel who strolled up to the Quarter Deck was a very different person from the woman who'd craved death for breakfast. The red hair was smoothed back into a chignon, and, always quick to tune into dress codes, her white trousers and sailor top looked straight out of *Dames at Sea*.

The Queen's Room had definite overtones of the hotel she'd left behind in London. As at the Savoy, a harpist sat in the middle of the public lounge – thrumming out a bit of Andrew Lloyd Webber. And waiters, in snowy mess jackets, carrying huge trays of minuscule sandwiches in their white-gloved hands, circulated between the tables.

'Sorrel, over here!'

Mickey, who had the ex-actor's appetite of a gannet, had already secured a big pile of the dainty cucumber sandwiches. 'I can't help it,' he said as he wolfed. 'It's the result of all those years of not knowing where the next meal was coming from. You already know Mrs Fiddler and this is Jack Lawless.'

I can't turn my back for a minute! thought Sorrel. But it had to be admitted that the American certainly knew how to behave because he was already on his feet and offering her a handshake that was pleasantly warm, and nice and dry.

'Feeling better?' asked little Mrs Fiddler. 'I managed with the tablets.' She was wearing a bright turquoise twinset, which made her grey hair look remarkably pretty. Her glasses gleamed, and there was no mistaking the fact that this was someone who obviously took great pride in keeping herself almost luminously clean.

Oddly enough, Mickey was thinking about cleanliness too. I know what he smells of: it's hygienically clean sweat and very good lemon soap; anybody who bottled that smell could sell it as an aphrodisiac. 'He' was, of course, Jack Lawless. The next thought was, this is ridiculous. The best thing I can do is to try and look innocently at Sorrel.

It didn't work. 'Have you been having a nice day?' she asked in a voice which threatened to descend into a guffaw.

'We all had lunch together.' This was really meant to mean 'Bloody well watch it, Starkey!'

'Isn't the doctor a price?' clucked Mrs Fiddler.

Mickey was glad of the chance to move things away from the unspoken subject. 'You didn't know that Mrs Fiddler was a big pools winner, did you, Sorrel?'

'That's right,' said their neighbour. 'Nothing modern, not the lottery. And I thought you was going to call me Polly.'

Jack Lawless, smiling in the teasing manner of someone who has purposely misunderstood, began to hum 'Hello, Dolly!', and Mickey said, 'We could restage the first act finale, here and now. There are certainly enough waiters. And d'you know what else, Sorrel? They talk amongst themselves in Polari.'

Polari was the old underground language of gay Englishmen, which had recently been enjoying something of a jokey revival. Actresses sometimes understood odd bits of it too because some of the words had been taken from the vocabulary of veteran performers.

The presence of Jack Lawless was causing the waiters to dance an extraordinary amount of attendance on the table. Two young man bearing silver platters of cakes all but collided, as they honed in on Jack, at the same moment. After tiny meringue swans and glazed strawberry tarts had been distributed, the waiters moved away – one murmuring to the other: 'Did you varder the cartse?'

'The cartse' was the Polari term for the most famous portion of Jack Lawless's anatomy.

'Eh, you! Come back.' This was a new Polly Fiddler. One who was bristling with indignation. 'Don't you dare polari about my friend's cartse like that.'

Had Mrs Fiddler suddenly broken into fluent Swahili, Mickey could not have been more startled. And a bewildered Jack Lawless asked, 'What gives?'

Polly Fiddler was ready with her answer. Glaring at the waiter, who looked as though he wished the floor would open and swallow him up, she said, 'This evil queen's got a mean screech on her, that's what gives.'

Once the poor waiters had evaporated away, Mickey spoke up again. 'If you don't mind my asking . . .'

'I used to work at the Old Garret in Manchester before they rebuilt it, when it was still a gay bar. Best years of my life! Knew all the queens: Jackie Carlton, Blond Eric, Greasy Violet . . . lovely lads, all of them. Nobody calls queers in front of me!'

'Excuse me . . .' The woman with the black hair with a white streak in it, the one they'd noticed the previous evening in the casino, had come up to their table and was reaching towards Mrs Fiddler's copy of the Daily Programme. 'May I?'

'Course you can, love.'

Once again the woman was with the haunted-looking husband. 'I told you it was two shows,' she said to him. 'One at nine and one at eleven.'

At that moment June Gee came trundling up the starboard passageway. She was still dressed in the pink tracksuit and the acupressure bands, and the look in her eye reminded Sorrel of how she'd once felt herself – in the years when she'd shivered in doorholes, waiting for the pubs to open.

'And once again she's kettled us,' said Mickey. It was all the talk of Polari that had caused him to use this term.

'No, I don't think she saw us,' said Sorrel.

'But that woman who just borrowed the programme saw *her*,' muttered Mickey. 'And if looks could kill, Miss June Gee would be dead. Thank you very much,' he raised his voice to a normal level as the Daily Programme was handed back by the handsome spectre of a husband. Mickey decided to have a look at the publication for himself. 'There certainly is something for everybody: there's a College Crowd Get-Together going on now, and the Freemasons met at three. There's also one man who must consider himself very special.'

'Why?' asked Mrs Fiddler.

'Because his friends are invited to meet him in one of the Grill Room Lounges, at five o'clock.'

'Let me see that,' said Sorrel. She suspected a coded message. And she was right. What's more, she was now extra glad that she had cancelled that five o'clock hairdressing appointment.

As Sorrel descended the staircase into the Grill Room Lounge she heard some familiar words which told that the meeting had already begun. Somebody was reading aloud from the Big Book: 'Alcoholics Anonymous is a fellowship of men and women who share their experience, strength and hope with one another, that they may solve their common problem and help others to recover from alcoholism.'

She slipped into an empty chair at the back of the windowless lounge, noted the suitability of an unmanned cocktail bar, and allowed more of the comfortable words to wash over her. Meetings always began with this reading, it was called 'the preamble'. And Sorrel had first heard it over a decade previously, in a scruffy room, up a lot of stairs, in a building beneath a leaking railway arch in Manchester.

Yet this had been the beginning of a whole new life

because the people in that room had taught her that the unthinkable was possible: one day at a time, she had learned to abandon that desperate urge to reach for alcohol. Booze had stolen her career, her looks, and her relationships. It had taken AA to hand her the whole lot back – everything and more. If she'd never climbed that ramshackle staircase she wouldn't have been on the *QE2* today: in all probability she would have been dead.

The people at her first meeting had been, for the most part, distinctly shabby. It had taken an old hooker to tell her 'it's alcoholism when drink costs you more than money'. And a man who was justly proud of the fact that he'd finally moved out of a tramps' hostel, and into a bed-sit, had said something else which struck home. 'We can have self-control in every other area of our lives but we can't handle drink. We're like men without legs who still insist on trying to walk.' When she got to know him better she discovered him to be a professor of medicine.

So who was here today? A frank gaze around the meeting was not considered bad form, everybody did it. The people sitting in this little lounge were as mixed as they would have been at any other AA gathering. Everything from American teenagers to an old woman in coffee lace.

She was sitting next to a big tough Broadway actor called ... Here he would just be 'Bill'. Nobody had surnames. And for the duration of the meeting, the two uniformed waiters, in chairs near the front, would not be obliged to call anybody Sir or Madam: absolute equality would prevail.

I'm home, thought Sorrel. And this is about the only place on earth I'd consider sharing out my pressing problem.

The reading didn't take long. The man with the book turned to the woman next to him and invited her to tell her story. This was usual procedure. Staying seated in her chair, the woman described her drinking days, told how she'd found her way to the Fellowship, and went on to describe her life today. She ended up by saying,

'Nowadays I don't have a drink problem, but I'm still an alcoholic so I have living problems – that's why I keep coming back to meetings.'

Me too, thought Sorrel, me too. This was the point where you could chip in, if you felt you'd gained any identification with what the speaker had said. Before Sorrel could open her mouth, a man piped up with, 'My name's Frank and I'm an alcoholic,' and he went on to describe the worry of a having a refrigerator full of Cunard's tempting alcohol in his cabin.

Two more latecomers came down the stairs – men. Their Brook's Brothers appearance caused Sorrel to tag them as perhaps advertising people or American politicians. And she wondered whether they were alcoholics or members of Narcotics Anonymous, who sometimes used drink-recovery meetings when their own weren't available – addiction was addiction.

'Anybody else got a pressing worry?' asked the man with the Big Book.

It was now or never. 'My name's Sorrel and I'm an alcoholic. When I first got sober I had the same problem as the last speaker, but it was with booze in hotel rooms. I found the only thing to do was ring for the maid and ask her to empty the fridge. It wasn't that I was going to drink it, it was just that I was haunted by the idea of it being so handy.' But that wasn't what she needed to say. 'I'm keeping something to myself. And it's not doing me any good.'

She could feel a perceptible quickening of interest coming from the people around her. It wasn't just idle curiosity, people were there to care. 'I've got this lump. Here.' She touched her left breast. 'Just by my armpit. I went to the doctor and he sent me to see a specialist. They've done a biopsy. I won't get the results until I get to New York. And I'm travelling with somebody who doesn't know anything about it. He really needs this holiday so I don't want him to know.'

It was out, she'd said it, and she already felt about a ton lighter. What's more she knew with absolute certainty that what she'd said would remain confidential. It always did. In the past, in AA meetings, Sorrel had heard people admit to having committed murders.

Nobody came out with anything like that today. But one young girl said that she hadn't realised that ocean liners were kept afloat to the accompaniment of popping champagne corks, and that it was driving her bananas – she got quite tearful. But everybody else stayed calm and more experienced travellers proffered practical advice.

A very late arrival tiptoed down the stairs and into the meeting. It was Jack Lawless. And Sorrel caught herself thinking that she wouldn't half mind hearing his story. Though she loved her fellow alcoholics she loved Mickey Grimshaw even more protectively. Lawless was too young for Mick: too young, too headily sexy, too obviously proud of being dangerous. And he had such wonderfully shaggy eyebrows!

4

The Gaiety Cinema on Peter Street had once been a famous theatre, but that hadn't stopped it from looking like a flat-fronted nonconformist chapel. For years, it seemed to Dinah, the building had housed *Gone With The Wind*. When the film finally moved out to the suburbs, the Gaiety started to play host to a downwards spiral of low-budget horror movies.

Would Rory consider her forward if she used one of the more horrific moments as an excuse to pretend to be frightened and clutch at him? That's what Dinah was debating as she walked from the bus stop to the cinema. But this was not her main concern. Would he actually turn up? That's what was really bothering her.

Instead of a canopy, the Gaiety just had long narrow strips of poster above both entrances. And each poster bore the fluorescent Day-Glo title of one of the films in the double-bill. *Breathing Slime* and *I Married a Teenage Hammerhead*.

Business seemed slack to the point of nonexistent. But her heart leapt at the sight of just one very smart and upright young man, standing between the two doorways, in what was obviously his best suit. Rory Brogan had added punctuality to the list of his attractions.

And only a real man could have got away with being caught with a dainty, little, quarter-pound box of Milk Tray in his hand. 'Here,' he said as he handed them over. In theory, all lads were meant to practise this nicety, but the fashion was dying out. In fact, these days, some boys even invited girls to the movies and then said 'I'll meet you inside'.

As they stood there in the evening sunlight, Dinah could already smell scented cinema-disinfectant. She just hoped it wouldn't be too hot inside the picture house. Casual clothes had yet to come into fashion in Saracen Street and she was tightly buttoned into the ice-blue two-piece costume that she kept for 'best'. Her mother was under the impression that Dinah was attending the crowning of a Primitive Methodist Rose Queen.

'I like the coffee flavour, meself.' Rory was nodding towards the box of chocolates, now in her hand. She always wore crocheted gloves with the blue suit. There was meant to be a half-hat too – blue petals – but tonight she'd nipped down the back entry and hidden it in the coal hole because it always made her feel like a bridesmaid.

Rory, it seemed, had run out of conversation. 'Oh yes,' he said, about nothing in particular. Or perhaps it was the chocolates. Obviously seeking further inspiration, he gazed up at the posters: 'Looks a bit lurid, doesn't it? I thought I was asking you to *South Pacific*.'

'That's at the Gaumont.' And you have the most beautiful mouth I've ever seen. Could lips be curly? His were. And, oh, how I'd like to block them out with my own mouth, she thought. But all she said aloud was, 'I think you have to book at the Gaumont.'

'We could always walk up there and see.'

'I don't mind lurid,' she protested.

He seemed more dubious. 'I've been looking at the photos; they all seem to be clanking around in tin suits. Let's stretch our legs.' He actually took her arm as he steered her across Mount Street; it struck Dinah that Rory must have been giving a lot of thought to how these things were meant to be done.

'Where does your mother think you are?' she asked him. The warmth of his arm, next to her own, was more than she'd been expecting this quickly.

'She thinks I'm at that big mating jig at the Holy Name.'

'Won't Cissie and Josephine say you weren't there?' The Midland Hotel was looming up on their right-hand side; the doorman was bowing a portly middle-aged couple, in evening clothes, towards the entrance. 'All right for some,' observed Dinah.

'Oh I'll get revolving doors, given time,' he assured her. 'There's no point in envying other people. You just have to slog at it and make things work.' He began to explain how his engineering apprenticeship at Metropolitan Vickers gave him day release to study at Salford Tech. And that this was deferring his National Service.

'I'm good at art,' she said. 'But if you go on to the Art School it's four years, and me dad says too many are doing it.'

'Don't you ever rebel?'

'Well I *am* here tonight.' She hadn't meant it to sound snappy but that was how it had come out. And it couldn't have happened at a worse moment because danger – massive danger – was heading their way.

Lily Jelly, the most notorious gossip in Saracen Street, had emerged from the side door of Boots All-Night Chemist's shop, bearing a large bottle of kaolin and morphine. She had already removed it from its wrapping, and, as she paused to peer at the directions on the label, her great bulk was well on the way towards blocking the narrow pavement.

Dinah's first thought was that she'd better turn round so Mrs Jelly wouldn't see her face. But Rory was already tugging her towards the kerb.

'Ouch!' She hadn't meant to cry out but his grip was suddenly painful. And the involuntary sound had been enough to alert the very woman they were trying to avoid.

'If I'd known you was coming to town, Dinah, you could have saved me a bus-ride.' Her beady black eyes were drinking the pair of them in. 'Poor Mr Jelly's in a terrible state – shocking! Hello, Rory.' She had obviously taken in the situation at a glance. 'If that poor soul's been down the yard once, he's been down it twenty times. I blame a bad whelk off Cross Lane Market. He's even made a temporary toilet for himself in the back kitchen. He's got the wooden clothes maiden up, with sheets round it. The poor soul's on a chamber pot inside.'

Spare us the details, thought Dinah. But Mrs Jelly was

sparing nothing. 'Of course I shan't say I've seen you, I won't breathe a word.' Considering she was known locally as Pathe Gazette ('The Eyes and Ears of the World') this seemed an unlikely assertion.

Rory took hold of Dinah's arm again. 'I hope he's soon better. Goodnight.' High above them, on top of an office building, the thousand separate light bulbs of the Bovril sign suddenly exploded into life.

It put Dinah in mind of flares dropping down, before an air raid. 'She'll say something, I know she will.'

'There seems to be a big queue outside the Gaumont,' was all he replied.

'And I bet they've got tickets too. It's "Booking in All Parts" for *South Pacific*.'

'Haven't the photos outside gone a funny colour? Mitzi Gaynor looks practically anaemic.'

'Rory, Mrs Jelly saw us! You don't seem a bit bothered.'

'I'm thinking about it.' That was when he asked the uniformed commissionaire about seats. There weren't any, even though the man congratulated Rory on winning an amateur boxing title. And the Oxford Picture House, next door, had a big sign up: Closed for Redecoration. 'This outing's getting us nowhere fast.'

By now she could tell that he too was becoming tense. 'Let's just have a walk,' she suggested miserably. 'Me nerve's gone. I bet Lily Jelly gets straight off that bus and starts broadcasting. I don't think I could settle down to watch a picture now.'

'Have a chocolate,' he suggested.

Her mother didn't let her eat walking along. But this was a minor crime when you compared it with being seen out with a Catholic. Getting the Cellophane off the box was no easy matter in crocheted gloves. Eventually she handed Rory a Coffee Creme and selected a Hazelnut Cluster for herself. Now she needed to get rid of the outer wrapping.

There was a rubbish can attached to a lamppost opposite Tootal's warehouse. A couple were standing necking on the marble steps of the building; the woman looked West Indian and she had red feathers in her hat. But the man, who was only half her size, was white. What's more he already had a wife of his own at home: they lived on Swinton Park Road, just near St Luke's Church.

Before Dinah could say anything about this to Rory, she caught sight of somebody else she recognised. It was that boy called Peter Bird, the one who'd said that The Place made him want to kneel down and pray. But he wasn't doing anything religious tonight; he'd grown a lot taller since she last saw him and he was tripping along with two other boys in very tightly belted raincoats. And one of them was definitely wearing black mascara. 'It's as though people come to town to lead a different life,' she said to Rory.

'If we go past the Ritz Ballroom there should be a way down onto the canal bank. Not that I want to live my life in the bloody shadows – if you'll pardon the French.'

She liked the fact that he'd apologised for strong language. That was gentlemanly. But she wasn't too keen on the idea of a canal bank. 'The thing is,' she explained, 'I can't swim. I had funny ears when I was little so I missed learning.' He was already leading her down an alleyway between two crumbling buildings. There was a strong smell of gas. 'As long as it's understood that, if I fall in, you'll come after me.'

'Okay.'

There were rough cobblestones under her feet, and as they walked round a corner she caught a first glimpse of the straight stretch of black water.

'You're all right,' he said. 'There's nothing to be scared of. I won't let anything happen to you.' This time he didn't link his arm through hers, instead he put it round her waist.

Tall warehouses loomed up on either side of the waterway and Dinah had never seen so many broken windows in her life. Even those with glass in them were murky. 'And why is steam puffing out of those pipes in the wall?' she asked nervously.

'No idea. Stay on the inside of the towpath and take

my hand.' At his touch, her own hand started to shake. 'You really are scared, aren't you?' he asked her.

It was easier to say 'Yes'. In truth, just so long as Rory stayed between herself and the inky water, she'd never felt safer in her whole life. Safe and . . . She paused, momentarily, to try and find the right word for the emotion and he urged her forward with 'Come on, I'll look after you.' Dinah immediately found herself overwhelmed by that top of Blackpool Tower feeling.

'Why are you shaking?'

'I'm not.'

'Feels like shaking to me.'

She needed to say something – anything – to change the subject, but she couldn't find any words. This was terrible! He was only holding her hand to be nice, yet she felt just as though somebody had poked a long hat feather up her best blue skirt. 'Do you go down canal banks with a lot of girls?'

'Not many.'

'How many?'

'None. You're the first. And if that sounds feeble, I'm sorry; but it's the truth.' They walked on for a bit and then he said, 'I spotted you years ago. I spotted you when you was almost too young for it to be decent.'

'Well you were younger then,' she said, making excuses for him.

'But I was nearly grown-up, I'd definitely what you might call "gone over the border".'

She paused for a moment on the towpath. 'I must be as old now as you were then.'

'D'you want us to turn back?'

'No.' She said this with absolute certainty. It was as though the conversation was going on at two levels: words that meant one thing could be taken for something else. This meant that every syllable would have to be weighed in the balance. Except, *Immaculate Heart of Mary be Praised,* enough must already have been said because his arms were around her, his lips had found her own, light was blocked out and she could feel the whole length of him pressed up against her.

And without a moment's hesitation she wanted to try the other kind of kissing, the sort girls talked about on the school bus. And his tongue was as urgent as the other thing she could suddenly feel pressing from beneath layers of clothing – right against the spot where she'd imagined the feather. It was as though – in one moment – she had grasped the whole idea of the infinite possibilities which could flow between two human bodies.

'Steady on,' he breathed. 'It's wonderful but . . .'

When they next came up for air she said, 'I didn't know I'd just know how to do it.'

'Me neither. Your eyes have gone all shiny.'

She rubbed her face. 'My chin's sore.'

'Sorry. But I only shaved at five o'clock. You can understand why people say you've got to watch it, can't you? It'd be dead easy to get carried away.'

She did know what he meant. 'I'm sorry for feeling the shape of your bottom.' There could be no pretending she hadn't done it because she had.

'I was having to stop me hands from going everywhere,' he said in wonder. 'By God, you *don't* need a book of words, do you?'

She wasn't sure she liked this. 'Me?'

'Us.' He said the word without any embarrassment. 'Us,' he repeated. And this time there was joy in his voice.

Before the kissing started, each time he'd taken her hand or put an arm round her waist it had felt somehow awkward; she had been reminded of signals, above a railway track, clanking into place. But now they were much more relaxed together. And as they continued with their stroll along the gritty towpath they swapped easily from holding hands to placing arms around waists, and sometimes they just leant into one another and smiled and laughed.

And the proximity would lead to yearnings, which were swiftly satisfied with more kisses. Except, the very satisfaction seemed to breed further longings of its own. But kissing was still enough of a novelty to turn Dinah's mind into a symphony orchestra, a fireworks display, a Grand Tour. Her feet felt inches off the ground and she could have been heading for the Piazza San Marco instead of the Rochdale Canal Basin at the back of Deansgate.

They were not alone on the canal bank. Dusk was beginning to fall and the world seemed to be out in twos. But that was something of a sweeping statement because the towpath was also playing host to stray men on their own. And if they were Peeping Toms they were only interested in one another because – after every dozen or so paces forward – they all seemed to cast one furtive glance back.

When Dinah voiced this theory aloud, Rory said, 'I think they're . . . you know.'

As a matter of fact she didn't know. But she didn't have time to think about it because her attention was seized by the sound of angry argument. As they got a few yards nearer to some lock gates the noise turned into two specific voices – a man's and a woman's. They belonged to shadowy figures, quarrelling beneath a stone bridge which was dripping mucky water.

'Either you go home tonight and say something or that's it.' This was the woman.

'I always mean to.'

'Then why don't you?'

'Because she always brings the state of her nerves into it and makes me feel a pig.'

'No, you're the one who's hiding behind her nerves. I'm beginning to think I'm just a convenience.'

Rory looked at Dinah and said, 'Let's never get like that.' By common consent they began to climb a set of stone steps, which brought them out opposite Knott Mill Station. It was colder now and the sun and the moon were in the sky at the same time, and on top of the viaduct, on the other side of the road, a train was busily puffing out white smoke. But there was nobody else about, nobody at all, so the world was still magical and all their own.

'I've been thinking,' said Rory. 'We might as well have the row sooner rather than later.'

'Us? Why?'

'The row with your mother and mine.'

'Why do they have to know?'

'Do you want a life on the sly?' he asked her. 'D'you want to risk ending up like those people under that bridge?'

'Oh but I think he already had a wife at home,' explained Dinah earnestly. 'At least that's how I read it.'

Rory looked her straight in the eye. 'Do you want to go steady?'

The only conceivable answer was, 'Yes please.'

'Then we'll have to tell the truth and shame the Devil.'

A Morris Minor rattled past them, quickly followed by a Ford Prefect, and one of the electric trains must have sneaked in silently from Altrincham because a whole lot of people suddenly came echoing out of the tiled tunnel of the station approach. The bubble of a world that had seemed to belong to nobody but Dinah and Rory turned back into plain old Manchester. Two groaning double-decker buses in an angry shade of red came heaving into view, and Dinah was immediately reminded of her mother and Mrs Brogan.

'If you set out to break my heart, Dinah Nelson, you've certainly gone the right way about it.' As always, when she was upset, Eva had reached for a duster. In fact the way she was polishing the black leaded range could have meant it was first thing Tuesday morning instead of ten o'clock on a Saturday night.

'Would you mind just going a bit easy,' said her husband. 'It's my weekend too.'

'And who's ruined it?' Eva was glowering at her daughter. 'Fat chance your father's got of relaxing with you around. And where's your hat?'

'In the coal hole.'

'Now I *know* you're mad. Did you know what that

70

boy was going to say when he come banging on my front door?'

'I was the one who did the banging,' protested Dinah, only too well aware that this was not the moment to bring up the subject of having her own key. 'I was nervous, that's why I rapped a bit hard.'

'I should think you *were* nervous! And as for you . . .' Eva had transferred her glare to her husband. 'What did you think you were doing inviting him in?'

'He asked whether he could have a word.'

Eva could have been sitting for a portrait of Sarcasm. 'I expect Hitler "asked whether he could have a word" before he grabbed Poland. You do know what that lad said, don't you? The sense of it has sunk in?'

'Don't talk down to *me*, Eva. The lad said: "Mr Nelson, I want you to know that I've been out with Dinah and we'll be going out together again." And if you'd not had hysterics he might have said a bit more. You do know you threw a bag of sugar on the fire?'

'He's a Catholic,' shouted Eva. 'He's a bloody Catholic.'

Her husband remained unabashed. 'So's the Duke of Norfolk but it won't stop him running the Coronation.'

'And who was supposed to be at the crowning of a Rose Queen at Pendleton Primitive Methodists?' asked Eva dangerously.

'I was. I'm sorry.'

'I think the Duke of Norfolk ran the royal wedding too,' put in Tommy.

'You used that word on purpose, didn't you? Wedding, I'm talking about – wedding!'

'Give them chance!' laughed her husband.

'Chance is what I'm not going to give them. It wants nipping in the bud, now.'

'You seem to be forgetting something.' It wasn't often Tommy Nelson put his foot down, but when he did you could always hear it in his voice. 'This is my house. I've already had apologise to the lad for your ranting and raving . . .'

'Which I did not appreciate.'

'And I didn't tell him he couldn't see her again.'

'Well you can just put your shoes on and go over the road and tell him now.'

'No way. And before you start again, these things are harder on fathers. But I can't fault Rory Brogan. He was always a lovable kiddie and he's turned into a thoroughly decent young man. Bit wild, but who wants a jessie for her. They're two kids, Eva. They just want somebody to go out with. Get your sense of proportion back.'

'It's all right for you,' she stormed. 'You didn't grow up in a street where it was all around you. I did. Bradys, Rogans, O'Connells, some of the biggest sinners in Salford. But off they went to Confession on a Saturday night, and come Monday they was knockin' buggary out of their wives again.'

'Times change.'

'Rome doesn't.' Her hatred was as old as the Manchester Ship Canal, which had caused thousands of immigrant Irish labourers to dig their way into Lancashire.

And that night Dinah's dreams were also of an historical nature. No less a personage than Good Queen Bess took it upon herself to walk out of the Gaiety Cinema, where she grabbed Dinah with a jewelled claw and hissed, 'You're going to the Tower.' But, when Dinah got there, it was Blackpool Tower. And Mary Queen of Scots was behind a microphone, in the ballroom, crooning 'Some Enchanted Evening'.

These dreams were more exhausting than no sleep at all and she finally awoke to the reality of the noise of the *Sunday Chronicle* being pushed through the letter box. When she got downstairs, her blue petalled hat was sitting in the middle of the kitchen table, a mute reminder of the events of the previous evening. And the morning remained silent: Tommy had already gone off to dig his allotment, Eva was refusing to speak.

The Brogans always went to High Mass at eleven o'clock. They generally came back about twenty minutes after St Luke's bell tinged out the midday Angelus. Dinah was more than anxious to hear how Rory had reacted to all the bawling and the sugar flinging; in fact she'd peered through the front parlour window so often that the pattern of the lace curtains had started to stay on her eyeballs after she'd stopped looking.

There's an awful lot of hanging around to first love. And when the Brogans did finally return it was only the women and Macushla and the baby who came back. That meant that this must be one of the Sundays when Rory went off to a Catholic pub, after church, with his father and his uncles. Love can also involve a deep knowledge of unprinted timetables.

Macushla was left outside, on the pavement, in her wheelchair. Sid, the lurcher, bounded out almost immediately to stand guard. By the time Dinah got out into the street he had settled at the cripple's feet. Although it was quite sunny, Macushla was wearing her pink woollen Sunday coat, and somebody had put a giant satin ribbon bow in her hair. A mistake. It only made the pale hair look even thinner. As usual she also looked as though she was feeling the cold. She even had a dewdrop quivering on the end of her nose. But – and most unusually – the eyes which gazed up at Dinah were wary.

'What's wrong?'

'Mrs Jelly started a story going, in the paper shop. She's calling you and our Rory "Romeo and Juliet".'

'Didn't he say anything himself last night?' He'd promised. He had definitely promised. He'd said, 'We'll tell yours, then I'll tell mine.'

'All you could hear in our house last night was a damn big row about Eamon de Valera. It went on till all hours and Daddy and Uncle Tim had to be pulled apart.' She treated Dinah to another cold blue gaze. 'Is what Mrs Jelly says true? Did she really cop you both necking on Oxford Street?'

Dinah could feel herself going bright red. 'No.'

'And the paper shop's owned by a Catholic lady. Me mammy's feckin' blazing.'

'Didn't Rory explain?'

'Him and the daddy and the uncles had already sloped off to the Britannia when the story got to St Luke's. Your names were being bandied right the way round the church garden.'

'People only ever stand at the front.' Dinah knew that for sure. She'd often seen them. She'd always watched anything – everything – which had even the remotest connection with Rory.

'Is it true?' Macushla's tone brought the Spanish Inquisition to mind.

'We weren't necking on Oxford Street.'

'But you were out together.' This wasn't a question it was a statement.

'He was supposed to be telling you himself.' Even to her own ears it sounded like weak repetition.

'You don't barge in on a row about Eamon de Valera. Not in our house. Are you sweethearts?'

'Would you mind?'

'Yes.' It was a cry from the heart. 'He's mine. He's my Rory, and I like you a lot but you're a Proddy-dog. My brother's good and he's beautiful and he deserves better.'

Dinah had been taking criticism since ten o'clock the previous evening. It was 'he deserves better' which finally caused her to see red. 'Would you consider the Virgin Mary good enough for him?'

'That is one of the most terrible things a human being could think of saying. Only a dirty Proddy-dog could say that about Our Lady.'

'Listen, you! I go to sleep every night wearing the green scapular!'

Macushla's eyes opened wide and her thin lips parted in astonishment. 'You do?' The Irish can change their attitude even faster than they can burst into song. 'You still shouldn't have said that about Our Lady.'

'I know. I'm ashamed. She's already been very good to me.'

'She'll understand. She's wonderful understanding about rage.' Macushla really had changed sides. 'Watch out for yourself, Dinah,' she hissed. 'I can hear me mammy creaking down the lobby.'

Anastasia Brogan was a brawny woman with a great sloppy bust, arms like hams, and a lot of vigorous, greying, curly hair. She was wearing a printed cotton frock and an expression of fury.

The sight of Dinah had turned eyes that were blue as her children's into icicles. 'Inside, Sid,' she said to the dog. 'And you're coming indoors too, daughter. As for you, Miss . . .' It was Dinah's turn in the tub. 'As for you, you'd better keep your luscious curves and your fascinatin' ways to your own side of the street from now on. At least that's what you'll do if you know what's good for you. You're scum. You hear me? You're nothing but a walking mortal sin.'

School started again on the Monday and Dinah came straight home and did her homework. There was nothing zealous in this. It was just that she needed something, anything, to take her mind off unleashed love. She had spent the day seeing Rory Brogan in everything – literally everything. In morning prayers she'd thought about his religion, in English Literature her imagination had managed to turn him into Prince Hal in *Henry IV Part 1*. Geography had sent them sailing up the Nile together. It was obsessive, it was awful, it was wonderful!

Painful too. Was everything still the same between them or had his family started working on him? When Cissie Brogan met the wrong young man, the priest had been called in and poor Cis had been packed off to the furthermost tip of Ireland for a whole summer. And why hadn't Rory left her a note or come round and banged on the front door?

He was definitely at home. She'd already watched through the curtains and seen the battered van drop him off on the opposite side of the road – the van that was always crammed with apprentices in boiler suits and had its back doors held together by an old clothes line.

Homework: the only thing to do was blot the whole thing out with more of her homework. All she had left to do was her biology revision – 'The separate parts of flowers and ferns'. Stems, bracts, petals, stamens; the notebook dated all the way back to the first form, and the illustration she had done then looked very tight and careful, compared with her drawings of today. If only she could go to the Art School and learn how to do this sort of thing full time, but her parents were dead set against the idea. They kept on pointing out that, if she'd been at an elementary school instead of Pendleton High, another wage would have been coming into the house a year ago.

Still, she supposed she might just be able to get some sort of job where she could use her drawing. She had always been keen on Biology because it involved diagrams and colouring – everybody said she was going to get the O level Biology prize and what the hell did it matter when thoughts of Rory Brogan were marching through her head like the Whitsuntide Walks – bands, banners, the lot!

This is awful, she thought. It's not to be borne. I'm like a boiling kettle with a blocked up spout. The only relief she could think of would be to draw Rory – yet again – in the painted diary.

Opening the cupboard at the side of the fireplace to take out the Windsor Castle biscuit tin, she accidentally knocked some books off the same shelf. *Five Go Off On An Island Adventure* and *Professor Petrulengo's Compendium of Astrology*. If everybody had their own, the latter belonged to Macushla. But she had allowed it out on 'a long lend' because she knew that Dinah had become deeply attached to the volume. And Catholics weren't really meant to have books like that anyway – which hadn't stopped it coming from the Knights of St Columba's jumble sale.

For perhaps the twentieth time, Dinah opened the compendium at her own section. She had been born under the sign of Cancer the crab, which made her 'mystical, a passionate dreamer, much influenced by the waxing and the waning of the lovely moon'.

But what was Rory Brogan's sign? And how did they match up? The book told her that, ideally, he should be Scorpio so she lost herself in reading that section. Lost herself so deeply that she must have missed a discreet rap on the front door, because, the next thing she knew, her father was in the room saying, 'He's out there asking for you.'

'Rory?' She jumped up off the floor, her arms went straight round Tommy Nelson, and she gave him a kiss that was made of joy.

All he said was, 'And don't think I've not been your age because I have.'

But she could tell he was on her side; though, as she got out into the lobby, she saw that Rory had been left waiting on the front step. In Saracen Street terms this was not an embracing gesture.

Neither did Rory seem about to offer her any kind of hug. He just stood there on his big feet and said, 'Wednesday night: it's mixed bathing at Swinton Baths on Wednesday nights. I could teach you to swim. Okay?'

'Yes.' Did her bathing costume still fit her? 'Thank you very much.' As he shifted his weight from one foot to the other she realised that he was about to move off. Did that mean that he would be out of her life again until Wednesday? She couldn't just let him go like that. Struck by sudden inspiration, Dinah asked, 'When's your birthday?'

'Christmas Eve,' he laughed. 'It means I only get one present. Or if it's two, the other one's always a new raincoat. See you on Wednesday. You'll have to bring your own towel because we change in separate parts.'

He'll have nothing on, she thought in wonder. Well, next to nothing, anyway. And that's how he'd be when he held her up in the water! But what about her own bathing costume? It was a terrible old thing, bought in an arcade on Blackpool front. In the time it had taken her to think these thoughts Rory had already put the street between them and was waving good-bye from his own front door.

I love the way he walks, she thought. Those long strides and the way he clomps his feet down. Christmas Eve, he was born on Christmas Eve.

Consulted immediately, the book said that this made him Capricorn. And when she flicked to the section that explained how Cancers got on with Capricorns, Professor Petrulengo proved to be very stern indeed. 'This is a 7–7 vibration,' he declared. 'In mathematical terms it is a negative. When Capricorn encounters Cancer he is destined to want to move away immediately.'

No, she thought, it can't be right. If the book was my own I'd throw it on the back of the fire. But Professor Petrulengo had been almost eerily accurate about everything else so she forced herself to read on.

'In perhaps one in a million of these encounters the two signs meet and touch, and instead of repelling one another they cause a massive explosion to take place. The resulting debris falls into a pattern which is rare and beautiful. It is best likened to a banquet. But from the very beginning the fear is that this will be a magnificent meal without a dessert.'

They *are* going to send him to Ireland, thought Dinah. It took real courage to read on. 'This fear is inevitable but both parties should rest assured that given time – and in its proper place – the dessert will arrive as surely as night follows day.'

Her heart singing, Dinah rushed out of the room and into the kitchen, where her mother was rubbing Goddard's powder into a knife blade as her father filled in his football pools coupon. 'Dad,' she cried, 'are you ready for another kiss?'

Dinah Nelson had often noticed that once her mother had slept on a new idea, she generally awoke with the matter pickled in vinegar. The trip to the baths was proving to be no exception.

'That Rory just wants the chance to see you in your nothings. What time of the month is it?' Eva shivered open the big cupboard door at the side of the black leaded range. Like the majority of householders in Saracen Street she kept a Co-op calendar behind it, a photographic view of their redbrick headquarters in Balloon Street, Manchester.

'You can close the cupboard door,' said Dinah. 'I'm not due to come on till next week.' Though the high school taught that menstruation was no barrier to exercise, Saracen Street retained more old-fashioned views.

Eva wasn't letting go of the matter of swimming. 'I'm very much against the whole idea. You've got ears, Dinah. I was forever traipsing you off to the doctor's with them when you were little. Go and put that costume on.'

'Now?'

'Now. You're all right, your father's working two till ten.'

'Why should that affect anything?'

'It means he won't see you in the nuddy. And while we're on the subject, I think you're getting a bit old for all that flinging your arms around him.'

'You're not stopping me loving my dad,' protested Dinah stoutly. 'I love my dad.'

'Strikes me you want to love the whole world. Go and get yourself into that bathing suit.'

Dinah's bedroom always looked as though the furniture had been chosen with a view to moving to a nicer house. Pastel pink painted furniture and rosebud curtains, and a distinctly middle-class Peter Rabbit rug: all of Eva's aspirations for her daughter were on view in the decoration of that attic.

The swimming costume was in one of the dressing table drawers. Dinah had chosen the garment for herself, two years previously, when elasticated waffle cotton had been all the go. Had she really – deliberately – settled on a pattern of blue Scottie dogs on a bright yellow background? And had the puckered garment always been as small as this?

She took off her clothes, climbed into the one-piece costume and her reflection shone back at her – three dreadful times – from the triple mirror which sat on top of the dressing table. She looked like someone who wanted sixpence for an ice-cream cornet – all that was missing was the bucket and spade! No, it was worse than that: she looked more like a grown-up doing a dreadful child-imitation. Dinah had grown a lot since Blackpool. This meant that the costume did wonders for her waist, but it made her bust look like two giant, squashed, poached eggs. 'And I wouldn't care but I've got a nice bust.' She actually said it aloud.

'People who talk to themselves get taken away in yellow vans.' Eva had stolen into the room and assumed the pose of official inspector. 'That should cool his ardour,' she said remorselessly.

'I'm not going in it.' There was flat refusal in Dinah's voice.

'Well then you're not going at all because you're not getting another.'

'I'll borrow one.'

'You will not. You're not wearing something that's been next to somebody else's private parts. You will not, Dinah. And I'm quite capable of following you to the baths to see whether you've defied me.'

She was too. Of that, Dinah had no doubt.

'What's that clanking noise?' demanded her mother.

'It must be in the water pipes.' The cistern stood in one corner of the attic, Eva had painted it apple green.

'It's been going on all day.' Her mother returned to the subject of the swimsuit: 'At least everything's covered up. That's the best that can be said about it. In fact it's about all that *can* be said about it.' And she began to laugh.

That night, Eva's laughter haunted Dinah's dreams. The hollow mocking sound was so horrible that it woke her up; that was when she discovered that the noise was really coming from the water pipes. Her *Three Little Pigs* alarm clock showed four in the morning. If she went back to sleep, Dinah knew that her dream would resume exactly where it had broken off: this was something which was always happening to her – always. But Dinah Nelson had her own foolproof way of breaking the pattern.

Climbing out of bed, she pulled her dressing gown over her nightdress and began to pad downstairs. Her mother was forever saying that her father could snore for England, though Eva was one of those people who went to bed and died.

I won't do it in ink, thought Dinah, I'll just use soft pencil. This was how she altered the scenarios of her dreams, she drew herself a new story. The cupboard door and the tin box always seemed to make much more noise at night. What did she want to dream about? Experience had already taught her that one thought of Rory would breed a dozen more. Far from encouraging pleasant slumbers she could be encouraging the feeling of being a mad steam kettle.

It was too late: he had already taken possession of her mind so she decided to draw his face. Except, suddenly, she couldn't remember what it looked like. Her mind's eye could only settle on separate bits: his curly mouth, the blue eyes, those shoulders . . . They were all floating past her like something in a painting by that crazy Spaniard, Salvador Dali.

I'll just do the mouth, she thought. And when I've done it I'll kiss it. And then I'll dream about him all night long.

Fat chance! One kiss turned her head into a Pandora's box of romantic possibilities. Dinah never even bothered going back upstairs. By five o'clock that morning she was only too well aware why people carved names on trees, why they wrote initials on the top of school desks, why grown men felt obliged to have women's names tattooed into their very skin. It was in the hope of *release*.

It wasn't that she wanted Rory out of her life. God forbid! Even the thought of it had her touching the green scapular, in her nightdress pocket, for protection. But if these all-embracing enrapturing thoughts were love, then even crossing the street was going to be dangerous.

When she judged it to be properly daylight, Dinah made herself a cup of tea; at seven o'clock she took up another pot, on a tray, to her parents – just for something to do. And when she got to school, everything was dominated by thoughts of seeing him that evening. It was as though she was living her life in monochrome. And it seemed as though it would stay that way until Rory – by his presence – brought back the colour.

The hands of the kitchen clock had never moved so slowly nor been inspected so frequently. And when the knock on the front door finally came, Eva was ahead of her down the lobby.

Without so much as a 'Good evening' or a nod she said to Rory, 'There can be no question of her going near the deep end. That's to be understood from the word go. And I don't want her floating to the middle on a rubber raft.'

He dived into his hold-all and produced a deflated life-belt. 'In case she's a bit nervous.'

'And have you got a puncture outfit too?' Eva was obviously determined not to be impressed.

'No but I've got a life-saving certificate.' He was more than up to her.

'Nine o'clock,' said Eva to her daughter. 'It's a week night so I don't want you in a minute later.'

'I'll have her back,' said Rory levelly.

'I was speaking to Dinah, not you.' It was as though she was defining the nature of her own relationship with the young man: all right, he was there, but if there was any way she could cut him out, she would. 'Nine o'clock, Miss. And dry yourself properly, afterwards.'

Eva's attitude gave them plenty to talk about on the way to the baths. Rory, it transpired, had been receiving Mrs Brogan's brand of stick, on the other side of the road. 'They'll get over it,' was the last thing he said as they pushed their way through the turnstiles and parted for the changing rooms.

These were individual cubicles around the edge of the pool, with half-doors, like a stable. The hinged wooden flap was carefully positioned to act as a modesty screen.

There you stood, wriggling into your costume, to the echoing sounds of a hundred screaming and shouting children. Everything seemed to be bobbing and swaying, and the smell of chlorine only added to Dinah's feelings of danger.

'Get changed,' he'd instructed her. 'Take your clothes down to the lockers next to the showers. All you have to do then is walk through some chemicals that wash your feet, and I'll meet you outside.'

She also had to fight her hair under a rubber bathing helmet which her mother had insisted on borrowing off Mrs Jelly – a former swimming champion. It made Dinah look like Amy Johnson ready to fly the Atlantic. A lot of the other girls, splashing in and out of the showers, hadn't bothered with bathing caps, but she supposed they hadn't got 'ears'. Come to that, there'd been nothing wrong with her own since she was seven! And now she was sixteen, and treading her way through a San Izal footbath to meet the man she loved.

He was standing waiting patiently, surrounded by a gang of fully dressed girls. They were taking it in turns to put their wet bathing costumes through the wooden rollers of an old iron wringing machine. But Dinah could tell that the young women's real interest lay not in their mangling but in the nearly naked Rory Brogan.

His woollen trunks were skimpy and old and washed-out but his body was breathtaking. 'Magnificent' was not a word which often sprang into Dinah's mind but it did now. Those wide shoulders, the swell and the depth of his chest, the beautifully sculpted arms and legs, and even the long fingers and feet, were all on a heroic scale.

One of the girls, more daring than the rest, had actually laid a hand on Rory's chest. As Dinah got nearer she heard her saying, 'You've got a better front than I've got but it's rock-solid.' She actually dared to trail a finger across one of his dark red nipples and Dinah could have sworn that the flesh rose up to meet her touch.

That did it! Exactly imitating Rory on Whit Friday she

marched straight up and said: 'I'll give you one second to stop that.'

'Will you?' The girl transferred her hand to one of his biceps and, smiling at Dinah, gave it a proprietary feel. 'You've had your second,' she said. 'So what do you propose doing about it?'

'This!' Dinah thumped her straight in the eye.

'Steady on,' muttered Rory, but there was admiration in his voice.

The fully dressed girl, the one she'd thumped, came lunging towards Dinah with fingers that had turned into claws. 'I'll bleedin' scrag you,' she bawled as her nails went for Dinah's face. It all happened in two quick flashes: one long tearing scrape downwards was followed by another one, going across.

This definitely wasn't fighting fair. But a memory of some old words of her father's came to Dinah's rescue: 'In a rough-house the only thing to do is knee them in the jimmy's.' The girl with the fingernails obviously didn't own jimmy's but Tommy Nelson's daughter raised her knee sharply, just the same.

Totally winded, her opponent collapsed onto the wet tiles at the edge of the pool.

'She'll never be able to have babies now,' screamed one of her friends. 'Moira, speak to me. Speak to me, Moira.' Another of the gang took a wild swipe at Dinah with a wet swimming costume. It hit her face with such ferocity that she saw coloured lights in front of her eyes in a pattern that was just like a Turkish carpet. And her ears were full of the sound of long shrill blasts on a whistle.

The pool attendant, a bald and burly pudding of a man in a white singlet and white flannels and damp tennis shoes, had panted into view. Removing the whistle from between his indignant lips he pointed an angry stabbing finger at Dinah. 'You. Get dressed and get out. You're barred for life.'

'It was just something that happened.' Rory was plainly trying to be reasonable.

He was wasting his time. 'If I hadn't stepped in, you

could've been telling that to an inquest. Is this fire-cat with you, Rory?'

'Very much so.'

The girl on the ground had recovered enough to shove in her own gasping two penn'orth: 'If I've had a prolapse, my mother'll be coming round to see your mother.'

'And I want no loose talk in my baths,' said the indignant attendant. 'The pea in this whistle's never jumped so hard in its whole life!'

Dinah trailed off to the tin lockers and collected her clothes. The baths had suddenly gone a lot quieter and it seemed as though a hundred pairs of curious eyes were all following her progress to the changing cubicle. She could taste her own blood; and when she started getting dressed, some of this blood went on her bra.

'I'm not looking in,' said a man's gruff voice. 'But I've brought you the First Aid box.' It was the attendant again. 'Are you decent yet?'

'Just a minute.' Eventually she turned round and looked at him, over the top of the wooden flap.

'Rory Brogan explained.' He sounded almost kindly. 'I can't have my authority flouted but I've decided you're only barred for a month. There's Germolene and plasters in the box. If you want hot water from a kettle you'll have to come to the office.'

She did her best with what was in the First Aid kit. She had to trail back into the showers to find a mirror to see what she was doing with the Elastoplasts – four separate strips. You could have played noughts and crosses on her face. When Dinah returned the red tin box to the pay desk, Rory was already waiting for her by the exit.

'Are you all right?' he asked.

'You could've done something to stop it.'

'It was a woman's fight.' He said it calmly. 'How could I join in that?'

'That's not what I'm talking about. She was touching you up.' And then Dinah said what was in her heart. 'She's touched part of you that I've never touched.'

'It's all yours, you should know that. All of it, every-thing – such as it is.'

'It's beautiful,' she assured him. Her mind began to project ahead and she envisaged their homeward route. It would take them through Victoria Park, which had a decaying mansion at one end and a cast-iron bandstand in the middle.

And in the shadow of that bandstand she finally got to trace her own fingers across the spot the girl had defiled. Rory's chest was indeed like rock, and the thought that he'd said it was all her own filled Dinah with such warmth and happiness that she could have wept at the wonder of it all.

'I think I'd better deliver you back to your dad, properly,' said Rory. They'd come downhill from the park and now they were walking hand in hand along Saracen Street. Dying sunlight was softening the blunt edges of the buildings; it was an evening of palest gold with umber shadows. Empty milk bottles, gleaming on top steps, had turned to bronze.

'Me dad won't be there. He's working two till ten.'

'Somebody's got to explain how you look to your mother.'

Eva would only blame Rory. 'I'll do it.'

'Sure?'

'Positive.'

She knew that the little kiss he gave her on her own doorstep was just a statement for the benefit of the rest of the world. Besides, his lips, his arms, those loving hands had already told her silent volumes by the bandstand. 'You make me happy.' She said it shyly.

'That's funny,' he sounded almost embarrassed himself. 'That's exactly what I said about you to me mother. "She makes me happy," I said. I'll see you on Friday night. Half past seven.'

'See you.' She let herself in and went down the lobby in a dream. Friday night at half past seven: the world would go into suspension until then. And he'd talked about her to his mother . . .

86

'Is that you, Miss?' It was her own mother. The lobby door burst open and Eva stood there in a dress and a pinafore and unaccountable wellingtons. 'I've had a lady here complaining you bashed her daughter. My God, whatever's wrong with your face?'

'I did bash somebody. But she started it.'

'You were never in a fight in your life, not till you took up with Catholics. That settles it. It stops. And tomorrow, after school, you go round to that girl's house in Penelope Road and apologise.'

'No.' Dinah meant it. 'She's the one who should apologise. She tried to finger Rory.'

Eva put her hands over her ears. 'I don't want to hear. Roll round in a barrel of muck and some's bound to rub off. And those Brogans *are* muck.' Now she began to wail: 'And I wouldn't care but my back scullery's like Noah's flood! That clanking noise was a pipe getting ready to burst. Mr Jelly's been in to look at it but the stop-cock's jammed and his tools are lent out to somebody who's not in.'

'Rory's got tools,' cried Dinah. He always carried a leather toolbag in from the van when he came home at nights.

'I'd wade round me scullery before I'd ask a Brogan. What am I talking about, I'm wading already! But you're not going for him.' She cocked her head on one side. 'What was that new noise?'

'Another sort of clanking in the pipes.' Together they rushed for the scullery.

'I've been to the phone box and rung the plumber and he's out,' wailed Eva. 'Oh my God, it's gone in another place.' The flooded scullery was a step down from the kitchen but – even with the back door open – water was beginning to seep over the coconut matting of the kitchen floor. 'The drains won't take it. And it'll ruin polished furniture – ruin it.' Eva gave in to self-pity: 'You scrimp, you save to get things nice, and you end up with a house like Agecroft Regatta. I do me best, it's just not fair.'

'Let me get Rory.'

'No.'

But Dinah knew her mother. 'You've not even finished paying for that sideboard yet, and it's going to be ruined. Your lovely sideboard, absolutely wrecked.'

'Get him, get him, get him,' snapped Eva. 'I won't like it but needs must when the devil drives. And don't just suggest he comes and has a look; get him to bring his toolbag straight over.'

Three minutes later he was there with a toolbag, a blow-lamp, and Sid the lurcher in attendance.

'What's that ostrich-dog doing paddling round my scullery?' stormed Eva.

'He likes being with me.' Rory was already kneeling in several inches of water. 'He's got wolf-hound in him, they're very fond of rivers.'

'Yes and he's got yellow eyes too,' said Eva darkly. But at that moment the water stopped pumping out and Dinah could tell that the fight had gone out of her mother.

Five minutes later Eva interrupted her own mopping up to ask Rory, 'What do I owe you?'

'Nothing.'

'I wouldn't want to be beholden to you.'

'You're not. It's all right for you to ask me to do things for you.' He seemed to be measuring out his words carefully. 'It's all right because you're Dinah's mother.'

'Yes and a nice state her face is in too.'

He remained unruffled. 'It wasn't her fault.'

'Oh it was yours, was it?'

'No.' This in a tone which simply had to be believed. 'No, it just happened. It was something or nothing.'

'It wouldn't have been something or nothing in my day.'

Rory turned to Dinah. 'I'll see you on Friday at half past seven then?'

'Yes.' She waited for an outburst from her mother but none came. All Eva said when Rory had gone was, 'Sly, it's not the word for you, Dinah Nelson!' And then she gave a nasty laugh. 'I'll tell you something else. Mothers can be very funny about losing their favourite sons. You won't find it so easy to wheedle your way round Anastasia Brogan.'

Dinah generally did her homework in the front room. On the Thursday of that week she found herself with a great knot of mathematics to unravel – both arithmetic and algebra – and she was hopeless with figures. And tonight the distractions were massive. On the opposite side of the street Macushla was out on the pavement in her chair; she was nursing the Brogan baby and he was howling like a banshee.

Whatever a banshee is, thought Dinah. And where's the square root of twenty-seven multiplied by sixteen gone? She could actually see the numbers inside her head. They had toppled over like a pile of playing cards, and getting them into any semblance of order would be impossible until she took a break to clear her head.

Fresh air might help. In fact it only took her nearer to the screaming baby. He was called Tyrone. 'Named for the county, not for the fillum actor,' explained Macushla as she tried to pacify the furious infant.

'He looks just like a little red tadpole.'

'Yes and he keeps grabbing for the titty and I'm as flat as a board.'

Dinah was only half-listening because she had suddenly realised that the baby on Macushla's knee was a miniature reproduction of Rory, a tiny Rory gone a bit chubby. 'D'you think he'd come to me?'

'I'd give him to tinkers.' Macushla handed the baby over. As it was another sunny evening Tyrone was wearing nothing but a nappy and an abbreviated vest. Dinah wasn't used to babies, and when she lifted him to her own front she was surprised to find that he was very warm; in fact it was like hugging a rubber hot-water bottle in a knitted cover.

'Watch out or he'll start sucking at your gym slip,' warned his sister.

But he just nuzzled up against Dinah and gave a little burp. 'I think he's smiling,' she said in awed wonder.

'Wind. They don't smile that young.'

'No, he is, he's smiling at me. He's beautiful, Macushla.' And I want one of my own, was the next thought. Just the feel of him was touching extraordinary places inside Dinah. Tender places and caring ones and protective ones. 'Doesn't love have a lot of departments?'

'I sometimes think you're a bit touched. You'll soon stop talking about sloppy love when he widdles down you.' It was one of those times when Macushla was looking particularly bony and angry with everything and everybody. 'What homework have we got?'

'Maths. But I have to do it for myself because you won't be next to me in the exam.'

'Bet you I'd slaughter it in two minutes. Watch out, here's me mammy.'

Stasia Brogan must have just washed her hair because it was hanging down in wet rats' tails to shoulders that were as broad as Rory's. 'What was he screaming about?' She didn't look best pleased at seeing the baby in Dinah's arms. 'I suppose he's hungry.' In a figure of eight movement she wrested the baby from Dinah and fished out an enormous breast. It was very white with blue veins running across it, and Tyrone went straight for the untidy splotch of purplish-brown in the middle. 'I'll just give him a couple of minutes on the top step,' she said. And she suited the deed to the word by sitting down. 'This is Catholic motherhood you're looking at, Dinah.' She spoke with grim satisfaction. 'Mr Brogan only has to throw his trousers over the bed-end and I'm having another!'

The baby wrested away from her had left Dinah with an inexplicable feeling of loss. 'Ten wouldn't be too many for me,' she said. And she meant it.

'They wouldn't? You might think a bit differently at three in the morning. This one goes on the bottle as soon as he gets teeth. You were a terrible chewer,' she said to her daughter. 'I was red-raw with you. But it's the men who never get over the titty.'

Conversation had never been like this on the other side of the street! And as the baby suckled, Mrs Brogan was looking at Dinah, looking at her hard, looking into her. Eventually she said, 'Are you planning on making a fool of my son? Are you playing games with him?'

'No.'

'I wonder.'

Something that had never been said to Rory obviously needed saying to his mother. 'I love him.'

'Oh you think you do, do you? Well take a good look at me. It might all begin in the moonlight but it ends up with the stink of boiling nappies. And something else has to be said: you're not a Catholic.'

It was Macushla who came to Dinah's rescue. 'She could be instructed. She could have Father Conklin's twelve lessons.'

'It wouldn't turn her into a cradle Catholic. Those bloody know-all converts! Catholics are born not made.' But she had obviously come to a decision: 'The baby likes you, I could tell that. And he won't go to just anybody.'

'I like the baby.' Dinah only hoped it didn't sound as though she was trying to curry favour.

'Ours isn't a tidy house like your mother's.'

'You can have too much of tidiness.'

'When I was having Tyrone your mammy was kind enough to lend me a chamber pot.'

The fact that it had never been returned had been the subject of much acrimonious comment.

'If you come inside for a minute I'll rinse it out and you can take it back. Ouch you little bugger!' she said to the baby. And with that she shoved the damp breast back into her flowered frock and led the way into the house. 'You'll just have to take us as you find us.'

Dinah found them to be almost embarrassingly holy. Even in the back kitchen there was a big, painted, plaster of Paris statue of the Virgin Mary, with a glass tear coming out of one eye. And next to her on the sideboard – but on a smaller scale – stood a chipped figure of an old monk in a brown habit, with a baby on his knee. The most spectacular sacred item of all was the huge framed and coloured engraving over the fireplace: Jesus Christ's heart was glowing through his nightshirt and dripping with its own blood.

In the months to come Dinah was to grow very familiar with this rickety household. The focal point of interest was always the ever-shifting mound of clutter on the big kitchen table. Many layers of anything from unironed washing to boxing gloves and bicycle clips, and a bottle of Amami setting lotion, and half-finished knitting. But it all felt jolly, it felt as though a lot of separate lives were going on at the same time. And to a carefully brought up only child, that back kitchen was as gloriously foreign as Paris.

Dinah's whole life may have been lived in the spotlight of her parents' attention but, in fairness to the Nelsons, they had gone to lengths to assure their daughter of a reasonable amount of privacy. Intimacy was the name of the game at the Brogans – enforced intimacy. It was as though the family spent their days on an open plain, midway between the constantly banging front door and the queue for the lav in the back yard. ('Come out of there, Macushla, we know you're only reading.')

Yet, despite all of this, Rory Brogan managed to lead a life which was almost curiously self-contained. And nowhere was it more evident than in his relationship with Dinah Nelson.

Since that first meeting outside the Sawyer's Arms he had never parted from her without the assurance that they would be meeting again, at a set time, in a set place. It seemed as though he had to have this assurance before he could go off and get on with his life.

And that was the trouble: Rory had just grafted Dinah onto the side of his existing programme. This made her feel as though she was left walking up and down Saracen Street with her heart in her hand.

Professor Petrulengo seemed to know all about it. 'For Cancer subjects, love is a full-time occupation. The male Capricorn is capable of returning affection at the most profound level – after the daily round has been completed, after the football match has been cheered to the echo, after every last piece of correspondence has not only been answered but also posted. Then – and only then – will he give Miss Cancer the all-embracing attention she craves.'

The in-between times were the problem. Rory liked the idea of her being around the Brogan household. 'Mucking in,' he called it. 'Getting them used to you. You'll need to stay friends with them when I go off to do me National Service.' But unless they were going out on a specific date, being around the house simply turned her into more female wallpaper. She was just somebody who could help busty Josephine get a hem straight, whilst Rory was a tantalising figure in nothing but underpants, demanding to know the whereabouts of his clean training shorts. There was no room for false modesty at the Brogans.

The one person who was very covered up, when he came home for the holidays, was Holy Paddy. This was Rory's irreverent nickname for his elder brother, the seminarian. In all weathers Paddy was obliged to wear a long black cassock, which covered him from Adam's apple to ankle.

'They're not supposed to start stirring up female passions,' was how Rory laughingly explained it. 'He's a lovely feller is Paddy, a lovely feller.'

And he was. He was Rory all over again, but a more gentle version with an inner kindness which shone out of him. Nevertheless he was a Brogan so it was only a matter of time before Dinah copped him in his underpants. And she was startled to discover that they were almost as disturbingly well-filled as Rory's own. It wasn't that she was looking . . . Oh, go on, she was looking. But his body didn't send her the same messages as Rory's did. It just seemed, to her Protestant mind, that it was a pity to think of all that strength and beauty being allowed to run to waste.

It took Paddy to effect a real change in his mother's attitude to the girl from number twenty-four. 'She's going to make a wonderful gift to Holy Mother Church,' he said. 'Stop looking like that, Stasia.' They mostly called their mother by her Christian name. 'The only sin will be if they *don't* marry. It's love and it's grand and where's me clean black socks?'

'You're as bad as Tyrone,' grumbled his mother. 'That child's bewitched by her.'

By now the baby was starting to form words, and his big brother's girlfriend was always 'Me Dinah'. He would chuckle with joy when Rory swung him up into the air but in next to no time he'd be holding out his arms to Dinah Nelson. The very act of taking him from Rory made her go gentle inside. One day, she would think, one day . . . ! And then Tyrone would love her and love her. And that would remind her of how much Rory was capable of loving her – on his bloody appointed hour, on the appointed day. And then she would wonder whether she should be thinking such things whilst she was holding an innocent baby.

Not that she and Rory ever went too far: that was the trouble. Steam built up and went nowhere. He'd once admitted that he sometimes felt forced to go off and 'take a hand' to himself. 'I couldn't go indoors sticking out like a bren gun!'

She hadn't dared to tell him that a vivid imagination and two fingers had been connected with other parts of her own body, that sometimes a pillow found its way down her narrow bed. But the pillow hadn't been Rory so it had never got her to the place she needed to get to. Couldn't get her there, because she needed to be where two people would lose their identities in one another.

Dinah Nelson sang the hymn 'Forty Years On' with the other girls who were leaving that year, got all the teachers' signatures in her autograph album, and that was the end of Pendleton High School. O level examinations were behind her, the results were yet to come.

'Your next stop's the Juvenile Employment Exchange,' pronounced Eva. She had already cut up Dinah's gymslip and pegged it into a rag rug, and now she was taking her scissors to a pair of outgrown hockey shorts. 'I'm not saying you've got to begin work straight away. You'll need your results to get the cream of the jobs.' However, that night, Eva did not fail to comb the Situations Vacant columns of the *Manchester Evening News*.

'Listen to this: "Prominent Salford herbalist requires trainee assistant. Knowledge biology and neat handwriting are musts." And there's a phone number.'

Dinah rang up the following morning. She made the call from a public kiosk on Bolton Road. It was drizzling outside, traffic was swishing past and two buses were grinding to a halt at the fare stage. As she pressed Button A and the four pennies dropped into the box she had to raise her voice to explain that she was answering the advertisement.

'Are you tall?' It was a woman's voice, she sounded old and peppery. 'And have you got long arms? Short arms won't do, they have to be long.'

'I'm five foot five.' She had added an inch. 'And I've never measured my arms.'

'You'd better come and see me. Come at two o'clock.' She gave Dinah an address off Cross Lane and said that the street was practically opposite Salford Hippodrome. 'You're not funny about ladders, are you?'

'I don't think so.'

'If you are you'd be better saying now. John . . .' The woman had raised her voice to speak to somebody at the other end. 'Not in the dandelion bin, John.' Now she was talking to Dinah again: 'Ladders was the last girl's undoing. No herb on earth can cure vertigo. You have to go up quite a long way,' she warned. 'Wear low heels.'

Dinah had already been planning on high ones, to compensate for the fictitious inch. In the end she settled on her new 'flattie ballerinas' with rubber galoshes pulled over the top, to stop them getting spoiled in the rain. She had her best blue costume on too, and a transparent plastic mac of Eva's.

This raincoat was very stiff and unyielding, and it

made sinister crackling noises as she got off the bus at Cross Lane. Rain, battering down onto the matching, clear plastic umbrella, added to the unmusical symphony. Dinah was not feeling confident.

What's more, she was nearly a quarter of an hour early. So she decided to shelter under the canopy of Salford Hippodrome, a battered music hall, which had two windows full of display photographs. The show they were advertising was called *We're No Ladies*.

Somebody else was also taking cover from the rain. It was a tiny old woman, a human rag-bag who sported a good quality man's cap above a grey Plasticine face, which featured a pair of curiously glittering eyes. She was drinking something called Dr Abercrombie's Chlorodyne Compound, straight from the neck of a miniature brown bottle. 'You'd never guess them girls was all fellers, would you?' This observation came with a nod towards the display case. 'What God 'as forgotten they've padded with cotton! Not a real woman amongst them.'

And not one of them who didn't look better than Dinah felt, inside her creaking plastic cocoon. Now she glanced at her own reflection in the glass of the showcase. She looked as though she ought to be on the stage herself, singing 'It Looks Like Rain in Cherry Blossom Lane'. Nobody could seriously hope to get a job looking like this – nobody. 'Is that Peplum Street over there?'

The woman took another swig of the compound. Dinah was sure you were only meant to have 'two or three drops in warm water'. The old wraith licked withered lips. And when she finally replied, it was in a faraway and dreamy voice; 'Peplum Street is nothing but common lodging houses and a herbalist's.'

'That's where I'm going.'

'You're going to see Mrs Tench? She's a tartar!' All dreaminess had vanished. 'Are you in a mess, love? Are you after penny royal? She won't sell it. Not Mrs Tench. Very strict about things like that.'

'What's penny royal?'

'Sorry, love, I mistook you for a girl in trouble. She's a

96

bad besom, that herbalist. Stopped me 'aving any more of 'er poppy syrup. Said I was getting too keen on it. Fastest road out of Salford, that's what that syrup was to me.' Tapping the last dregs of the contents of the chemist's bottle onto her tongue, she glazed away into her own reveries.

The faint odour of chloroform was making Dinah feel queasy. Better early than late, she thought. 'See you,' she said as she put up her umbrella again and darted between a brewer's dray and a bus marked 'Docks'.

The horses pulling the dray were steaming in the rain. And a delivery boy on a bike labelled 'Turner's Prime Pork' just missed her ankle as she reached the opposite pavement. Looking back over his shoulder as he rode on, he shouted out, 'You need glasses.'

'Oh get off and milk it!' she yelled back. Dinah Nelson might have been down but she wasn't out, though the rain had suddenly decided to stop, which would make her look even more of a fool in this ridiculous outfit.

Peplum Street was only short: it was just a dead end, with a view that looked over railway tracks, towards a group of iron gasometers on the horizon. The houses were older than most Salford terraces. They were Georgian and must have once belonged to professional people. 'Good Lodgings For Working Men' was painted on the brickwork of one double-fronted dwelling, and a similar sign on another bore the additional words 'No Irish'.

The street had plainly fallen on bad times. Just one tall thin house boasted clean windows and recent paintwork. But the brass sign on the front door looked nearly as old as the street itself: 'Tyrell and Tench – Practising Herbalists – Push'.

Dinah wondered how many generations of Salford children had automatically obeyed that injunction and then run away, laughing. She didn't feel a bit like laughing herself, she felt distinctly nervous. Nevertheless she gave the door a tentative shove and found herself looking down a narrow passageway where gloom met cleanliness. Stepping inside, she nearly fell over an ancient black bicycle. It was an upright model with no crossbar, and it was chained to one arm of an oak settle.

'Yes?' A little glass window marked 'Enquiries' had flown open and a head was poking out.

Anybody who had ever seen *Professor Codman's Famous Punch and Judy Show* would have recognised the figure immediately. But this Judy – pixie hat, hook nose, thin lips and all – was genuine flesh and blood. And she was obviously the owner of the peppery voice which had spoken to Dinah on the telephone. 'Are you the girl?' she squawked. 'Carry on up the hall. You'll find a door on the right-hand side.'

By the time Dinah edged her way there, the door was already opening and she was afforded a full-length view of the woman who was about to interview her. Pixie hood, jumper and skirt were all knitted in that multi-stranded brown and fawn wool known as 'mingle'. Her shoes were brown too, men's lace-ups.

Noticing Dinah glancing down to these, the woman barked, 'I'm not a collar and tie job if that's what you're thinking. My late husband took a pride in being very well shod. I don't believe in waste.' She stepped back to appraise the girl in the transparent raincoat. 'Well you're certainly not another midget. Come in, come in.'

In the same way that some rooms are lined with books, this one had mahogany drawers from floor to ceiling, and all of them were labelled with the names of herbs in faded gilt lettering. It began with Aconite in the top left-hand corner, way above the black marble fireplace, and ended down by the far skirting board with a drawer marked Yarrow.

Mint and Myrrh were either side of the window onto the street. And two zinc dustbins, labelled Dandelion and Comfrey, stood on the scrubbed wooden floor. Indeed there so many names of herbs in the room that it was like being in the middle of a completed crossword puzzle.

'I see patients upstairs,' explained the woman. 'That's how it's always been since Father's day. I was a Miss Tyrell, now I'm Mrs Tench.'

Dinah wondered why a herbalist didn't know about tying horsehair around warts; there were quite a few that needed attention. And if she drew the nose in the painted diary tonight, she would have to remember the downwards swoop of a tomahawk. The mouth was just a straight line, the eyes two nasty brown beads. What's more they were boring right into her as Mrs Tench asked, 'Where are you working at the moment?'

'I've just left Pendleton High.'

'I was there when it was still called Summerfield. Doesn't that coat of yours crackle? Sit yourself down, dip the pen in the inkwell, and write something for me.'

'On this bit of scrap? What shall I write?'

'Suit yourself.'

Dinah tried to think of some poem with herbs in it – tried and failed. The only thing that seemed to come to mind was a short verse by Hilaire Belloc. So without really thinking what she was doing, she began to write it down.

'Not that I'm apologising for the pen,' said Mrs Tench after a while. 'I never apologise. But it was the last girl who chewed the end of it to bits. Would you believe it, she said I made her nervous!'

Yes, Dinah did believe it. And she was suddenly realising the full meaning of the words she had just written down. She had once been made to copy them out, fifty times, in a detention period at Pendleton High; that was how she came to know them so well.

'Let's have a look.'

'I think I'll just cross it all out and write something else,' said Dinah wildly. 'It has capital letters in funny places; they're meant to be there but you'd probably get a better idea if I wrote out a hymn.'

'No. It's my paper and my ink so don't think you can defy me.' Mrs Tench snatched up the page with one hand, grabbed a pair of wire-rimmed glasses with the other, and using the spectacles as a magnifying glass, she began to read aloud.

> *'Lord Finchley tried to mend the Electric Light*
> *Himself. It struck him dead: And serve him right!*
> *It is the business of the wealthy man*
> *To give employment to the artisan.*

'You certainly don't lack spirit! Let's see how cocky you are about climbing ladders.'

It was only now that Dinah noticed the wooden library stepladder, leaning against one of the walls of drawers. 'I'll have to take my galoshes off first.'

'Naturally. I want you to climb as far up as the word "Arnica" and then look down.'

It seemed that the only thing to do was to obey her and Dinah began to ascend towards the whitewashed plaster ceiling.

'Any feeling of giddiness?' called out Mrs Tench, when Dinah reached the top. 'Any swaying sensation or general unsteadiness?'

'No, I just feel as though I'm up some ladders.'

'Stop where you are a minute. Those aren't regulation Pendleton High School knickers.' Her tone was accusing.

'Well I've left.'

'If you were to work here you'd need drawers with elastic at the knee. You'd be spending a lot of time aloft and men come in, travellers et cetera.'

At that moment, the door from the corridor opened and a member of the male sex – he was wearing a long white medical overall – did indeed enter.

'You don't have to worry about him,' barked Mrs Tench. 'That's not a man, it's a fully qualified herbalist. I'm trying her out for vertigo,' she explained to the new arrival. All Dinah could see of him was the top of a pair of ears and some pink scalp. 'You can come down now, he's not the kind who looks up young women's skirts.' It wasn't that he was balding, just that he had baby-fine blond hair. 'This is my son, Johnnie.'

As Dinah creaked her way down the ladder she was able to get a better view of Johnnie Tench. He belonged to the breed of slim young men you sometimes saw on the tennis courts in Light Oaks Park. No amount of exercise would have turned him into anything but a drink of water. He had kind eyes though – washed-out blue. And had nice hands too. They were a bit sturdier than the rest of him, and he was holding one out as he said, 'How d'you do?'

'She'll do very well,' replied his mother. 'The hours are nine till five thirty, and one o'clock on Saturdays. The pay's two pounds seventeen and six a week. You can start next Monday.'

Eva insisted on Dinah taking sandwiches to work. 'I don't like the idea of a young girl roaming round, looking for a meat pie, on the Barbary Coast.' Cross Lane led down to the docks, at the inland end of the Liverpool-Manchester Ship Canal. But before you got that far you came to another branch of Tyrell and Tench, on Eccles New Road.

It was a big shack rather than a proper shop, opposite Stowell's Memorial Church. And the window display featured glass bottles containing tapeworms pickled in formaldehyde. Mrs Tench's father was said to have extracted the largest one from the innards of a Bengali seaman. This branch was also noted for owning a white parrot. It sometimes lived in a brass cage in the shop window. More often it was allowed to flap its disconcerting way around the inside of the shop.

There were no mahogany drawers at the Stowell's Memorial branch, just wholesale-sized biscuit tins of herbs, with their names inscribed on gummed luggage labels. Neither was there a consulting room at this shop, and only basic remedies were dispensed over the counter. But things went on here that didn't go on at Peplum Street.

The establishment was under the sole jurisdiction of a man known all along the Barbary Coast as 'Dickie Pop'. The wooden shack led into another, which opened into some old brick stables. That's where the gaseous herbal drinks were brewed, and then siphoned into stone bottles: ginger beer, saspirella, dandelion and burdock. Dickie Pop's real name was Eugene Gannon. Brewer, bottler, the Stowell's Memorial branch was his kingdom – his empire. But he didn't own it, Mrs Tench did. And he cordially loathed her.

'Call me Eugene, it'll make me feel younger,' were the first words he ever said to Dinah. He had a sing-song, Irish, country person's accent, a bit of a lisp, dyed black hair, and he looked as though he was wearing dabs of rouge when he wasn't. Or perhaps he was.

Eugene darted and dived so quickly, adjusting bubbling glass pipes here, tapping the bung into a barrel there, that it was difficult to fix on a complete picture of him. It was equally hard to put an age on the man. Thirty-five, forty, fifty? With his sleeves rolled up to reveal long white forearms covered in fine black hair, Eugene was a lot like a jerking marionette. He had a foxy little nose and lips that were the same shade of red as you see in old tattoos, and if snakes could speak they would surely have sounded just like this guardian of the herbal brewery.

'Mrs Tench is the devil's daughter.' Tap-tap went his little wooden mallet. 'Ask the girls at the Eccles branch. Both those sisters have had to go to Salford Royal for electrical shock treatment. And why?' He began to screw in a stopper. 'Edna Tench, that's why. Never trust a woman with mustard breath, Sonia.'

'My name's Dinah.'

'Yes but you've the look of a Sonia. Did you know that Tyrell and Tench got bricks through their windows in the First World War? German blood. Wouldn't surprise me if that Edna wasn't descended from the Kaiser. Him or Adolf Hitler! Ah well, dictators rise and dictators fall . . .' One hand flew out to turn up the gas jet which was bubbling under a concoction in an iron pot. 'The days of Tyrell and Tench are numbered. Of course, her father was a genius; he was what we call at home "a wise man". She's just a witch. No, she's worse, she's a bitch. And that's a Sin of Uncharity and

I'll have to confess it on Friday; pass me that wooden spoon.'

He hadn't finished his tirade. 'The Eccles branch is crumbling to bits, the front shop here is held together by courtesy of a pound of four-inch nails; the only thing this business has got left is the inherited herbal knowledge inside that old cow's head. That and the secret formula for the Gentlemen's Remedy.'

'What's the Gentlemen's Remedy?' asked Dinah, fascinated but mindful of the fact that she had been sent to Stowell's Memorial to collect a box of ointment jars from the bottle store. 'What does it do?'

'How can I put it delicately enough for a maiden's ears? Tyrell and Tench's Gentlemen's Remedy is known from here to Port Said. Sailors always come in and ask for "the cobra pills". It's a powerful arouser that can lead to Mortal Sin.' Whenever he used Catholic phrases he always made them sound as though each word began with a capital letter. 'Mortal Sin. Get my meaning?'

Dinah immediately thought of Rory and his bren gun. 'I think so.'

'She's had men come from as far as London to try and buy the formula. Beechams Pills was even said to be after it. While she's the only one who knows the formula she's got power. And Edna loves power. Look how she's managed to cut the plums off that poor son of hers.'

'Has she used herbalism on him too?'

'She has not. All he had to do was spend the twenty-six years of his life with her. Get these jars round to Peplum Street before she puts a spell on you too. I must get on, I've got me holy brasses to rub clean.' As well as working for Mrs Tench, Eugene acted as unpaid sacristan at a tiny Catholic church, nearer to the docks and much frequented by foreign seamen.

Outrageous as his conversation always was, Dinah felt that it would have been even more unbridled had it not been for his religion. 'In a purely spiritual way . . .' he would say thoughtfully. 'In a purely spiritual way, did you notice that Spanish sailor and wasn't he bloody lovely? I'm only speaking from the head, you understand; there's no sin in admiring beauty.'

But when Dinah mentioned Rory Brogan, Eugene all but licked his chops. 'The Rory Brogan as is light heavyweight champion of Adelphi Lads Club?' he cried. 'What a wonderful thing it must be to be a young woman. Does he take you to the dances at the Holy Name?'

Dinah would have preferred not to think about those dances. Her one visit to the big church hall off Oxford Road in Manchester had been a disaster. She had assumed that ballroom dancing – like kissing – was something which just came naturally. As far as Rory was concerned this was indeed the truth. But to the fiddle and accordion accompaniment of Finnegan's Dance Band, Dinah had learned that the fairies at her own christening had dumped two left feet in the cradle. If her thinking had gone Irish, it could have been because bold-eyed beauties, with great clouds of black hair or tumbles of bright ginger ringlets, had been quick to notice her inability, and had whirled Rory off ('You don't mind, do you? I'm a friend of his sister Cissie's'). Wantonly whirled him into the midst of the jigs and the reels.

'I can teach you those,' said Eugene Gannon, afterwards. 'I've medals galore. But I've no knowledge of the passion dances,' he added sternly. 'I'm not your boy for the waltz or the tango. You'd have to go to Madam Jones's ballroom at Pendleton to learn the passion dances.'

The swimming lessons continued. Dinah had her own private name for them – 'Aqua Rapture'. And if it sounded like a Van Johnson and Esther Williams movie, there was certainly a lot of underwater twining and embracing. As often as not lusty Rory was obliged to keep his nether regions hidden in the water, long after Dinah had departed for the ladies' showers.

There she would often find herself debating the wonderfully amazing differences between men and women. It took next to nothing to get Rory worked up. So how did Holy Paddy, his celibate brother, cope? Locked, as he was, inside that long black soutane with the row of little buttons down the front.

Poor Paddy didn't come home often. And when he did, he seemed to be hemmed in by a whole lot of sacred restrictions. He hadn't even been able to allow himself to go and see Joseph Locke in *Aladdin*, although Macushla had assured Dinah that the sides of the stage would be packed with Irish priests, listening to the Irish tenor on the sly.

Paddy was very far from being a killjoy, you could tell that by the gleeful way he played the accordion. Whenever he came home, Gervase Pollock did too. He was another seminarian, whose family lived near to the Eccles branch of Tyrell and Tench. 'Both boys are so nice-looking,' she would say to Rory. 'It seems such a waste.'

The herbalist's at Eccles was run by two nervous spinster sisters. It was not true that they 'both had to have electrical shock treatment'.

'Eugene romances a bit,' said Avril Porter, who also worked in the Eccles shop. 'He thinks life's a colouring book. There was *talk* of one of the old biddies having it, and that was enough for Eugene to add it to old Ma Tench's list of war crimes.' In truth Avril didn't say this, she shouted it instead. Avril shouted everything. Words were forever exploding from the sounding board of her generous body. She looked Slavic, with high cheekbones and slitty grey eyes. She also had a big bust, a small waist, and legs with highly developed calves. 'Eugene thinks nobody hates Ma Tench like he does but he's wrong. I hate her worse.' Yet Avril was an affectionate creature. Half the dogs and cats on the road to Patricroft could bear witness to that. Animals were forever arriving at the Eccles shop, just to say hello to her.

In the painted diaries Dinah always drew Avril Porter as Mother Earth, but there could be no denying that she had bad adenoids and that she shouted. She was also very frank, so being out with her could be embarrassing. 'Didn't that woman pong of old chip fat?' she would bawl. And, 'Don't look now but that man's got one arm shorter than the other.' Her least varnished comments were reserved for Edna Tench. 'She's bad. It's as simple as that, she was born bad.'

As one year of employment gave way to the next, Dinah was forced to concede that Eugene and Avril were right. For a start, the girl from Irlams o' th' Height had been hired as a trainee: Edna only passed on training that was useful to Tyrell and Tench. Dinah may have learned to brew an extract, to compound a poultice, but she never acquired an entire process. Old Edna would always step in, like some member of a medieval guild of alchemists, and add secret finishing touches. It was as though the trainee must never to be allowed to absorb anything which she could take away and use in a rival establishment.

Even volumes like *Culpeper's Complete Herbal* and *The Apothecaries' Almanac* were locked in a bookcase, behind a wire netting grille. It was precisely this secrecy which magnetised Dinah to the establishment. Jobs were easy enough to find in the 1950s but she was blowed if she was leaving Peplum Street before she could carry away something of value.

Edna Tench had one salutary effect on Dinah Nelson's life. Compared with her mean-minded employer, she began to view her own mother and Stasia Brogan in an altogether more favourable light.

She even began to understand how the ever-shifting pile of oddments on the Brogans' kitchen table had grown up. Stasia Brogan's life must have been like perpetual participation in that movement known at barn dances as 'the grand chain'. One thing always led to another. Just as she was stitching on somebody's missing button, the cry would go up for the iodine bottle, and another of her daughters would be demanding that Stasia should cast sixty-eight stitches onto a pair of aluminium knitting needles – immediately. And with all those people in the house, all of them separated from even more of the family in Ireland, the postman never missed a visit. Envelopes and snapshots and catalogues were forever being added to the table-top confusion. And Dinah was much shocked by the casual way in which they opened one another's letters.

'Rory's got to go on a course in London SE23.' Macushla was out in the sunshine, in her wheelchair.

Dinah was just coming home from work. 'He never said anything.'

'He doesn't know yet. It's hostel accommodation and a rail voucher.'

'How long will he be away?'

'Twenty-eight days and a certificate at the end of it. Oh Dinah, I do miss the way we used to do our homework together.'

'I've just been to the big library in Peel Park, and guess what I found? *Culpeper's Complete Herbal*.' Dinah pulled the book from her shopping bag. 'Ma Tench's not got the only copy in Salford.'

'And you can learn all the wonderful secrets,' cried Macushla. 'Dinah, would you ever let me have a lend of it? Just during the days.' Sid the dog added his pleading gaze to Macushla's own.

'Course you can.' It was hard to refuse her anything. Macushla was even thinner than she'd been in their childhood, her hair more like a piece of yellowing white silk that had been pulled through a nit comb.

But she still embraced life with abandon, her own life and other people's too. 'While Rory's away, you could finally have some ballroom lessons. Madam Jones has been advertising in the *Reporter* again.'

'No, I'll go to the Broadway in Eccles with Big Avril. She might be hefty but she's like thistledown on her feet, and I won't mind making a fool of myself with her.'

Later that evening she repeated this idea to Rory, but he was more interested in talking about his forthcoming course and how it might affect National Service deferments. 'I know it's all supposed to be over, but they've still got the right to call up engineers who've not done their time.'

Dinah manoeuvred the conversation back to ballroom dancing. 'The reason I don't want to go to Madam Jones's

107

is because it's all girls at the start, but after a bit she mingles you. You could find yourself flung up against anything.'

They were walking near the duck pond in Light Oaks Park. It was dusk but there was still enough light to see the towering stems of giant hemlock, which were making black Spanish lace canopies over the water's edge. And this was one of the years when the hawthorn flowers had stayed late in the bud. May blossom in June. And now that it had finally flowered it seemed doubly scented.

'That's a smell that's got a lot of lads in trouble,' observed Rory.

'How?'

'It does things to you.'

Quack, went a duck as it waddled towards the wooden shed on the island in the middle of the water. Quack. There was a crescent moon in the water too, a curve of tarnished silver, shimmering between the big flat leaves of the water lilies.

'On a night like this you could nearly believe in romance,' said Dinah.

'Why only *nearly*?'

'Because it's still Irlams o' th' Height.'

'That's the first time you've ever shocked me,' said Rory. '*Nearly*,' he repeated the word disconsolately. 'Aren't I good enough for you?'

She answered him with arms and lips that sought his own. When they came up for air she said, 'I do believe in romance, I paint it and draw it all the time. It's just that we don't seem to be getting anywhere. I mean, how long have we been marking time? It's more than two years, nearer three.' Suddenly she understood what he'd meant about the fecund smell of the hawthorn and she began to kiss him again, this time more urgently. What's more, her fingers were feeling him, *really* feeling him.

'You're going where you shouldn't,' was the thrilled Catholic response.

'So are you,' was the eager Protestant reply.

'I've got to kiss them,' he said. Her cotton frock was

108

already undone so that moonlight shone on the half-naked breasts.

'There.' Now she had them fully exposed for him. They'd never gone this far before. It was 1955 and people didn't. Or, if they did, they kept very quiet about it.

Rory was weighing the pale mounds in the palms of his two hands, his voice sounded much younger and more Irish than usual as he said, 'I can feel them going heavier on me. And look how the beautiful ends have a little life of their own. Can I suck?' The wonder in his voice had turned to terrible yearning: 'I want to be a baby again, I need to suck.'

The touch of his lips on her nipples, that flickering tongue, sent her soaring to regions which belonged to God. Everything of course belonged to the Almighty, but this was somewhere special. It was like a thousand times stronger version of the feeling she got near the stone at The Place – at the side of the Packhorse. She was on a roller-coaster ride through the heavens and one of her hands was holding on to his iron bar for safety.

For safety? No, it was need, terrible inexplicable need. Something ought to be going up and down and in and out. And because her hand was there . . .

'Stop it,' he gasped as the buttons came undone. 'No. Don't! Christ Jesus, if this is mortal sin it's bloody lovely.' Nevertheless he forced her hand away. 'Marry me,' he breathed. 'Please, please marry me.'

'Because we went that far?' She knew she shouldn't have said it but the words were out.

'Marry me because it's the only thing that'll stop me going insane.'

Once again they were in a deep embrace. And Dinah was surprised to find that she was weeping with relief. 'I didn't think you'd ever ask me.' She had finally admitted it aloud. But that was one species of relief, and renewed proximity had revived demands for another. She wanted them to be one person, and, to this end, she pushed herself right up against him.

'No.' There was no mistaking the firm decision in his

voice. 'We can't. You're marrying a Catholic. There are rules and we've got to stick by them.'

Quack-quack went the duck.

'Ah come here, Dinah,' he groaned. 'But just hands. Our Lord surely can't mind your fingers helping me have a bit of an accident.'

'I need helping too. Touch me.' She guided his hand as she had often done before, in her imagination, alone in her bed at night. 'There. It's all right to touch me now. I'm yours.' She just prayed that the quacking duck would not ruin the moment. And it didn't.

'Keep looking up,' said Avril. 'We'll only see them if we look up.' The newspapers had been full of stories of flying saucers. 'Two cigar-shaped ones are supposed to have followed the whole length of the Ship Canal.' Avril and Dinah were walking along the main street in Eccles. They were heading for the Broadway Ballroom; you got in by a side door next to a picture house of the same name. The steps that led upstairs were of the same kind of compressed chipped marble as you found on the way to the lav in the cinema. And during the day the ballroom was called the Broadway Cafe. By night, the pale green and silver basket chairs were rearranged around a sprung dance floor. One of the cinema usherettes was shaking French chalk, from a canister, onto the floorboards – and then treading it in.

They could see her doing it as they exchanged their half-crowns for mauve admission tickets. The orchestra was tuning up too. Strictly speaking it was a quartet: four men in pre-war dinner jackets and wing collars with ready-made dicky bow ties.

These musicians looked much older than the boys in best suits and brilliantine, already gathered together at one end of the ballroom. Once female patrons had dumped their coats in the cloakroom, they milled around at the other end. It all reminded Dinah of a discreet film they'd once been shown, without comment, at Pendleton High School – *Mating Habits in an Insect Colony*.

'What do I do if somebody asks me to dance?' she asked Avril in sudden panic.

'Just say "No, thank you" but smile nicely.'

Somehow this didn't seem quite enough. 'Should I point to my engagement ring as well?'

'Why should you? It's not meant to be a bloody chastity belt.'

Oh she did have a loud voice! Avril was wearing a drawstring peasant blouse and a dirndl skirt, cinched in at the waist by an elasticated belt. As usual she had managed to look like a Slavic refugee from the Whit Week walks – all that was missing was the red Wellington boots. 'Let's go and peer out of the window,' she said. 'We might just see one going over the rooftops.' The newspaper stories had started in America, and now the more sensational English papers had alerted the British public to the possibility of the arrival of visitors from another planet.

'I thought we'd come here for me to learn to dance.'

Avril was that rarest of creatures, a good person. But she wasn't boringly good, she was still capable of taking umbrage. 'Right,' she snorted in nasal tones. 'Let's be the first two on our feet. Let's get straight up and make an exhibition of ourselves!' The quartet of piano, bass, drums and violin, were already playing a syncopated fox-trot version of 'How High The Moon'. 'Do you want to lead or follow?' she demanded imperiously.

'Let's go and look at the sky,' said Dinah miserably. A boy in a Harris tweed sports jacket and grey flannels had already begun steering a girl, wearing an impressively full-skirted frock, around the floor. 'I'll never be able to swagger out like that, never.'

'You said the same about swimming. We'll just go and have a bit of a look upwards till the floor fills up. The *Daily Sketch* is offering five hundred pounds for a genuine photo.'

'We've not got a camera.'

'You're all criticism,' said Avril. 'You've been nothing but doom and gloom since Rory went to London.'

The quartet chose that moment to swing into the gloomy strains of 'Lover Come Back to Me', and Dinah reflected that Rory's absence was, indeed, colouring everything. The musicians were fronted by a singer, a woman old enough to be every one of the dancers' auntie. She was trussed into a big net frock and she had a beauty spot painted on one rouged cheekbone.

> 'Every road I've walked along,
> I've walked along with you . . .'

She was crooning her misery into a pedestal microphone. Through the window, sudden rain had turned the slates on the roof of Redman's Cafe into shades of deep and shining purple. Where would Rory be at this moment? The two weeks he'd been away felt as stretched out as chewy toffee; except they were cut up into fourteen separate pieces, and each one had taken forty-eight hours to pass.

Because her mother didn't have a phone, Rory had arranged to ring Dinah at the box outside the Elite Hairdressing Salon on the Height. But, at the appointed hour, she had arrived at the kiosk to find a man already ensconced within.

'If you don't come back to me, Joyce,' he was saying, 'I'm going to take tablets.' And then there were a lot of threats of what he was going to do with a brick to somebody called Arthur. Dinah didn't even pretend not to be listening. After playing audience to his end of the conversation for fully twenty minutes, she tapped on one of the windows and pointed significantly at her wristlet watch.

It did no good. The man just carried on saying that, as far as he was concerned, the hire purchase people could whistle for the debts Joyce had run up. 'And by what right did you take two pedigree pups away from their mother?'

It could only have been a local call because he hadn't

put any extra money in: you could stay on all night for four-pence if you felt like it. The air inside the red kiosk was blue with cigarette smoke. And every now and then he wafted the door open and shut, to let a bit out. At one point, just as Dinah was ready to scream with frustration, he actually poked his head out and said, 'This is likely to take a while.'

By this time she had memorised every stitch he was wearing; she would have no difficulty in recalling the trilby hat, the gaberdine raincoat, the ragged turn-ups sitting on square-toed shoes, when she came to draw them in the painted diary. But at the moment when her very being had started to cry out for the sound of Rory's voice, all it actually got was, 'I've kicked the glass of this phone box in, Joyce.' A lie. 'I'm just going to slash me wrists.' And then the man in the greasy trilby replaced the receiver, leaned out of the box again, and said, 'Have you by any chance got three pennies for a thrupenny bit?'

Rory's call never came.

But two days later there was a picture postcard of Battersea Funfair, bearing the hand-written message 'Couldn't get through.' Just that. No 'love', no nothing. And Dinah had sent off daily reams of intimacies to the address in London SE23. He did write some letters but they were . . . she couldn't think of the right words – stilted, formal. The most abandoned they got was 'it won't half be nice to see you again'. Yet in Light Oaks Park she'd heard this same man's soul singing.

Dinah comforted herself by looking down at her engagement ring: two diamonds with an aquamarine in the middle. And then she looked out of the Broadway window again . . . no sign of flying saucers.

The very next moment, high above Montague Burton the tailor's, a bright white light began to pulsate in the evening sky. 'It's the Martians,' bawled Avril in that nasal voice which sounded as though it was coming through a megaphone. 'There *is* life on other planets.'

Somebody nearby said, 'Take no notice of her, she works in a herbalists – they're peculiar people.' But a whole lot of other people, who were sitting out the fox-trot, crowded towards the big window. And this caused curious dancers to leave the floor and join them. Eventually, even the band laid down their instruments and came over to see what all the fuss was about. The throbbing white light appeared to be coming ever-nearer. The elderly female crooner, the one with the mascara beauty spot, breathed, 'It gives you some idea of how they must have felt in Bethlehem.'

It took the pianist to say, 'It's just a weather balloon.'

Hardly anybody wanted to believe him. Indeed, a slightly hysterical girl in a limp white semi-evening frock chose that moment to demand to be taken home – because if she was going to die she wanted to die with her mother.

The pianist was not to be deflected. 'I work at Barton Aerodrome during the day. Them balloons are silver rubber; that's what makes 'em glow.'

A disappointed sigh went through the sky-gazers. Nevertheless, they continued to look upwards. Dinah was looking down to see whether anybody in the street below had noticed the drifting silvery sphere. Eccles was deserted except for a 28 bus and two lads on foot; they were crossing the road and heading towards the ballroom.

Avril, who was lad-happy and looking for love, must have noticed them too. 'Why d'you think they're both wearing their trousers at half-mast? Can it be a new fashion?'

Dinah was privy to the answer. 'They might not be their own trousers,' she said carefully. 'Or then again, they could be trousers that haven't been out of the wardrobe for a while.'

The pianist chose that moment to try to turn the proceedings back into a Saturday night dance. 'We will now have a Ladies-Excuse-Me-Waltz,' he announced, in the voice he saved for moments between dances when he acted as Master of Ceremonies. 'Do you know any waltz with space-ship in it, Charlie?' he asked the drummer in altogether more realistic tones.

They mustn't have been able to come up with one

because, eventually, the musicians drifted into 'Oh How We Danced On The Night We Were Wed' as the two men in peculiar trousers entered the ballroom. Seen closer up, the sleeves of their jackets were definitely a bit on the short side too.

'They're still bloody lovely,' breathed Avril. 'The one like Errol-Flynn-without-the-moustache has spotted me.'

Just don't let the other one spot me, prayed Dinah. Aloud she said, 'I'm going to hide in the Ladies.'

'When he's got a friend? Don't be so daft.'

It was the friend that Dinah was worried about. The friend was more than familiar, the friend bore a marked resemblance to Rory Brogan. Which was not surprising because it was his brother – Holy Paddy.

And Paddy must have spotted her because she could hear him saying to his companion, 'Hang on a minute, Gervase.'

Avril Porter was not skilled in social graces. 'Why are you dressed like something out of *Our Gang*?' she asked, by way of introducing herself to Gervase Pollock.

'Why are you?' Dinah addressed the same question, very quietly, to Paddy Brogan.

He led her to one side, and then seemed worried about even having touched her arm. 'We're in his brother's clobber. Two of his brothers, to be strictly accurate.' Paddy had gone very red. 'We got changed in their hen hut. It seemed a lark at the time.'

His voice had trailed away so miserably that Dinah blurted out, 'I won't say anything. I promise. You're all right with me.'

'We sort of saw it like fancy dress. And there was such a rumpus going on at home that I was glad to get out. Did you hear they mistook him for me? Thought he'd dressed himself up as a seminarian.'

All this talk of dressing up had left Dinah at sea. 'Who?'

'Rory. Somebody's surely told you that the redcaps came after him tonight? Thought he was at home, didn't know he was down South.'

Weren't 'redcaps' the military police? 'But what's he meant to have done?' she demanded frantically.

'Not done, more like. His call-up papers came and he never went.'

At that moment Avril whirled past in Gervase Pollock's arms. Dinah felt like shouting out 'You're mauling a man of God' but she was more concerned about Rory. 'He never said anything about his papers coming.'

'He never knew. Somebody threw the letter onto the kitchen table and it got swallowed up in the mess. The army need engineers again; some military ructions have started in Cyprus.'

Remembering geography lessons at school, Dinah cried out, 'But Cyprus is the gateway to the Middle East . . .' If this much of the three weeks he'd been in London had seemed an eternity, what was an international separation going to be like?

5

On board the *QE2* the Alcoholics Anonymous meeting was heading towards its close. Seated on her little gilt chair, Sorrel made a mental note never to bring these new white slacks to a meeting again. They had to be real linen because they'd started to accordion behind the knees. An idle glance at the sunray clock above the closed shutter of the cocktail bar revealed that there were fewer than ten minutes left to go. She only hoped that nobody was going to choose them to leap into prominence – like the final starring act at the London Palladium. Her first friend in the Fellowship, all those years ago in Manchester, had always maintained that they seemed to be saying, 'Now I'll show you how it *really* ought to be done.'

'My name is Gary and I'm an alcoholic.'

But he wasn't known to the world as Gary. Outside this meeting he was Jack Lawless the porn star. And he certainly didn't look like somebody who was craving the closing spot: he looked like any old member of the Fellowship who'd spent the meeting with a head full of problems, somebody who'd just taken a deep breath and decided to open up.

'I said I was an alcoholic but I'm an addict too. I did drugs.'

Anywhere else, this admission might have caused people to sit up. But nobody here was in any position to sit in judgment so they just relaxed in their gold chairs and allowed somebody else's story to work its healing spell on themselves.

'My addictions don't stop there, either. I can get hooked on coffee, food, people . . . anything.'

Me too, thought Sorrel. In fact we should be singing 'And So Say All of Us'. In recent years addiction had come to be seen as an all-round problem. And Jack Lawless did not look the same arrogant aristocratic Elvis she'd first noticed with Mickey at Southampton. Instead, he suddenly looked defenceless.

'I don't talk much in meetings,' he said. 'Back home, in the States, I mostly go to gay meetings . . .' His voice trailed off. And then he tried again with, 'Except I don't know where home is. I know my address in West Hollywood but I don't know where home is. I don't know where I really belong.'

This was what the meetings were really about – identification with the person who was speaking. Sorrel got it now as she recalled her own lonely years of not belonging. Of sitting holding onto a hated glass in the furthest corners of licensed bars, with a pile of shillings for the juke box in front of her on the table. Juke boxes had been the final thing over which she'd had any control. And the music had always had to be dreamy and sad.

Jack Lawless, newly revealed as Gary, was still talking. 'I'm in the adult entertainment industry. I screw for cash. And now . . .'

'My name's Lila and I'm an alcoholic.' The woman who'd interrupted was English and red-headed. She had very shiny legs; there was a lot of them on view because she was wearing shorts and a tee shirt and an inappropriate pearl necklace. 'I felt I just had to come in and interrupt for a moment because I really don't want to listen about sex. I come to meetings to talk about my drinking.'

The chairman for the day, the middle-aged American man who'd opened the proceedings with a reading, stayed serene. 'Thank you, Lila, but we're all of us here to talk about anything that could cause us to reach for that first drink. We all of us know that if we don't have that first drink we can't have the second one, or need the ninety-ninth. Go on, Gary.'

These interruptions had plainly thrown the handsome young man and he began to pick his words more carefully. 'When you do the kind of job I do you compartmentalise sex and love. One doesn't necessarily go with the other.'

He's articulate, thought Sorrel. But her actress's ear had

caught something else. 'Jack Lawless' wasn't American at all, he was English. What's more, he had originally come from Lancashire. Now she was doubly interested in what he had to say.

'As I was getting on this ship I saw somebody . . .' For a moment his eyes flickered, worriedly, towards Sorrel. 'I'd seen him before on a documentary, on British TV. The guy's old enough to be my father. A shrink once tried to tell me that I wasn't gay at all, that I was really just looking for my dad.' As he examined these confusions within himself, the rest of the room must also have realised that his accent had left America for England, that absolute honesty, the whole basis of the programme of recovery, had taken over.

And he's got to be talking about Mickey, thought Sorrel. But I don't think he's being manipulative. All of this isn't specially aimed at me so I'll go and tell Mick. This lad is in too much of a state for that. And anyway, nobody with any real recovery ever told outsiders what went on in meetings – they all had too much to lose.

'I've talked to him, four times I've talked to him. God, I remember every word! And he's so *nice*.' There was longing in that last word. 'Nice and sharp and funny, and tough where it counts – inside. But the trouble is that I know me. I'm hooked on the idea so I'll go to any lengths to make him like me.'

You won't have to, thought Sorrel. I don't see the problem.

Out it came. 'Sex in front of the cameras is nothing. Neither is sex for cash. When it comes to that I can blank out, I'm just a gifted robot.'

Mickey wasn't above paying, Sorrel knew that. This wasn't to say that she liked it or even understood it. But his argument had always been 'Look at all those men who bought me dinner when I was young. Why shouldn't I pay my dues and buy a few dinners back.'

Jack Lawless's next statement was defiant enough to prove that he could only be a relative newcomer to the Twelve Steps and the Twelve Traditions. 'I'm a thousand bucks a trick. And I don't need to pay agency commission, I get them direct.' His burst of bravado fizzled out as he said, 'I'm falling in love with this guy. And the one thing he's going to expect isn't how I celebrate being in love. The most I want to do with people I love is put soft music on and light candles, and say "Listen to the rain on the window". And then my body locks itself up and I yearn.

'It can't lead to the other because I already sold out on that. There's one way I *can* handle it. If I smoke a joint, I loosen up. Hash makes me as loving as real people. And if I get away with smoking a joint I'll try a line of coke, and before you know where we are we'll be on to the brandy and fine wines.' His voice had turned back into self-mocking American. 'Thank you,' he said to the meeting at large. The ship was beginning to pitch again as he added, 'I feel better for just having got it out into the open.'

'My name is still Lila and I'm still an alcoholic,' said the woman with the shiny legs and the pearls. 'And I just wanted to say, Gary, that I'm sorry I tried to stop you sharing. God knows, all any of us can do is get things out into the open – it certainly cuts them down to size.'

Gary did not look one hundred per cent convinced of this. But the chairman chose that moment to say, 'Shall we close with the Serenity Prayer?' Just as other people must have been doing, at the same moment, in other rooms around the world, all the members rose to their feet and joined hands as they said,

> 'God grant us the serenity to accept the
>   things we cannot change,
> The courage to change the things we can,
> And the wisdom to know the difference.'

The meeting had worked its wonders, worked them to such an extent that Sorrel felt guided to go over to the handsome adult entertainer, and to take his hand and say, 'You're okay; I don't have to tell you that what you said

120

within the meeting is going to stay within the meeting.' But even deeper in her heart she was realising that Mickey Grimshaw had landed himself with a big problem.

'The trouble is,' said Jack Lawless miserably, 'there's another guy on the ship. And he's a raving fan of mine, and he keeps on offering me little wraps of hashish.'

Whilst Sorrel was in her meeting, Mickey had been to visit the ship's library. It was also the book shop. Tomorrow he was due to give a lecture in the *QE2* Theatre. There was to be a book signing session afterwards, and he wanted to be sure that Jane Marazion had plenty of copies of his latest novel in stock. Marazion was her married name: Mick had first known her when he was earning himself a reputation as a wild young man in London. In those days Mrs Marazion had been a mannequin. And Mick, yet to become an established writer, had padded out his income from acting by working as a male model. Indeed, they had once appeared together on the front of a Paton and Baldwin's knitting pattern.

Nowadays Jane Marazion spoke in lowered library tones ('If we are closed, Madam, you can always post your book into our letter box'). She even wore horn-rimmed glasses.

But at night . . . At night Mrs Marazion slipped in her contact lenses and wore little Jean Muir dresses which had been cunningly copied in Hong Kong silks. At night she sparkled for her admirers and fended the younger ones off with: 'I'm just a librarian and a grandmother.'

At midnight Mick might have chosen to tell her what had put a frown on his face and a spring in his step, for previous shared voyages had proved Mrs Marazion to be the perfect confidante. But this was only the cocktail hour. You actually caught yourself thinking in terms the like of 'the cocktail hour' on the *QE2* because baroque hairstyles had begun to emerge from the Steiner Salon, and white tuxedos and shimmering evening dresses were beginning to speed the footsteps of those passengers who were still in shorts and shirtsleeves and canvas deck shoes.

In her library, if Mrs Marazion sensed that you wanted to talk, she generally led you towards the door – so as not to disturb the people sitting reading in the big leather club armchairs.

'You never cease to amaze me, Grandma,' said Mickey happily. 'You've got all the hottest best-sellers on your shelves.'

Mrs Marazion began to look ahead for him. 'You can sign copies of *A Town to Remember* after you've done your lecture about *Angel Dwellings*. We'll save your new novel for when you talk about writing the books.' She took her career very seriously, and Mick was always aware that she worried he might go off like a firework on her peaceful premises. But she softened the fact that she was giving him the elbow with, 'Are you free for a drink in the Chart Room, late on? Call me in my cabin. Somebody's waiting with the new Joanna Trollope in their hands. It's absolutely flying out of the shop.' She was gone.

But the fact remained that, give or take a year or two, she was his own age and men still found her highly attractive. So if it could happen for Jane Marazion . . . Oh God, he thought impatiently, it's a well-publicised fact that Mickey Grimshaw is wedded to his readers. And, in a way, this was no less than the truth.

The novels had brought a satisfaction into his life which writing for television had never done. The *Daily Mail* had once quoted him as saying, 'I make love to my readers, I've only ever had sex with my viewers.' He had handed the woman journalist that line because she had been trying to question him about the split-up with Joe.

'Do me a favour,' he'd said. 'Would you leave the grisly details about Joe out of your piece?' And the alleged lady-dragon had promised she would, and been as good as her word. Mickey wasn't like Sorrel, who hated the press: he had real friends who were journalists. They'd helped make him a name. He acknowledged that and he was grateful to them.

This hadn't always been the case. There had once been a time when they had used hints of his unorthodox sexuality as a stick to nudge their readers into sniggering. Shoving in lots of 'darlings' when he'd never said them, and using phrases like 'the willowy young bachelor script-writer'.

But they never actually came right out and said he was gay. It was as though *Angel Dwellings* was such a sol-idly British institution that it would have been unseemly to acknowledge that it was the creation of a homo-sexual.

Writing the novels had changed all of that. The first one was about an out-of-the-closet scriptwriter, and his publicist had said, 'You're laying yourself wide open. If you don't want them probing and rooting you've got to spell out the fact that you're gay in interviews.'

'It's the world's worse-kept secret.'

'Yes and you've told everybody but Fleet Street. You can't blame them for hinting. I'll set up interviews with people we can trust.'

Angel Dwellings had always brought him a vast cor-respondence. Some of these letters were full of praise but there was also a lot of anonymous abuse about the programme. Newspaper revelations about his sexuality brought not a single unpleasant word.

His mother had refused point-blank to believe this. 'Why do you have to write about people like that?' she'd moaned over and over again. 'Why, why, why?'

'Because I've translated everything into the convenient terms of your world for years and years and years. People always used to ask Somerset Maugham why he never wrote plays about himself and he said: "I do. But Gladys Cooper generally plays me." '

From that moment on, interviewers had never hesitated to bring up the subject of his acknowledged life-style. Nat-urally enough, some of them wanted to know about his prime relationship. Joe had always had broad shoulders in every way. And when Joe went, it had been Mickey's friend from the *Mail* who'd said, 'You'll fall in love again.'

'Not me.'

'You will. I'm telling you. You've always idolised Noel Coward and he didn't hesitate to fall in love again at your age.'

'Not me.' He'd been adamant about that. Only now it was happening. The black despairs, the wild elations, all the things he thought he'd put behind him . . . There was a record player in the cabin and he was having to restrain himself from going to the hi-fi shop on board. He suddenly desperately wanted to hear Diana Ross singing 'Every Time You Touch Me I Become A Hero'. And he wasn't even a fan of Diana Ross's!

It was just that he was remembering Jack Lawless's arms going around him as he'd adjusted the cumbersome life jacket. And how they'd stayed there a fraction of a moment longer than was strictly necessary. And he was remembering Jack's eyes across the table in the Queen's Room at teatime. And Mick was thinking about the surprise he'd had when he encountered need – yes childlike need – in the hustler's glance.

No, he told himself firmly. It wasn't need at all. He's the best in the world at it. It was just one of the tricks of his trade. Only why was bloody Diana Ross still singing inside his own brain?

Because you're crackers, he told himself. Sorrel always said that swallowing all those vitamins would catch up on you in the end, and it has done. And, anyway, I'm not Deborah Kerr flying down a street, I'm a man walking along a ship's deck.

Strictly accurately, it was more of a covered causeway, carpeted too, at the side of the *QE2* pub – the Golden Lion. People were streaming out of Stella Artemis's early evening lecture. She might not have been using the dreadfully magical old name of June Gee to drag them in, but the occult was obviously still a big draw.

His thoughts did not stay on that subject for long

because, heading towards him, came . . . Dear God, I've never been tongue-tied in my whole life but I know I'm going to be now. Does he know I'm half-looking for him? Jesus, I wouldn't want him to think I was some sort of lunatic fan!

'Hi,' said Jack Lawless. The suntanned arms emerging from the tight white tee shirt could have belonged to the Belvedere Apollo.

But porno stars don't blush, thought Mickey. And this one is definitely blushing. I'm *not* deluding myself, the crackle on the air between us is almost visible. Find a mirror, Mick, he told himself. Take a good look at yourself. Remember how old you are.

He didn't want to remember his age. He just wanted to turn round and get another look at the figure hurrying away from him. No. The professional side of Mickey Grimshaw could be very stern with the real Mick. You mustn't turn round because people are watching – watching both of you.

He'd had so many years of debatable celebrity that he could tune out the perpetually interested glances he got from members of the general public. Now it was Mickey who was looking around for something to stare at. Something, anything, which wasn't Jack Lawless.

His gaze rested on the woman with a white streak in her hair, the woman Sorrel said she remembered having seen around when they had all been children.

Now the female had noticed him staring, so he felt obliged to say, 'Excuse me but do you by any chance come from somewhere called Irlams o' th' Height?'

Dinah Nelson looked at Mickey coldly. 'Yes.' And then she realised that it had been very coldly so she felt forced to add, 'I know who you are but I'm afraid I never watch your show.'

This statement left her feeling a complete idiot. What she had really meant to imply was that she didn't want to seem to be sucking up to somebody who had been a recent subject of *This Is Your Life*. And being quite honest with herself, the Height or no Height, Dinah Nelson wasn't much interested in Mickey Grimshaw. She had bigger things to dwell upon because – not five minutes before – the adult Dinah had decided that the time had come to kill somebody.

6

Avril Porter lived in Monton, which was only a 27 bus-ride away from Saracen Street so she often came round to spend the evening there. And Dinah would marvel at Avril's gift for friendliness. It verged on genius. She even managed to get Eva Nelson ('My face has never seen paint nor powder') to try lipstick. Dinah's dad thoroughly enjoyed teaching the visitor to 'vamp' on the piano, an accomplishment he had never managed to pass on to his daughter. Vamping was a method of playing a few chords of accompaniment which sounded much more accomplished than it really was.

'Imagine I'm in a big black velvet gown,' said Avril to Dinah, as she sat down on the piano stool and lifted the lid of the Nelsons' upright. This instrument had inlaid marquetry angels set inside its front panels; they were holding on to brass brackets – originally intended for candles. The night outside being cold and wintry, the dark red chenille curtains were tightly drawn, and the gasfire, in the black-leaded fireplace, was making gentle popping noises. 'Imagine I'm in *On With The Show* on the North Pier at Blackpool.'

'Just don't sing "Faraway Places With Strange-Sounding Names",' warned Dinah.

'You were the one who mentioned that, not me.' Avril went into 'Begin The Beguine'. As her friend sang about nights of tropical splendour, Dinah was thinking about how much the words of popular songs colour everyday life. And then her mind moved back to a faraway place with the strange-sounding name of Famagusta. It had come into a poem at school; something about having seen ships in the harbour there. And it was where Rory was stationed.

The war in Cyprus was almost beyond her comprehension. The Greeks said the island had always been theirs, the Turks maintained that it was just a bit of their own country, separated from the mainland by a narrow strait. A sinister-looking old priest came into it too, Archbishop Makarios. Anastasia Brogan maintained that this pontiff made the late Pope Pius the Twelfth look like Cary Grant.

English soldiers were only over there because the War Office in London saw the island as, somehow, British. By what right? fumed Dinah inwardly. Why should Britain thinks it's got the right to go telling people what they should and shouldn't do? Boiled down, what she really meant was, how dare they annexe her Rory.

What was worse, his last letter had said: 'If I do three years in the army instead of just the two, I will come out with a qualification I'd never get in Civvy Street.' No question of discussion, he'd just spelled it out flat. His letters did not bring Robert Browning to mind.

When she plucked up the courage to write and say that he never sent her words of love, she got a note back which told her everything he'd eaten for a week. But it ended, 'I cannot write sloppy but Our Lady knows to keep you safe for me.' And for the first time he'd put some little tiny kisses beside his big signature.

He prays for me, Dinah had marvelled. Somebody in Cyprus is praying for me. In its own way the thought enfolded her as firmly as the memory of his strong arms.

'I'm sick of being a lady at the piano,' announced Avril. 'I've brought the new *She* magazine. I left it with your mother in the kitchen. You stop where you are, I'll get it.' She rose up from the stool and headed for the door.

'I'm not reading the Evadne Price page,' Dinah called after her. Evadne Price was the magazine's regular astrologer.

Avril must have chosen not to hear what she'd said because, when she returned, she was already intoning: '"Absent Capricorns are faithful and true. The tap root of their being goes deeply into the life of their chosen partner." What more can you ask for than that?'

'Ten days' leave, that's what I could ask for. The army

should start giving them proper leave.' He had never been home since he sailed away on the troopship. Still, at least she'd got to see Southampton. She'd stood on the quayside and waved the great grey ship good-bye. 'Avril, did you do a poem at school about tall ships and Famagusta?'

'I went to a mixed school so I never really concentrated.'

Dinah told herself she really would have to find the poem and read it again. Southampton had been where the woman next to her on the quayside had said, 'The rumour is they won't be back till it's all over. I'm going to drown my sorrows in a sherry. Fancy joining me?'

Though the almost tubercularly thin woman had worn a fur coat, it was one with big Joan Crawford shoulders so Dinah had decided that she couldn't be an officer's wife. Very dyed blonde hair, too. In next to no time this grieving wife had shoved her handkerchief into her pocket, reviewed her make-up in the mirror of an Outdoor Girl powder compact, and led the way into a pub which was more like a milk bar that sold alcohol.

Two sailors had immediately tried to engage the pair of them in conversation. At first the skinny blonde had fended them off with lines like, 'You remind me of a man I used to know but he was fully equipped.' However, after a surprisingly short while, she accepted an invitation from one of them to go off to somewhere called the Mambo Club.

'Well you've got to have a bit of consolation, haven't you?' she'd said to Dinah, as she departed on the smiling sailor's arm.

The one left behind had very slightly bowed legs and sad eyes. I'll only stay for as long as he keeps the conversation general, vowed Dinah. But she needn't have worried because he was soon producing snapshots of his girlfriend in Torbay.

'She gave a qualified optician his ring back because of me,' he said proudly.

In her turn, Dinah showed him a photo of Rory in big boxing shorts and a white vest. She could have produced another picture of him, in just his swimming trunks, but she thought the vest kept things a bit more reserved.

Today, these same photographs were in little frames, upstairs in her bedroom. And they'd probably been kissed more than she'd ever kissed the man himself. Oh those real kisses! After seventeen long months of separation, just the thought of them was enough to set her yearning. But Rory had written that the engineers would be the very last people who could hope for leave, that sometimes they were on 24-hour stand-by.

Dinah's mother now burst into the room. The fact that she was wearing a small velvet pincushion, strapped around one wrist on a petersham band, could only mean that she was dressmaking. 'Anybody seen the pinking shears? I've got your poor father standing in the middle of the kitchen being a stuffed dummy for me.'

'They're on the mantelpiece.' Dinah had used them, the previous evening, to cut an angry serrated edge round a drawing of Mrs Tench. It was now stuck into the painted diary.

'If I've told you once I've told you a thousand times, put things back when you've finished with them. And *that* wants putting in the bin.' Eva was indicating Avril's copy of *She*. 'There's stuff in there that's only suitable for married women.'

'But you're broad-minded, Mrs Nelson,' teased Avril.

'I'm not *that* broad-minded! I'll wait till I have the change of life, thank you very much; I'm sure I don't want them to tell me about it.'

'But the article on foreplay was good,' persisted Avril, wickedly.

'Mr Nelson has protected me from anything like that. And I can't believe that ladies allow men to kiss it, I just can't. Whatever am I saying? It's you, it's you, Avril Porter! You're altogether too freewheeling.' But she wasn't really being critical. Avril only had to cross the threshold and the whole atmosphere in the house lightened up.

As Eva departed with her pinking shears, the girl with

the Slavic cheekbones and the hourglass figure said to Dinah, 'Let's go and see what gives at the Brogans'.' In many ways she had been Dinah's passport to an easier relationship with her boyfriend's family. The fact that Dinah had chosen to make friends with a girl with the 'freewheeling' quality mentioned by Mrs Nelson, had caused them to relax their guard with Rory's fiancée.

It was dark and cold out in the street, but as usual the front door of the house opposite was only on the latch.

'Who is it?' yelled Stasia Brogan, as the two girls creaked their way down the lobby.

'Us,' called out Avril.

'Come on in, it's a titty factory!' Anastasia Brogan proved to be speaking no less than the truth. 'Excuse us all being in our bust-bodices but we've turned the kitchen into a beauty saloon.'

Tonight, Cissie and Josie, both of them as full-fronted as Old Mother Riley's 'beautiful daughter Kitty' in the comedy films, had got huge amounts of wet hair constrained within complicated arrangements of crossed kirby-grips and fierce iron curlers. The pair were hovering over their mother. Her great bottom was hanging over the sides of a bentwood chair and she had a striped towel around big bare shoulders.

'Pour on the Amami,' cried Josie to Cissie, who already had the bottle of green setting lotion at the ready.

'Dear God in heaven,' moaned Mrs Brogan, 'it smells just like Woolworth's bath salts.'

Tyrone Brogan was no longer a baby, he was a proper romping little lad. 'Pick me up, pick me up, pick me up,' he pleaded with Dinah.

Once he was in her arms he nuzzled up against her cheek. 'Kiss,' he said, and he gave her one. Then he started pretending he had a hammer, with which he was meant to be knocking the kiss home.

'He'll soon be too old for the sight of all this semi-nudity,' observed his mother. Which struck Dinah as odd when she considered that one or other of that family was always in a state of partial undress. As she held the small boy close it suddenly occurred to her that he was made of exactly the same ingredients as Rory – bits of Mr Brogan and bits of Mrs Brogan. She had once caught herself thinking something similar as her hands had gone under Rory's shirt in Light Oaks Park. For a moment the thought had chastened passion's fingers.

But it had only been a moment. Why had the pair of them never gone the whole way? Why? Why? At the very worst she could only have ended up with a beautifully sturdy child like Tyrone. Now she was remembering a hot day with Rory stripped to the waist. 'You've got very silky skin,' she'd said. 'Make the muscles go hard again for me.' And she'd traced the outline of his iron chest with her fingers.

'Have you heard from the lad?' bawled Stasia. 'Avril, put that tube of hair-remover down. I saw what you was looking at in the mirror. Don't even think of using Veet on your upper lip. Believe you me, there's nothing the gentlemen like more than a wicked little hint of a meestache. Have you heard from him, Dinah?'

'Not since the last postcard.'

'We've had a whole letter,' swanked Josie. Cissie was the kindly sister, Josephine was always just a little bit beady. 'They've been given leave.' She pronounced it leaf.

Dinah treated Tyrone to a rapturous hug. 'When does he get home?' Life was suddenly amazingly valuable.

'Who said anything about home?' Josie's tone was as sharp as the point on the tail comb she was tugging through her mother's grey tangles. 'They're all going off to some island paradise.'

Life was even drabber than it had been before. 'But if he's got leave, why isn't he coming home instead?'

'You cannot get a number 19 bus from Cyprus,' chuckled Stasia. 'Talk sense, Dinah.'

You could hitch your way on a ship or an aircraft carrier; that's what I'd have done, thought Dinah. I'd have swum if I had to! And why had he chosen to tell them this first and not her? Because he was ordered Rory, everything to a solid timetable, and it hadn't been her turn for a letter.

'Heartsease, that's the herb you need,' put in Macushla. The little wraith had been sitting, all the while, in a corner – reading Dinah's copy of *Bright's Herbal Dictionary*. 'You need an infusion of heartsease.'

No I don't, thought Dinah. I need your brother. I need his arms around me and all that strength pressed up against me and – I don't care – I even need him inside me. Why had they never done it?

'You won't believe this, Dinah,' said Stasia. 'But when Mr Brogan first came to England for the building work, and I was affianced to him but stuck in Kilkenny, I nearly went berserk with longing. Jesus, he was a glorious figure of a man in those days! That was before the beer got to the belly. Mind you, he's still got a full head of hair, and he's given me good daughters to wash me own.' She looked just like a beached whale with a Turkish towel around its neck. 'The Brogan men are rotten letter writers but they're true to their word. When he gets to this island paradise, Rory won't be gallivanting off with no hula-hula maidens.'

Dinah hadn't even thought of that but she did now. Men were men and seventeen months was a long long time.

'You were six pounds seven ounces,' said Eva Nelson. 'And you were born with a thatch of black hair, like a little Japanese doll.' It was Dinah's twenty-first birthday. The postman had already brought her cards and now she was opening her presents. Her parents had produced a satin-lined canteen of stainless-steel cutlery. The Brogans' present was also intended for her bottom drawer. They had clubbed together to buy her a huge Prestige pressure cooker – it was practically catering sized.

'Which only goes to show how many children they're expecting you to have,' observed Eva darkly.

But Dinah failed to rise to her mother's bait because

Josie Brogan had also dropped off a bulky parcel covered in triangular Cypriot stamps and marked 'Don't take to Dinah's house until morning of July 9th'. Dinah was saving that one until the last. 'But who's this from?' she asked her mother. The package she was pointing at was a peculiar shape but somebody had contrived to Sellotape it, very tidily, into *Snow White And The Seven Dwarfs* wrapping paper.

'I don't know how old he thinks you are. It's from your father. It's something he sneaked off and got on his own, on Saturday.'

Dinah broke the seals and pulled out a highly coloured figure of Black Sambo standing on his hands. It was made of glazed pot and it was awful. But she knew she would never be able to part with it because Tommy Nelson had always read her 'Little Black Sambo' stories when she was little herself. In its own way, his present was a monument to the best part of her slightly chilly childhood.

'Oh my God, not tears!' said Eva. 'Both you and your dad have got eyes that are too near to your bladders. Come on, Dinah, open the one from Rory. It's nearly time for my bus.'

Only now did the birthday girl allow herself to look at what he'd written on the customs declaration form, which was stuck underneath the stamps. 'Cloth' it said. Just that – cloth.

'From the size of the parcel, if it's a table-cloth he must be another one who's expecting you to have four sets of twins!'

Dinah already had the brown paper open. The next layer of wrapping was flowered foreign wallpaper, tied up with narrow green ribbon. This came off to reveal white tissue paper with Greek words printed on it in silver. And Rory had added a ball-point message: 'For your wedding dress.'

'Oh God, what if it's awful?' moaned her mother. 'Men have no taste, look at your father. Open it, go on, get it open.'

Beneath the tissue lay a huge bolt of hand-embroidered white lace.

'That'd be ten guineas a yard in Kendals,' breathed Eva in near disbelief. 'Feel how crunchy it is. And there must be enough for a crinoline. Oh Dinah . . .' her voice grew even more wary, 'however did he afford this? It's just to be hoped he's not running some soldier's racket.'

'He's always said everything's dirt cheap over there.' As soon as the words were out she wished she'd not applied them to this white-encrusted gossamer. 'Oh I do love him.' It was her birthday so she dared to enjoy the luxury of just saying it aloud.

And for once Eva chose to pay Rory a compliment. 'Not many men would have the guts to go into a shop and choose something as delicate as this. It's very Deanna Durban; we'll put it over white taffeta. And the veil ought to be plain tulle to show it off. Look at that clock! If we don't get a move on we'll both be out of a job.'

Together they hurried towards Bolton Road where they waited at bus stops on opposite sides of the road. The last words Eva mouthed over to Dinah before she stepped onto her bus for Swinton were 'Plain white satin court shoes'.

On the top deck of the number 21 for Cross Lane, Dinah began choosing hymns. Except she supposed they would have to be Catholic hymns. Holy Paddy would be able to advise her; these days he was known in the family as Father Paddy – he'd been ordained the previous spring. Dinah had found the service extraordinary. The young ordinands had all prostrated themselves on the High Altar like a row of men having swimming lessons on dry land. And once the Holy Spirit was deemed to have descended upon them, and the officiating bishop had departed, the new priests' families had all queued up to get a 'first blessing'. Macushla had said that this brought you the best luck in the world.

Nowadays Paddy was a curate in a parish at Weaste. Dinah had been dreading the famous 'twelve lessons' off fierce old Father Conklin, at St Luke's. But he had been quite happy to agree to allow Paddy to instruct her in the Faith. Sometimes she went to Paddy's presbytery and sometimes he walked uphill from Weaste and talked to her in her mother's front room.

Dinah already knew the *Penny Catechism* by heart. And when she told the young priest how the green scapular had got Rory to look at her for the very first time, he had smiled and said, 'You seem to have been born with a natural devotion to Our Lady. Why you're almost a Catholic already.'

These days she went and sat through the mysteries of Mass with the Brogans on Sundays. Lesson by lesson the young priest explained them to her. Soon she would have to make what Paddy called her 'life confession'. But she was going to Father Conklin to do that. And before she made her first communion she would have to be officially received into the Church.

Eugene Gannon, the man who tended Mrs Tench's herbal pop depot on Eccles New Road, was in ecstasies about the whole business. 'You know you get to choose an extra name for your confirmation, don't you? How about having Veronica? She was the lady who lent Our Lord her pocket handkerchief to dry his tears.'

'I'm having Mary.'

'What name is greater?' he said piously.

She hadn't the heart to tell him that the Mary she was calling herself after was the one who dried Jesus's feet with her hair. She quite fancied the idea of trying it with Rory: she could imagine it leading to all sorts of other excitements.

The bus reached Cross Lane. These days the Tyrell and Tench premises were rather more crowded because the Eccles Branch had been shut down. The two 'nervy' sisters, the ones whose flat went with their jobs, had been dumped in an almshouse at Clifton. And Avril had been shunted down to join Dinah at Peplum Street. There were two new boys in the back of the premises, as well. Twins. They had dreadfully ginger hair and they helped John Tench with the growing wholesale side of things.

'Happy birthday to you,' carolled Avril, as Dinah flung off her cardigan and struggled into one of the new white laboratory coats. It really was 'all change'.

But some things stayed the same. 'Another minute and you'd have been late,' said Mrs Tench. July or no July she was still wearing her pixie hood and one of the home-knitted two-pieces – today's was in maroon and grey. The passing years had added another wart on top of the largest one on her face.

Once Avril had finished singing, she said, 'You get your birthday cards and things at dinnertime. Eugene's coming up. We're having a bit of a do for you.'

'And I want no crumbs,' put in Mrs Tench. 'Bring me a bag of verbena from John's shed,' she said to Avril. At the oak workbench, in the middle of the room, Edna Tench already had her Bunsen burner lit.

'There's verbena down there.' White-coated Avril was pointing towards one of the gilt-lettered drawers.

'I need fresh. I'm doing an unguent with figwort for eczema.' Dip-dip went her fingers into a couple of the mahogany drawers; she could slide these wooden compartments in and out so nimbly that you were left with no idea of what she'd gathered together. And now she waited until the door was shut behind Avril before she said, 'I *could* have managed with the verbena in here but I wanted a word with you, Dinah. There's been more of that silly giggling on the back corridor, this morning. D'you think Avril's setting her cap at my Johnnie?'

'No he's not meaty enough.' It was out before she realised what she'd said. And the phrase was Avril's not her own.

'She called him sweetheart.'

'She calls everybody sweetheart.'

Mrs Tench began rubbing dried leaves, which Dinah recognised as myrtle, against a broad iron file. 'Has she got a man?'

'I don't know.'

'You do.'

'All right, she's got her eye on somebody.' This was

137

the most that Dinah could admit without breaking a promise.

'It's Johnnie, isn't it? There might not be much meat on the bone but he's still a very good bet.' The powdered myrtle was tipped into a glass gas jar. 'Johnnie will inherit all this and the Gentlemen's Remedy. And that's as good as saying he's got a pension for life. Believe you me, I'm going to choose his wife very carefully. I need two drops of belladonna.'

'Mrs Tench,' ventured Dinah cautiously, 'if that's got myrtle and belladonna in it, are you sure it's for eczema?'

Mrs Tench stared at the gas jar in near disbelief. 'Whatever am I doing? I'm making something Father used to compound for horses' hooves. It's all that Avril Porter's fault, she's got me distracted. But she'll not walk down the aisle with him. She shan't!' Suddenly she was more like Punch than Judy, and she should have been banging a wooden stick. 'I'll dose her with monkshood before I'll let that happen.'

At dinnertime (they never called it lunch) Eugene Gannon appeared with freshly blackened hair and a lady's wicker shopping basket over one arm. Its contents were covered by a linen tea towel. 'All my own work,' he cried as he drew back the cloth. 'I love mauve icing. And the little silver balls are guaranteed edible.'

There were twenty-one candles too, in purple icing-sugar holders. As the cake was placed reverently upon the central workbench, and John Tench moved forward with a cigarette lighter, his mother observed, 'Icing sugar's the worst thing on earth for anybody with catarrh.'

'What a miserable thing to say at a jollification.' Eugene was the least scared of her of the lot of them. 'And here's your present, Dinah.' It was a white mother-of pearl rosary. 'Blessed at Fatima,' he breathed.

'Now mine.' The parcel handed over by Avril looked like a book, and it was. '*Married Bliss* by Marie Stopes. I always wanted to see the inside of Stewart's Surgical Stores,' she confided.

John Tench handed over an envelope containing a two-guinea gift token for Boots. His mother went over to the cast-iron safe, unlocked it, drew out a cash box, extracted a half a crown piece and passed it to Dinah. The recipient couldn't help feeling that either more or nothing would have been more appropriate. But at least she'd got to see the inside of the safe, the sacred hidey-hole of the Gentlemen's Remedy.

'You've not opened your cards,' boomed Avril, who was not to know that it would be months before Dinah did.

Somebody must have crept noiselessly up the corridor outside because rapping was suddenly to be heard on the frosted glass window of the hatchway. From inside the room all you could see was a shadowy outline against the word 'Enquiries' spelled backwards.

Even though it was the official dinner hour Mrs Tench was never one to miss the opportunity of making a farthing so she snicked back the catch on the little window and opened it.

The sight of Father Paddy, peering anxiously through the gap, immediately reminded Dinah of her impending 'life confession'.

'Yes?' snapped Mrs Tench, who didn't know the priest and never made any bones of the fact that she had no time for Christianity. 'What is it?'

'I've come to take Dinah home.'

'Home?' squawked the herbalist. 'It might be her birthday but there's still half a day's work to be got through.'

'Something's happened. Something serious. She'll need to get her coat.'

'I didn't bring one,' said Dinah. Why did it suddenly feel as though all the shadows inside the room had gone blacker? 'What is it, what's happened?'

'May she leave?' Paddy was addressing Edna Tench.

'If she must.'

For some reason of his own, John Tench had continued to light the miniature candles, and now all twenty-one flames were dancing as crazily as Dinah's thoughts. What could be wrong, what could be wrong? What? 'It's not Rory, is it?' By now she was outside in the corridor.

'Please be good enough to shut your little window.' Paddy was talking to Edna Tench.

As it closed, Dinah could now see 'Enquiries' the right way round. 'Just tell me what it is.'

'You're going to have to be very brave. A telegram's come from Whitehall. Rory's missing in action.' He gazed at her anxiously. 'You might as well have the lot: they think he might be dead. "Presumed killed."' He was obviously quoting from the official communication.

'No.' She didn't know she'd even said the word but she must have done because she could hear her own shout echoing around the narrow hallway. 'No, no.'

He put a comforting arm around her. It felt for all the world like his brother's arm and she longed to bury herself in the black serge front so as to feel the whole length of Rory again. Except this was a priest and . . . he even smelt like her dead lover.

Paddy must also have recalled his vocation because he withdrew the arm. And that was the moment when she knew that the last hint of Rory Brogan had truly gone away from her. Hopeless tears began to flow.

'They sent for me.' Paddy said it awkwardly. 'Stasia's in a terrible state. He was always her favourite – the special one. I borrowed a car . . .' He seemed to have run out of words. 'Come on,' he managed eventually. 'I'll take you home.'

Home had been in Rory's arms, that's where home had been. Dinah had never known that tears could be as scalding hot as this. Her whole body was shaking uncontrollably and she could feel her shoulders going up and down as though they were leading an independent life of their own.

Eventually she managed to gasp out, 'None of this is real, is it? I *am* going to wake up in a minute, aren't I?'

'Just step outside and get in the car. There was nobody much around when I came in.'

Dinah's thoughts were still flying wildly. He won't say

it's not real. Perhaps if I walk back into the big room it'll just be my twenty-first birthday with mauve icing and little silver balls on the cake. She pinched herself – hard.

It was real.

The car proved to be a half-timbered shooting brake. It must have been borrowed from somebody who had recently been plucking chickens because bits of brown feather kept floating through the air. And all the way to the Height, inside her head, Dinah could hear the antiquated woman crooner from the Broadway Ballroom singing 'Lover Come Back to Me'.

> *'Every road I've walked along*
> *I've walked along with you,*
> *I'm so lonely . . .'*

Dinah remembered having made exactly this same journey with Rory, time and again, and especially on that first Saturday night – when they'd met outside the Gaiety. In her mind's eye she could still see him standing there, chocolates in hand, in his best suit. And then she remembered Swinton Baths and 'Aqua Rapture' and Rory with next to nothing on, and how loving him had got her into a fight with a girl from Penelope Road.

'He was mine,' she sobbed.

'It's only *presumed* killed.'

'Only?' Once again she found herself shouting when she hadn't meant to shout. '*Only?* I can remember things we did but they're like history now. And when I go for the feeling of the real Rory, inside my brain he's not there any more. I can't find him. I'm frightened.' It was weird – awful. 'He's misted out altogether, Paddy. I can't even see what he looks like.'

'He looked like me.'

'I'm not meant to look at you. You should know that, you're a priest.' She had to pause to spit out a fragment of feather so she sneaked a look at Father Paddy anyway. For all the thick curly hair and the wickedly blue eyes were almost identical to his brother's, he would never be in any danger from Dinah. 'Rory was the only person I ever fancied.' The feather hadn't quite gone so she had to spit again.

'Look, everybody's got him dead and buried when . . .'

'When what?'

'Who knows.' He said it wearily, he'd obviously had a morning of it. And as he turned the car into Saracen Street Paddy added, 'I'd no way of getting hold of your mother. Come into us for a cup of tea.'

That afternoon the Brogan household seemed to have taken on an atmosphere of Ancient Greece. For a start, the sacred front parlour was in use. The great ruin of Stasia lay prostrate on the horsehair settle and she was being attended by a group of women neighbours. All of them darkly clad, as though death was their special forte, they would have been more properly described as a group of St Luke's female parishioners.

> 'Holy Mary, Mother of God,
> Pray for us sinners now
> And at the hour of our death,
> Amen.'

Then they went right back to the beginning: 'Hail Mary full of grace . . .' It was just a kind of background hum with the odd rattle of rosary beads. Dinah suddenly remembered that she'd left all her birthday presents at Tyrell and Tench. Once in a while the women did the odd concerted 'Our Father' and 'Glory Be'. The eerie thing was that they all seemed to know which came when.

Though Macushla, in her wheelchair, was part of the praying, Stasia was more like the altar. Just occasionally her lips moved along with the rest, but for the most part she was just lying gazing into some terrible middle-distance. And every now and then she would shake her head in disbelief.

'Dinah's here,' ventured Paddy.

'I saw.' Her voice was as cold as Connemara marble. 'If it wasn't for her, Rory would be here too.'

This statement was enough to drag Dinah back from the fearful plateau of her own grief. 'Me?'

'You.' Stasia was obviously a woman who had been waiting to vent anger. 'He only stopped on to do that extra time so he could give the marriage a better start. "A better start," his own words.'

'That's not what he told me.'

'You're not his mother; it's what he wrote. And I just hope you're contented.'

'Stasia,' Paddy remonstrated gently, 'the girl's in bits.'

'What's her grief compared to mine?' she snapped. 'Have a son, Dinah. Have a son and lose him and then you *will* know what grief's about.'

> *'Hail Mary full of Grace,*
> *The Lord is with thee . . .'*

The Irish piety continued in the background in just the same way as stray Catholics always seemed to wander in, during the middle of Mass, to light votive candles at the side altars. Dinah had always found this disconcerting but Paddy had explained to her that it was simply living proof that the Faith ran right through the centre of everything.

Now, for the first time since he'd arrived to collect her, Rory's brother asserted his priesthood in her direction. 'Would you not want to pray with them?'

'No. Praying got me into this.' Her own anger was as strong a thing as Stasia Brogan's. 'It's all the fault of the bloody green scapular!'

A chorus of Glory Be's drew to a startled halt. The woman leading the devotions, the one in unrelieved black with the amber rosary, said to her immediate neighbour, 'Did you hear that, Philomena?'

'I did.'

'She's distraught,' said Paddy.

'She's a Protestant,' said Philomena. And then she saw fit to add, 'Father.'

Before Father Paddy could say anything back, Stasia Brogan sat bolt upright on the slippery settle. 'You threw yourself at him, Dinah Nelson – absolutely threw yourself. Your mother should have taken you in and slapped you. Time and again you should have been slapped. No, I won't stop, Paddy. I can't. She killed him.' She looked straight at Dinah. 'You killed him.'

One word exploded out of the girl: 'How?'

Stasia's hail of answers could have ricocheted out of a machine gun. 'He wanted you to have everything that Protestants have. He wanted you to have it like the Ideal Homes Exhibition at the City Hall. You dragged him off there and he came back with ambitions. I was making cocoa at the time he told me. At nights he always told me everything. He was still a babba to his mammy.' The memory halted the barrage of words by bringing on a great wave of sobbing grief.

'I'll take you over the road, Dinah,' said Paddy.

'I can take myself thank you . . .' Sid the lurcher chose that moment to haunch himself out from beneath the settle. Fixing Dinah with his yellow diamond gaze he handed her a melancholy paw. 'Oh Sid,' she wept, 'at least you're still nice.'

> 'As it was in the beginning,
> Is now and ever shall be,
> World without end
> Amen.'

The words of this Glory Be were still echoing through her mind as she got outside. If she went home the only person in the house would be her father. She'd heard him creep in from his night shift at six o'clock that morning so she knew his teeth would be in the glass, on top of the chamber pot cupboard, by the side of the big double bed.

Only last week she had herself gone into Albert Johnson's, the Height furniture shop, and given a double mattress a tentative prod. Perhaps God had thought she was dwelling too much on that side of things – perhaps that was why he had chosen to separate them. And why had she further tempted Providence by shouting abuse of the green scapular?

Remembering that Paddy had told her to pray, Dinah decided to go to St Luke's to do it officially. She saw this as a bit like paying your electricity bill at Electric House – rather than entrusting a postal order to the mail.

As she passed the display cases and swung open the door into the church itself, the smell of incense wrapped her in its sacred embrace. At one time she had thought of it as the scent of her love for Rory, but in recent months it had converted itself into being just part of Mass. She'd even been taught the name of the thing it was burned in – a thurible. And the youth who swung it was a thurifer and did any of that really matter?

Considering the building was really a glorified shed, the Catholics had certainly managed to invest the place with a lot of gloomy mystery and winking candles. Mary and Joseph were either side of the High Altar, and somebody had bequeathed the Holy Virgin a Brussels lace wedding veil and a real diamond ring. Lace, lace . . . the word had seemed wondrously beautiful when she opened the parcel from Cyprus – could it only have been this morning? Now the word 'lace' had started to make her think of shrouds.

Where would his body be? In some Rupert Brooke 'corner of a foreign field'? Or, worse still, like something she'd once overheard, after a lorry knocked down a young lad on Bolton Road: 'All they could do was scrape him up.'

'Don't let him be dead, God,' she prayed. 'Just let him be alive somewhere and let there be another telegram saying it was all a big mistake.' She was down on her knees and her eyes were tightly closed against the sight of the larger than life blood-stained figure on the cross.

Dinah suddenly felt the need to try to do something to get in good with Heaven. Honesty, she felt, would be the best policy: 'I'm sorry I'm no good at proper Catholic praying. I know there are set ways of doing it, and I ought to have a rosary and a rapt expression.

But I'm not anything any more: I'm not what I learned at Sunday School and I'm only halfway to being someone who can receive communion . . .' It felt as though she was in the right company but seated on an awkwardly placed chair.

'Wait for me,' she said to God, right out loud. 'Just give me a minute and I'll be with you – head on.' As she fled from the church she realised that she had failed to observe any of the Catholic niceties. No genuflection, no blessing herself with holy water, instead she had just run out of the front door and up Swinton Park Road, and now she was haring past the gentlemen's toilets and veering sharp left.

She was at The Place. 'I'm back. Sorry to have kept you waiting . . .' She was talking to Heaven again. In truth she was gasping through clenched teeth – a bit like a ventriloquist – because two women, laden with oil-cloth shopping bags and wicker baskets, were taking a short cut across the patch of open land. As it was July, bright spikes of golden rod were flowering around the grey stone thunderbolt.

This is my church, thought Dinah. It called to me when I was dead little. I may only be a half-trained amateur Catholic but whatever-this-is runs right through me.

And, amazingly, it seemed to be saying that everything was still ordered, everything still meant, that the whole song was in tune.

Now she didn't care about women with shopping. 'Even Rory?' She was talking right out loud again. 'Even Rory?'

But you never got actual answers. Not in words. Just the feeling that something benign and all-powerful was well disposed towards you.

Somebody else was toddling towards her, across the open croft. It was the little woman Dinah had first met under the canopy of Salford Hippodrome, on the day she went for her interview at Tyrell and Tench. The old dame in the cloth cap, who'd tapped the last of the contents of the Abercrombie's Chlorodyne Compound bottle onto her tongue.

Today she was wearing an old straw picture hat at a sedate angle. 'They won't sell it me in the Height,' she said, as though she had somehow been privy to Dinah's thoughts. 'I have to make do with kaolin and morphine.'

The same potion Lily Jelly had been buying on the night that she and Rory had first gone out together. 'Is it your bowels?' asked Dinah, as the gnome-like creature in the soiled raincoat settled herself down on the thunderbolt.

'Is it buggery.'

Dinah resisted the temptation to say, 'Would you mind getting up because you're sitting on God.' Anyway it wouldn't have been strictly accurate: the stone was only the centre of the most concentrated part of the unique atmosphere of The Place.

The woman shook her bottle and unscrewed its cap. 'This stuff messes the bowels up,' she observed. 'Blocks 'em solid. I only go once a week and then I do a brick.' The swig she took from the neck of the bottle was all but sacramental.

Dinah found herself both repulsed and fascinated. 'Why do you take these things?'

'To forget.' The mixture was leaving pale fawn sediment in the corners of her mouth. 'I wasn't always old. You've been crying,' she said accusingly.

Within the safety of the aura of the stone, Dinah felt strong enough to say, 'It's my twenty-first and everything's gone wrong.'

'I was eighteen when the rug was pulled from under me. But I never tell people. Doesn't do.'

'I told you,' said Dinah indignantly. She was surprised that any emotion other than grief was capable of rising to the surface.

'You only told a bit. You've got lovely 'air. Only twenty-one and a white streak already!'

'I got it at eighteen.'

'Don't mention bloody eighteen!' She took another swig. 'I loved somebody and they never came back. Drove an ambulance in the First World War. They had

147

wooden wheels in them days. Came home on leave once. Told me all about it. Mud, blood, the lot. Then they went off again and never come back.'

'Don't!' It was all too near to home. 'Please don't.' She felt obliged to attempt more. 'And you still miss him?'

'Who said anything about *him*?' snapped the woman. 'Got you there! I always get 'em there, when I do choose to tell. Always. "Oh, just a friend," they say, "just a bit of a woman friend." That's all they know! And they wouldn't even let me have a ticket when Princess Alice came to Salford to unveil the war memorial.'

There was silence for a moment and then she said: 'People used to call her "mannish". P'raps she was.' The old wreck sounded like somebody who had been trained to be ashamed. 'But when I have a swig of this, and it hits the right spot, I can feel her standing right next to me. And she's generally humming "The Piccadilly Johnny With The Little Eye-Glass".'

'Perhaps if you'd met a man . . .' ventured Dinah.

'That's where I *would* have been wicked because it wouldn't have been love. Not with a man. No, I'm built irregular but I'm true to me principles.' She suddenly came out of her reverie and looked around in amazement. 'Whatever made me tell you all of that?'

'It's this place.' Dinah was surprised at how calm her own voice sounded. It was as though The Place had reinforced the faint possibility that Rory Brogan might still be alive. And something seemed to be encouraging her to release her own story in return for the one with which she had just been entrusted. So, very slowly, going right back to those early days when she had willed Rory to simply look at her – when that in itself would have been Heaven on Earth – Dinah told the sorry tale to her new-found friend.

'We're both of us unacknowledged widows,' said the old woman. 'Unacknowledged war widows, that's us.'

*   *   *

148

No more news came from Whitehall. Many months passed and one evening Dinah found herself edging the latest page of the painted diary with a narrow black border – just like old-fashioned mourning stationery. This only echoed what was going on inside her head. Dinah was obsessed with thoughts of death. They haunted her days and seeped into her nights to an extent where she would find herself getting up before daybreak, to make sure that her father was still breathing.

Generally she just tiptoed in and out, but one night she was surprised by a voice in the darkness asking 'Who ish it?' Tommy Nelson hadn't got his teeth in.

'Only me.'

There was a rattle of dentures against glass and then: 'What ails you?'

She wished she was still young enough to be able to say, 'Can I get in with you?' But she wasn't. And at his side, her mother, who must have been lying on her back, was emitting rhythmic siffling noises, which every now and then climaxed into a genteel whistle.

'Come on, Dinah, what's up?' whispered her dad.

Even in her blue woollen dressing gown it was cold for October. 'Nothing.'

'Then why are you roaming? Shall I get up and make us a cup of tea?'

The room was still in darkness and he must have swung his legs over the side of the bed because the springs were arguing noisily. This caused her mother to stir in her sleep and to say, 'I'll take a quarter of a pound if you'll cut it from the middle.'

You could carry on complete conversations with her and Tommy replied, 'No, Missus, I'm not cutting it from the middle.'

'Then I'll go elsewhere.'

'Suit yourself.' Tommy and Dinah tittered their way to the landing. Once the bedroom door was closed he switched on the overhead light. 'Come on, what's all this about?' He didn't own a dressing gown, he always wore his old army greatcoat instead.

'I just wanted to make sure you were okay.' Khaki was a dangerous colour at four in the morning. Army uniforms went with tears.

'Are you missing him?'

'All the time. Every minute.' Now the tears did begin to flow. 'And I can't stop thinking about death. Even dead leaves are enough to get me going.' She hardly liked to add that discarded chip papers also had the same effect. 'Why does everything have to die?'

'It just does. And shush, we'll talk in the kitchen.' When they got there he looked at the clock and said, 'Well I'm on early turns so another half-hour and I'd've had to be up anyway. Matches, where are the matches?'

Dinah felt obliged to explain something. 'I keep dreaming they've taken the parlour door off and you're laid out on it.'

'Well you've dreamed wrong.' His hair was tousled and his face was sleep-crumpled, like a little boy's. 'Anyway, when I die, we've already arranged what you've got to do. You just crook your arm and I'll come back and link it. You won't be able to see me but I'll be there. And that's a promise.'

Dinah could only regret that she had never reached some similar arrangement with Rory. 'Dad,' she asked hesitantly, 'do you think he could still be in the land of the living?'

'Tea caddy, tea caddy . . .' He was searching more awkwardly than was strictly necessary.

Now there was silence and Dinah pounced upon it, 'You don't! You don't think he's still alive.'

'Fifteen months is a long time on an island that size.' Three spoonsful of tea went into the little aluminium pot.

'Me mother'd go mad if she knew you'd put water from the hot tap in that kettle.'

'I love you,' he said.

'I know or you wouldn't have got up.'

'And I'd do anything for you. You know that.'

She nodded. What was coming?

150

'Does that give me the freedom to speak me mind?' he asked.

'I'm not going to like it, am I?'

He looked her straight in the eye. 'You've got to pick up the pieces and move on.'

'But he was *all* of the pieces, Dad. I only came alive when he was around.' Somewhere outside in the darkness a bird began to chirrup, as the kettle came to the boil. 'No sugar in my cup, I'll have saccharine instead.' Dinah had spent the past year eating for comfort and now she was supposed to have put herself on a diet.

'Are you getting in training for the next lad along?' asked her father brightly. Too brightly. 'There's no need to look at me like that.'

'There isn't going to be any "next lad along".'

The boiling water finally hit the tea leaves. 'Life has to go on, Dinah.'

'You sound just like Avril.'

'She's been a good friend to you.'

A new voice said, 'Yes and Avril's ruining her own chances by pandering to your grief.' It belonged to Dinah's mother. The sound of their conversation must have woken her because she had now materialised in the kitchen, wearing a passion-killer of a nightdress in sprigged winceyette and an apple-green slumber hairnet. Unhooking a cup for herself she continued speaking. 'Avril could have had boys galore and all she's done is sit in that front room with you, night after night.'

This wasn't quite the truth. As Dinah allowed her mother to steer her back upstairs, she reflected that Eva had never been privy to the girls' deeper conversations.

The fact of the matter was that Avril Porter had spent the last two years nursing a hopeless passion for a married man. 'I know you think it's sordid,' she would say to Dinah. 'But I just have to settle for crumbs from his table.'

This had caused her to buy a Woolworth's wedding ring, and to allow herself to be signed in as Mrs Johnson at a family and commercial hotel in Fleetwood.

'Gulls kept tapping on the window with their beaks,'

she told Dinah afterwards. 'And he wears funny vests with off-white rubber buttons down the front. Of course *she* chooses them for him.'

'Did you know that Johnson is the most common name used by people with something to hide?' Dinah had read this in *Readers Digest*.

'I know that I'm five days overdue. Mrs Smart should be at this party and she isn't.' It soon became ten. And it was nearly a month before she got her period. In the interim Avril had lost all respect for 'Mr Johnson'. She described him as 'shivering with terror and demanding to know how much I'd got saved up in the post office'.

'You need a whole new life,' said Dinah.

'Too true. I should never have trusted a man who buys his cigarettes in packets of ten. But if I need to come out of the shadows, so do you. What we really need is a good fortune teller.'

'Father Paddy'd go mad.' Dinah knew the Church was very strict in these matters.

'You hardly ever see him,' pointed out Avril reasonably.

Since the awful day of Rory's death, relations with the Brogans had been somewhat strained. Macushla sometimes wheeled herself over the road, but not often because it involved finding a passer-by to trundle her up the kerbstone. And these days she had something wrong with her bony chest. She coughed a lot and she seemed to veer between the brink of tears and unrealistic optimism. Eva Nelson had been known to mouth the letters TB. And after Macushla had gone, Eva would rinse out the girl's teacup with Dettol.

'Of course Spiritualism is one up on fortune telling. It's a religion,' said Avril. 'There's that man who does seances, over a chip shop, on Cross Lane. They're always hauling him up in court for it.'

Dinah had not quite abandoned her own conversion to Rome. 'It's just that you remind me too much of Rory,' she'd explained to Paddy as they sat drinking strong tea in the presbytery parlour. 'I can't listen to what you're saying for thinking of him.'

152

'We could find you another priest.'

'No.'

'Tell you what, for the moment, just keep on going to church.'

But, after a while, even that had fizzled out, until she was back where she started – simply repeating the printed prayer on the green scapular.

'Yes, we could become Spiritualists,' said Avril importantly.

'Over a chip shop?' Dinah was mildly scandalised. 'We'd never get the smell of fat out of our clothes.'

'That medium's not the only pebble on the beach. There's a young woman who rents the Co-op Hall, at Pendleton, on Thursday nights. They say she's so good she can even tell you how much small change you've got in your purse.'

'Oh I don't know.' Dinah was still dubious.

'You *never* know. Let me be the one who knows. We're going.'

Strictly speaking the public hall no longer belonged to the Co-operative Wholesale Society. The whole building had been sold off to a firm who made remoulded tyres, and the hall above their shop was let out, on a nightly basis, to anything from jujitsu clubs to the Al Jolson Appreciation Society.

But on Thursday evenings a properly made plastic sign, with stuck-on lettering, hung over the street-level entrance. It read: 'DEATH? DON'T MAKE ME SMILE.' And in smaller letters, underneath, it said: 'Clairvoyance at 7.30 by Mrs June Gee. Admission half a crown.'

As Dinah and Avril mounted the bare wooden steps of the staircase the air was heavy with the smell of rubber tyring. 'Madam Jones from the ballroom does her Christmas pantos here,' said Avril 'She's got a daughter called Gypsy Jones, she's semi-professional.'

June Gee the clairvoyant was wholly professional. That much was evident by the way the body-builder, on the door, didn't let anybody in before they'd handed over their admission money.

Inside the hall, the words 'Death? Don't Make Me Smile' were in evidence again, embossed in purple felt on a lemon satin banner, which hung above the stage. And yet again, on properly printed greetings cards. These were being sold by a constipated-looking middle-aged woman, who was manning a little bookstall.

'It's all very go-ahead for Pendleton, isn't it?' Though Dinah was impressed, the free and easy use of the word 'death' had started to alarm her.

'All right, I'll own up. I've been before on the sly,' said Avril. 'It was a real eye-opener. Mr Muscles is the husband, and the woman with the bad breath, selling pamphlets, is her mother. They keep June hidden till it starts. She sort of bursts on. It's just that I thought it might bring you a bit of comfort.'

'I *have* always liked the smell of new tyres,' conceded Dinah.

Avril clicked open a big red handbag. 'I brought Bassett's Liquorice Allsorts.'

'I thought this was meant to be a religion.'

'You'll see,' said Avril confidently. 'It's a bit like *Five To Ten* on the wireless. "A message of hope and comfort for those who are afflicted."'

''Ave you ever 'ad one?' A woman in the row in front had turned round to address Avril.

'One what?'

'A message off June.' The speaker's hair had been set in rigid waves, and it had not one but two hairnets pulled over the top of it. She must have been a good-hearted soul because she was handing out eating apples to a man with a deaf aid on one side of her, and to a male hobgoblin, bent over a white stick, on the other. 'He's hoping for healing,' she nodded towards the wearer of the pink plastic ear piece. 'Deaf people can be very snappy,' she mouthed in a style that proved she had learned silent speech inside a noisy cotton mill.

'Have you ever had a message?' Avril asked her.

'I did *claim* one, the week before last. But when I got home I decided I might've been a bit too handy.'

'It's easily done,' observed the blind man. 'Some of the things she gives out can be very general.'

All attention now switched to the stage because a rubicund gentleman, who brought the Michelin tyre advertisements to mind, had seated himself at the upright piano.

'That's her dad,' explained Avril.

'It's a rotten piano,' observed the woman in front.

Avril lifted a pink seed-covered Liquorice Allsort to her mouth, but it stopped halfway as June's husband mounted the steps from the hall to the stage. 'Oh Martyn, you're all man,' she murmured appreciatively. He had dark hair and bright eyes, and the lavish muscles were straining through the pearl-grey gaberdine of an American-drape suit. 'They do say he puts it about a bit.'

'Stop it,' muttered Dinah, embarrassed. She judged the man to be twenty-five or twenty-six. And she would have to remember his blue shirt and the yellow silk tie for tonight's page of the painted diary.

Now the running commentary was taken up from the row behind. 'He's definitely not got false teeth, Lizzie, they're just not quite genuine.'

Martyn Gee, who was beaming down at the audience, said, 'Here we are again,' in tones which implied that he was working class like themselves but that he'd got on a bit and what was wrong with that? 'Here we are, ready to confound the sceptics. And before I get the proceedings under way I'd like to answer the person who's been writing the critical letters to *Psychic News*. Somebody has been following us around. And, God knows, they must have worn out some shoe leather because my lovely lady wife is passing the message seven nights a week . . .'

'They've got a two-tone Zephyr,' breathed Avril.

'Following us around from public hall to public hall and making notes. It seems that June is too razzmatazzy for them, too show-biz. Not enough of the philosophical side of the Movement.'

'Shame,' shouted a girl at the front. 'Shame on them!'

'Are you for us or against us?' beamed Martyn from the platform.

'For you, every time.' It was the same voice and it struck Dinah as rehearsed.

But somebody else at the front started singing

> 'And so say all of us,
> And so say all of us . . .'

And a lot of others joined in. There seemed to be a bit of ragged dissension as to whether it was 'he' or 'she' who was the jolly good fellow but the audience applauded themselves anyway, at the end.

'There's nothing like a vote of confidence from your own.' Martyn appeared to be manfully concealing emotion in a larger-than-life way. 'We're not having a piano solo, from Mr Monk, tonight. Instead, we've got a special treat for you. Last week, at Clitheroe Town Hall, June was able to bring evidence that there is no death to a young lady who was very much in need. But it wasn't just any young lady. It was Miss Olive Farrell who has recently stood in as deputy contralto with the BBC Northern Orchestra, conductor Charles Groves. And tonight she has consented to come here and . . .'

Before he could get any further a white miniature poodle rushed onto the stage, jumped up on its back legs, and pirouetted towards him.

'Peppy,' shouted a girlish voice from the wings. 'Peppy, come back!' A big blonde with a beehive hairstyle, a very short skirt, and jaunty legs, teetered onto the stage in a state of pretty agitation.

'Too much make-up,' observed the man with the deaf aid, loudly. 'Eyes like piss-holes in the snow.'

'Peppy, come here.' She was talking to the dog but smiling at the audience.

'Ladies and gentlemen,' barked Martyn, 'I give you the one – the only – June Gee.'

'But it's not my turn yet,' she protested modestly. 'Olive's waiting to sing.' June caught the dog and lifted

156

him up in a way that brought animal acts at Salford Hippodrome to mind. 'Olive's wonderful,' she confided to the audience. 'Wonderful.' She just mouthed this last word – you always got a lot of mouthing in Pendleton.

'Miss Olive Farrell,' declaimed Martyn.

At the piano, Mr Monk raised his pudgy hands and crashed them onto the yellowed keys in a manner that was positively grand operatic – thrum-thrum-thrum-thrum. A woman in a brown evening gown with a rust net picture skirt and a spray of suede flowers at the waist, walked gloomily to the centre of the stage. 'It is an honour to be with you in Pendleton,' she said.

'Thank God she didn't say Bolton!' observed June, roguishly, from left of centre of the stage.

'Mrs June Gee has particularly asked me to sing "Nobody Knows The Trouble I've Seen".'

At this point Dinah expected June to leave the platform. Not a bit of it: the clairvoyant just handed the poodle into the wings, retreated only halfway into the shadows and began to observe the audience closely – very closely.

Brown was the right colour for Olive Farrell; she was the kind of contralto who wrung her hands as she moaned low. And all the while June was standing studying the rows of people as they sat on their uncomfortable wooden seats. At one point she even produced a pair of upswept spectacles with diamanté trim.

'She generally puts those on before she starts,' whispered Avril. 'I think it's to make her look more intellectual. Come on, Dinah, clap the singer, she wasn't *that* miserable.'

But the song had taken Dinah down to the depths and she couldn't shrug off the feeling that the clairvoyant had been watching her.

Miss Farrell was not allowed to acknowledge her own applause. The moment it rose to its height June moved back to the centre and said 'Thank you'. Pointing dramatically towards someone in the front row, she added, 'In a moment I want to come to you.'

First the singer had to trail her skirts out of view. And

as she went, June observed, 'I want you all to know that Olive Farrell's done this for nothing. Well, not quite for nothing; she was here tonight because I've been able to give her wonderful evidence of her father's survival. You.' The pink-lacquered talon was again pointing towards the youth in the front row.

Dinah could only see the shoulders of a duffel coat and mousy hair and the back of a neck which looked young and defenceless. But June could see more. 'My guide is telling me that you are very much drawn to the Spiritualist movement. He says that you were one of the first people waiting outside tonight. Does the name "Maggie" signify anything?'

In the 1950s half of Pendleton would have known a Maggie. The youth replied, 'It was me Gran'ma.'

'Not was. Is. She's with you. She's here. She's talking about when she used to make you hotpot in a brown-stone dish.'

Dinah muttered to Avril, 'I could do as well as this.'

'Shut up.'

June was rising to greater heights. 'I'm seeing Gran'ma opening her purse and giving you money and saying "Don't tell your mam". Right or wrong?'

'Correct.'

'Who's Jim?'

'Me uncle.'

As she studied the boy, June could have been a blonde snake charmer. 'But he's in the body, isn't he? He's on this side.'

'Oh yes.'

'Thank you. Gran'ma's saying that he's due for a bit of luck on the football pools.'

'He won fifty-seven quid on Vernons last Saturday,' shouted the boy.

June only had to spread her hands modestly for her audience to erupt into applause. Dinah noted with fascination that these same pudgy hands were a size smaller than the rest of June Gee.

As the clapping subsided, the medium appeared to be

addressing a whole host of invisible people around her. 'Just a minute,' was said to one. Another got 'Yes, in the third row, by the aisle.' And 'I can only give one message at a time, Madam.' June returned her attention to the paying public as she said, 'They're pressing in on all sides. I'm afraid I'm going to have to ask my guide to get them in order.'

Again she addressed the unseen: 'Are you there, Navarna? Lovely to see you, but could you get them into a queue?' To the audience in the hall: 'What a thing to say to one of the greatest philosophers of this or any other age!' Yet again she conferred with the invisible: 'Ta, Navarna.'

Having restored order on the Other Side, June turned into a woman who could have just removed her own elasticated girdle. Great rolls of deceased aunts and uncles and cousins came flooding through. There was also a Lily Woolley and a Norman and a border collie called Patch, plus a Mrs Dodds whom nobody could 'claim'.

'All hold on to that name,' cried June. 'It'll come to somebody when they get home.'

'Harry Jepson,' called out a woman.

'I beg your pardon,' said the medium.

The person who'd interrupted was a pallid soul with a prominent goitre. 'Last week you gave out Harry Jepson and when I got home my mother said he was a man she nearly married.'

'Well there you are.' June spread her little hands for more applause. As it died down she pointed towards Dinah. 'You.'

'Me?' squealed Avril excitedly. 'What've you got for me?'

'A Woolworth's wedding ring, chucked down a grid! I'm talking to the girl next to you.'

June Gee descended the steps from the stage and began to make her way up the central aisle. Half of Dinah was much afraid, but the other half was wondering why an appearance-conscious woman like June had never gone in for contact lenses. The magnified mascara, and the dark blue shadowing round the eyes that gazed through the diamanté-rimmed spectacles, gave the medium the appearance of a panda. And Dinah recalled reading that pretty pandas could be dangerous.

The over-curvaceous figure pointed a tiny finger towards Dinah. 'I've a feeling that tonight's this young lady's first visit. Am I right? Just "yes" or "no" please.'

'Yes.'

'And I've a feeling that your friend with all the hair brought you here. I'm getting a public transport vibration – I think you came by bus.'

Just as Dinah was about to dismiss the whole experience as ridiculous, June snapped, 'Who's in the army?'

Dinah could feel herself beginning to tremble, in exactly the same way she'd trembled on her terrible twenty-first birthday.

'Just nod or shake your head if you're overcome by emotion,' said June. 'First I was shown khaki, then it was foreign writing on a whitewashed wall. Not the same alphabet as ours – could be Greek.'

And still Dinah tried to dismiss this 'evidence' as a lucky fluke.

'I can *see* him now,' said June with authority. 'He's never communicated before so Navarna's having to tell him how.' Turning to the people on the opposite side of the aisle so as to allow them a better view of herself, June continued, 'He isn't half handsome!' Addressing the ether she said, 'Come on, Mr Soldier, dear, just do as Navarna tells you. You think it in your brain and I'll get your voice in my head.'

Revolving, to give the whole audience chance to see her, she added, 'I'm just a living radio receiver. My husband always says I should have Pye stamped on my forehead. Ah! We're getting somewhere now.' Her attention swivelled back to Dinah. 'Who's Roy?'

'Rory?' She'd corrected her before she knew she'd done it.

'That's right, Rory.' To the hall at large, June observed, 'That was really strange. He was saying his name on the Other Side and she was saying it here.' Her beam of interest landed on Dinah again. 'He got a massive bang on the head, didn't he?'

'I don't know.'

'You do now. Massive. He's showing me himself wandering and staggering. And then he fell against this wall with lettering on it, and that's where he made his transition.' For a moment June looked genuinely puzzled. 'Now I can see him out of uniform. He's very spruce in his best suit – could be outside a picture house – and he's holding a little box of chocolates.'

It was the mention of that 'little box of chocolates' which caused Dinah to rise to her feet and run from the hall.

7

Cabin 2142 had taken on more than a slight resemblance to a West End dressing room. Sorrel, clad in one of Cunard's white towelling dressing gowns, was seated in front of the dressing table's illuminated mirror. She was busy applying the final brush strokes to her right eyelid.

'There's something curiously attractive,' she said, 'about a man in a white evening shirt and black trousers; I sometimes think it's a pity the jacket has to go over the top at all.'

'White or black?' asked Mickey. 'Tuxedo or dinner jacket? What are you wearing?'

Something with long sleeves to cover my secret lump, she thought as she got to her feet and began to make her way to the walk-in wardrobe. Not that the lump was really visible. But in her mind's eye it was perpetually sailing towards her like an iceberg. And if I can finger it and feel that much above the surface, what must be happening underneath? 'A dinner dress,' she said. 'Classic, high neck, very covered-up.' She pulled aside the curtain of the dressing area. 'Honestly, Mick, the tatty state of your luggage! It's a disgrace.'

'No it isn't, it's just experienced. I can't find the little box that's got my cufflinks in it. Let me see the frock.'

It was pale creamy-beige. Draped jersey, she reflected, never looked anything on a hanger.

'Oh dear,' said Mickey.

'Oh dear, what?'

'You'll look like a living digestive biscuit. I don't want to be critical, Sorrel, but the second night out is always the full grand swank. Could you straighten my bow tie? Maybe the cufflinks are in my carpet bag.'

Why have I never strangled him? she wondered as she

162

tugged the black silk bow into a better shape. 'Stand still,' she commanded.

'I'm only trying to put this CD on.' The portable record player was on the little shelf, by his bed.

'And I suppose that Miss Diana Ross is going to tell us that every time he touches you, you become a hero – for the umpteenth time!' She threw off her robe, slipped into the frock, and climbed into a pair of high-heeled bronze sandals. 'If you want swank, Mickey Grimshaw, I'll give you swank.'

He didn't have to be asked to zip her up, after all these years it was automatic. And he was confident enough of their relationship to add, 'People will only say you're trying to disguise an antique neck.'

'What I propose wrapping round my neck will blind them.' She marched over to the wall-safe and punched in the correct combination, 3534, the telephone number of the London flat they'd shared at the very beginning of their careers. In some ways she was as much married to Mickey as she'd ever been to beautiful Barney Shapiro.

'I just hope you haven't been to that place at Blackpool again,' Mickey said accusingly. 'I hope you haven't been buying more of those tacky drag queen rhinestones.'

She searched for a withering comment but could only come up with 'Oh shut up'. Besides, Sorrel knew she was about to produce her trump card. She took a heavy brown manila envelope from the safe, ripped open its industrial Sellotape fastening, and extracted a flat red leather box. It was a little worn at the edges but it still bore two royal coats of arms and the discreetly gilt-lettered words 'Wartski – Crown Jewellers of Bond Street and Llandudno'. Mickey's mouth fell open. It really did fall right open and Sorrel gloried in the moment.

'If those are what I think they are,' he said, 'they ought to be in the bank.' He was remembering the fuss there'd been when Ruby Shapiro died and left Sorrel the necklace.

Sorrel clicked open the red leather box. 'The Wartski diamonds.' In the years it had taken her to get old their blue-white fire had remained undiminished.

'I'd forgotten how amazing they were,' marvelled Mickey. 'Memory can't cope with that kind of relentless blaze. You're never going to actually wear them?'

Sorrel was already lifting the shimmering collar to her neck. Probably for the last time, she was thinking. But she wasn't about to tell him that. If the lump was really growing . . . 'Just fasten the catch. And you'll find there's a tiny bolt under the big sapphire at the back.'

'Come where there's more light.' The long wall mirror reflected dancing shafts of iridescence and a very worried Mickey Grimshaw. 'Sorrel, they were worth a quarter of a million when you got them.'

'They must easily have doubled,' she assured him. Actually they had trebled in value, and the insurance was ruinous. 'So do I still look like a digestive biscuit?' And then all theatricality vanished as she said, 'Mick, if it wasn't you, I'd swear there was a distinctly sentimental look in your eye.'

'It's just that I'm remembering the flat in Cornucopia Mews, and the way we had to take the empties back before we could afford to buy ourselves a packet of ten fags.' And he was also remembering that he had been young and indefatigable in those days, rated as one of the most attractive boys in London and very much pursued. At the time he had counted this as little more than a nuisance: he had only wanted to have his work taken seriously.

Well, they'd taken it seriously. And now – as Diana Ross rose to yet another crescendo – he wanted everything the other way round. He didn't want to be famous, he just wanted to be fancied. 'I'm a fool,' he said as he switched off the sound system. 'I haven't really got a sentimental bone in my body and I still can't find my cufflinks.'

'You said the carpet bag.'

'Elaine might just have slipped them in there.' Elaine ran his house in Manchester. But he didn't want to open the bag, which was full of research material. 'Joe packed it. Months ago. It's got all the stuff I need for the next book in it.'

Joe had always been good at filing the many and

164

various oddments that Mickey's authorly instincts told him to save: letters, newspaper cuttings, video tapes of potentially useful documentary programmes. All of these had always gone into a selection of box files. The one that came out of the carpet bag was labelled 'Occult'.

'Oh Joe, why did you go?' sighed Mickey.

'To clear the decks for your present adventure.' The Wartski diamonds seemed to have filled Sorrel with positivity.

'I thought you were dead set against it.' Mickey was already halfway down the bag. Blank workpads, boxes of pencils, a brass pencil-sharpener – no cufflinks. 'Anyway, this dream affair could be totally one-sided; it could all be in my imagination.'

'No it isn't.' It was out before she'd realised what she'd said. But she wasn't free to reveal any more because she'd learned it within the walls of an AA meeting, so Sorrel immediately wished that she hadn't said it with such certainty.

He seemed not to react. 'I need to make a new will.' Mickey was still down on his knees. 'If we drown at sea, Joe will still cop for the lot.'

'Who will you leave it to?'

'You've got enough and more. I wonder whether Elaine could have slipped them into the box file? If she hasn't I'll just have to use paper clips. Haul down my white tux, Sorrel.' He carried the file over to the bed. 'Success!' A pair of knitted gold links were in place in seconds.

As Sorrel helped him into the white tuxedo he was still rummaging through the file. 'Joe really was wonderfully painstaking. Look, he'd put together every single thing I could possibly need for this new book about the woman who finds she's psychic and wishes she wasn't. Oh my God!' Mickey was holding up a sound tape cassette. 'I have the strangest feeling that this should go into the safe.'

'Why, what is it?' Sorrel cursed herself for having asked so directly. Now, inevitably, he would tease her by throwing a veil of mystery around the item.

165

And he did. Into the safe it went with the cryptic comment, 'Just something.' The door clanged shut.

'And I bet you won't tell me who you're going to leave your money to, either,' sighed Sorrel.

'I've just had an inspired thought about that. The people who've always called me outrageous are going to have a field day when my will is published!' The white bedside telephone had started ringing but Mickey reached into the bathroom and picked up the extension there.

'Hello,' said a woman's voice. She sounded as though she should have been on *ITMA* on the wireless, a long time ago.

'Who's that?'

'Your girlfriend, I've been shopping. It's Polly Fiddler from the next cabin. Could you just step out into the gap? I've got something to show you.'

As Mickey rattled open the cabin door, the one opposite was rattling open too. And the Polly Fiddler who stepped out into the little hallway was a woman transformed. The perm and the spectacles were exactly the same, but she had added a bright blue dress. A caftan, which was . . . the only word that sprang to Mickey's mind was a French one – *étincelant*. This had always seemed to him to add tinsel to glitter, and the dress had done the same thing.

'Bought upstairs,' said the tiny woman proudly. 'The lady in the shop said that each frock keeps a family beading for a week.'

'I can well believe it.' He was trying not to notice what she had on her feet.

But she was too quick for him: 'Nobody can say they don't match. Plastic paddling shoes, bought for comfort, in Rhyl. People will just have to take me for a rich eccentric.'

'But you are a rich eccentric,' Sorrel assured Polly. The actress's diamonds were sparkling away at the side of Mickey's white linen shoulder.

'Eeh,' went their glittering neighbour appreciatively. 'We look just like a couple of Christmas trees, don't we?'

It wasn't *quite* the effect Sorrel had been aiming for. And Mickey Grimshaw, who had been imagining himself and his leading lady swanning through the ship like Noel Coward and Gertrude Lawrence, tried to get used to the idea of being part of a trio that would include the late Hylda Baker in a scene-stealing finale frock.

Once again Polly Fiddler proved herself ahead of him. 'You two tall ones stick together,' she commanded as Sorrel turned the key in the lock. 'I've got to count four doors along.'

'Who lives there?' asked the actress as she reminded herself that the skirt of the beige dress had a very slight train. It would take a bit of managing as she went round bends.

Everybody seemed to be reading everybody else's minds: 'Just kick it behind you, like Danny La Rue,' advised Mick.

'I knew him when he was a chorus girl called Danny Carroll,' called out Mrs Fiddler. 'When *Misleading Ladies* came to Hulme Hippodrome the boys always called into the Old Garret for a drink of a Sunday.' It seemed as though all the blue sequins had gone to Polly's head because she was now banging on a cabin door like a Lancashire knocker-up. 'Bring out your dead!' she cried enthusiastically. And then she confided, 'I've already had two of those miniature gins from out of the fridge.'

Mickey was just telling himself that she wasn't like a proper knocker-up (because they had a special professional pole) when the cabin door opened to reveal Jack Lawless wearing the exact double of Mickey's own white tuxedo.

'Now I *know* you're a matching pair!' exclaimed Polly Fiddler. 'What a good job I phoned down to the head waiter and asked him to put our tables together tonight.'

The devil entered into Sorrel Starkey: 'We'll walk a couple of paces ahead, Polly. If the boys come behind us, nobody can tread on my trailing bit.'

'Don't they look handsome?' observed Mrs Fiddler as she moved forward.

Mickey could have kicked himself for his previous 'Hylda Baker' moment of snobbishness. And he was wondering why another name – Heather Jenner – was running through his mind. But only for a moment: Heather Jenner had once run a Bond Street marriage bureau.

'Hi,' said Jack Lawless quietly. 'I didn't know about the table. I hope you don't mind.'

'No, I don't mind.' He risked a sideways glance. Like many men with dark hair Jack Lawless had a swarthy beard line. But, freshly shaved, it had taken on an expensive-looking gleam. And tonight he didn't smell of hygienically clean sweat, instead he smelled of 'Vetyvert' – exactly the same cologne as Mickey had just slapped on.

'I never thought that gay men would go back to aftershave.' Mickey was remembering the years he'd spent stomping round San Francisco in plaid shirts and Levi's and work boots. He could even recall sending to England for Wright's Coal Tar Soap. 'My goodness me but we took the butch bit about as far as it would go!'

'And tonight the pair of us smell like Kendal's ground floor again,' laughed the porn star.

Like Kendal's ground floor? If there was a more Manchester expression than that, Mickey couldn't think of it. 'How on earth do you know about Kendal's?' he asked in wonder.

'I was born in Stockport. If the American act is convincing it's because it had to be. My first five years in the States were illegal.'

Mickey simply had to ask something. 'How old are you?'

'For real?'

'For real.' Only don't ask me my own age.

'Thirty-three.'

Thirty-three: I was twenty-six when he was born, thought Mickey. *Angel Dwellings* was just about to start. And this whole madness has to stop here and now.

'You've got to be sixty.' Jack was still smiling that extra-happy smile. 'I've read everything that's ever been written about *Angel Dwellings*. My mother's a lady who's

168

not too happy with my way of life; sometimes, instead of a letter, she keeps in touch by sending me cuttings about your show.'

He's a fan, thought Mickey gratefully. That's okay. I know exactly how to keep fans at a respectable distance.

Not this one. 'Sixty makes me feel safe.'

Mickey chose to misunderstand. 'Good.'

Jack halted, the women continued to move along the lengthy gangway. Mickey hesitated for a moment, then he too stayed where he was. It was the Stockport-American who spoke. He said, 'I don't often ask people to be friends.' But he sounded like somebody who had often been hurt. 'Just for this trip, couldn't you forget what I do for a living?'

'Could you?' Where had that hateful line sprung from? Most unusually, Mickey cursed his own quick wits and his fast tongue.

'I could try.' There was no hint of reproach in this, it was just a statement of fact.

'Okay,' said Mickey. But what was he saying okay to? And why had he immediately felt as young and light-hearted as Jack Lawless was suddenly looking. 'This is madness – madness,' Mick actually came right out and said it aloud. And at the same time he was trying to control an irrepressible grin which was threatening to spread itself from ear to ear. Noel Coward? He felt more like Mickey Rooney!

'Are you negotiating a contract for him?' Mrs Fiddler called over her shoulder. She and Sorrel had paused at the entrance to a staircase.

'Yes,' called back Jack. 'We've decided I'm going legitimate.'

Ho-ho, thought Sorrel. Ho flipping ho!

It was Baked Alaska Night in the Britannia Grill. At the two tables turned into one, only Mickey Grimshaw understood the significance of these words at the top of the menu.

Things had already got off to something of a festive start. Once they had settled themselves down, Jack had announced that it was his party and had insisted upon ordering champagne. Not just any old champagne – vintage Bollinger. And in the grill rooms it was possible to order items that were not listed on the menu, and he had called for Beluga caviar.

It arrived in one of those containers that always reminded Mickey of a silver inkwell surrounded by cracked ice. And a second waiter was proffering a silver tray of those tiny Russian pancakes called blinis.

Jack had also ordered sparkling mineral water. 'I don't do alcohol,' he explained easily.

'So why the fizz?' asked Mickey.

'Because I get off on other people drinking it.'

Sorrel could understand this; the drinks she served in her own home were always generous; it was as though she was still pouring them for the Sorrel Starkey who had drunk herself into oblivion. Guests had been known to leave the house reeling.

If this is an attempt at seduction, thought Mickey, it's all gloriously old-fashioned. And then he dismissed the idea. The deal was that he and Jack were going to be friends. The sane side of his mind could already read the story in the *News of the World*: 'Mickey Grimshaw, the self-confessed gay father of television's wholesome *Angel Dwellings* has a new companion . . .' But the sane side of his mind was not in charge tonight. What exactly did 'friends' mean? And how had Jack Lawless earned the money for the party? He didn't have to search hard for the answer: one way or another, Jack had earned it with his legendary charms.

Similar thoughts must have been going through Mrs Fiddler's head. 'Nobody ever calls rent-boys to me,' she said as she allowed the waiter to refill her glass. 'If this is caviar, all I can say is our cat might quite like it. Did you ever know a boy in Manchester called Ten-bob-Terry?' she asked Mickey. 'Always bought the bar staff at the Old Garret beautiful Christmas boxes. I've still got a Jacqmar scarf he lifted from Affleck and Brown's. And then there was Blond Eric who did it as a lady. Aren't we having a nice little time? "A life on the ocean wave,"' she quoted merrily. '"Where there isn't a girl in sight."' She then dug Mickey in the ribs and asked, 'Aren't you glad now that I got the tables shunted together?' Oh, she was well away! 'Don't thank me,' she continued solemnly. 'It was the least I could do. I must have seen your name go over that screen a thousand times but I never thought I'd get the chance to play Cupid for you.'

Mickey choked on his champagne as Polly Fiddler raised her glass to the next table and said 'Chin-chin'. He didn't dare look at Jack so he gazed instead at their immediate neighbours – Helene Kramer the white-haired American psychic and her husband, Art. They were dining with a US Army General, who had the kind of blonde wife who must once have looked much younger than her rubicund husband.

'Dinkey,' he kept calling her. In fact he had already bellowed 'Dinkey darlin'' over and over again.

'I thought I was going to be Gloria for this trip,' she complained. 'I mean, it is my name.'

Sorrel, who had been thinking that the woman must once have been a beauty queen, gave herself up to unabashed eavesdropping.

'No, you're my Dinkey, the fairest girl who ever stepped out of a bubble bath. And I know you want to ask Mrs Kramer a personal favour.'

'Well I do.' The ageing blonde hitched up her strapless top. 'Mrs Kramer, can you "see" anything for me?'

'She's closed down,' said Art Kramer in the automatic tones of a man who'd been obliged to repeat this too many times. 'Helene only opens up her abilities for six months of the year, and these ain't they.'

'He's quite right.' Helene Kramer was somebody else who was sticking to Perrier water. 'But the sea always has the strangest effect upon me. Like a lot of natural psychics I was born under the sign of Cancer. That makes me a water subject, and the sea always seems to open them up again. Not,' she added hastily, 'that I'm about to sit here and go into a reading.'

But why, Sorrel wondered, was elegant Mrs Kramer glancing across at Mickey in that perturbed fashion? In the same moment yet another empty plate was placed in front of her. This one must be for the Dover sole, and then there would be a sorbet to refresh her palate, and experience had already taught her that the eventual main course would be accompanied by vegetables that were so tiny and perfect that you could only think of them as 'new-born'. As she continued to eat, Sorrel's inner-self rebelled.

The *QE2* was presenting her with an excess of riches. All these people were spoiled, spoiled, spoiled – she had just heard somebody complaining that their prawns hadn't been peeled for them. And all this over-pampering only made real-life problems seem grimmer by contrast. I won't think about that fucking lump, she told herself. I won't. Instead she thought about mucky Salford, before the Clean Air Act, when bright sunlight had only showed up the cracks to worse effect.

In an attempt to change the direction of her ruminations she looked out of the picture window. All she could see was the shifting black satin Atlantic. Why were there no white horses on top of the waves this far out to sea? She had come a long way from Blackpool.

'Are you okay?' murmured Mickey.

'Just remembering.' Her mind had gone all the way back to the housing estates of both of their childhoods, to a world where you could set your watch by the postman's arrival and predict – with absolute accuracy – where each family on Rookswood Avenue would take their summer holidays. All the exterior woodwork had been painted green and cream, mostly bottle green – emerald had been considered as daring as arriving home in a taxi. You weren't meant to do anything to draw attention to yourself. And Sorrel had done plenty! Except, in those days she'd been called Sheila. Sheila Starkey who ran away from home because she wanted more.

Well she'd got more. It didn't take the reflection of the Wartski diamonds in the window to remind her of that. And now the necklace was filling her with guilt as she faced up to the fact that half the world's population didn't have enough to eat.

Mick, she realised, was looking at her again, and his eyes were filled with concern. She tried to reassure him with, 'It's just that it's all a bit phoney, too grand.'

'It takes a dive in a minute,' he promised her gleefully. 'The final plate of all is meant for your baked Alaska.'

'Why have all the lights gone out?' she asked him.

'You'll see. It doesn't mean the ship's going down, it means your pudding's due to arrive.'

Cymbals suddenly began to crash and the air was filled with the pre-recorded strains of a Souza march. To this accompaniment three-quarters of the waiters trooped back in bearing flags of many nations. The remaining waiters processed in a line – down the middle of the flag-bearers – carrying platters of flaming Baked Alaska surrounded by fizzing sparklers.

'How very odd,' said Sorrel to Mickey, 'I was just thinking about Blackpool and it's exactly like being there.'

'In a minute you'll think you're switching on the illuminations again!' Chefs in tall white hats had emerged from the kitchen to set alight more banks of sparklers on metal stands, strategically placed around the grill room.

The indoor fireworks were reflected in the lenses of Mrs Fiddler's glasses. 'It's just like being in Fairyland!' she exclaimed. 'If you'll excuse the expression,' she added hastily.

And both Mickey and Jack guffawed in such a similarly gleeful way that Sorrel was surprised to find herself conceding that they were a far from ill-matched pair. The pudding itself proved to be made of chilled ice-cream surrounded by boiling hot meringue. Its arrival had been such a grande finale that everybody was left wondering what to do next.

'I want to get a seat for Paul Daniels in the Grand Lounge,' said Mrs Fiddler.

'Me too,' Sorrel rose to her feet. 'I love a good conjurer.' The game of after-dinner musical chairs had begun and it was already spreading to the next table, where the General and his wife and Art Kramer started heading for the exit, with much noisy talk of Monte Carlo and the gaming tables.

'And I have to see a guy in the Crystal Bar,' said Jack Lawless, rather to Mickey's surprise. The last thing he'd expected to be was dumped. Then Jack added, 'Why don't you come and have a brandy there in about half an hour?'

'I might.' Who was the man? Jealousy of this kind was an emotion he had never expected to have to handle again.

'He's just a fan. He's the kind who won't take no for an answer.'

An answer to what? But Jack was already heading towards the staircase.

Similarly abandoned at the next table, Helene Kramer leant across and said to Mickey, 'Ain't nobody here but us chickens. But you'll be too young to remember that song.'

'I feel old enough to recall the Spanish Armada.'

'Yet young enough to jump over the yard-arm.' Beneath her white fringe, Helene's canny old eyes were observing him closely. 'Feel like a walk round the deck?'

'Will you be warm enough?' She was in a slim gold and white dress, it looked as though it had been tailored out of a sari.

'It has its own coat.' She reached for the back of her chair.

Mickey got up from his own and helped her into a white wool jacket which had a little collar in the same material as the dress. 'I'm worried about Sorrel,' he said. 'She shouldn't be roaming round the ship in all those diamonds.'

'The diamonds are not her problem.' The words had turned Helene Kramer into a woman who looked as though she could have willingly bitten her own tongue. 'It's the sea,' she said awkwardly. 'It opens up my sensitivities.'

174

'What is Sorrel's problem?' The head waiter was already beginning to bow them out.

'Forget I said it.'

'I can't. She's been harbouring a secret since the Savoy.'

'Well you won't get me to spy into her mind for you.' Helene was leading the way up the stairs. 'We'll need to go higher up in the ship if we want to get out on the open deck.'

Their leisurely stroll took them past display boards of photographs of groups of passengers, embarking at Southampton.

'My God, she looks just like a bloated Phyllis Diller.' Helene was pointing a white-gloved finger at a glossy print of June in her dusty black travelling outfit.

'Either the brain's gone too or she keeps on cutting me and Sorrel dead.'

'No, look at those poor old bloodshot eyes. She probably can't stand the pain of her own contact lenses.' The gloved finger touched the photograph. 'There's a lot of pain inside that heart too. I have to stop this, Mick, I'm supposed to be closed down. Here and now I have to stop it. Let's cut through the Grand Lounge.'

It was almost like a theatre, with a packed audience watching a stage full of bespangled and feathered dancers. 'Why do they invariably open with "That's Entertainment"?' Mickey wondered aloud. More spectators were standing watching from a balcony, which ran round three sides of the lounge. But Mickey and Helene edged their way towards the back of the huge room, and then climbed the grandiose staircase to the Yacht Club.

'Oh my God, they've turned it into a disco!' exclaimed Helene. 'Where's the glass grand piano gone? I just hope these heels will make the Boat Deck.'

They did. Here everything was painted white except for the polished wooden boards of the open deck itself.

'A moon and a very slight breeze,' said Helene contentedly. 'You *had* to do that, didn't you?' Mickey had reached out and touched the varnished handrail.

He found himself admitting something he'd never told

a living soul. 'Sometimes I feel forced to reach out and do it, actually feel her. Touch the ship, I mean.' He trusted Helene enough to admit, 'There's love in it – real love. This was the first big liner I ever sailed on. It took the *QE2* to teach me that ships have souls.'

'And you adore her.' It was a statement not a question.

'Ridiculously. I even hate the fact that they've taken that great big horse-shoe staircase out of the Grand Lounge. I think she minds.' Helene Kramer, he reflected, was very good at leaving the sort of long silences which called for further explanation. 'This ship always tells me things about myself,' he admitted. 'Things that even I didn't know. I should have forgotten all about ambition and gone to sea for a living. It's as though I missed out on my one chance of being perfectly contented.' He came back out of his dream. 'I'm not sure whether the sea could have my bones,' he said more realistically. 'Although sailors who've nearly drowned often claim that the rapture of the deep beats imagination.'

Helene Kramer continued to gaze over the ocean. 'I won't let you open me up,' she said to the heavy black swell. 'I don't need it. I don't want it.'

Mickey must have waited a full sixty seconds before he asked, 'What's it telling you?'

She shook her head. 'This is the six months when I don't do it.'

But she had forced something out of him so he needed something back. 'What is it telling you?' he persisted.

Helene gave a little sigh. 'Maybe, if I get rid of this one bit, it'll let me go.' The wind stirred her hair as she turned to face Mickey. 'That young man, the one who was paying you so much attention . . .'

'Jack?' he asked eagerly.

'The spectacularly handsome one at your table.'

'Jack.' Even repeating his name brought Mickey pleasure.

'This is very hard to explain.' Her voice began to drone. 'He's two separate people. One is made of light and one was fashioned in murky shadows. He knows it, he's brave, he tries to fight for the light. But somebody on this ship is trying to take him right down into the darkness.'

'And?'

'You're at the cross-roads. It's up to you. Stick with him and you might develop something that's above rubies. Or, then again, he could ruin you.' Her voice returned to normal as she said, 'Well you did ask.'

The Crystal Bar was yet another example of the ship's refurbishments. It obviously took its name from the Art Deco, moulded glasswork behind the lavishly curved bar. This translucent wall looked as though it might have come out of one of Cunard's pre-war liners. And the shimmering sound of one of the distant dance bands playing 'Transatlantic Lullaby' only added to the feeling of being in a time warp.

Something else belonged to the past too. This low-ceilinged cocktail lounge was reminiscent of a gay bar of yesteryear, of a time before the harsh English homosexual laws were partially relaxed. Mickey was remembering the nights when men of his kind were obliged to colonise the darker corners of straight establishments. And here they were again, in cautious twos and threes.

The other passengers might not have realised, it took one to spot one, and Mickey was spying plenty. Pairs of handsome young men simply having a good time. Here a dinner jacket that was a mite over-tailored, there a pair of eyes which could not resist following the trail of a handsome waiter – who was equally well-aware of being in on a secret.

And it didn't all belong in the past, either: Mickey had spotted something he had got too used to seeing in the Castro in San Francisco, on Canal Street in the Gay Village in Manchester – the strangely beautiful holocaust face of a boy with Aids. These days, wherever there was luxury, in the very best hotels, on the Orient-Express, you saw these frail men on walking sticks, bravely dressed to the nines in the cause of reaching for one last infusion of the high life.

That was the moment when the night handed him back Jack Lawless. He was seated at a nearby table with a pudgy man in a rose brocade smoking jacket. Even from here Mickey could see the puncture marks above the stranger's peeling suntanned forehead, indications of hair grafts that had failed to take root. And he also noticed the solitaire diamond ring on a strong-looking finger that was pushing something across the table-top.

Now Jack was pushing it back. As Mickey got closer he felt as though he was observing a game of chess because – once again – the small white envelope had been moved in the porn star's direction.

'Okay,' he heard Jack say. And then he sighed, 'Anything for a quiet life. But listen, you've got to be more discreet. We need to talk. And away from here.'

The other man was old. That was the moment when Mick realised that the champagne and the exchanged glances in the Britannia Grill must have deluded him into thinking that he, himself, had shed decades. In reality the man was probably his own age – and Jack Lawless liked them mature.

Jack rose to his feet, the man did the same. He wasn't really fat, it was just that he was heavy-jowled, and that formal tailoring offered no favours to his kind of bulky gym-built body.

Registering the fact that Mickey was advancing upon them, Jack threw him a highly professional lazy grin and said, 'I've just got to go and sort something out, Mick. Order yourself a drink on my tab. I'll be back in a minute.'

Not in my minute, thought Mickey savagely. God knows what's going on but I'm not even going to waste sixty good seconds in finding out. Jack Lawless could piss up his own leg and slide down the steam!

As the porn star and his burly companion made their way towards the head of the stairs, they all but collided with a chubby female figure in a black wig and a general effect of spangled black veiling.

It was dreadful June Gee, and she wasn't quite alone because she was being stealthily followed. Mickey's mind immediately went back to the fans of *Angel Dwellings* who had waited outside Buckingham Palace. The most intense of these admirers of the show were little short of stalkers. Thirty years in the public eye had taught Mickey a good deal about people with all-absorbing obsessions. There was a look to them, a style he could spot instinctively. And June Gee was definitely being stalked by that woman with the white streak in her hair – the one who originally came from Irlams o' th' Height.

8

By 1964 most people had forgotten the song 'Lover Come Back To Me'. In real life Dinah was somebody who couldn't carry a tune in a bucket. But, inside her head, she was the possessor of a light but true soprano; this was the voice that – even now – sometimes sang

> 'You came at last,
> Love had its day.
> That day is past,
> You've gone away . . .'

And Rory wasn't coming back; June Gee had made that abundantly clear. So Dinah stayed on at Tyrell and Tench – mostly for the company she enjoyed there. People who work together closely are often privy to far more intimacy, during the daytime, than they would ever dream of indulging in at home. And from nine to six on Mondays to Fridays, and until closing time came at one o'clock on Saturdays, Dinah learned everything there was to be known about her fellow employees: the state of their finances, their bowels, their love lives.

Avril Porter was the Sadie Thompson of the establishment. 'Men just view me as a slice off a cut loaf,' she would moan nasally at Dinah, as she lurched from one disastrous love affair to another.

And Dinah would chide her with, 'If it's not difficult you're not interested.'

All of this was done in lowered tones. The men knew exactly what was going on but you had to keep up the pretence that they didn't.

By now the red-headed Turnock twins, always known as 'Ham' and 'Bud', had stopped being all wrists and ankles and acne, and emerged as a handsome young duo.

Tall and slim and full of mischief and energy, their main preoccupations were watching stock car racing at Belle Vue and downing copious quantities of Holts's bitter beer. They were also on a perpetual search for another pair of twins – female ones.

'But they've got to be blonde,' beamed Bud.

'And they've got to be good for a laff,' put in his equally affable brother.

'Doesn't it matter what they look like?' asked Avril, who took a motherly interest in the two young men.

'Not as long as they're blondes,' they replied in unison.

'Ah well, they do say that blondes get dirty quicker.' Eugene Gannon was somebody else whose interest in the Turnock twins verged on the motherly. 'You pair of dirty snickets!' he would add lovingly.

His hatred of Edna Tench had deepened into something which was little short of obsessive. Eugene's greatest delight was to snatch up the knitted tea-cosy, place it on his head, and launch into a virulent impression of his employer.

He could make the woollen cosy look exactly like Edna's pixie hood. And from beneath it he would squawk out such typical lines as, 'Whoever marries Johnnie doesn't just get him – she gets a feller who's going to inherit the Gentlemen's Remedy!' Reverting to his own voice he would add, 'And she'll bloody well need it. She'll need to slip it in his tea if she wants results.'

It was considered all right, indeed natural, for men to make passing references to sex. Just so long as they didn't go too far. Not that the girls viewed Eugene as much of a man. He was more like their resident pantomime dame. Mother-Goose-before-she-got-the-money was how Dinah drew him in the painted diaries. And on the Irishman's more masculine days he would be transcribed onto the cartridge paper pages as an angry little Rumpelstiltskin.

He plainly saw John Tench as a fool who had allowed himself to be dominated by an overbearing woman. Dinah viewed him in a more kindly light. In her opinion John had little choice in the matter. If his mother was riddled with nastiness, there were equal amounts of kindness within her son. And he was no dope. Dinah was of the opinion that his apparent docility was John's way of maintaining some serenity within his life. But you'd only to see the way he knocked hell out of a tennis ball to realise that there was more to him than met the eye.

She knew about the tennis because – unbeknown to his mother – he had been giving her lessons. Not at solid old Monton Cricket and Tennis Club where John was a member like his father had been before him. No, Dinah had only been prepared to make a clumsy fool of herself in Light Oaks Park, where the use of public tennis courts cost sixpence an hour. Besides, she didn't have the proper clothes.

'Caught the boss's son's eye, have you?' her father had said darkly.

'It's not like that,' she had protested. And, in absolute honesty, it wasn't. The lessons were the result of the Nelsons getting their first television set. This was 1964, and, that year, in the middle of every evening of Wimbledon fortnight, the BBC had shown telerecorded highlights of each day's events. As a result, there was hardly a girl on Saracen Street who didn't long to be dressed in a trim white tennis top and a pair of tailored shorts by Colonel Teddy Tinling – the designer who had revolutionised the look of post-war women players by putting white lace on Gorgeous Gussie Moran's panties.

Those Wimbledon telerecordings inspired a lot of people to head for Light Oaks Park. Soon there were barely enough public courts to go round. And the owner of the greasy second-hand shop at the bottom end of the Height must have been delighted to find that his cumbersome old tennis rackets – some of them dating back to the days of Suzanne Lenglen – were suddenly at a premium.

Dinah did not have to invest in one of these back-attic relics. Once she had expressed envy of the girls who were out on the courts, John Tench produced a lightweight racquet made by Grey's of Cambridge and came up with his first tentative offers of coaching.

The courts in the park were not grass, they were surfaced with red shale – their white lines delineated in heavy linen tape. Dinah, who had often peered through the wire netting to see what other girls were wearing, put together an outfit of navy-blue beach shorts and white blouse; she finished it off with the black and white-speckled plimsolls she had last worn for gym classes at Pendleton High. But the John who arrived to pick her up was dressed in proper, close-fitting tennis whites. A little green Fred Perry emblem sat on the knitted cotton shirt which covered a chest that was nothing like as dramatically sculpted as Rory's had been.

But the abbreviated shorts revealed long, slim, pale-golden legs. And she was startled to find that his lightly muscled arms were not without a beauty of their own – in fact they made her fingers itch for a carefully sharpened 2H drawing pencil. And because it was summer he had recently had his fine blond hair cropped so that it no longer looked sparse. It looked endearing – almost like a little boy's hair.

It's still just Johnnie Tench, she told herself. But a slyly snarled 'Johnnie' was his mother's way of diminishing him. Tonight he looked his own man, and very definitely 'John'.

And out on that red shale tennis court, for the first time she saw him as a figure of authority. As a coach he was firm but kind. All around them, on the other sunken courts, inept enthusiasts were crying out 'Your service' and 'Deuce' with no real idea of what they were doing.

In fact these young men in old cricketing flannels, and their girlfriends who appeared much given to the kind of green eye-shades that cost a shilling at the newsagents, were merely knocking old grey tennis balls in over-enthusiastic approximations of the right direction.

In the midst of this maelstrom, John Tench was a rock of disciplined calm. The whole of the first lesson was devoted to teaching her how to get used to the feel of the beautifully fine racquet. How to hold it, to raise it, to be sure that each arm movement led pleasingly into the next.

As he adjusted her grip on the leather-covered handle, Dinah was once again aware of the very first thing she had ever noticed about him – his hands. Not only were the fingers long and slim, they were also the kind of super-clean that you would expect to find in an operating theatre.

There was complicity in these meetings of theirs on the public courts, opposite to the brick and wooden wind shelter, which was topped by a fretwork bell tower – shaped like an overgrown birdhouse. The bell only rang when the park was about to close. Tennis lessons over, with dusk about to fall, they would collapse onto one of the wooden forms, which stood within the recesses of the shelter, and talk about who *knew*.

Knew what? That they were out together, however innocently. Tommy Nelson's dark fears about bosses' sons and working-class daughters had grown to such an extent that Dinah had felt obliged to ask John Tench to refrain from calling for her. The racquet was supposed to have been handed back. Eva, who had many ambitions invested in her daughter, did not share her husband's views. Given half a chance, she would have had John Tench to Sunday tea on a regular basis. In fact, before he stopped calling, she'd even gone so far as to invest in a silver-plated pickle fork.

These days Avril had a bed-sit in a big Edwardian house on Fallowmeadow Road. This was just near to the park so that was where Dinah kept her shorts and her new white Dunlop tennis shoes. John kept the racquet in his Jeep. By now it was understood to be, quite definitely, her own racquet. Mrs Tench would have dropped cork-legged!

So Avril was in the know, and Eugene Gannon – who never missed a trick – was busy being over-careful not to ask too many questions. It was the Turnock twins who added a new threat to these clandestine meetings.

Saturday mornings at Tyrell and Tench were much

more relaxed than the rest of the week. Old Edna only came in at one o'clock, to cash up. That was when she would cycle over from her home in Eccles on the black-painted bicycle which generally spent its days chained up in the entrance hall. Her Saturday absence always reminded Dinah of a jolly line from the song 'Nymphs and Shepherds Come Away', often to be heard on *House-wives' Choice*, and always sung by the Manchester School Children's Choir.

'For this is Phoebus' hol-i-day.'

On Saturdays John Tench would often stroll in wearing a blue Jaeger pullover and fawn cavalry twill trousers. Eugene remained in his eternally penitential black suit, but the twins dispensed with neckties; underneath their brown warehouse coats they sported open-necked shirts.

The painted diary contained a wicked drawing of Eugene gazing at the twins in Saturday-fascination. Obviously Dinah hadn't been able to draw him looking at both twins at one and the same time; not unless he'd been standing a long way back – which he wasn't. No, she'd shown him with those Irish eyes – the colour of alligator skin – fixed in rapt fascination on the small triangle of flesh exposed by Bud Turnock's unbuttoned shirt collar. Bud was the more vigorous and assert-ive of the two boys but both had the same crest of bright ginger body hair, sprouting right up to their collar bones.

The sight of this was always enough to set Eugene's tongue flickering nervously over his thin tattoo-red lips. His eyes would flicker from Bud's ginger triangle to Ham's ginger triangle and then back again. Dinah had once caught him murmuring 'Thank God it's Saturday'. She knew that Eugene went to Confession on Saturdays but it was still a bit puzzling.

'You live at the Height, don't you?' Bud Turnock asked Dinah. 'Ever get on the tennis courts?'

Panic set in. 'Why?'

'Twins,' said Ham. 'Girls. A lad we know's seen a pair there.'

'You wouldn't like them,' said Dinah hastily. 'They're not what you're looking for; they've got brown hair.'

'We know.' Ham was doing the talking this time. 'We were told. We thought we might have a go at talking them into turning blonde. Do they look good for a laff?'

'No, they're very serious. I think they're Methodists.'

But the Turnock twins, it seemed, were refusing to be deflected. 'Perhaps they want cheering up,' grinned Bud. 'We might have a ride up there one night, on the tandem.'

And ever since then, out on the courts, Dinah had had difficulty in keeping her eye on the ball. She was forever losing her concentration by glancing in the direction of the park gates as she anticipated her troubles 'coming not singly but in pairs' and expecting to see them astride a green Raleigh tandem bicycle.

'Stop worrying, it may never happen,' said John. He was standing behind her, adjusting the angle of her arm. She was meant to be practising her service. Dinah didn't mind him touching her, it was companionable not erotic. Even as close as this he didn't give off any waft of masculinity. Instead he was surrounded by an impersonal aura of Tyrell and Tench's Patent Oatmeal and Cucumber Body Scrub, with just a hint of Listerine mouthwash.

And Rory had always smelt of . . . Rory. In his day, deodorants for men had yet to come into fashion. So, however hard he washed and scrubbed himself, something gloriously animal had ever been present. Not sweat – just essence of Rory. Even now the memory was enough to give Dinah that breathtaking 'top of Blackpool Tower' feeling.

But propriety didn't allow her to luxuriate in the sensation, not whilst John Tench was adjusting the angle of her elbow! She pushed memories of old passion from her mind by asking, 'How would your mother react if the twins did see us and said something?'

'Let's worry about that when it happens.'

But she noticed that her words had caused him to move a pace away from her.

'You take these three,' he said, handing her a set of balls that were much whiter than any of the ones going plip-plop on the other courts around them. 'Give me a minute to get round the net and then start sending me down quick smashes.'

Her game was definitely improving, John had seen to that. But as he returned her third serve with more testing vigour, the ball hit her racquet at an awkward angle and went flying over the top of the wire-netting which surrounded the courts. It landed in a flower-bed, up on the higher level.

'My fault. I'll go,' called out Dinah. You had to watch how you opened the metal-framed gate, it was easy to catch your fingers.

Beneath the flower-bed, on the gravel pathway, stood a park bench. And seated on it was a familiar figure. It was the little old rag-bag who doused her troubles in patent medicines. She was always popping up like a jack-in-a-box around Salford, and she always gave Dinah a running commentary on which pharmacies she'd visited and on what opiates she had managed to acquire.

'Nothing today,' she said. 'So I'm just sucking a chlorodyne lozenge.'

'How do you afford it all?' The tennis ball was quite forgotten.

The dried-out wraith bristled indignantly. She was sporting an equally dried-out Bangkok straw hat, with a wreath of threadbare cloth daisies running round the crown. That and one of those cotton duster coats which you sometimes saw in sepia photographs of Edwardian women sitting up in vintage motor cars. 'I'm not without,' she said. 'My friend who died in the First World War was a moneyed person. You're looking at somebody who came into streets of houses.' She patted an old leather handbag, big and brown, with a raised sunray design on the front. 'What d'you think I've got in here?'

187

'Your empties?'

'Don't be so cheeky. Rents, that's what I've got in here, tenants' rent money.'

Today, the muscles of her face seemed to be leading a life of their own. They were giving convulsive little jerks, under their casing of dried chamois leather skin. 'I've got the jim-jams,' she said gruffly. Her little brown eyes could have belonged to a dog at the vet's. 'Not had enough of my stuff.'

The tennis ball was still lying in the flower-bed, a white intruder amidst mauve and orange zinnias. Dinah hopped up onto the higher level and retrieved it. As she turned to climb down again she saw John Tench, way down on the lowest level of all. He was leaning against one of the posts of the tennis net, waiting for her patiently.

Though he smiled and gave Dinah a gentle wave of acknowledgment, she knew there would be no need to rush back. She also knew that he enjoyed watching her doing things. She'd often noticed it, at work. There was never anything salacious in the way he observed her – just kindly interest.

How did she feel about him? Really feel. The thought which sprang to mind surprised her. Dinah often spent evenings with Avril in her first-floor bed-sitting room on Fallowmeadow Road. Evenings of deep discussion. They always had hot buttered toast with Marmite on it, and real coffee, made in one of the new electric percolators. It was a welcoming room, even though there was a New World cooker in one corner.

Avril had hung travel posters over her landlord's splodgy oatmeal wallpaper, and converted two empty Chianti bottles into table lamps with gingham shades. And sometimes, when Dinah was leaving the house, she would look up to the firstfloor window, and Avril would be looking down, waving. I've got a friend, Dinah would think, with real gratitude. I've got a friend.

She was beginning to have similar feelings about her employer's son. He was kind and considerate and treated her respectfully. Almost as though she was a young widow, which, in a way she was.

'I'm surprised at you.' Salford's oddest female drug addict was staring at her reproachfully. 'I thought you was like me. I thought you was true to the memory of that dead soldier.'

'I am.'

'Then what you doing out tennising with a man with bare legs? And you're in your scanties too.'

'It's just what you wear for it,' said Dinah. 'It's so you can run.'

A spectacular tremor ran through the little woman's whole body. It even set the flowers on her hat quivering. 'I'm bad today,' she muttered to herself. 'Real jim-jams.'

'What would stop them?'

'Some stuff.'

Dinah's mind went to her mother's kitchen cupboard. It flew straight up to the second shelf where she saw a half-filled bottle of liquid and sediment, standing next to the Optrex and the blue eyebath. 'Would kaolin and morphine help?' Did this offer, she wondered, turn her into a dope peddler?

But Dinah Nelson was about to be treated to some of the most lavish gratitude she had ever received. 'May God bless you,' said the woman. 'May he bless you and keep you and make his countenance to shine upon you . . .'

Dinah, who had only ever heard a clergyman say these words before, was distinctly startled. 'Where are you going?'

'Not me. Us. We're going to get that stuff.'

'But I'm playing tennis,' protested Dinah.

'You've got the stuff and I've got the hab-dabs.' If there was pleading in her tone, there was also iron resolution. 'Anyway, the park-keeper should be tinging the bell in five minutes.'

This, Dinah reasoned, was true enough. 'But I can't go home in shorts,' she remembered. 'We'll have to call somewhere else, while I change.'

'Why?'

'Because. Just because.'

'Are you deceiving somebody?' One shrewd glance at Dinah's face had obviously been enough to give her the answer. 'Does your mother know where you are?' She made a gruff 'Hmph' noise. 'You'd have been better off being true to your memories.'

'Do you *want* that stomach bottle?' said Dinah threateningly. The way she'd barked this question had quite surprised her, made her realise that she was in a position of power. Power she did not want.

But the woman did want the bottle, oh how she wanted it. 'Please,' she pleaded. 'I'm so shaky today.'

Whatever have I fallen into? wondered Dinah. All she said aloud was, 'Wait here, I won't be a minute.' With this she began to head back for the tennis courts.

Plip-plop went four different sets of balls. Plop-plip. Plip-plop. Plip-plop. Only now did she register just who was playing singles on the court next to their own.

It was the girl twins, unskilled with their racquets and hampered by rope-soled espadrilles. Two gloomy blobs in identical, limp, rayon frocks. Which of the two of them could manage to run the slower? That seemed to be the only real competition in their match.

Dinah had just begun to call 'I'm coming, John' when her words were drowned out by a metallic crash. A tandem bicycle, its wheels spinning, had fallen to the ground. Its frame had jade green paintwork, the perfect contrast to ginger hair.

Here was Ham and there was Bud, spying down on the courts. Dinah could have been Eugene Gannon as she tried to avoid their eyes and registered the bright red triangles of young chest hair. They looked for all the world like a pair of cockerels.

Laughing eyes took in Dinah, glanced down at John, and then looked back at her again with new understanding. In one voice they both said the same amused words. 'Don't worry, we won't tell anybody.'

*　　*　　*

190

By now the little woman was more than nameless drift-wood. She had revealed herself as Daisy Carver. And asked where she lived she had replied, 'In a shed.'

It was John Tench who had elicited this information, en route for Avril's in his Jeep. The herbalist and the addict were still sitting waiting in the parked vehicle. Dinah was upstairs, changing back into her lemon cotton frock – a newish one with a Peter Pan collar.

John had obviously asked the questions in order to make polite conversation. But he had neither hesitated to act as chauffeur nor questioned Dinah as to why they were carrying this unusual passenger. John Tench just liked doing things for Dinah Nelson – it boiled down to that. And Dinah knew he *liked* her to take advantage of him.

Normally this filled her with uneasy guilt but, today, she was using him in the cause of an errand of mercy. As she changed her clothes it suddenly occurred to her that there might be no need to raid the cupboard at her mother's. 'Avril, have you got kaolin and morphine?'

'No but I could beat you up a raw egg. There's nothing finer for an upset tummy.'

'It's not my tummy.' She passed a broad white leather belt around the waist of her frock and began kicking off her tennis shoes.

'You'd never get John Tench taking anything from a chemist's. Who's it for?'

Off came the white ankle socks. 'Tell you later. You could do with running the vac over this carpet. You've let crumbs get in it again.'

'I've lost interest,' sighed Avril. 'This place was got as a love nest. But nobody shows me any respect so I've lost interest in my surroundings.' She treated Dinah to one of her frankest looks. 'You've got him on a plate. You know that, don't you?'

'Well he can stay on a plate.' Dinah pushed her feet into her white sandals.

'Aren't you the least *bit* interested?' There was no jealousy in this. Avril was too big for that.

But there were no secrets between them, either. Dinah

paused whilst she considered her true feelings. Eventually she said, 'You know when you were little and your dad was off work, and he came to meet you at the school gates, and you felt lovely and safe . . .'

The Slavic eyes widened in surprise. 'And this is the man who means nothing to you?'

No secrets. 'I just can't imagine him up against me.'

'I certainly wouldn't mind two penn'orth, not since I've seen those pale gold legs. And you know what they say about long fingers.'

'You'll never go to Heaven, Avril Porter!'

'*On a plate*!' were the words Dinah heard repeated as she hurried down the mahogany-panelled staircase. The house had definitely come down in the world.

Daisy Carver and John were still sitting, high up, in the Jeep. 'Move over so I can get in.' The front seat was a long bench. 'And then drive to the corner of our street, John, and wait there.'

By now they had turned into the posh end of Claremont Road, where smug semi-detached Edwardian villas were set up on grassy mounds. This was where she first noticed that Daisy Carver was trembling violently again.

'I'm always like this when I know I'm getting nearer to it. Sometimes it's all I can do to hand the money over the counter. You sure your mother's got that bottle?'

'Positive. Have you explained to John?'

'Didn't see the need. Thought it was between you and me.'

He did not react in any way. There is such a thing as too accommodating thought Dinah. Once again she was looking at his hands as they rested on the wheel, looking at the length of his fingers.

By now the villas with stained-glass panels set into their front doors were behind them. Big terraced houses, with front gardens that were little more than a narrow gap, hedged with privet, had taken over. But soon they would be reaching Saracen Street where you stepped straight in off the pavement, where niceties were considered soft, where bold questions were always the order of the day.

'This is going to take a bit of handling,' she said to John. 'Drive just past our house and wait on the corner of Bolton Road.'

'Your wish is my command.' And that was the trouble. Polite and considerate was one thing but you liked to know that somebody had a bit of fight in them, that they were capable of standing up to you in a scrap. If they couldn't work themselves up for that, however were they going to be able to manage to . . .

Whatever am I thinking of? she wondered in alarm. It's sex-mad Avril who's got me going like this. John is good and he's kind but he's never going to replace Rory Brogan. 'Park there,' she said. 'By the Elite.' This was a hairdressing salon which also sold umbrellas. 'I'll be back as quick as I can but I'm going to have to be a bit sneaky.'

These days she had her own front door key. Her parents viewed this as a major concession; they still thought of her as sixteen.

The bottle, the bottle, I must get the bottle. This pressing thought gave her some understanding of what it must be like to be Daisy Carver: that the little crone's every morning must be centered round the need to get at the dreamy syrups which took her back into the past.

As Dinah opened the kitchen door she saw that her mother was standing ironing, right in front of the kitchen cupboard. There could be no question of just sneaking the bottle out; she would have to invent some excuse for getting it down from the shelf.

'Though I say it meself, that lemon frock turned out well,' said Eva who had made it. 'All you need is a bunch of corn and a basket of eggs.'

'What would they do for me?'

'Turn you into the girl on the Ovaltine posters. I've just made the mistake of trying to press a crease into the sleeves of your real nylon blouse.'

'Is it wrecked?' asked Dinah. Not that she'd ever liked the garment. But a guilty Eva might be more amenable, less likely to ask too many questions.

'The nylon melted. I had to take a table knife to the iron. It's just to be hoped I've not bared the element.' Still ironing, she went straight into a story she'd heard at work. One about a woman who'd been photographed in a nylon wedding dress. 'And when the pictures came out, she was standing there in nothing but her bra and her pants and her suspenders.' Nylon, it seemed, did not 'take'.

Was Daisy Carver's every morning like this? Did she too have to nod and smile and listen to everything she was handed, before she could get at what she needed?

'Mother, Avril's got the runs.' Dinah, who wasn't given to telling lies, was surprised at how easily this one had left her lips.

'There's a bug about.'

'I said I'd take that stuff of ours over. I'll need to get behind you, into the cupboard.'

Eva made no effort to move. 'Oh no,' she said as she began to iron the strings on an apron maddeningly slowly. 'Corking herself up could be the worst thing she could do. It's better out of the system.'

'She's got a date tonight.' Where were these stories coming from?

'Who with?'

'Some man.' Now she was actively resisting the temptation to embroider.

'Well it's to be hoped he lasts longer than they usually do. She's been through more men than I don't know what.'

'No,' said Dinah loyally. 'They've been through her.' God, that sounded terrible! And could any one apron pocket deserve that much attention with an electric iron? 'If I could just get inside that cupboard . . .'

Eva did not move. 'Word spreads you know. Men talk amongst themselves. I'm not saying she *does*. I've a lot of time for Avril. But she looks as though she does.'

'She's stuck on the toilet at the moment.'

'You can be very vulgar.' But Dinah must have finally conjured up an urgent enough image to cause Eva to move to one side.

Her daughter opened the cupboard door and reached for the stomach medicine.

'Don't let her take more than one tablespoon or else she'll end up in the Land of the Happy-Daft. That's drugs, that is. And put it in a paper bag, Dinah.'

As Dinah wrestled open the top drawer, where paper bags were kept, the lobby door creaked open and her father walked in. He was carrying a clanking shopping bag, which meant that he must have been to Tong's, the off-licence.

'Guess who I've just seen?' he said.

'Can I get back to my ironing now?' Eva asked Dinah. 'Who?' she said to her husband.

'That John Tench. He's parked just past the cobbler's. By God, money sticks with money!' Dinah's father not only hated capitalists, he believed that they were privy to some special secret which amassed them wealth. In his view they all belonged to a mysterious order, from which working men were forever disbarred. 'Tench was with Dirty Daisy.'

'Not the one who's supposed to count gold in a shed?'

'She's up on his front seat.'

'And him so hygienic!' Eva was plainly filled with wonder.

'I'm going now,' said Dinah.

'Where?' asked her father. 'And where's my kiss?'

She knew if she hugged him he'd feel her guilt so she just gave him a quick peck on the cheek, instead. He must still have known her too well because as Dinah dived up the lobby she heard him saying to her mother: 'Summat's up. She's keeping secrets.'

Daisy Carver was no longer in the Jeep. She was standing trembling on the pavement, her little brown eyes fixed anxiously upon the advancing Dinah.

'Got it?'

'Here.'

Without even removing the paper bag, Daisy unscrewed the protruding metal cap, raised the bottle to her lips, and downed the entire contents in seven desperate slugs. You could tell she'd consumed the lot because she tapped the bottle onto her tongue to get the benefit of the last dregs. 'There is a God.' She said it gratefully to the evening air. 'Oh yes there is a God. And that bottle definitely came from Boots. I can tell it without so much as looking at the label.' She took a deep breath, all trembling had ceased. 'You see before you a new woman.' A much more talkative one too. 'I'm back inside me own skin. I'll go and find meself a form to sit on. I like to be on a form when I'm dreamin' me dreams. And in a bit, when the stuff gets to work on the brain, Jessie'll come out of the past. My lady. And I'll be beautiful and she'll be comical and I'll feel like a peach in cotton wool. Thank you for your kindness. It will not go forgotten.'

She was already toddling off. And Dinah noticed that the little woman's bunioned feet were leading her in the direction of The Place.

John Tench spoke for the first time since Dinah's return. 'I'm going to have to disinfect this van, I just saw a little, black, specky thing jump.' His tones were matter-of-fact and not unpleasant. Now they turned serious: 'I'm not criticising you but I've a feeling she's led us into something very wrong.' He looked really worried. 'Somehow or another I think we're going to have to pay for it.'

The following Friday morning Dinah was late in getting into work. Allowably late, she had been to the dentist's for a filling. After he had accidentally probed against an exposed nerve, three separate injections of cocaine had not stopped the drill from hurting. But they had given her some understanding of Daisy Carver's addictions. The cocaine had left Dinah feeling distinctly unreal: detached, smoothed-off round the edges, capable of coping with anything.

But this was to be no ordinary Friday morning. In fact, by the end of it, she would have welcomed a general anaesthetic.

Pendleton Church had already struck ten o'clock by the

time she finally got to Tyrell and Tench. To her surprise nobody was working. Instead, they were all sitting around the central bench, sipping coffee.

'Where's Ma Tench?' she asked Avril.

'Slammed off out.'

'John?'

'She'd already sent him off to Ruskin's to get a ledger back. That was before it all started.'

Ruskin's were the firm's book-keeper's. 'Before what started?' There was a lot of smirking going on. Mind you, the twins had been doing that non-stop since the encounter by the tennis courts. 'What's going on?'

It was Eugene who answered. 'All hell has broken loose. You know how she gets a free copy of the *Salford City Reporter* . . .'

'Because of the firm's advert, yes.'

'Well she came in here, spread out the paper on this very work bench, the advertisement was there. All fine and dandy so far . . .'

Avril grabbed the climax of the tale. 'But then she rustled through a few pages and went berserk. Screaming, shouting – your name came into it – cursing, the lot. And the twins didn't help matters any. Ham couldn't stop laughing and Bud offered her a packet of sulphur tablets to cool her blood.'

'But why did *my* name come into it?'

'God knows.' Eugene helped himself to a Marie biscuit from the communal tin. 'It was all jibber-jabber. She was dancing up and down like somebody in bare feet on hot sand.'

'Haven't you looked what was in the paper?'

'No, Sonia, we have not looked what was in the paper.' He still called Dinah that when he was being tart. 'We couldn't. She kept it clasped to her flat bazooms.'

The cocaine was causing Dinah to listen to human voices as though they were instruments in an orchestra. Sounding just like a moaning cello, Avril said, 'I went up to Tripp's to get another. But there was a sign on the door saying Closed Due to Bereavement.' A cello with catarrh.

'This whole business is going to be *somebody's* funeral,' observed Eugene darkly. He was definitely an Irish harp.

'Why say funeral and look at me?'

The harp made a few more glissandos: 'Belladonna, aconite . . . she listed five separate poisons she was thinking of using on you.'

'Stop it, Eugene, just stop it. I thought you liked me.'

'He likes drama even more,' observed Avril on a low note. 'Sometimes he puts me in mind of Joan Crawford.'

'How dare you,' snorted the dyed-haired elf. 'If I'm anybody, it's Vivien Leigh in *Gone With The Wind*. "I will return to Tara,"' he quoted dramatically.

And Dinah suddenly realised, with absolute certainty, that he must have done the same thing, many times before, in front of a mirror. But she was more concerned with her own problems. 'Whatever am I meant to have done?'

'I'd say you'd got yourself into the papers,' was Eugene's reply. 'It's only a guess I'm hazarding, Sonia, but that's what I'd say. The way she stuffed that *Reporter* into her bicycle basket was a sight to behold.'

'And she even cycled off with a flat tyre,' put in Bud Turnock. 'You could hear the rim of the wheel clattering over the cobbles.'

Another sound had broken into the conversation. The telephone was ringing.

Eugene answered it. 'Tyrell and Tench.' It was easy to make these name sound prissy. 'It's for you.' He was holding the receiver towards Dinah.

'For me?' she ask incredulously. You weren't meant to have phone calls at work, not unless it was an emergency.

'A man.'

She took the phone from Eugene. A voice was already saying, 'Is that you, our Dinah?'

Her father always got flustered when he had to use the telephone. He didn't really understand how it worked. Tommy Nelson was on late turns; in her mind's eye, his daughter could visualise him inside the phone box on Bolton Road. Imagine him having puzzled over the printed directions. 'What is it, Dad? What's wrong?'

'You're what's wrong,' he said sternly. 'Very, very wrong. If you wanted to break my heart you've gone the right way about it.'

'But I don't want to break your heart.' This was awful – unbelievable – and people were listening.

Tommy Nelson was still talking. 'I've not cried since your gran'ma died but I don't mind admitting I shed a few this morning. And what kind of fool am I going to look at work? I work with men who think I can trust you.'

'But what am I meant to have done?'

'You know. Or you should.'

'I don't.'

'I've got to go,' he said in the coldest tones she had ever heard him use. 'Somebody wants to use the box. And to think I went round boasting you'd do anything to please me!' Click. Dialling tone.

It was such an unusual morning that one of the twins dared to switch on the radio. The set was always tuned to the Light Programme in readiness for the dinner break – the only hour when it was officially permitted to be used.

The old-fashioned room was flooded with the modern sound of Zav Hankey singing 'Puzzles on the Pavement'.

'He's from the Height too, isn't he?' asked Bud innocently. Too innocently.

'Zav? He's from our street.'

It was Ham who said, 'Oh, I thought he came from nearer Light Oaks Park.' Adding hastily, 'Only because he mentions the bandstand. There's all sorts in that park, isn't there? Swings, a duck pond . . .'

'Sporting facilities.' Ham was grinning merrily.

Dinah just thanked her lucky stars that the boys were basically good-hearted. They might tease but they would never blackmail. Nevertheless, she did not want Eugene finding out because he would be incapable of keeping it to himself.

'Quick! Get that wireless off,' he hissed. 'She's coming clattering over the cobbles again, on her bike.'

'It still sounds as though the tyre's right down on the

rim,' said Ham. 'You'd need to be mad not to get off and pump it up.'

'Mad or very very angry. Oh Sonia!' Though he sounded sympathetic, Eugene looked like somebody who was just about to pull the Cellophane off a box of his favourite chocolates. Someone with an extra-sweet tooth.

Bang: the front door had obviously been crashed open. Clatter: that had to be the noise of the bicycle being flung against the oak settle in the corridor. The next sound was generally the rattle of the chain as she secured the padlock.

Not today.

As everyone pretended to resume work, Edna Tench marched into the room quivering with fury and brandishing a rolled-up newspaper.

As always she brought a Punch and Judy show to mind. And this morning, thought Dinah, that jutting chin makes her look like both of the leading characters rolled into one. Dinah's own jaw was still totally numb from the effects of the cocaine, and now she waited to hear which musical instrument Edna would resemble.

'Back street slut!' A wildly discordant violin. 'You're nothing but a social climber. In my day we paid to go to Pendleton High School. There were no scholarships. We could afford it.'

The door opened again and in walked John Tench. He was carrying a big bound ledger. 'I've just picked your bike up off the floor, Mother. Kids must have got at it.'

'No. You got at it, John,' she said icily. 'Or at least you got at me. Here . . .' She handed him the rolled-up paper. 'Spread that out, and open it at page five.'

'Our advert's always nearer the back.' But he did as she bade, he always did whatever she asked without question. 'Page five . . . Oh.'

'Well you might say Oh, you deceitful little boy.'

Dinah was just enough drugged to feel free to protest, 'He's thirty-six.'

'I don't recall asking your opinion,' snapped her

employer. 'Perhaps you might like to tell me what you think of *that*.' Her index finger was jabbing angrily at a photograph in the newspaper.

In her semi-anaesthetised state Dinah chose to read the caption first. 'Autumn Idyll: a young couple take advantage of the outdoor facilities in Light Oaks Park.' The photograph was of herself and John, either side of the tennis net, rackets raised. By some trick of the light the photographer had managed to make the ball look just like a tiny flying heart.

'It's more than obvious what's been going on,' snorted Edna. 'Idyll, young couple, a bouncing heart! And you said you'd joined the Territorials, John.' From the sound of it, her bitterness knew no bounds. 'I should've known they wouldn't let you go this long without a uniform. Where've you been sneaking off to change your trousers, that's what I want to know.'

'I don't see why I should tell you.'

It was the first time Dinah had ever heard him stand up to her. 'I wonder if I could get a proper copy?' she mused aloud. Though God alone knew what she'd do with it because this self-same picture must have been what had annoyed her father. On weeks when he was on late turns he was always the first to consume the local rag. 'It's caused trouble in our house too,' she assured Mrs Tench.

'Presumably because your parents know their place. "A proper copy"? I've been all the way to the *Reporter* office to make sure they'd not got the picture in the window display.'

'It's a very nice picture,' said John 'We both look good in it.'

'Oh it's We, is it?' stormed his mother. 'And where else have we been exhibiting ourselves? Picture houses, public ballrooms? I might as well have the whole story.'

'There is no whole story,' he said quietly. 'What you see is all we've done.'

'I don't believe you.'

'Ask Dinah.'

'I wouldn't stoop to ask that class of person anything. They're not known for their love of the truth.'

John went bright red in the face, whether from anger or embarrassment Dinah could not tell. But he certainly sounded icily annoyed as he said to his mother, 'We've told you the truth. I've always wished there was more to it but there hasn't been.' Now he turned to Dinah. 'I'm sorry to ask you like this but I won't stand by and see you hurt.' He took a deep breath. 'Will you let me take you out to dinner tomorrow night?'

Saturday afternoon and Tommy Nelson was sulking. He was sitting in the rocking chair, between the kitchen table and the wall, glowering unhappily into space.

Eva was on the other side of the table, knitting. 'It's a horrible habit, Tommy, horrible. He gets it from your Gran'ma Nelson,' she said to Dinah. 'She once cut me dead from New Year's Eve till Shrove Tuesday – all because I forgot to return a china pie funnel.'

'Dinah knows why I'm not talking.'

'You just did,' said his wife, as she knitted in a bit of red; she was on the sleeve of a Fair Isle jumper. 'She's going out to eat dinner with him, she's not off on a dirty weekend.'

'I only said I'd go to annoy his mother.' Not quite true. Immediate acceptance had been the reward she had handed to John for his display of courage. Mrs Tench had immediately threatened to sack her, so Avril had said that if Dinah was leaving so was she. And the Turnock twins had startled everybody by saying that jobs were ten a penny and they would leave too.

'How annoyed *is* Mrs Tench?' asked Eva.

'Very. But she didn't want to lose us all in one go so she just climbed down and muttered a lot.'

'Well I'm annoyed too.' Eva dropped a stitch, glowered at her husband, and said, 'Now look what you've made me do.'

'Aah, don't go for him,' protested Dinah who hated to see Tommy unhappy.

Eva grabbed hold of a crochet hook, to help pick up the stitch which had already started to run. 'I'm annoyed, Dinah, that you were placed in a position where you felt you had to fib. And I'm annoyed that you must have paid full price for those tennis pumps when I could've got you discount at our shop.'

'Unless he paid for them,' came from the rocking chair.

'Oh it can speak when it's nastiness,' observed Eva.

'I paid for them, Dad. I did, I paid for them myself.'

'Ignore him,' said her mother. 'Oh I hate it when he goes feminish like this. Dinah, don't . . .' She was trying to give Tommy a hug but he only pushed her away. 'I could've told you that would happen.'

'He's never sulked with me before.'

'He's never accepted you as a grown woman before. What are you going to wear tonight?'

'I don't know that I'm going; not if it's going to cause all this aggravation.'

'Course you're going. Why don't you nip round to the Elite and see whether they can give you a quick shampoo and set?'

'They do it too tight.'

'I'd pay.' Eva now had four knitting needles on the go at the same time, and they were flashing around in a manner which indicated high satisfaction. 'I'd pay for you to go to Lewis's, in town, if I thought you could get an appointment.'

Tommy Nelson flashed his wife a black look, picked up the *Daily Herald* and stomped off into the back yard.

'And you can bet your bottom dollar he'll be sitting on that cold toilet seat for hours! The way he hates bosses is most unreasonable, he's like a throw-back to the General Strike.' Her tones grew more cautious: 'Does . . . er . . . John, does he always keep his hands to himself?'

'Always.'

'Well that side of things can be very over-rated, I'd rather have a tin of Quality Street.' Nevertheless Eva sounded relieved. 'Your father's a most contrary creature.

Fine about Rory Brogan – God rest his soul – but ructions when you went into mini-skirts. Will you be wearing your cyclamen?'

'I'm thinking of going down to the box and ringing him to say I'm not going.'

'You might get her.'

'You could go for me – say I'd got a cold.'

'I'm telling lies for nobody. I want you to look me in the eye, Dinah.'

This always made Dinah feel about six years old but she obliged her mother in the cause of a quiet life.

'It's a chance, Dinah, isn't it? A genuine chance.'

'I suppose. But it's not one I want.'

'That's what you think now.' Eva brought her fifth and final knitting needle into play. 'You might feel quite differently once you've viewed him across the salt and pepper pots.'

Mancunians who charged items to accounts at Kendal Milne and Co. generally celebrated red letter days at the Midland Hotel. Those who paid cash at solid old Affleck and Brown preferred the Grand.

These were the thoughts which were filling Dinah's head as she sat nervously on the edge of her chair in the hotel dining room. When older Affleck's customers bought woollen dress material they sometimes asked the sales assistant to set fire to a tiny sample – the resulting smell was meant to prove whether the fabric was one hundred per cent genuine. Here, at the Grand, they seemed to apply the same principle to meat: some of the cooking was accomplished over little spirit lamps at the waiters' white damask-covered service stations.

The room was oak-panelled and gloomy, the hotel servants elderly; male diners were a bit 'best suit' and their wives were the kind who boasted one good diamond ring and Clark's shoes. 'But at least the menu's in English,' said John.

'I did French at school.' Dinah was feeling a mite

over-sensitive. She had deemed it best to wait for him on the top step of her mother's house, and Stasia and Macushla had been observing the proceedings though the window, opposite. And when the Jeep arrived her father had burst out and made a speech about trusting John would behave himself as a gentleman.

Fat old Mrs Jelly, walking past with a string bag full of empty beer bottles, had seen fit to throw in, 'That's right, Tommy, you tell 'im. Mind you, she doesn't want to end up a spinster.'

I'm twenty-eight, thought Dinah. And there can be no denying that they've started calling me 'Miss Nelson' in the Height shops. It won't be long before I have more than just a white streak at the front.

'You do look nice,' said John. 'I think I'll start with the prawn cocktail.' He looked nice himself, a bit like an advert for Kendal's, in a Prince of Wales check suit.

'I'll have the grapefruit.' She was wearing 'Mary Quant exclusively for readers of *Woman*.' Her mother had used the paper pattern to produce a little shift in material which looked like deck chair canvas. Black and white. People were prone to say 'Very Jackie Kennedy'.

'I must admit I'm not much inspired by the idea of chicken in the basket or speciality gammon with individual pineapple ring,' said John. 'If we'd driven out to Prestbury there's a retired ballet dancer who does *cordon bleu*. Him and a friend. But the food is superb.'

Fancy his knowing people like that! And the discreet Paisley tie he was wearing had to be genuine foulard silk. Greatly daring she ventured to ask, 'How did your mother ever come to let you have anything as dashing as a Jeep?'

'I came into a bit of money from Uncle Arthur Tyrell. And he left me the Growing Grounds, too.'

Eugene had always described this herbal garden as 'Eden in Swinton – romantic as a birthday card and a hundred times more valuable.'

'I never knew you owned that.'

'It's not long been settled. Mother felt obliged to contest the will. It made mealtimes very awkward.'

'I think I'll go for the mixed grill.' Dinah was dying to ask him why he continued to put up with Edna Tench.

He seemed to have anticipated the question. 'She's a brave woman, you know. Left a widow early. She could easily have gone under if she'd not had that cast-iron courage. Which is not to say that she isn't a terrible old cow.' He treated Dinah to a smile like the sun coming out.

He was also about to prove himself much more adventurous than she had ever realised because he suddenly said, 'Do you really want that mixed grill? Couldn't you fancy something a bit more daring?'

'There isn't anything, not unless you count lemon sole.'

'There is at Prestbury. It's still early. Shall we just drive out there and see whether they can have us?'

Dinah was immediately struck by a new worry. Prestbury was in Cheshire, and Cheshire was meant to be très à la posh. 'Would I be dressed right?'

'It never matters what you wear. It's time somebody told you you're beautiful.'

The depth of feeling that went into this unexpected compliment left her dazed but she still said, 'I wouldn't want to show you up.'

'You're not capable of showing me up.'

Don't look at me like that, she thought worriedly. I know love when I see it and that look is made of real love.

He was already on his feet. 'Let's go.'

They took the Oxford Road out to Cheshire but before they crossed the county boundary he insisted on stopping in Withington, a suburban village turned pale golden in the autumn evening sunlight, to buy her a bar of chocolate: 'So you don't come over faint for lack of food.'

Kind. So kind. The shadows lengthened as streets gave way to country lanes and John began to hum the words of 'The Piccadilly Johnny With the Little Eye-Glass'.

'The only other person I know who can sing that is Daisy Carver.' Dinah had her white cardigan back on again because it was blowy inside the open Jeep. Fortunately, her hair was up in the new beehive style, which meant it was held in place with plenty of lacquer.

'Daisy the addict?' John called out above the thrum of the engine. 'One day we'll have to do something for her.'

'What sort of something?' she called back.

He slowed the vehicle down a little. 'I once got a man at the tennis club off morphine. He was first prescribed it as medicine in the Far East.'

Got a man off drugs? This new John Tench was full of surprises. It was as though each mile they drove away from Manchester was another mile away from the constraints imposed by his mother. But nearer to the beginning of this journey Dinah had caught sight of the little bridge on Oxford Road. The bridge over the canal. Through the gap between the tall buildings, down the old stone steps, onto the towpath . . . that was where Rory had first kissed her. For years now the memory of this life-changing event had caused her to keep a quarter to eight on a Saturday evening as a sacred moment. But it had to be admitted that for the same number of years her life had virtually stood still.

Cheshire was like the pretty songs in the musical *Salad Days*: manicured grass, neat white fences, fake milkmaid's cottages. Wasn't there a song in that show about not looking back? 'We Said We Wouldn't Look Back', that was it.

But I'm only half of a 'we', thought Dinah. There's no Rory to not look back with me.

But there was John Tench and he was steering the Jeep into a gap between a Jaguar and a Bentley, in front of a sign which said 'Parking Reserved for Patrons of the Whitethorn Cottage Restaurant'.

A brawny figure, a man with grey hair and rolled-up sleeves and a butcher's striped apron, was standing on the doorstep, under a rustic archway. 'Thank God you've not brought your mother,' he said briskly to John. 'You're welcome any time but I'd throw food at that critical old wretch before I'd serve her again!'

'We're not too late?'

'Not so long as you'll have what you're given.'

What they were given would eventually inspire Dinah to embark upon a new passion for cooking. The herbalist in her recognised that the Mediterranean fish soup was scented with saffron, that the golden sauce over the chicken breast had been subtly enhanced by lemon balm and garlic: 'And this dessert tastes as good as it looks; you could get drunk on all the brandy these baby strawberries have been soaked in.'

John had ordered something called Lutomer Riesling to go with their food. 'Tito piss!' called out the proprietor contemptuously, as he bustled between red and white gingham-covered tables and began defeating dusk by lighting candles in crystal holders – shaped like stars. 'What do you think of my new painting? It's an Alan Lowndes.'

Why did it have to be a picture of the Whit Week walks? It was as though the ghost of Rory Brogan was trying to make itself felt from the end of a long tunnel. 'But is that a real Lowry, next to it?' she asked in wonder.

'They're all real, thank you,' he said, banging an antique silver coffee pot onto the table. 'Bought them early, got them for coppers. And that's a Magda Schiffer. She used to come and do a bit of cleaning for me, when she first fled from Germany.'

The owner of the restaurant was also the chef and his name was Matthew Haygarth. For some reason this irascible ex-dancer seemed to have taken a shine to Dinah. He even sat down with them and called for an extra cup and did the pouring out himself.

'Know what his mother did?' he asked, indicating John. 'She leant across to the next table, asked Sir Basil De Ferranti whether he had a bad heart? And then she announced that my good bay leaves could be the death of him.' He was observing Dinah closely. 'You've been a bit heavy-handed with the hair lacquer,' he said. 'Pat Phoenix has the same failing.' One wall was covered in framed photographs of celebrities. 'You don't want to go looking like a taxi-dancer.'

You couldn't be cross with him and anyway he was right about the lacquer. 'What's a taxi-dancer?'

Big Matthew began humming 'Ten Cents a Dance' and then he rose to his feet and rushed off to scrawl out somebody's bill.

'I didn't know places like this even existed,' she confided in John. It was as though the owner of the establishment had imbued her with his own confidence, let her see that he himself hadn't always been posh, drawn her in, made her feel as though she had every chance of being part of it all. It was heady stuff.

John too had grown in confidence. 'Dinah, would you consider coming out with me on a regular basis?'

Her eyes were suddenly drawn back to the painting of the Whit Week walks: outside a pub, pint pots in hand, a gang of men had emerged to watch the procession – just as Rory had once watched the Catholic procession on Deansgate.

'Would you?' asked John.

9

The second morning at sea Mickey did not breakfast in the Britannia Grill. Instead, he settled for the snatch and grab of the self-service counter in the Lido. Down in the grill he could have found himself confronted by Jack Lawless. However, this was proving to be a straight case of frying pans and fires because June Gee had chosen to settle herself two tables away. And now she was attempting to catch Mickey's eye, as she sucked on a cup of coffee and brought Bette Davis to mind by stubbing out a cigarette in somebody's abandoned fried egg.

I'm too experienced in the ways of this wicked world to allow her to succeed, he thought. But last night I wasn't experienced enough to prevent myself being taken for a ride by over-available masculine charms. Left waiting whilst Jack waltzed off with an obvious punter! Every inch of Jack Lawless is for sale in every dubious video shop on earth and I was daft enough to start thinking in terms of hearts and flowers.

The word 'daft' meant that Mickey's inner voice had reverted to the faintly Lancashire tones of his childhood. But that childhood had given him the ability to create *Angel Dwellings*, and the resulting whiff of fame had kept him in the sexual arena for a lot longer than most of the rest of the gay Englishmen of his generation.

But there's no fool like an old fool, he reminded himself. Jack wasn't just involved with a punter: a little packet – which had to be drugs – came into it too.

Through the glass picture windows the sun was shining down on a sea that was as calm as a boating lake. Once again, chubby old June, an object lesson in why sequined blouses should not be worn in the daytime, was attempting to attract his attention.

As Mickey avoided her eye, his own gaze rested for a

moment on a man who was watching him with interest. Too much interest? Could he be a tabloid reporter? Was this whole Jack Lawless business some newspaper's attempt to set up a scandal? These thoughts were not precisely paranoia; three decades of *Angel Dwellings* had imbued Mickey with suspicions which would never occur to members of the general public.

I'll have my second cup of coffee somewhere else on the ship, he thought. If the man follows me he's the press, if he doesn't, I'm an idiot.

In the event Mickey proved to be an idiot.

But that was the trouble with fame: if they stared you still wondered why. And if they seemed to fancy you, you wondered whether it was for yourself or your name. But people went to gyms to make their bodies more attractive so why should building a reputation not be of equal value?

By now Mickey Grimshaw was thoroughly annoyed with himself. Over the years he must have been through these thought processes a thousand times. A line from that piece of inspirational writing known as 'Desiderata' sprang to mind, that piece of prose which was always turning up, tastefully framed, in gift shops. 'Surrender unto youth those things which belong to youth.'

The dreadful June had also gone in for inspirational writing in her day. By now his introspections had carried him as far as the balcony which fronted the shops, the one on the upper level of the Grand Lounge.

'And a one, and a two, and a three and kick.'

A rehearsal was taking place on the stage, down below. The curtain was raised and a group of young performers, who presented a series of nightly shows, with titles like *Transatlantic Cocktail* and *Broadway Nights*, were pounding their way through an energetic dance routine. They were also miming to the pre-recorded words of the song 'There's No Business Like Showbusiness'.

I'm home, thought Mickey gratefully. This is what I fell in love with when I was little. In the greater scheme of things it might be regarded as shoddy and valueless;

but I wanted to make audiences laugh and cry, and I did it.

One of the dancers, a boy who could have been Mickey himself at nineteen, looked up at the balcony resentfully. Instinctively, Mick knew that the youth didn't want the performance to be seen until the show was ready. The creator of *Angel Dwellings* suppressed a mad urge to shout down, 'It's all right. I've been in the business since I was twelve – I'm one of you.'

But the youth was probably thinking he was just some leery old man, leaning over the rail to get a sly peek at young bodies in tight jeans.

Nobody's going to make mistakes like that about me in the future, thought Mickey grimly. I shall go through life like a nun, with lowered gaze. I shall observe 'custody of eyes'.

This was the moment he caught sight of June Gee looking up at him from the floor of the auditorium. 'Stay where you are,' she called out as she began to advance towards one of the stairways.

Beyond the shopping promenade there was a row of Boat Deck Staterooms which were rather more luxurious than the cabin occupied by Mickey and Sorrel. These were the province of rich passengers who did not see the point of spending the extra thousands demanded for a penthouse. Nevertheless, cunning planning had turned the quarters into near-suites with massive square portholes, sitting and sleeping areas, and marble-lined bathrooms.

The kind of people who occupied these cabins knew ships, understood cruising, were already aware of how to get the best possible use out of every facility on board. The former Dinah Nelson, once of Saracen Street, had evolved into just such a passenger.

Prior to departure from home she never worried about rushing evening clothes to the dry cleaner's. Instead, everything came on board in bin bags, stowed inside well-travelled cabin trunks, and was sent straight down

212

into the bowels of the ship to be cleaned and pressed by Filipino experts.

And now Anna, the maid, was carrying back the last of the polythene-covered items – a scarlet dinner dress and Dinah's husband's black velvet smoking jacket.

'They should have come to less than yesterday's because they weren't Express.' Dinah checked the tickets pinned to the wrappings. 'Rip that stuff off and hang them up.' It wasn't that she was tight with money, the years had simply taught her how to handle it. Anna and her husband, Janos the valet, had already been tipped once, before the ship set sail, and been promised a further gratuity ('If you look after us properly') upon arrival in New York.

Dinah always took care of these things herself. And she had found that this manner of tipping established a working relationship from the outset, and generally guaranteed good service. 'Take these clothes into the bedroom, Anna.'

The sitting area was light and airy with white leather sofas and a fake Regency writing desk with a huge painting of the *Queen Mary* above it.

Dinah followed the maid round the bend into the sleeping area where there was more white paintwork and white carpets and thankfully – oh so thankfully – two large single beds. 'These wardrobes are practically a cabin in themselves,' she said. 'Whilst you're in mine, would you take out the grey chiffon. I caught my heel in the hem last night; you'll need to give it a couple of tiny stitches.' Did the woman understand this much English? 'Where are you from, Anna?'

'Bosnia-Hercegovina.' The maid's hand went straight up to her own mouth as though she'd said something she shouldn't have done. She was a squat motherly-looking woman, with a fawn birthmark on her face, dark eyes, and brown hair pulled back into a bun. 'Please, you forget I said that?'

'Said what?'

'Bosnia.' She looked as though she hated repeating the word. 'Janos and I have four children. We need the tips.'

Whatever was she going on about?

Anna obviously felt the need to explain. 'This war cost money, cost lives. Some passengers, if they know, they no tip.'

Dinah was horrified. 'I can't believe it.'

'Is so.'

'You can rest assured I'm not that sort of passenger. That's the grey dress I meant. Here's where I caught it, look.'

'I do it. I beautiful at sewing. You won't say nothing to Janos that I tell?'

'Of course not.'

'And not to your husband.'

This was getting ridiculous. 'Not to him either.' The fact of the matter was that she wasn't even speaking to him. Didn't want to think about him. This didn't alter the fact that soon, very soon, they were going to have to have a frank conversation. Time had taught Dinah to recognise the give-away signs. And unless her husband was held in check, she knew that he was liable to embark upon a course of behaviour which would turn him into the talk of the whole ship.

It was curiosity which had kept Mickey on the balcony – in front of the duty-free shop – waiting for June to heave her way up the staircase. Why had she suddenly decided to acknowledge his presence on the ship?

Even as he was thinking that she must want something, and that there might still be time to give her the slip, he was kept rooted to the spot by a snatch of overheard conversation.

'You think you've got problems of your own and then you stop and think of the state poor Sorrel's mind must be in.' The speaker was an Englishwoman wearing shorts over particularly shiny pink legs.

And that pearl necklace at this time of day makes her look as though she doesn't trust the safe in her cabin, thought Mickey. But this was only secondary to his major

214

concern: what was supposed to be wrong with Sorrel? He didn't have time to dwell upon it because June had finally reached the upper deck and she was making her way towards him.

The passing years had slowed that once electric pace so he had plenty of time to observe the spangled blouse, the black crepe slacks which strained over the big hips and flared lavishly at the ankles. And as she got nearer he tried not to stare at the puckered cleavage and resisted the temptation to say 'Baby Jane, I presume'. Instead, he simply waited for her opening gambit.

It came in the shape of, 'Isn't it time we all remembered how much we used to love one another?'

You soil the very word, he thought, as he sought for a reply that she couldn't use to quote against him. 'The sea's a lot calmer this morning, isn't it?'

'You see you've never faced up to the great issues of life, have you, Mickey? Never.' The false little girl flirtatiousness of her youth had given way to tones of boozer's gloom.

'I'd say I joined the grown-ups a long time ago. How else would I have managed to resist your attempts at blackmail?'

'That line is actionable.'

Mickey remained unyielding. 'I'll be quite happy to see you in court.'

It was June who crumpled. 'Don't mention the dock to me,' she sighed. 'I spent weeks on end there, being misunderstood. The reality's nothing like a Joan Crawford picture; they never show you Joan bursting for a tinkle. That judge must have had a cast-iron bladder. Either that or he wore a special appliance!'

This attempt at black comedy had left her looking older than her mother had ever done. But Mickey reminded himself that June was probably just pausing, breathlessly, to sharpen her dagger, prior to coming in from another angle. He didn't dwell on this thought for long because the taped rehearsal music changed to a song he recognised as coming from *Les Miserables* and he only hoped that it wouldn't go into his unlucky one, the song they'd played at Buckingham Palace – the one that reminded him of Joe.

'Well you've certainly fulfilled all the prophecies about lonely old queens.' June had grabbed the advantage.

'Whose prophecies?'

'It's written all over you.'

'Please don't summon up your spirit guide,' said Mickey firmly. 'I don't think I could bear Navarro this soon after breakfast.'

'Navarna,' she corrected him.

'June, why have you changed *your* name?'

'Because people stood up and told lies about me and I went to prison. Not that I'm knocking Holloway,' she added loyally. 'Everybody should do a spell inside. I always say that six months in Holloway would have been the making of Princess Diana. I shared my cell with a Mayfair madam who could split a safety match into four.'

She's luring me with stuff that she knows will fascinate me, thought Mickey. As much for his own benefit as for hers, he said, 'You tried to get thirty thousand pounds out of me.'

'No. You misunderstood me. They all misunderstood me. I'm a good woman. All I wanted anybody to do was invest.' She must have deduced that this line of defence was not working because – perhaps of old habit – she began to drone on, in psychic tones: 'You've been down a long and hard road, Mickey.'

When Helene Kramer, the American psychic, gave him messages he always felt that the angels might just have taken a step nearer. Whenever June started, he felt like smacking her one.

She was still at it: '"Is it worth going on?" That's the question you've often stopped and asked yourself.' Now she rose to a dramatic crescendo. 'Men have let you down!'

'How's Martyn?' he asked matter-of-factly. Mickey was remembering the glowingly handsome body-builder who had turned June into Mrs Gee.

'Dead,' she said. 'On the other side,' she corrected herself. 'He couldn't resist dabbling with steroids. And by the time they came onto the market he was hardly a boy.' Her face began to register the first genuine emotion of this whole shipboard reunion – horror. 'Those injections atrophied his private parts. And you know how Martyn loved his bit of rumpy-pumpy.'

'I always liked Martyn,' said Mickey quietly. 'And the children?'

'Two more rats who fled the sinking ship. When I think of the money that was lavished on their private education . . .' This last phrase had set her talking posh. 'Foreign travel, the best hotels . . . Doesn't the wind whistle round the penthouses on this ship?'

'I wouldn't know.' And neither would you, June, because you're tucked away in some cabin way below the water-line.

'It absolutely howls,' she assured him. 'Penthouses? They're more like Portakabins, super-glued to the top deck!'

In truth, she's not actually saying she's in one, thought Mickey. It's the same kind of cunning dissembling that goes into her alleged clairvoyance.

Out of the blue June suddenly wondered, 'However did you manage to write so brilliantly about old age when you were young? Those characters like Red Biddie: how could you have known what was going to be waiting down the road for all of us?'

The odd thing was, for the very first time in his life, he had asked himself that question not half an hour ago. And that was the trouble with June. Just as you were ready to dismiss her as a fraud, she always managed to throw a hand grenade underneath your defences.

It didn't stop there. 'What's wrong with Sorrel?' she asked.

She must read minds, he thought. Telepathy, that's how she does it. He tried to block June off with, 'I think she's still missing Barney.'

'It's more than that.' She said it with absolute certainty.

June flipped back the cover from the face of a flashy diamanté wristlet watch. 'Can you see the time? I've not brought my glasses.'

Mickey essayed a bit of mind reading of his own. 'The Yacht Club bar should be just about opening.'

'Yes I do need a drink. I'll level with you: I need a drink and I need a friend.'

Not me, he told the sentimental part of his own personality. I'm the wrong person. You're the woman who did terrible things to Sorrel: I could never be your friend again.

Once again it was as though June had ventured inside his own head. 'Pity me.' She said it quietly. 'You could surely manage a bit of pity.'

And he found he could. The gurgling, blonde, sexual lighthouse which had once been June Gee was now a slack-bodied wreck in a dusty black wig. At least he'd lasted better than she had. So, yes, he could afford a bit of pity.

'I need your help,' she said. The whites around the old blue eyes were crisscrossed with tiny red veins.

Just like the map of a council estate – he could use that some time in a short story. Not that June had ever lived in a council house: Rookswood Avenue had been distinctly 'private'. Oh he and June went back all right! Far enough back to know that the streets of Manchester had once been littered with the corpses of people who had been foolish enough to attempt to help June Gee. Not literally, of course. And it might be interesting to know what kind of mess she'd got herself into this time.

'I've got a stalker.' Frightened as she obviously was, June had not resisted the temptation to invest this statement with simple pride. It was as though she saw herself as back in the running again – she had her own stalker.

'I know. I saw her watching you yesterday.' The words were out before he realised they could draw him further into June's clutches. She actually seized hold of him physically, grabbed his arm. Like a blast from the past he caught a whiff of that sweet French perfume

218

of hers – the scent called 'Joy'. But it was stale: last night's joy.

'So you know who I'm talking about?'

'Would you please let go of me?' He could smell June's breath, it was appalling. And, this near, you could see where the china caps ended and her own front teeth started.

'I'm desperate.'

'Then why don't you go and tell the captain?'

'Not enough real evidence,' she muttered angrily. 'Anyway, she's a Queen's Grill passenger; Cunard practically *expect* them to get away with murder.'

'You could always ask Navarna for advice.'

'Doesn't work for myself.' She was still muttering. 'Never has done.'

There was a wicked side to Mickey Grimshaw, one that was filled with curiosity, the part of him which wheedled out stories which might make plots. 'June, I'll help you on one condition.'

'That being?'

'I'll help you if you'll confirm for me, once and for all, that you're a fake.'

'No way! The *News of the World* once offered me fifty thousand to say that.'

It must have been a long time ago, he thought. 'Perhaps she's just a fan of yours.'

'I haven't got any left.' The utter defeat in this statement was terrible to hear. 'If there was a farthing left to be wrung out of the name June Gee do you think I'd have changed it Stella Artemis? No, that woman is going to kill me. You'll be sorry when I'm dead.'

'But surely your life's work has been to convince us that there *is* no death?'

'So you're saying you won't help me?'

A middle-aged married-looking couple passed them on the balcony. The pair were full of talk of the sun being over the yard-arm, and of 'it being time for a snifter'. This and the sight of a steward carrying a large bunch of keys towards the Yacht Club suddenly appeared to be much more important to June than any thoughts of her own imminent demise. 'Anyway, your novels will never be as good as those early scripts you wrote for *Angel Dwellings*,' were her last words to Mickey as she hurried off to answer the call of the distilleries.

Poor cow, he thought. And then he wondered whether he should have been kinder to her. But June had reminded him of an out-of-work actress; the kind who will promise eternal devotion in return for a part – any part. The kind who always ends up by turning the rest of the cast against one another. That sort had used Mickey as a ladder in the past and he could still feel their footprints.

But Sorrel was a totally different proposition. Never pushy, she'd always had to be pushed. Pushed and protected – mostly from herself.

Whatever kind of mess can she be in this time? he wondered as he began to make his way back to their cabin. And how come a woman in inappropriate jewellery knows about it before I do? Of course, pink legs could mean high blood-pressure, and that could have been caused by booze. Perhaps the woman belonged to Sorrel's reformed alcoholics' mumbo-jumbo society. Though she had explained to him how AA worked, she would never tell him what was said in meetings. Never. And that infuriated Mickey because he regarded Sorrel Starkey as his own property.

It was in this mood that he turned the key in the door of Cabin 2142. His leading lady was sitting at the writing desk between the two portholes. The sound of the door opening had caused her to swivel around in the revolving chair.

'Where did you have breakfast?' she asked. 'Jack Lawless was looking for you.'

Ignoring her question, Mickey said, 'Something's up. Other people know all about it and I don't.' Only now did he concede to himself that this had actually left him feeling hurt. 'What's wrong with you, Sorrel?'

She had rehearsed all sorts of ways of telling Mickey and now they all flew out of her head. 'It may be nothing. I

. . . I found a swelling. Well it's a lump. A hard lump.' The tears which had begun to fall were made of sheer relief.

'Where?'

'Here.' Her hand went to underneath her arm.

'Let me feel.' Though sexual strangers they were entirely familiar with one another's bodies. 'There?'

'No. Just underneath where my tit starts curving. Let me guide your finger . . . there.'

At first he could just feel that sloppy feminine softness which always made him wonder what straight men found so attractive. And then the tip of his finger found something as definite as a hard glass marble – beneath the surface.

'Pull your jersey off. Let me look.'

'No point. You can't see.' How many hours had she spent with her arm raised in front of mirrors? 'The only way to find it is to prod.'

'We need a doctor,' he said decisively.

'I've seen two. They've done a biopsy.' She finally voiced aloud the image which had been haunting the whole voyage. 'The surgeon said he'd cut a little bit out, and now they've got it on a glass tray in some medical laboratory; they're trying to see whether it grows.'

Mickey's arms went tightly around her. 'I'm hugging you for me and for Barney,' was all he could think to say.

'I might be seeing him sooner than I expected.'

'Shut up!' The thought of life without Sorrel didn't bear thinking about. 'Don't say things like that.'

She could feel him shaking, and when she looked into his eyes she was amazed to find that they were bright with unshed tears. 'Mick,' she said in wonder, 'you're nearly crying.'

'No I'm not.' It was his childhood that was responding: he might have been queer but he'd never been a cry-baby. 'I love you,' he said dully. 'I've always loved you. I don't want you to go away and leave me.' And now the tears began to roll in earnest.

Sorrel was still weeping herself as she attacked him with

her handkerchief. He was always my child, she thought. I never realised it before but that's what he's always been – my lovely infuriating boy. 'Blow your nose,' she said helplessly. 'You're awash.'

'This handkerchief's only big enough for an elf,' he grumbled. 'Are you sure you've seen the right doctors, the best ones for the job?'

'I did marry into a Jewish family,' she said reproachfully. 'Zillah's husband swears that Schachter sent me to the best man in Harley Street. That's what I was doing the afternoon before the investiture.'

'And all those people in AA knew and I didn't.'

'They're my family now.'

'Which makes me?'

'Probably the most important person in my life. That's why I kept you in the dark about this awful waiting game.'

'When will we know the results?'

'New York. They're going to fax the Algonquin.'

The Algonquin Hotel, he reflected bitterly, had always been part of their dreams. When he'd been a boy in the Central Reference Library in Manchester, reading every theatrical biography he could get his hands on, he had thought, one day Sorrel will star in a show of mine, and we'll be the kind of people who have lunch at the Ivy in London and stay at the Algonquin in New York.

'It's this growing old,' he said, stuffing her handkerchief into his jeans pocket. 'The minute I got that bloody MBE I started to feel my age. I never did before – never.'

'No wonder you understand actresses so well,' she marvelled. 'You're just like one yourself. You've just swivelled the spotlight right back on yourself!'

Things were returning to normal. And though they did not know it, life was about to take a little turn for the extraordinary, for somebody was knocking at the cabin door.

'I'll go,' said Sorrel. 'You look like a commercial for hay fever.' She opened the door to find herself confronted by enough flowers for a West End first night. Red roses with great long stems. And from the look of them, far more than the traditional two dozen.

'Thank you so much,' she said to the invisible owner of the pair of hands that were clutching the white porcelain vase. 'Could you put them on the dressing table?'

As the flowers were carefully manoeuvred into the cabin, Mickey saw that they were all but dwarfing a red-jacketed Filipino steward. 'For Mr Grimshaw,' he giggled.

'Is there a card?' asked Sorrel loftily.

By way of reply the steward pointed to a glossy photograph, pinned into the middle of the display.

'How bold,' was the best Sorrel could manage under the circumstances. The picture was of Jack Lawless stripped to the waist. And the message scrawled upon it, in thick Magic Marker, said 'Forgive me? Let's be more than friends.'

Sorrel blurted out, 'Well he's certainly changed his mind!' before she realised that she was breaking an Alcoholics Anonymous confidence.

'Just what do you mean by that?' The arrival of the floral tribute had obviously left Mickey furious.

'I can't tell you. Don't ask me, Mick. I simply cannot tell you.'

10

In later life Dinah Nelson would look back and try to recall the moment she knew she was going to marry John Tench. The fact of the matter was that there was no specific moment – they just drifted into the idea.

But, if it was a drift, it was an inexorable one. The summer of 1964 was the season they played tennis in the park. By the late autumn of that year he was taking her to dances at Monton Cricket Club, a considerable suburban statement in itself.

As the dark nights came in, Edna Tench grew daily more pinched and withdrawn: a woman who was apparently refusing to concede that anything significant was happening. But Eugene Gannon, who spent a lot of time alone with her in the upstairs office, maintained she was forever muttering Dinah's name to herself.

Dinah's father was somebody else who remained several chilly paces away from her. 'You might expect me to accept the situation,' he would say, 'but it doesn't mean I have to like it.'

'There's nothing to accept,' his daughter would try to reassure him.

Eva Nelson knew different. She was a woman who had always worked, always saved, and on her half-days she would slip down to town and invest in items intended to further Dinah's chances.

'This blouse is only a little Dorothy Perkins but with the buttons changed nobody will know.' Eva had natural good taste.

'I don't know why you've suddenly started ruining me at twenty-eight!'

'Precisely because you *are* twenty-eight.'

'Don't make me feel desperate,' said Dinah hurriedly.

'I don't want to rush into anything in the cause of sheer desperation.'

'Then you do admit there's something on the wind? I got buttons and lipstick to match.'

'Mother, it's not a cattle market!'

'That's where you're wrong. And stop glowering, Tommy. This life *is* a cattle market, and Ellesmere Park is an altogether better class of cattle pen.'

'I liked Rory,' said Tommy stubbornly. 'I can't feel sure this chap's got all the right parts.'

'Rory wasn't to be,' snapped his wife. 'And you are tackless, Tommy. You're really tackless.'

In truth, Dinah had stopped comparing John with her great lost love: the qualified herbalist was something quite different. Only Avril Porter was privy to the juicy details.

'Do you kiss yet?' she demanded nasally. (The recent operation on her adenoids had failed to alter the timbre of her voice.) 'What's he like at kissing?'

'It's all a bit respectful,' was the only answer Dinah could come up with.

'No tongues?'

'You couldn't think of that and him in the same breath.'

'Doesn't he press up then?'

'Only once. And he apologised afterwards.'

'But everything's where it should be?'

'Oh yes.' Dinah started to laugh. 'I'm not laughing at him,' she added hastily. 'I'm laughing at myself for being surprised. He's too decent to see as a joke. He makes me understand what the word "cherished" really means.'

'I wish somebody'd bloody carry me round like that,' said Avril gloomily. She had recently embarked upon an affair with a young man who spent the remainder of his free time in the YMCA gymnasium.

'But you've finally got what you wanted, you've got "meaty". And at least this one's not married.'

'Yes but he's keener on all-in wrestling than he is on me. That bed-sit of his is like a shrine to Billy Two Rivers!'

John Tench's friends were as polite and mild-mannered as

he was himself. When Dinah portrayed them in the painted diaries they were always tinted in her palest water-colours. John was thirty-six and most of his contemporaries had married in their early twenties. By now, the majority of their wives boasted diamond eternity bands next to their engagement rings.

Jeweller's shops had started to figure in John and Dinah's lives. At first they had just walked down these illuminated arcades to look in the second-hand window because he collected silver card cases. Latterly, they had taken to straying towards the other show-cases.

'Look at that silver teddy bear,' said Dinah. The pair of them were arm-in-arm. 'I love it.'

'It's a baby's rattle.'

She was so embarrassed that she tugged him along to look into the next spot-lighted display, only to discover that this one was full of engagement rings.

'I gotta horse!' yelled a voice out on Market Street. It belonged to Prince Monolulu, a Negro racing tipster who often tramped through Manchester wearing a long gaberdine raincoat and a high ostrich-feathered head-dress. 'I gotta horse.'

'Do you like that ring?' asked John. It was a big solitaire diamond.

'Who wouldn't like it?'

'Do you want it? With a view to us getting the silver teddy bear later.'

It was now or never. There could be no mistaking the fact that this was a genuine offer. Dinah looked at him. He's kind, she thought, and he's good. He will, of course, expect the other. But he'll make a lovely daddy. 'Yes please,' she said.

'We'll come back when the shop's open tomorrow and get it.'

'I gotta horse,' was Prince Monolulu's repeated cry.

Yes and I've got a fiancé, thought Dinah. And goodness but this kiss is a lot thinner than Rory's used to be.

* * *

The niceties were about to be observed.

'Strictly speaking, I think the bridegroom's mother should be coming to us.' Eva Nelson and Dinah were upstairs in the big front bedroom, with the curtains drawn and the electric light on. Eva was trying on the outfit she had bought especially for the forthcoming high tea. This was scheduled to take place, on the following Sunday, at Mrs Tench's house in Ellesmere Park. 'It's a very good class of two-piece,' Dinah's mother explained as she buttoned up the mulberry stockinet jacket. 'I got it at Roland and Rivkin. Bit less than King Street prices but definitely on a par with Kendal's. What do you think?'

'You look belting.' And she did.

'So what's the matter?'

Dinah didn't answer straight away because a big bang had gone off somewhere outside. It was an early November evening and children were already letting off fireworks.

'I said, what's the matter?'

'It's her. Ma Tench, I mean. She must have been able to see it coming but she's behaving as though she's suddenly been struck by a plague of boils.'

'Your father's the same.' Eva opened a trinket box. 'Does this cameo go with it?'

'It doesn't need a brooch.'

'I had to practically frog-march your dad into Weaver-to-Wearer. I finally prised him into ready-made grey worsted. He was just like a little lad: wouldn't try anything on as though he meant it.' Another banger exploded outside. 'It's not as though you'll be living with her after you're married.'

'John's got the deposit from his uncle's money, but he'll definitely need a rise to cover the mortgage.' A surveyor had already been commissioned to submit a report on a semi-detached house on Dovesway, on the Ravensdale Estate.

Whoosh ... this sound was followed by a terrible crashing noise. 'I think a rocket's just hit that window,' said Dinah in near-disbelief. She had already rushed for the curtains and now she pulled one aside. 'Tyrone Brogan's belting off down the street.'

'Stasia cut me dead this afternoon,' sighed Eva. 'I suppose they saw the engagement announcement in last night's paper. How about these earrings? No,' she decided. 'Too flash.'

'I should have gone over the road and told them myself. But ever since the Jeep started arriving they've got colder and colder with me. I still want Macushla to be a bridesmaid.'

'In a wheelchair?' Eva looked scandalised. 'She'll draw all the attention away from you.'

'I don't care. I want her.'

'I wouldn't bank on it. She's not good.' Eva put the trinket box back in the dressing-table drawer. 'Mrs Jelly says they've had the doctor out twice in one week. I've bought your father one of the new drip-dry shirts – a Tern in its own box. He won't even try the thing on.' Eva began to climb out of her mulberry skirt. 'So far his only contribution to Sunday has been to make me cut through the double-stitching, on the buttonhole, on the lapel of his new suit.'

'Why?'

'So he can get his enamelled union badge into it. Don't worry, he's going to find that badge has gone missing by weekend.'

'If he wants to wear it, why shouldn't he?'

'Because it looks like a meeting outside the dock gates. And I don't want him fulfilling Mrs Tench's worst fears, that's why.'

The air was rent by another loud explosion. Incredibly, it seemed to be within the house itself.

'Bloody little bastards!' Tommy Nelson shouted along the lobby, downstairs. 'They've put a banger through the letter-box,' he yelled up the stairway.

Dinah rushed and opened the bedroom door and met a smell which took her straight back to her childhood – November gunpowder. 'Don't go after them, Dad,' she called warningly; he had already opened the front door. 'It's Tyrone. He's upset.'

'Do you wonder?' he asked bitterly. 'Do you bloody wonder?'

That did it. 'Right!' flared Dinah. 'Let's have it out, once and for all. What've you got against John?'

Her father's face glared up the stairs. 'He's never got his hands dirty in his life. He lacks spunk, that's what I've got against him. He lacks spunk.'

'What word did you just use?' screamed his wife from the bedroom. In seconds she was out on the landing. 'I've had just about as much as I'm going to take from you, Tommy. Hear me, once and for all. You are going to Mrs Tench's tea-party, and you are damned-well going to enjoy yourself. Understood?'

On Sundays there was no bus service to Eccles so they were obliged to go by taxi. Well, by Baldwin's Private Hire. Mr Baldwin's car was an Austin Princess with little chromium-plated vases attached with rubber suckers to the rear passenger windows.

'Saw the happy news announced in the paper,' he said hopefully.

But Dinah knew that her mother wouldn't take the bait; she had already decided to have Len Dobb's Limousines for the actual wedding. ('They have a Daimler that once belonged to Queen Mary.') There had already been much discussion of the forthcoming nuptials. The bride's parents would obviously be expected to stage the wedding. The big question was, as Dinah was about to go up in the world, could Mrs Tench be asked to make a contribution towards the expenses?

'I'd rather have it small and paid for by us,' was what Tommy had said.

But Dinah's mother had other ideas. 'I'd like the "A" menu at Binn's Cafe, and all the trimmings.'

Obviously, none of this was being discussed in front of Mr Baldwin, in the car. As he turned it onto the private road which ran through the middle of the grandiose Victorian housing development known as Ellesmere Park, Eva observed, 'They say that Joan Stone, the novelist, used to live round here – I like a nice Joan Stone. Mind you, she's got a bit sexy of late.' She must have been nervous because she was jabbering and the sight of large detached villas, up driveways, had sent her voice a tone posher. 'Of course, everything's got sexier, really. I never thought I'd have skirts up to my knees again. I wonder what Mrs Tench will wear for the wedding?' They had never met.

'She'll probably just make do with something she's already got.' It was Dinah's turn to feel apprehensive.

'Begging your pardon,' said Tommy.

'What for?' asked his wife suspiciously.

'I just farted.'

'Wind down the window, Dinah. And could that please be an end to your vulgarity for today, Tom?'

'Kidney beans have always acted on me as shirt-lifters,' he said unrepentantly. 'Wasn't Joan Stone's uncle the man who went to prison for funny business with other men?'

'I said no more vulgarity! Just look, roses still in bloom in November.'

The Victorian merchant mansions had given way to labour-saving villas built in the Twenties and Thirties. Double sunray gates and long lawns and miniature black and white Tudor gables above moneyed expanses of russet brickwork.

'And look at that lovely stained-glass window,' chirruped Eva. 'A little Dutch boy and a little Dutch girl!'

'Yes and a few bob spent on tarmac wouldn't come amiss,' was all her husband offered in reply.

'Did you just fluff again? You did. Sorry, Mr Baldwin.'

'I'm getting it over before I get in.'

'It's to be hoped you are. And stop easing that collar with your finger. What did you say the house was called, Dinah?'

'Comfrey.'

'What a funny name.'

'It's a herb they found, growing wild, in the garden.'

Eva's hands went up to pat her own hair as she said nervously, 'There's John's Jeep. We're here. They might've found that herb but she's not got much else growing.'

The front lawn of the house, which was semi-detached in a bigger than average way, was like a long narrow bowling green. And the noise of the car stopping, and of Tommy insisting that Mr Baldwin must accept over the odds ('So you can have one on me tonight') soon brought Mrs Tench out onto the front step.

'Are you sure she's expecting us?' Eva whispered to her daughter.

'Course she is.'

'Then why's she dressed for out?'

'No, she always wears knitted costumes and a pixie.'

As the trio from Saracen Street trooped up the driveway Edna Tench made no attempt to crack open a smile. She just stood on the top step, summing them up.

'I see you've had your paths concreted,' Eva called out socially.

Oh God, she's putting it on already, thought Dinah. 'Concreted' had come out as 'corncreted'. Her mother always made a meal of words when she was trying to be fancy.

'Would you mind leaving your boots on the step?' Mrs Tench said to Tommy Nelson. 'I've got a lot of parquet to consider.'

'Actually, they're not boots, they *are* a shoe,' Eva assured her.

'It's still parquet,' was the implacable answer. So Tommy's shoes were removed and left standing beside a cast-iron foot-scraper. 'Nobody round here will pinch them.' John's mother led the way into a gloomy oak-panelled hall, just as John himself emerged from the first door on the right, carrying a copy of the *Sunday Times*.

In the past Dinah had only ever seen this newspaper on shop counters, never in anybody's hand. It seemed to emphasise the social gap between them. She also registered the fact that he was wearing camel house slippers with his more familiar cavalry twill pants and a navy jersey.

231

Somehow, the slippers and the newspaper made him look like an old advertisement for gas fires.

There was a coal one burning in the big oak and pewter fireplace in the lounge. Goodness but the room was dark! More of the panelling to halfway up the walls, and the only pictures were black and white steel engravings – views of Chester.

'I've lit the paraffin heater in the dining room,' John said to his mother. 'I thought sherry in here, first.'

'You're the one who bought it.'

It didn't bode well. And Dinah noted that her father had already sat down without waiting to be asked. You could see the word 'Wolsley' printed in white, on his new black socks.

'Take a pew,' said John to Eva. And then, greatly daring, he smiled at her and added the word, 'Mother.'

At this, Edna Tench – still on her feet – recoiled; it was for all the world as though she had been struck an invisible blow.

Rather than stare, Dinah took in more details of her mother-in-law-to-be's lounge. The plain leaded lights in the transoms of the bay windows were echoed in a bookcase, which stood on top of a bureau. Copious quantities of bound volumes by Sir Walter Scott sat side by side with the works of Dornford Yates and Harrison Ainsworth.

'I see you've kept your picture rails,' said Eva. 'A lot of people are getting rid of them.'

'Are they?' said Mrs Tench. 'Are they indeed.'

Silence fell: the kind of silence which made Dinah feel as though they had all turned into flies trapped in amber. Except, the daylight in the room wasn't orange, it was pale November grey.

Dinah racked her brain for something to say, found nothing, so she just adjusted her engagement ring – a new habit she had recently fallen into.

This movement had not gone unnoticed by Mrs Tench who closed her eyes for a moment – a moment in which she resembled a lizard.

'Did somebody mention a drink?' Tommy Nelson had brought the world back to life again.

'Why don't we just go straight through?' suggested John. 'The decanter's on the trolley in the dining room.'

'I hope you've washed the glasses,' said Mrs Tench accusingly. 'They've never been out since your father's funeral.'

Dinah inadvertently caught her own father's eye, and he treated her to a very tiny but very wicked wink.

'I'll lead the way,' said John. 'It's just cold cuts and salad. I roasted the meat yesterday.'

'Oh you're quite the Philip Harben, are you?' Eva's reference to the television chef was less chirpy than her earlier social efforts had been.

If I ever get round to sketching us trooping into this dining room, thought Dinah, I'll have to make us look like a band of unsuccessful strolling players. That was the moment when Mrs Tench managed to tread on Tommy's stockinged foot.

'Bleedin' hell fire!' he exclaimed. 'Mind me bunion.'

'I've never heard you use such language in my life,' said his wife.

'Course you have. I do work at the Dry Docks. Oh look, a piano!' And without further ado, he sat down on the stool, lifted the lid, and played the opening bars of the Dead March in *Saul*. 'There's nothing like the jolly ones, is there?' he asked innocently.

'Stop it, Tom,' said Eva sharply.

But he was not about to obey her instructions. Instead, improvising a few chords of accompaniment, he began to address Mrs Tench in passionate song.

> *'Speak to me, speak to me,*
> *Speak to me, Thora.'*

The dining room was the lounge all over again. Except, it had French windows which looked out onto a forbiddingly plain back garden, relieved only by a concrete bird bath with sea-shells stuck into it.

'Come to the table,' Dinah hissed at her father.

Actually, the sight of the table made her want to weep. Somebody had set it carefully and tried to brighten things up by arranging a few late nasturtiums in the same kind of chilly little silver vases which Mr Baldwin had sported in his hire-car. And that somebody had not been Mrs Tench because she was obviously looking at the frost-bitten flowers for the first time.

Poor John, had he also had to iron the drawn thread-work table-cloth, polish the engraved silver knife blades, rub up the bone handles? Not for the first time, Dinah was left wondering just what she had got herself into.

'Look how your pickles match my two-piece!' You had to hand it to Eva for trying. And, indeed, the glass-lined silver bowls were full of beetroot and pickled cabbage in exactly the same shade of red as her stockinet suit.

'Aren't these new short skirts awful?' she ploughed on gamely. 'But you've no choice in the matter; not when it's all there is in the shops. Will you be having your wedding outfit made?'

Mrs Tench stared at her for fully five seconds. 'No.' She closed her mouth and then opened it again to allow her tongue to flicker over those thin lips. And once again she brought a lizard to mind: a lizard in a room that smelt of paraffin and was as cheerless as any rock.

'May I help you to cold lamb?' John began to pile the sliced meat onto one of the impressively old, blue and white plates, talking all the while to Eva. 'Mother was feeling a little dickey this morning. I wanted her to have the doctor but in this house we generally save him for broken bones. She concocted something up for herself, instead.'

Dinah's father now entered the conversation with a question directed at their hostess. 'Wasn't it your dad who used to get worms out of people's innards?'

'Tommy, not at the meal table!' protested his wife.

'My father was practically a saint.' Edna let out the words very slowly, as though they had some huge inner significance for herself – some message that she wanted to pass on to the whole world.

Dinah had never heard her speak like this before. And John said worriedly, 'You're perspiring again, Mother. She's been complaining of a swimming scalp,' he explained to the others.

'My father . . .' Something inside her seemed to be seeking to add even more weight to these words.

'Your dad, what?' asked Tommy, not unkindly.

As Edna opened her mouth again, to answer, she actually rose to her feet, and Dinah noticed that the lizard lips had turned a colour which was midway between cobalt blue and violet, and that her face had gone whiter than one of her own parchment lampshades. The swaying wraith was, indeed, gazing upwards at the three-branch wooden light-fitting.

Suddenly she hadn't got any eyeballs. They had swivelled back into her head to an extent where just the whites were on view.

And that was the moment when Edna pitched forward, head first, so that knives and forks and silver vases and a crystal condiment set, all went flying. In a matter of seconds she was slumped face-down into a great pool of magenta pickle vinegar, shaped like a map of Europe, even to the little boot for Italy.

Now the map was going out of shape and pandemonium ruled. The final knife had not finished clattering before Tommy started yelling, 'Give her air! Give the woman air.'

Dinah rushed to open the French window.

'It bolts at the bottom,' called out John as Eva enquired, 'Does she have a history?'

'Only dating back to this morning. I feel awful about it, I thought she was just playing up.'

'You'll have to get the doctor,' said Eva decisively.

'She's funny about having him.'

'John,' by now Eva was speaking none too patiently, 'your mother's in no position to argue. That's if she's still with us.'

'What a thing to say!' Dinah had finally brought one of the French windows shuddering open. If she sounded shocked it was because she, herself, had been thinking something similar; in fact she'd been trying to remember the name of the nearest undertakers – Laithwaite's, that was it, Laithwaite's of Eccles Old Road.

From somewhere in the distance that most melancholy of Sunday sounds, the recorded chimes of a distant ice-cream van, rang through the cold draught which was coming in from outdoors.

'Get the doctor,' repeated Eva.

'All right.' With this he left the room.

'John sometimes needs instructions,' mother said to daughter.

'I know.' Dinah only dared whisper the next bit. 'Is she dead?' Her mother knew more about these things than she did.

Knew enough, it seemed, to open her own handbag and bring out a small vanity mirror. 'Just lift Mrs Tench's head up,' she said to her husband. 'Go on, lift it.'

Once he'd obeyed her, Eva held the little mirror in front of Edna's mauve mouth.

'She's a goner,' said Tommy.

'What, when this is misting over? No, she's still in the land of the living.'

'There can be no backing out now.' Tommy was speaking as though Dinah had every intention of cutting and running. (It had to be admitted that the events of the past two minutes had contrived to multiply the potential weight of her future responsibilities.) 'The engagement's been in the paper,' he continued severely. 'We've been to tea . . .'

'Well, just about managed to get over the doorstep,' put in his wife.

'She's near as damn it your mother-in-law, Dinah. Engagement? More like a cruel rod for your own back!'

'They must be her own teeth,' observed Eva. 'Or if they're false she's got them well glued in.'

* * *

236

Edna Tench sorely tested the patience of the staff of Hope Hospital. Indeed, Dinah, arriving one day with John at visiting time, was surprised to find no less a personage than the matron of the hospital at her employer's bedside.

This tailored figure of authority, her outfit topped-off with a high starched cap that tied, with white strings, under her chin, was delivering a speech designed to constrain even the most difficult of patients. 'You were very seriously ill, the heart attack was massive – massive. But we've got you over the hump of the bridge and the time is past when we had to consider your whims. I would remind you that this is a National Health hospital. If you want to throw your weight about you will have to go elsewhere and do it privately. And I will not have a hat worn by a patient on one of my wards.'

'It's a pixie hood,' snapped the patient.

'*We* wear the hats round here.'

'Then I'll go to the nuns at St Joseph's.'

A bell sounded which meant that visitors were supposed to leave. But Edna did not allow hers to go without detailing a list of instructions, both personal and professional.

'Is she bald?' Dinah asked John, as they got out onto the car park.

'I don't know. She did once send me to Monton, with a little bottle, to get piano oil; and the bottle was labelled "Krink's Never-Fail Hair Restorer".' They had finally reached the stage where they exchanged confidences of this nature.

'She's loaded,' he said. 'Absolutely loaded. And all I've got is Tyrell's Growing Grounds and expectations. My actual salary's a joke.' He let out a deep sigh. 'Do you think I'm meant to ring the doctor about St Joseph's, or do I get straight on to the Mother Superior? I wouldn't care, she hates Catholics!'

But the good nuns did not hate Edna Tench back. In their little hospital at Whalley Range they treated her like a deliciously naughty child. When Edna spat out their creamed tripe they presented her with coddled eggs. And when she hurled a bed-pan through a window-pane they simply sent for some workmen and promised to pray for her.

From time to time the engaged couple felt obliged to consult the old harridan about the forthcoming wedding arrangements.

'I don't know why you bother asking,' she would grumble to the ceiling. 'You'll go ahead whether I want it or not. And it's not as though there's anybody I'd care to invite.' She turned her face to the wall. 'Have what you want, you will anyway. And I'll sit alone in the front pew on our side of the church.'

When Eva heard about this she said, 'Never mind, there'll be all of Monton Cricket Club behind her. Take no notice. Listen, Dinah, there's one question we can't carry on avoiding. Your frock. Are you going to use Rory's lace?'

'No.' The word had come out as a sharp cry. And she was surprised by the thought which had accompanied it: getting married to Rory would have been a real wedding. Panic set in. Uncontrolled panic. 'Mother, I'm not sure I'm going to be able to go through with this.'

'Everybody feels like that; I know I did. The way to get over it is to make plans, get things moving. The frock: why don't you settle for something really good in ready-made, and let me do the bridesmaids?'

'Whatever you say,' answered Dinah dully. Inside a golden bubble, within her mind, she was seeing a vision of herself and Rory being married by Father Paddy. 'Does it have to be church?'

'Do you want people thinking you're expecting? There's supposed to be good shopping at Bolton; we could try Joan Barrie's. Now then, how many bridesmaids?'

'Avril, and I'll have to at least ask Macushla.'

'Don't be so ridiculous,' snorted Eva. 'When the doctor's been brought out to her, in the middle of the night, twice in the last week? Talk sense!'

'I've still got to ask her. I always promised.' Rather than argue further, she headed for the door to the lobby.

'Where you going?'

'Over the road.'

'Are you mad?' A scandalised Eva had followed her into the hallway. 'They've practically got straw down in the street. That girl's on her way out.'

'Well at least, when she gets there, she'll be able to tell Rory that I did ask.' It was all too much: Dinah burst into tears, grabbed her old grey coat off a peg on the wall, and opened the door on to the frosty street.

The stars looked very bright and near as she crossed the cobbles. It was one of those nights when the moon was enormous.

The Brogans' door was, as always, just on the latch. Did she still have the right to barge in unannounced? Dinah hesitated on the threshold of their lobby. They had acquired St Joseph, framed in passe-partout, since her last visit, and the air was heavy with the sweetly sweaty smell of a chicken on the boil.

For the first time ever she actually knocked at the living-room door.

'Who dat?' Stasia's voice, from within, sounded scared.

'Only me.' Dinah pushed the door open to reassure her, and then wondered whether she would be landed a clout for her pains.

But the Stasia stirring the blackened pan, on the fire of the cast-iron range, was a woman made of big defeated curves which were only too obviously obeying the pull of gravity. 'I asked the poulterer for an old hen,' she said, 'and by God he took me at my word!'

'How are you?' Dinah was surprised to find she really wanted to know. Time could have stood still in that kitchen, where the table looked like a small corner of a public tip.

'How am I? Weary. Yes, weary. We thought we'd lost her last Tuesday night but dawn broke and she rallied.' Stasia fished inside her blouse and brought out the lengths of tape and the stitched linen tab of the green scapular. Lifting it up, she pressed down her chins to kiss the image of the Virgin Mary.

239

Dinah's own scapular was still in the same cupboard as the painted diaries, tucked inside an old box of Windsor and Newton drawing inks. In the early days she had hidden the Catholic item from her mother, now it was half-hidden from herself – lest it should conjure back too many guilty memories of having prayed for Rory's attention.

'The child's poor father's not drawn a sober breath in a week. The Britannia's profits must have soared. It's just his way of coping. Paddy's sitting with her presently. Would you like to step up and make your farewells?'

Dinah had not realised that things were as bad as this. The only possible answer was 'Yes'.

'We've done a shunt around; you'll find her in the big front bedroom. That way I can take a fire up, on a shovel.'

Upstairs a red electric light bulb was burning in the bedroom. Dinah had expected Paddy to be sitting by the side of the bed, reading from his breviary. Certainly he was on a bedside chair but he was turning the pages of an old brown cardboard photo album. 'And here's Cousin Philomena Begley on the day the goat broke loose and ate your sun bonnet.'

Bony Macushla already looked like a death mask, and the red light was also illuminating her finely tucked and smocked linen night-gown. For a mad moment Dinah caught herself wondering whether they'd already got the patient into a shroud. Everything about the bedroom was, somehow, makeshift: the bed-covers had once done duty as a pair of brocade curtains and there was no wardrobe – just piles of clothes spilling out of old trunks and suitcases.

Stasia's promised coal fire burned in the little cast-iron grate. And on the mantelpiece stood two statuettes which Dinah would once have thought of as 'a monk' and 'some child in a crown'. She now knew them to be St Anthony of Padua and the Infant of Prague.

The man who had taught her these differences closed the photo album and said, 'We're really glad to see you.'

If Dinah had been busy looking around the ruby-shadowed room, it was because she could hardly bear to look at Macushla: her small face was pinched down to nothing so that the nose was more of an angry beak than ever. But the eyes . . . oh those eyes! They looked bigger than ever, and even more all-seeing.

How on earth do I ask somebody, who's breathing like a saw cutting through wood, to be a bridesmaid? That's what Dinah was wondering. She knew she should simply be abandoning the thought but she had made a promise – and she always kept her promises. Perhaps just mentioning the idea as a possibility would get her off the hook. Or would that be a wicked piece of self-indulgence?

Macushla helped her out with, 'I saw the announcement in the *Evening News*, they brought it up to me.' When she spoke, the rasping noises all but vanished and she merely sounded weak and faraway. 'I want to tell you something.'

'Easy, Macushla, don't get worked up again,' said her brother. 'Pull up a chair,' he suggested to Dinah.

The wooden one she found could have been mistaken for a stool – its back was missing. Perhaps there were better ones but it was hard to see because Paddy had got up and switched off the overhead bulb so that the room was only lit by the flames from the fire and the glow of a little night-light which sat on an upturned apple-crate, at the side of the bed.

'This is nicer,' he said. His black suit brought funerals to mind. 'This is a better light for talking. Let me just put a few more of these drops in your eyes, Macushla. They get a bit dry,' he explained to the visitor. 'And then there's the little men inside her chest and the way her owd bones rattle,' he said affectionately.

And Dinah thought of Rory, someone else who had not been afraid to allow tenderness to shine through strength. She couldn't help it, she began to weep.

'No,' said Macushla. 'Don't. You mustn't. I'm only going home.' The hand which had reached out and seized

241

hold of Dinah's felt as though it was made of coral. 'I've been there once already, in the middle of last Tuesday night. But it wasn't my time so they sent me back.'

'Does she mean she's been to Heaven?' Dinah had addressed the question to the priest because she felt it was his department.

'She does. And who are we to question the experience?'

Suddenly, unaccountably, the bed-clothes started stirring, wriggling. As the last bit of conversation had been about a holy happening, Dinah was immediately reminded of the Red Sea parting in *The Ten Commandments* but reality intruded in the shape of a young dog's head emerging from under the covers. This lurcher, who was little more than a pup, was gazing adoringly at Macushla.

'He thinks he's a bleddy stuffed toy,' laughed the priest.

'He's descended from Sid.' Macushla named Rory's old dog in a gasp.

'Do you want to know a funny thing?' Paddy asked Dinah. 'We showed this young feller-me-lad Rory's photo and he wagged his tail like he already knew him.'

The animal kingdom and the human one had never been very far apart in this household. Now it seemed that neither were Heaven and Earth because Macushla said, 'When I came out of the tunnel and I saw it all, Sid was there with Gran'ad Brogan. And Gran'ma was having a laugh with the dead ice-cream lady who used to be on the concrete front at Bray. Jesus, it was beautiful, Dinah, bloody lovely.'

This last word was grabbed from Macushla by a fit of coughing. But after Paddy had helped her to a sip of water she came back with: 'There's geography to Heaven. There's trees and streams and everything. I was taken there and shown it but they said I couldn't be part of it – not yet.'

'She still seems to have a lot of strength,' Dinah whispered to Paddy.

'False energy,' he muttered. 'You often see it near the end; it's just the doctor's drugs.'

She's really going to die, thought Dinah. I'm looking at somebody who'll soon be in the cold ground.

But that wasn't the future Macushla was envisaging. Not a bit of it! She was convinced she been vouchsafed a glimpse of Eternity. 'Never think your prayers don't count, they do. The people there gather to watch them coming up, in the shape of beautiful mauve gases, and they're really pleased you're praying.'

Dinah found herself fascinated enough by all of this to dare to ask a very basic question. 'Did you get to see God?'

'No,' it was Paddy who answered. 'But she says she was told something that will surely thrill the Muslims.'

'The dawn?' Macushla asked him wildly. 'They told me to watch the dawn, Dinah. They said it was important to get up and see the break of day with people you love.'

Could any of this really be true? Dinah tried for something more prosaic. 'Was there food?'

'Just steamed fruits with their skins on. Hell's real,' Macushla attempted to sit up. 'Vast it is, and no colour and no real light – just little slithers. Enough to see them boring themselves silly with whatever it was they did that was wrong, when they were here.'

'Wheesht, calm down,' soothed her brother.

But she wouldn't be stilled. 'They try to dig their way out of Hell but they just break into more tunnels, and there're always dead ends.'

'Let me plump your pillows,' said her brother. 'Just support her back, Dinah. She's a terrible old tin-ribs.'

Dinah was glad he'd warned her; Macushla seemed to have little control left over her body and she felt like an unwieldy bundle of knitting needles. But nothing, it seemed, could stop her jabbering. 'All the promise is true, Dinah. Heaven is made of love. Jesus, when they're talking, they sometimes melt into one another out of sheer bliss!'

'Lie her back,' advised Paddy.

Even as they did, the recitation continued unabated. 'Gran'ma was there and little Gran'ad and Shelagh O'Hare who fell under the wheels of a bus . . . I knew tons of 'em, tons. But Dinah, I have to tell you this.' Once again she attempted to sit up. 'Somebody was missing. Somebody who would have crawled over broken glass to see me. Rory wasn't there, Dinah. He just wasn't there.'

Dinah Nelson had spent enough of her life at the cinema to have formed firm expectations of what a wedding day should be like: rolling ringing church bells, the sharply focused moment of 'I will', and then great flutters of confetti tumbling through shafts of sunlight. In the event, her own personal nuptial montage proved to be nothing like this at all.

It began at the hairdresser's. Carroll Arden ('Stylist to the Stars') was well enough known to be able to afford to have a salon that was a good half-mile away from the fashionable shopping district. In his rise to prominence, this one-time child of the back streets had dyed both his name and his hair.

There wasn't a lot of the latter but it was tinted to exactly the same shade of auburn as Elsie Tanner's. The actress who played the character, Patricia Phoenix, was a favourite client of the hairdresser's. And she was standing by the reception desk, arguing, as Dinah walked nervously off Oxford Road and into the salon.

'You've dyed my hair and my fake piece two different colours,' stormed the actress. 'And Sorrel Starkey told me you did the same to hers. It's all this black light you've got in here.'

'Oh shut up,' was his unperturbed reply. Carroll Arden's skin was the pale whitish-pink colour of belly pork, and he had plucked eyebrows and several chins and upswept spectacles. 'Sophie Tucker's coming back to Manchester on Monday and I'm having dinner with her at the Midland,' he boasted.

Evidence of his genuine friendship with the famous was much on view in the shape of lavishly affectionately signed photographs on the wall of the open salon. It was, indeed curiously dark, with just pin-spotlights aimed down onto each stylist's chair.

'Are you for me?' he said to Dinah. 'Are you the bride? *Bride of Frankenstein* more like, with that white streak at the front!'

'Take no notice of him, he's a bad bugger,' said Pat Phoenix as she stomped out. 'Good luck, love,' she called back over her shoulder.

'She won't need luck,' Carroll Arden shouted after the departing star. 'Not with me doing her hair! Come on, let's have a look at you.' He led the way towards the central chair.

As she sat down, Dinah only hoped that he would not prove to be one of those stylists who began by lifting up a handful of hair disparagingly. Instead he lifted up a tail comb and did a bit of deft rearranging. He must still have been thinking about Pat Phoenix because he said, 'Her and her bloody piece! How tall's your fiancé?'

'Quite tall.' Even this small amount of combing had significantly improved her appearance.

'Have you brought the head-dress?'

She had it in a paper bag – silver laurel leaves. And she explained that her plain white tulle veil was designed to fall down to meet the train of the dress.

'Quite classic,' he nodded approvingly. 'Lorraine,' he called out. 'Take her coat and bring some coffee. And bring some dark brunette pieces whilst you're at it.' Returning his full attention to Dinah he said, 'We'll build it up like Marie Antoinette. By the time I've finished we should be able to perch a ship on top of it.'

Dinah only hoped he didn't mean this literally. 'And I'm not in the market for buying a wig,' she added hastily. False hair was all the go at the moment.

'I'm too soft-hearted for my own good,' he announced acidly. 'I'll lend it you. Are you an orphan?'

'No.'

'Then your mother can bring it back on Monday.'

'I'm not sure I . . .'

245

He took a step away from her. 'You're very welcome to go elsewhere.'

A first visit to Carroll Arden's had always been one of her bridal ambitions. 'No. Do what you want.'

'I always do what I want,' he sniggered. 'Especially after hours. Of course I've had a lot more fun since we went Unisex.'

It was bit like being attended to by another woman. Even the plump little hands were feminine; they were absolutely hairless and they had brown liver spots on the back of them. But oh how they could wield a comb!

It had never looked so good in her entire life. 'Couldn't you just lacquer it like that?' she asked.

'Couldn't you just shut up? I'm the artist!' A craftsman too: he even insisted upon steaming her whole scalp, inside a clear plastic dome. 'My new Swiss conditioner,' he explained.

As Dinah's interest grew so did her confidence. When he finally lifted the plaited coronet of false hair onto the back of her head, she said, 'How much is all this extra attention going to cost me?'

'I'll never be a bride myself so you're getting it for the price of a re-style and blow.' With this he burst into song.

> 'This aching heart of mine is singing
> Lover come back to me.'

And as suddenly as he'd started he stopped. 'Whatever's the matter, love?' He was addressing Dinah's reflection in the mirror. 'Whatever have I done to bring that look into your eyes?' The memory of this frozen reflection would always remain with her as part of her personal wedding montage.

Making an obvious effort to change the subject, Carroll Arden asked, 'Are you newly-weds going in for your own home?' Once again he was confronted by a portrait of gloom. 'We were,' said Dinah, 'but the building society found something wrong with the foundations.'

'What's a bridesmaid meant to do?' asked Avril. She had arrived, ready and dressed, a good hour ahead of the wedding. Since then she'd been hanging round the kitchen in ankle-length, old gold, watered silk.

'Do? God alone knows. I thought my mother was never going to get in that car for the church. I certainly didn't expect her to cry.'

'Where's your father?'

'There's another one who's probably blowing his nose, he's gone down the yard.' Tommy Nelson had been much moved at the sight of his daughter dressed in a billow of white tulle over ivory satin.

Avril began to check off the traditional list: 'Have you got something old?'

'No. Everybody's been on at me about this. I've got nothing borrowed and nothing blue, either. I'm not going in for any of that.'

'You're not a bit bridal,' sighed Avril.

'Don't blame me, blame the Lancashire and Cheshire Affiliated Building Society. They back out and we have to come straight home from the honeymoon to his mother's!'

'Why couldn't you come here?'

'With no bathroom? Talk sense.' In the distance the outside lavatory cistern was refusing to flush properly, it was just giving out a series of clanking noises.

'Are you sure I'm meant to go to the church in a car of my own?' queried the bridesmaid.

'Last one before me. And you could have had an escort; I did offer you Paul. Don't sit down, Avril, you'll only crush the back of your frock.'

'Paul doesn't need me to give him any false ideas of his own importance.' Avril had dipped down to peer in the sideboard mirror. She was adjusting the set of her head-dress – gold laurel leaves to complement Dinah's silver ones. 'Your hair looks nice.'

'Yes but it's piled too high, makes me feel like a Bluebell

Girl. That girl at the florist's wants shooting – these bouquets are ten times too big.'

'Not a bit bridal,' repeated Avril reproachfully. The distant cistern flushed again, this time successfully.

'What's meant to be wrong with Paul Snowden?' He was a driving force behind Aquarius Galactica, a much more modern firm of herbalists, who bought a lot of basics, wholesale, from Tyrell and Tench.

'Too like his own name: beautiful-looking but something locked-off and chilly inside. You've not got your button-hole in, Mr Nelson.' Tommy had finally returned from the yard, looking distinctly alien in hired black jacket and striped trousers.

'What've you done with it, Dad?' Dinah asked accusingly.

'It's on the bread bin. I'd rather just wear me badge.' He sounded just like a defiant little boy.

'Come here,' said Dinah. And instead of pinning the carnation back into place she seized him in a deep hug.

'You'll squash all that net!' cried Avril.

'Who cares? It's me dad who matters. You can wear a paper hat for all I care,' she said to him. 'Just don't start blubbing again,' she added sternly.

Avril, obviously recalling that she was meant to assist the bride, asked, 'Could you do with going down the yard yourself, while I'm still here to help you lift up all the petticoats?'

'No but I've got to go up to me bedroom for something.' She slipped off her shoes. 'Too slippy for stairs,' she explained as she headed for the lobby.

'You should scrape those new soles on gravel,' Avril shouted after her.

Dinah called back, 'That bang at the front door's the car for you.'

'See you in the church porch, Dinah.'

'See you.' But she had somebody else to see first. Somebody who lived behind a sheet of glass, inside a varnished wooden frame.

Most of her things had already been packed up and driven over to Ellesmere Park. The framed photograph of

Rory, forever smiling in the sunlight of 1955, still stood on top of the pink-painted chest of drawers.

'I'm leaving you here,' she said it aloud. 'It's not because I don't love you, you know that. It's just so we can always have a place that's ours. I'll come back often, I promise.' As she kissed the cold glass she remembered the warmth of his reality, the strength of those hard muscles beneath the silken skin. And she remembered what a *man* he'd been. 'Oh Rory . . .' was the most she could manage.

'Are you all right?' It was her father calling up the stairs. 'My kidney stone's playing up. Dear God in Heaven, whatever's that?'

Even from up here Dinah could hear wild scrabbling at the front door. The only thing she could find to dry her eyes was a dressing-table doily but Eva always kept everything spotless so it was just as clean as a hankie. She still had it in her hand as she got out onto the landing.

The sound of the mysterious scrabbling had intensified. Tommy was already opening the front door as she began to descend the staircase.

A grey streak with yellow eyes darted round her father's legs and came barking its way down the hall. It was the Brogans' new lurcher.

'Mind it doesn't claw at your wedding gown,' shouted her dad.

But the dog had frozen in its tracks so that all it was doing now was gazing at her, gazing helplessly and reproachfully.

'He won't do you any harm,' said a voice which was both young and masculine. It belonged to Tyrone Brogan. He was hovering in the doorway looking exactly as she remembered Rory at the age of ten. Except, at that age Rory had never had blue jeans and a Beatle haircut. 'I don't know what got into him,' said the lad. 'His fur suddenly went up and he bolted for your house.' Tyrone ambled down the hall and grabbed the dog by its collar. 'Come on, Jethro. We're not wanted here.'

'You are,' said Dinah indignantly. 'Always. All of you.'

249

'Then why was none of us invited to the wedding?'

'Because we thought you were still getting over Macushla.' The matter had been the subject of considerable discussion.

'We could still have been invited.' He was obviously repeating something which had been discussed on his own side of the street. 'The other car's come back for you.'

'Are you going to wave me off?' asked Dinah hopefully.

'No. Come on, you.' He led the dog out into the sunlight.

That was the second image Dinah retained for her memory album. 'You can't do right for doing wrong,' she said helplessly to her father. He had his white carnation back in his button-hole and he was proffering her bouquet. As Dinah took it from him she said, 'Tyrone didn't even shut the door.'

'No need. We're off.'

Not a large show of neighbours were out on the pavement to wave her off. Just Lily Jelly and Mrs Hankey from up the street, and a few other women who had always been in the background of Dinah's life but never figured enough to be invited to the church.

Through the cries of 'good luck' the bride distinctly heard Lily Jelly saying, 'Another twelve months and she'd have been too old for white.' But behind her veil, Dinah didn't have time to dwell on this because a uniformed Mr Dobbs was already out of the Daimler and holding the rear passenger door open for her.

Just before she got into the car, Dinah glanced across the road at the Brogans'. All the curtains were drawn as firmly as they had been on the day of Macushla's funeral. To make matters worse, the parish church only had one bell – Dinah could already hear it tolling – and there is no way of making one bell sound anything but doleful.

Tommy wasn't much help when it came to getting the big skirt stowed inside the car but Mr Dobbs knew all the ropes. 'And we don't want to be dead on time,' he said as they drove towards the Claremont Road end of the street. 'Let's keep them in suspense for a few minutes. It's a bride's prerogative.'

'I've come out without Woodbines,' announced Tommy.

'The beer-off on the corner sells them,' suggested the chauffeur. So that was where the car headed. And on the way her father and the driver talked about whether Georgie Best was ruining his own chances. Dinah didn't feel at all central to the afternoon, in fact she felt like something that had been grafted on.

When they got to the little corner shop, both men decided they needed to make purchases. 'You'll be all right, won't you?' were Tommy's last words before he left her alone in the back of the car. The upholstery was in fawn felt and the same material lined the walls and went up over the ceiling.

From where she sat Dinah could see The Place. A familiar figure was sitting on the stone boulder. Despite the fact that she was bathed in spring sunlight, Daisy Carver was still buttoned into a long tweed overcoat, and this afternoon's hat looked like Davy Crockett's – without the tail.

The men emerged from the shop. They had brought the owner out to see the bride. 'My God,' he said, 'it doesn't seem five minutes since I was serving her with sherbet fountains!'

The motor purred back into life and they continued their journey towards the church. Daisy Carver didn't look up as they passed. Lost in thought, she would have made a perfect subject for a drawing in sepia ink.

As the car came to a halt at the bottom of the steps up into the churchyard, a cloud passed across the sun and bystanders were noticeably putting up their coat collars. Seconds later, rain began to fall, and Dinah was obliged to wait inside the limousine until Mr Dobbs had been round to the boot and pulled out a big umbrella.

Opened up, the word 'Guinness' was revealed, printed across each of its black silk panels. 'Good job this isn't the Methodist Chapel,' laughed the chauffeur. 'I took my good one fishing and it got nicked.'

My good one got nicked too, thought Dinah. My good man. I had the very best and now I'm settling for safety and convenience. If I kick off my shoes and start running away, which direction shall I go in?

The house is locked and I've got no key. I could always go to The Place. Daisy Carver would understand why I'd bolted. But what would I do after that?

She didn't know so she allowed Tommy to guide her up the steps. A lot of other umbrellas had gone up but there were still plenty of murmurs of 'Isn't she beautiful?' and cries of 'Good luck, love'.

Avril, who was waiting inside the entrance, gave her a startled look. 'Seen in here you don't half look tall. I've found greenfly on the dog daisies in this bouquet.' She had also chosen to rip out some of the asparagus fern which had added to the size of the giant posy, and now she was looking for somewhere to dispose of it.

'*Too* tall?' Without waiting for a reply she said, 'I think I'll pull some fern off mine too. They must have thought they were making them for a pantomime.'

'There's no central aisle, you know,' said Avril accusingly. 'Just two side ones. I've already had a peep round that stained-glass partition thing.'

'Come on, Avril, be a proper bridesmaid. Take this greenery, and yours, and shove it under that hymn book table.'

'Them flowers cost good money,' said her father.

'How much extra were the choir?' Avril asked him.

'Four and sixpence each, and the organ was three quid.'

It chose that moment to begin playing 'Here Comes the Bride', as the verger, in a long black cassock, motioned them towards the top of the left-hand aisle.

Avril must have been seized by some childhood memory because she began to hum

> '*Here comes the bride,*
> *Forty inches wide.*'

I just hope my hair's not forty inches too tall, thought Dinah, as they began to process towards the altar. St John's didn't smell a bit like St Luke's: nothing incense-laden and holy at all, in fact it just smelt of old prayer books.

She could already see John, waiting with his best man; they were standing with their backs to her, at the bottom of the chancel steps. And on the left-hand side of the aisle she was catching glimpses of distant relations who were usually just signatures on Christmas cards.

Something caught her attention on the right. Whatever were rosary beads doing in this most Protestant of parish churches? They were being fingered by Eugene Gannon, who was already awash with happy tears. And he was definitely wearing eye-black because – even through her veil – she could see a dark streak running down one of his rosy cheeks. The Turnock twins, in electric-blue suits, sported bright ginger sideburns to set off their new Beatle haircuts.

And here in the front pew – on the left – was her mother, resplendent in a beige lace picture hat which had been hired at the last minute, for a guinea, from a new shop called La Boutique.

The pews on the other side of the aisle were only narrow. Edna Tench had the very front one all to herself. Her outfit offered no concession to the event, none at all: she just looked like she did in workaday Peplum Street.

Old Edna's eyes took in the outline of the bride, and went straight to the top of Carroll Arden's ski-slope of a hairstyle. Next they transferred themselves to the top of her son's head. And only then did she allow a smile to play around her narrow lips.

In that moment Dinah realised, for certain sure, that she was going to tower over her bridegroom by a good three inches.

If carrying the exact memory of somebody's height inside your own head is difficult, it is even harder to try to position yourself so as to look shorter. Dinah barely heard the words of the service until the vicar got to the part where they were expected to repeat various bits. 'With my body I thee honour,' said the minister.

That was when she had a vision of John without his clothes on. And in the same moment, in her mind's eye, she saw all the assembled male members of Monton Tennis Club without theirs: suntanned arms and legs and dead-white middles.

Nevertheless she nudged John and muttered, 'You're meant to repeat it.'

'Would you mind just saying it again for me, please?' he asked the vicar.

'With my body I thee honour,' and the parson added a smile which was almost roguish. If that was awful, so was the thought that John would soon be expected to put the affirmation into practice. As he slid the ring down her finger Dinah thought about it even more – but it was too late to pull her hand away.

Rory, what have I done? Whatever have I done?

As the congregation struggled with the hymn 'O Perfect Love', and the bridal party started heading for the vestry door, Edna Tench was heard to say, 'I'll stop where I am, thank you, I've seen registers signed before.' Another chilly moment for Dinah's personal wedding montage.

The vestry boasted an inhospitable printed notice about refusing communion to those who were 'not in good standing with the Church of England'.

'I'm sorry my hair came out so tall,' Dinah said to John.

'It's worse now your veil's lifted back.'

He minded, she could tell that. It wouldn't have been too tall for Rory. As they signed their names in the parish records, rain was still battering against the ugly, yellow, stained glass of the vestry windows.

'What are those cans of Heinz beans for?' her mother asked the vicar brightly.

'We are not a rural parish; throughout the year I ask the choir to amass canned goods for the harvest festival.' Turning to John he said mock-reproachfully, 'Fancy you forgetting your words.'

Dinah marvelled that this portly man in a dog collar

was calmly expecting them to use their bodies to honour one another, that evening, at some presently unrevealed honeymoon address. And that, just because the Anglican clergyman represented the Church, he had been able to request this exotic assurance in public without anybody fainting dead away.

'If we're all set,' continued the vicar, 'I'll just press the bell for the organist.' In seconds, another wedding march – Mendelssohn's this time – started rising up in the distance.

'Off you go,' said her father sadly. 'I've given you away now.'

She couldn't even give him a last hug because she knew that the safe familiar feel of him might dissolve her into unstoppable tears. *What have I done, Rory? Whatever have I let myself in for?*

They processed, through smiles, up the aisle and back to the porch. The rain had stopped, and the verger was striding around outside, bearing a hand-lettered placard which read 'No Confetti By Request'.

'By request of who?' asked Edna indignantly.

'Me,' he said. 'I prefer a wedding to a funeral – less mess.'

But his inhospitable statement had been overheard, so people ignored the attempted ban and sent multi-coloured confetti and little, tiny, silver paper horse-shoes flying through the air. The invited guests even included one of those irritating women who are never happy until they've hit the bridegroom over the head with the empty confetti box.

'Well, we did it,' said John, as they settled into the back of the car.

'Yes.'

'Wasn't it awful of the photographer? Fancy him just not turning up.'

She had heard some discussion of this but the content had barely sunk in. 'Never mind, people got snaps.' She was attempting to re-enter real life. 'I'm afraid he did pile my hair a bit high, didn't he?'

'Don't give it another thought.' He reached over and took her hand.

I've just cold-bloodedly married a decent man, she thought wildly. I never pretended I loved him – never. But I bet I'm going to pay for doing this. And tonight, not just that fat vicar but the whole congregation will be thinking of us making love. I bet Mrs Tench doesn't sleep a wink!

By now they were driving past The Place. Daisy Carver was still on her rock, and looking bedraggled enough to set Dinah wondering whether the poor old crone had been there right through the heavy shower of rain. 'Could you stop?' she called out to Mr Dobbs.

'Here?' he said over his shoulder.

'I want to show her my frock.' In truth Dinah was again thinking of cutting and running.

'The old lady was part of our courtship,' explained John.

Dinah tried to hate him for being pompous but she couldn't. She liked him too much for that. But was liking going to be enough?

He was already leaning across and winding down the window. 'Mrs Carver,' he called out.

'Miss not Missus,' came back implacably from the boulder. Registering the wedding car and its occupants, Daisy rose to her feet and began dragging one of the new tartan shopping trolleys towards them. It was the first time Dinah had ever seen her with anything brand-new.

'So you finally did it,' said Daisy Carver.

Even those few words were enough to tell the bride that the old wreck was having a bad day – not enough of 'the stuff'.

'None today,' she announced, as if in confirmation. 'They've got it at Bairstow's but they won't serve me.'

'Perhaps I could slip in for you,' suggested Dinah obligingly.

'In your wedding dress?' John sounded scandalised. 'Anyway, it's drugs.' He didn't even attempt to keep his voice down for the chauffeur's benefit.

'I wish I'd never taken that first spoonful.' There was no mistaking the sincerity in Daisy's voice. 'The bloody stuff's turned round and bitten me. You see adverts for getting off heroin but there's no way off this. And it doesn't get me there any more.'

'Get you where?' asked Dinah.

'To where love is.'

'So why have it?' John could have been wearing his white coat instead of a black jacket and striped trousers. 'Why bother?'

Looking deeply ashamed, she said, 'To stop the shaking. When I don't have it, each minute takes ten to pass.'

'I'll go into Bairstow's.' Dinah repeated her offer without hesitation.

'You won't,' decreed her husband. 'I'm blowed if the first time you sign your married name is going to be in the poisons register! If anybody's going in that shop, it's me. But when we get back from the honeymoon, something's got to be done about this. You need herbal help. Understood?' he was addressing Daisy.

'I bend my knee to no man.'

'Then I can only suggest you carry on shaking.'

'Just get me the stuff,' she pleaded. 'Just get it. Could you really set me free?' The look she was giving him could have belonged to a little brown-eyed dog in a cage.

'I could try. After the honeymoon.'

Oh that honeymoon!

'Surprise me.' Dinah had been the one who had said this, weeks before. She had hoped it would encourage John to dream up something original. 'But not Blackpool, and not abroad because I haven't got a passport and we'll soon be needing that sort of money for carpets and curtains.'

His idea of a surprise proved to be Buxton. Night was falling as he parked the Jeep on the Georgian curve of the spa town's sandstone crescent. As he got out, and took the bags from the back, she realised that this would be the last time the pair of them would ever travel with everything packed in separate suitcases.

She felt as though she was saying good-bye to a life she had never, previously, regarded as enviable. 'Why Buxton?' Dinah had clambered out herself by now. 'And hasn't it turned chilly?'

'The mist comes down off the peaks. Dr Blakeney said we shouldn't risk going too far in case the wedding affected Mother.'

That figured. At the reception, Edna Tench had been even more noticeable than the wedding cake. Her unsmiling appearance had dominated the top table like the proverbial 'death's-head at the feast'.

'But Buxton!' cried Dinah. 'She's only to get on two buses and she can be here.'

By now they were under the dimly illuminated colonnade which fronted the crescent. The St Ann's Hotel must once have been houses and it appeared to have two separate front doors.

'This one I think,' said John. 'Could you take my wicker picnic basket?' He was already assuming the falsely jovial tones which some people save for reception desks.

The porter did not rush to help them. A tall skinny youth in a black uniform, he was yet another young man who sported a Beatle haircut. 'The restaurant's closed.'

'We're already quite replete.' John was even using funny words to match his phoney good cheer.

His nervous new wife was covertly looking around the entrance hall. It was genuine old-fashioned posh, with an orange marble fireplace and big oriental vases and faded Persian rugs. John, signing the register, looked exactly the part, in a good tweed hacking jacket and cavalry twills. Dinah could have wished that she had not allowed her mother to talk her into white court shoes. And she only hoped that her little navy and white suit was not shouting out 'going-away outfit'.

The porter, it seemed, had other preoccupations. Whilst John's whole demeanour was bent on proving that they were suitable guests for this 'Ashley Courtney recommended hotel', the boy in uniform seemed to feel the need to declare that he was somebody with a whole life away from the establishment. 'I'm only doing this to help out,' he said. 'I'm really in a group. We're being watched by Decca.'

Dinah moved closer to the desk. 'What's there to do in Buxton?' she asked him.

'Damn all. And they've just closed the Opera House again.' He took down a set of keys from a green baize board. 'Room ten on the first floor, sir; if you'd be kind enough to follow me.'

The old hydraulic lift groaned. The Turkey-carpeted upstairs corridor creaked. The bedroom, which looked as though it had been revamped when the 'contemporary' style of decoration first came in was all wrong. Embarrassingly wrong.

After the porter left the room Dinah was the first one to speak. 'He's done this on purpose. And you even put your hand in your back pocket and tipped him.' The cause of her hopeless anger was a pair of dainty twin beds with box-pleated valances. 'Far be it from me to dot the i's and cross the t's, John ... But married people are meant to sleep together. That porter's got Youth Culture written all over him,' she stormed. 'These days, if you're not nineteen you don't mean a thing.' What she was really thinking about was a pair of naked feet, padding across the gap between the divans. And those feet would have a body attached to them. And that was the wrong body she was meant to bloody well honour.

'A little nervousness is only to be expected,' pronounced John. 'I've read a manual on the subject.'

'Oh well, it's probably all for the best. I expect you're as tired as I am.'

'We could always push them together.'

'What, and spend the whole night with the sheets and blankets falling apart?'

'I'll phone down for another room.'

*   *   *

259

This one was at the back of the hotel. It bore no trace of modernisation. In fact the big mahogany bedstead looked as though it had not been used since Mr and Mrs Gladstone stopped off in Buxton. Big? There was enough room for all of the Brogans. And why was she thinking of them?

'Don't tip him, John,' she insisted, perfectly audibly. 'Not again.' The wedding ceremony seemed to have turned her into her own mother.

The porter went off in a huff. Dinah sat down on the bed. It let out agonised protesting noises. 'There's no way I'm going to try out the facts of life on this. And if that's bold, it's bold. This is 1965 and we're here for a purpose.' She jiggled up and down again and the noise of the springs brought Boulting Brothers comedies to mind. 'I'd rather die wondering than lose my virginity on this instrument of torture.'

'The way you face up to things is marvellous.' He had gone quite rosy with embarrassment. 'We could always put the mattress on the floor.'

'We're right over the public lounge, John. We'd risk bringing the plaster down on people's heads.'

'Of course there's no law that says we've got to do it tonight.' He could have been examining the idea of hand-addressing a hundred circulars. 'What say we stretch our legs and go for a bit of a walk?'

I'd bring the plaster down with you, Rory, she thought ruefully. With you, I wouldn't care if the floor gave way – just so long as we were together. 'A walk? Why not?'

It took them to St Ann's Well, opposite to the hotel. The Buxton waters came gushing out of a lion's head, and there was a tin cup on a chain so they both tried a free sample. But you couldn't get worked up, it was only water.

'We're going to need something stronger than this, John. I think we'd better find a pub and have a few.' Now she sounded like her father!

They couldn't find a public house. Instead, they went

into another hotel – the Old Hall. Modern revolving doors, but once you got inside it was all low ceilings and nooks and crannies, and the seats were oak settles with pads that weren't quite thick enough. 'This is where Mary Queen of Scots stayed when she came to Buxton for her rheumatism.' John was proving to be the kind of person who reads guide books beforehand.

I know so little about him, she thought. As the boss's son he had been obliged to keep himself to himself at work. And the rest had just been tennis courts and restaurants, where they had always been chaperoned by other members of the general public.

We're in no way qualified for the years to come, she thought. 'I think I'll have another of those gin and tonics.'

Altogether she had six, and two packets of salted peanuts. After his third brandy John went on to Coca-Cola. ('But you have what you want, Dinah.')

Conversation got livelier as he remembered the wedding reception. 'Who was that man who got up on the table? The one who put his thumbs in a big leather belt and sang 'Try a Little Tenderness'.

'Somebody me dad works with. Your mother's face was a picture when he started yodelling. John, how long do we have to live with her?'

'Only till we sort things out. Avril seemed to be getting on very well with that chap from Aquarius Galactica.'

'Paul Snowden? She hates him.'

'No, the other one. The one who always counter-signs their cheques. I don't like Paul Snowden either.'

'He's lovely-looking – very *now*.'

'I don't say he's a queer,' said John thoughtfully, 'but you wouldn't want him in the same changing room.'

This thought took her right back to the worrying idea of taking her clothes off in front of her new husband. Drink-emboldened she plucked up the courage to ask, 'Have you got stage fright too? Well, bedroom fright.'

'Of course not.' But his panicked eyes told a different story.

'Come on,' she said. 'Let's get back.' Just so long as she felt she was helping him out she was fairly sure she would be able to cope.

The Old Hall was only round the corner from their own hotel. They rang the bell for the night porter. Then they had to ring it again. The door was eventually opened by the same youth as before. This time John fished into his ticket pocket for a coin, and a whole lot of confetti came out too. It had been emerging from both of their pockets all evening.

'The post office rang up with a late telegram. The message was "Don't do anything we wouldn't do", it was signed Marie Stopes ...' he consulted a piece of paper, 'and the Turnocks.'

This extra publicity didn't do much for Dinah's newly found courage. They didn't bother with the lift, they went straight up the stairs.

The first-floor corridor, dominated by a big china dragon, suddenly seemed much shorter than it had done on the way out. Dinah tried to stretch out their journey by walking more slowly. But in next to no time John had the key in the lock, the door was opened, and Dinah was again confronted by that most expectant of beds.

In their absence, somebody had been in and switched on the bedside lamps, and turned down the sheets at both sides. 'Oh my God!' exclaimed Dinah involuntarily. The rearranged bed looked just like an altar. 'I feel as though I'm in the middle of an "X" film.'

'Let's unpack,' said John.

'No, let's not. And let's not start arguing about who has the bathroom first.' That would only be putting off the evil moment. She had downed enough alcohol to allow boldness to be her friend. 'Take your clothes off,' she commanded. 'All of them. I'm going to do the same. Let's get right over this hurdle, straight away.'

He looked frozen to the spot. 'You don't make it sound very romantic.'

She had already unzipped her skirt and now she stepped out of it. 'Have you ever done this before?'

'No.' Obviously trying not to look at her, he had begun to unknot his tie. 'I once came very close with an ATS sergeant but she backed off at the last minute.'

'You won't find me doing that,' said Dinah firmly. More than ever she sounded like her own mother. 'If I start a thing I see it through.' Skirt and jacket were already over the back of a beechwood chair as she dropped her waist-slip.

'God, you're beautiful,' he said.

'You've got too many clothes on, John. Show me what you look like in a changing room.' Her bra came undone leaving her in nothing but flesh-coloured tights and the white high-heeled shoes. Take your jacket off, John.'

He did.

'Now kick off your moccasins.' Quite unexpectedly, she was finding herself filled with a sense of power. 'Unbutton your shirt.' He wasn't wearing a vest. As the shirt came off she saw the remains of a tan on his arms, but the rest of the revealed skin was palest cream, his nipples light brown. 'Unzip your pants.' He hesitated. 'Come on, John, get them off. Now look me in the eyes.' His own were steel grey and she could actually see the black pupils dilating. Without breaking their gaze she said, 'Keep on looking at me and take off your socks.' He obeyed. All that was left were the white underpants. 'Take them off.'

'If I do you'll have more on than me.'

She kicked off her shoes. 'Take them off.' The atmosphere in the room had changed, it was as though the very air had thickened.

So had John's voice: 'If they come off I'll stick out.'

'Just keep looking into my eyes and do as I say. Thank you. Now you take off my tights.'

She stayed standing, he chose to kneel down. The final moment of unveiling, the one she'd dreaded was causing something to shimmer out from her inner being, something she sensed as age-old – yet it was still unexpected. As he knelt before her and his hands reached out to the elasticated waistband, she heard herself say, 'My eyes, John. I said, look into my eyes.'

But now his own masculinity was vying for control of the proceedings. 'Christ,' he breathed reverently, as her secret parts came into view. 'My God, I could spill over just looking at you.'

And now she recognised the bodily sensations for what they were. Cruder cousins of that 'top of Blackpool Tower' feeling. The realisation filled her with terrible confusion – tremors of that kind had never been unleashed by anybody other than Rory Brogan. But she'd started this and now it had to be seen through.

'Can I touch?' He was almost begging.

'Why ask? Just do it.' That which had been erotic was now threatening to bring the unpleasant mists of the Crescent indoors. All she could think was *Rory, Rory, why isn't this you? Why isn't this us?*

'Let's get on the bed,' breathed John.

If he did that, she was determined she would take Rory with her. Once again she could hear her own voice speaking to John. 'I'm going to close my eyes now.'

'I won't hurt you,' he promised. 'I wouldn't hurt you for worlds.'

It won't be John anyway, she told herself. It's going to be Rory's hands, Rory's lips, Rory's tongue. Rory's finally going to find his way inside me.

I'm touching you again, she thought as her hands went over another's muscled back. *I'm finding you. I'm feeling you*. And when John's ardour proved less passionate than remembered memories, she told herself that Rory must be feeling a bit under the weather. This thought released such waves of loving tenderness that John must suddenly have found himself swept into her ecstasies.

'Durex,' he suddenly said urgently. 'I've got to go in the case.'

The spell was broken. She had to have it back. 'Forget about that,' she said, 'just forget about it.' Her arched back lured him into fresh abandon.

Rory returned. An amazing rainbow-shaded soap bubble began to shimmer around her. But it had its own silk-gloved fingers and they were right inside her. Two fingers that were reaching out to touch one another. And when they did, she knew that she would have finally found her way to rapture.

'Oh my God, oh God, my God,' roared John. And then he collapsed on top of her, like a belly-flopped diver.

Alas, the inner fingers had failed to touch. And now they were turning into almost hurtful crab's claws, and leaving Dinah with a terrible feeling of desolation.

I've been unfaithful, she thought. She wasn't even sure to whom. And then it dawned upon her: she had been unfaithful to herself.

John had wanted to hug up after they had done the thing they did – Dinah didn't even want to put a name to it. But she had suddenly felt in desperate need of a bath.

She must have washed her nether regions half a dozen times. Never before could they have had so much soap and water slopped in and out of them. She lost count of how often she'd turned on the hot tap, but, eventually, she climbed out and slipped into a virginal white nightdress. 'There's a laugh!' She said it aloud and wryly.

There was still one bedside lamp lit in the other room. Face-down and stark naked, John had already fallen asleep on top of the ruby candlewick bedspread. For some reason which Dinah did not quite understand, she dived into her weekend case, took out a pair of clean knickers and slipped them on beneath her nightgown.

Her thoughts in the bath had verged on the metaphysical: could Rory's spirit have entered into John's body – to give her pleasure? Being careful not to disturb her husband, she climbed under the covers; although she was next to him, there were sheets and blankets between them.

Her mind was full of muddled guilt. I've used you, she thought. You think you've just made love to me and you haven't. My mind was in flames and you were just the poker in the fire.

Could that be where the vulgar expression 'poke' had come from? And she'd do it again, she knew that! She already had some inkling of the fact that, once those inner fingers connected, electric sparks would fly.

John's rounded buttocks were as neat as twin moons. These were the last things her eyes registered before she switched off the light.

In the darkness, the memory of that last sight reinforced the memory of the effects of his thrustings. Should she own up to what had really happened? No, it could only bring John unhappiness and it might cut off her chances of conjoining with Rory again.

I'll be the perfect wife in every other way, she vowed. He'll have knife-edge creases in all his trousers, and I won't just cook him Elizabeth David recipes, I'll improve on everything in her cookbooks. She managed to find a modicum of sedative in this thought, clung on to it, and gave herself up to sleep.

The next thing Dinah knew, a dream about going round and round on the Waltzer on Silcock's travelling fair was interrupted by a man's voice saying 'Hello. Hello? Reception, are you there?'

Just one curtain was partially drawn back to admit strong sunlight. John, telephone receiver in hand, was already up and dressed. 'Sorry,' he said to her, 'but I'm getting nowhere fast with this phone. I've been up hours. I went to Holy Communion; somehow it seemed appropriate.'

'What time is it?'

'Late. Breakfast's over. I thought it better not to disturb you.' He sat down on the edge of the bed and took hold of one of her hands. 'Are you all right?' he asked happily.

Was she? She didn't know. 'Fine.'

'Not sore or anything? I've got a little tube of Savlon in my razor bag.'

'No thank you very much.' As she moved her hips around, experimentally, she was made aware of a certain tenderness but it wasn't one she wanted examining in public.

The John sitting on the edge of the bed was a man who had grown very considerably in confidence. 'Of course it was only used for what it was designed for. And it's quite an elasticated region, isn't it?' He seized hold of her. 'God, it was amazing, wasn't it? Fancy another go?'

'Not just at the moment.' Her own voice had sounded as though it was refusing the offer of an After Eight mint.

'I was even thinking about it in church. Right up at the communion rail.'

Dinah nodded towards the telephone: 'Who were you trying to ring?'

'The Blue John Mines at Castleton. I wanted to know which one you can go round in a boat.'

London would have been nice, she thought. There'd have been more choice. 'I'll get up now,' she decided aloud.

A quarter of an hour later they were downstairs in reception. Amazingly, the Decca youth was still manning the desk. 'I hope you've not been trying to make any calls,' he said. 'The whole switchboard's gone kaput. We're not getting anything in, either.'

'Could somebody rustle up some coffee for my wife?' It was the first time John had ever used the word in general conversation, and you could tell. He had gone ever so slightly pink.

'To be quite honest, you'd get it quicker by walking up to the Pavilion.'

This proved to be just beyond the Old Hall. It was a small version of the Crystal Palace – tacked onto the side of a miniature opera house.

'Buxton's a bit of a swizz, isn't it?' Dinah said. They were proceeding past rows of trifles in waxed paper cartons, and green jellies in the same shape as the domes on the theatre outside, but topped with mock cream blobs. Once John had paid for 'just two coffees' she began to elaborate on her criticisms of the spa town. 'I expected it to be full of old colonels with gout. This lot look as though they're in on a day trip from Ashton-under-Lyme.'

There was a pause whilst she unwrapped a cube of sugar. In the interim John must have been looking around for evidence of gentility. 'That's a genuine sheepskin overcoat, over there. And those two women

– the ones unwrapping their own sandwiches – they're dowdy enough to be proper aristocrats. It's my fault,' he said miserably. 'I thought a quiet atmosphere would help get us used to the physical side of things.'

Now she came to think about it, on their very first date he had also settled for something safe and sensible. And when the Grand Hotel in Manchester had proved to be too boring, John had whirled her off to that wonderful restaurant in Cheshire.

Just as John's energy levels had seemed to shoot up when confronted with the challenges of that drab evening, so they did again this morning. 'There's no law that says we have to stay here. Why don't we just pack up and head for Brighton?'

Anything had to be better than coffee slopped into thick white saucers. 'And the bed-springs at the St Ann's are like something out of a cartoon! I thought somebody was going to pop up at the end and say "That's all folks".' Now she was married she could voice such thoughts aloud. 'I'm the first to admit it's the poshest place I've ever been in, but Brighton does sound as though it might have a bit more *go* about it.'

'Right you are then, Brighton it is.'

This was never to be. Even at that moment two figures were crossing the threshold of this section of the series of palm houses, moving past a pool full of drifting carp with much more purpose than anybody else in sight.

'It can't be,' said Dinah in near disbelief.

'It is.'

The intruders were Eugene Gannon and Bud Turnock, and they were plainly looking for somebody.

'Over here,' called out John.

'Thanks be to St Anthony.' Eugene removed his black trilby in Dinah's presence. He had never done this in his life before so it was the most married she had ever felt. 'I knew he'd find you for us, he never fails.' Eugene was as usual dressed in his crowblack suit.

With his sideburns and his fringed shirt Bud looked like

an amateur cowboy. 'Actually it was the hotel said you'd be here.'

'It's your mother, Johnnie.' Eugene's whole demeanour was as funereal as his suit. 'I'm afraid she's asking for you.'

'Well she can't have me. I'm on my honeymoon. Any minute now we're heading South.'

'If this place is licensed,' said Bud, 'I think I'll have a pale ale.'

'I could do with a livener too.' Eugene sniffed a dewdrop off the end of his white nose.

'It isn't licensed,' said Dinah. 'Not this part anyway.' Her voice began to rise in anger: 'Why should she think she's got the right to see him?'

John didn't help matters any by going, 'Shush.'

'I will not shush. Why should she be pandered to?'

'You tell,' said Bud to Eugene.

This was plainly a task that was much to the Irishman's taste. 'Can you sit down here without buying anything?' He did anyway, crossing his legs just like Marlene Dietrich in *Blackmail*. 'How was the wedding night?' he asked greedily.

'Just tell us what's happened,' said Dinah.

'Mayhem. Absolute feckin' pandemonium. You will recall that we all stood outside Binn's Cafe waving you off.'

'All except her,' remembered the bride.

'Precisely. Madam was upstairs enjoying self-imposed solitary confinement. And when we got back she'd slumped to the floor, like Fay Compton in *Escape Me Never*.'

'We should have took her straight to Hope Hospital, then,' observed Bud.

'Well we didn't. I, for one, thought she was play-acting. We propped her up on a hard chair instead. And being as how she'd never been cheerful, nobody noticed the difference.'

'She's never dead?' cried Dinah.

'And calling for her son from beyond the grave? That'd be a first!' snorted Eugene. 'No, she's flat on her back at home. And they daren't risk moving her because of the potholes in the road. One private nurse has already walked out, and her relief says she's not stopping beyond nightfall.'

'So we've got to go back,' said John quietly. 'I've spent my whole life in chains.'

'She's got two slaves now,' said Eugene.

A little over an hour later the Jeep was bouncing its way along the deeply rutted private thoroughfares of Ellesmere Park. It was the first time Dinah had ever seen Axminster Road on a Sunday lunchtime: the whole place smacked of newly washed cars, and of people returning from either of the two golf courses. She had definitely gone up in the world. This was the land of the big Sunday joint and three veg, and, 'Could I trouble you for the gravy boat?'

She knew better than to expect such comforts at Comfrey – a house named after a herb which Culpeper had described as 'having leaves so hairy or prickly that, if they touch any part of the face, hands or body, they will cause it to itch'.

Eugene and Bud had only motored behind them as far as the top end of Eccles Old Road, where they had disappeared in the direction of a pub called the Bowling Green.

Even before the newly-weds had set foot on the concrete driveway, the front door was opened by Avril Porter. She was already making the kind of motioning gestures which betokened, 'Hurry up and come here, I've got all the latest dirt.'

Dinah was the first to reach the doorstep. 'How is she?'

'Very weak but she's still managed to sack the other nurse. That's what I'm doing here. She's wired-up to a television set that goes peep-peep-peep. Dr Blakeney says he can't force the nuns to have her again.'

'So who will?'

'You.' Registering Dinah's face she said, 'I'm sorry, love, but that's what it looks like.'

'Just tell me one thing,' asked Dinah. 'Why, in the midst of all this chaos, are you looking so radiant?'

Avril's skin was glowing and her eyes could have advertised Optrex.

'God bless Aquarius Galactica.'

'Paul?'

'No the other man, the one with all the hair. I have *not* been wasting time. In fact he's probably still mooching around in my dressing gown at Fallowmeadow Road. Good morning, John.'

'It's afternoon.'

'She's upstairs.'

Old Edna was ensconced in the first-floor front bedroom. The one with old heraldic shields in the transoms of the leaded windows. Prior to the honeymoon, this had been the room marked down for the newly-weds. A lot of Dinah's clothes were already hanging in the dark walnut wardrobe, her trinkets stored in the drawers of the matching bow-legged dressing table. There was even a framed photograph of her dad on top of the tallboy.

But flat on her back, in the double bed, lay Mrs Punch. She was indeed connected by wires to a television monitor; it stood on an unfamiliar chromium trolley. And for the very first time ever, Dinah was seeing Edna Tench without her pixie hood.

She was revealed as not quite completely bald: stray strands of white hair hung down from a pinkish-grey scalp. 'You see before you a broken woman,' she announced. Looking straight at her son she said, 'You did this to me.'

In that moment Dinah knew for certain sure that the pixie hood had been specifically removed to add pathos. Nevertheless, she managed, 'How are you?'

'Old and unwanted.' Her energies were plainly returning.

'Of course you're wanted.' John was attempting joviality.

'Prove it,' she snapped.

'How?'

'Send her back to her mother's and you stop here and

271

look after me.' The next words came out as a terrible cry: 'I thought we were happy together.'

'It's a miracle you're not queer,' said Avril to John. 'A bloody miracle.'

Edna treated her to a malignant look. 'You can go now, Avril,' she said.

Peep-peep-peep: the fully-automated television monitor seem to be mocking every bit of flesh and blood in the room.

'I see they've got you linked up to a Marconi,' said John interestedly.

'Yes and when that stops bleeping I'll be dead. And then where will you be?'

Free, thought Dinah. We'll be free. This thought got her as far as the bedroom door.

On their way down the stairs Avril pointed to a vase full of dried honesty pods, on the half-landing window-sill. 'I always think there's something chilly-looking about those.'

'This whole place puts me in mind of an ice rink. Christ, Avril, what've I got myself into?'

'Did he rise to the occasion, last night?'

Half of her longed to tell Avril what had happened, to describe how one person had become another. But the part of the brain which dealt in magic and mystery, the part that had spent years committing people and events to the painted diaries, knew that revelation would dismiss the potency of the sexual spell. 'It was all right,' was all she managed.

'Nobody's even taken in the newspaper.' Avril pulled the *Sunday Times* out of the letter-box.

'We already had it earlier, in Buxton.' When life was simpler, she thought. Yesterday I was wanting Friday back, and now I'd prefer to be still in this morning. Was this new life going to be one long series of ever-diminishing returns?

Avril smoothed out the newspaper. 'I expect this one's too posh for horoscopes.'

Dinah thought of Professor Petrulengo's fortune-telling

volume. It was stowed with the rest of her books, beneath Edna's bed. Professor Petrulengo was the author who had fuelled her fever for Rory, the writer who had solemnly promised her an 'eventual banquet'.

'Fuck horoscopes!' said Dinah.

'I've never heard you use such a word in my life!' Avril sounded genuinely shocked.

'Have you ever seen me in this sort of mess before? That scene upstairs was straight out of *Oedipus* at school. How can I stay here after that?' Equally, how could she go?

'Dr Blakeney's coming back in a bit,' said Avril. 'I'm off home to have another jump. I really do think that your wedding might have brought me Mr Right.'

Avril left on foot. Upstairs the mutterings and the rumblings and the peep-peep-peep continued unabated. Dinah just sat in the lounge like a visitor listening to a ticking clock and gazing into a hopeless future.

Eventually John came downstairs and said, 'She's demanding barley water. I'll have to nip down to Peplum Street for it. Can you hold the fort?'

The best she could manage was a dispirited, 'I suppose so.'

Though the leaded windows she watched him walking towards the Jeep. Suddenly, keys in hand, he halted and headed back to the front door.

'Dinah?' He was inside the house again now.

'What?' she called out. But before she could make any sort of move towards him, he was already over the threshold. 'What's the matter?'

'Can I just put my arms around you?'

'Why ask? Just do it if you want to.' Even as she said this she knew she must have been sounding as frosty as all of Edna's off-white paintwork.

Nevertheless he held her close. 'Do you know what she used to do to me when I was little? She used to say, "One day you'll come home and find me gone. I'll take all the food and all the furniture, and I'll vanish."'

Dinah could even hear a frightened child within the

man's voice. And when she looked at him, she could see the boy within the man's face.

'All of this wouldn't make you leave me, Dinah, would it?'

'No. I already told you: if I take a thing on, I see it through.'

'I love you, Dinah.'

This was the first time he had ever said it, and the only truthful response she could give was, 'I know you do.'

'We'll manage,' he said. 'Somehow we'll sort our way through it and we'll manage.'

He had the good sense not to attempt to kiss her. Once the Jeep had driven off the only thing to do was listen out for the doctor's car. But the next vehicle to park outside Comfrey was Bud Turnock's second-hand white Mini.

As its owner, and Eugene, came up the path they appeared to have been much invigorated by their visit to the Bowling Green. Eugene was making a great show of tiptoeing and Bud was blowing up an empty crisp packet, which he proceeded to explode against the palm of one hand.

Dinah led them from the hall into the kitchen. 'She won't be able to hear us from here. Do you want coffee?'

'Is she still in the bay window bedroom?' demanded Eugene. 'That was nothing but an act of willful defiance. The doctor was all for us bringing a bed downstairs. But would she have it? "I shall reclaim my rights" was what she said. Lips the colour of gentian violet and she was still determined to have her own way!'

'Is there anything to eat?' asked Bud.

Dinah didn't think there would be. 'It's always struck me as a boiled egg kind of a house,' she explained.

The front door bell rang. Not a true ring, more a deep flutter – like a bird shaking its feathers.

Dr Blakeney proved to be big and bald in a navy chalkstriped suit. 'Mrs Tench junior?' he asked. 'I thought I recognised you.'

'How?'

'From the engagement picture, the one she ripped up in front of me last December. That was just a symptom of her last little do; this is an altogether bigger one.' He sounded bluntly Northern but educated; Dinah was not surprised to register a Manchester University tie. 'How is she now?' he asked.

Honesty seemed the best policy. 'I've been banished.'

'If she carries on like this,' he sighed, 'the only person left to nurse her will be her guardian angel.'

'She gave the doctor a terrible time last night,' said Eugene in a telltale's voice. 'She said the Chamber of Horrors at the waxworks was full of physicians who'd poisoned their patients.'

'Is she taking the tablets?' he asked Dinah.

'I'm sorry but there's no point in asking me anything. I just seemed to be red rag to a bull.'

'You mean a cow,' observed the normally equable Bud Turnock.

'Ah Bud, no!' cried Eugene. 'Don't let her fill your heart with Sins of Uncharity.' He plainly meant this. 'I'm somebody who's going to Hell anyway.'

'As far as I'm concerned Hell lies up those stairs,' said the doctor. 'I'll just go up and see how she is.'

The only snack they could find for Bud was two ancient arrowroot biscuits.

When the doctor came back into the kitchen he was already taking a fountain pen from his inside pocket. And now he brought out a prescription pad. 'It's not looking too good,' he said. 'I'm inclined to change her medication. Could somebody get this to Boots' emergency branch in town?'

'Would you give me a lift?' Dinah asked Bud. 'I could do with a change of scene. That's if you don't mind stopping with her, Eugene.'

'Would I get away with smothering her whilst you're out?'

Dr Blakeney indicated that Dinah should follow him out into the hall. Closing the kitchen door on the two men, he said in lowered tones, 'All joking apart, she is a

very sick woman. She must not be crossed.' Before
Dinah could react he held up his hand for further
silence. 'I know it's going to be difficult; Mother
Superior at St Joseph's always called her "an exercise
in tolerance". Just try and remember that she is your
husband's mother.'

And look what she did to him, thought Dinah. Look
what she reduced him to.

Bud's white Mini was soon following the doctor's navy
saloon car along Axminster Road. They parted company
by the Ellesmere Park lodge gates, where Bud took the
road for town. The hands on the little steering wheel were
long and spindly, and he had red knobs on the outside of
each wrist.

To think I began this morning musing about losing my
virginity, thought Dinah. And suddenly I'm jerked back
off my honeymoon and turned into Nurse Merryweather.

'We found them,' said Bud.

'Pardon?'

'Another pair of twins. They were dancing round their
handbags at the Ritz. Heidi and Trudi they're called:
they've sent their pictures up to London for the Toni
Twins competition.' He was talking about a brand of
home permanent waving kit whose advertising slogan
was 'Which Twin Has The Toni? (And which one spent
seven guineas at a leading Mayfair salon?)'

'Could they win?'

'They've won us. We're getting engaged at Easter.'

It was spring – mating time. Avril had found her man,
the twins' dreams were coming true . . . 'How long have
you known them?'

'Since Friday night. We couldn't see them again yesterday because of your wedding.'

'But you can't just say you're getting engaged on the
strength of one sighting.'

'We can. We have done. We always knew we'd know
when the right pair came along. And they said they'd
always felt the same way.'

And who am I to criticise? I knew when I was eight

who the right one was. But I had to settle for a substitute, and that's what's landed me with a gorgon of a mother-in-law.

On Broad Street a motor horn tooted at them from the other side of the road. It was John in his Jeep, with one hand he was holding up a brown stone bottle of Tyrell and Tench's Ready-Mixed Barley Water.

There was hardly anybody in Boots Cash Chemist's. The prescription was filled in a matter of minutes. Filled almost too quickly for Dinah, who was quite enjoying the respite of a silent sit on a canvas and tubular steel chair.

Bud had stayed outside in his car. As she settled herself back in the front seat again, and he swung the Mini into a U-turn, Dinah saw the sight that would haunt the whole of the rest of her life. It was so awesome, so unbelievable, that she heard herself let out a terrible cry of the most real pain she had ever known.

11

Jack Lawless had not sent Mickey two dozen red roses, all counted there were thirty-three of the long-stemmed hothouse blooms.

'Easy come, easy go,' Mick said to Sorrel. 'What a ridiculous thing to send to a man of my age. To send to a man anyway!' He was half flattered and half wondering whether they were meant as a sprat to catch a mackerel. 'People always think I'm richer than I am.'

'I could smack you,' she said. But Mickey didn't know the whole story. And it was privileged information, gained within an AA meeting, so she was in no position to be able to enlighten him. 'Couldn't you just give the lad a chance?'

'What's far more to the point is the fact that I've got to give a lecture this morning. What do I wear?'

'A smart suit. It shows respect for the audience.'

Mickey pulled back the velvet drape which concealed the dressing area and began to rattle his way through coat hangers. 'When I was little I always wanted a suit like Danny Kaye's in *Wonder Man* – pearl-grey gaberdine with a big drape jacket. Well now I've finally got one and I'm really a bit long in the tooth for it.' Nevertheless he carried the suit into the cabin and dumped it on his bed.

'All this going on about your age is getting boring. The suit's perfectly all right – depending on what you put with it.'

'You choose for me.'

It was Sorrel's turn to push her way past the cabin trunks. She emerged with a grey silk shirt and a maroon tie.

'Are you mad?' He quickly substituted a tie in yellow and swapped the shirt for one that was bright blue.

And that, she reflected, was the trouble with Mickey. He would ask for your suggestions and then cast them to the four winds. As he changed his clothes she began looking through the Daily Programme. 'You're on the front cover: "Mickey Grimshaw remembers The Road To Angel Dwellings". I could call out a few interesting questions at the end of that!' she mocked.

'You're not coming,' he warned her. 'I know you and your so-called musical laugh.'

'I've far more interesting things to do,' she scoffed. 'Why, in the Golden Lion pub, somebody called Gwendolyn Burrows is going to reveal "Thirty-Six Tricks With A Headscarf". What chance do you think you stand against that?'

Mickey always wrote his lecture notes down on postcards. As he tucked them into his jacket pocket, and made his way to the lift, he reflected that the *QE2* Theatre was one of the world's most acid tests of any celebrity's drawing power. At least three times a day, big names were on offer to an audience which had already been everywhere and heard everyone. It was extremely unusual to play to a packed house. The most you could realistically hope was that you wouldn't find yourself confronted by *too* many empty rose velvet seats.

Forty-eight hours of being on public view with his leading lady, together with that recent showing of *This Is Your Life*, seemed to have upped the numbers on the first lecture of this present voyage.

Mrs Marazion, from the bookshop, performed the introduction. Waiting in the wings, the man she was alleging to be 'as entertaining as he is talented' was trying to see who was in the audience.

The first person he spotted was the woman with the white streak in her hair (at her age the rest must have been very expensively dyed around it). June had rolled in too. She was sitting by an exit, which presumably meant that she could roll out again if she felt the Crystal Bar beckoning her.

The next thing Mickey saw was a pair of sculpted pectoral muscles inside a tight black tee shirt. A blue and black bandanna worn pirate fashion, and dark Ray-Ban glasses, in no way disguised the presence of Jack Lawless.

Mickey did his best to try to see the porn star's outfit as ridiculous. But it wasn't ridiculous, not with those features and that physique. If it was too West Hollywood to be true, it was also highly alluring.

'. . . so may I please ask you to welcome Mickey Grimshaw.'

At that precise moment, just as he began to make his way towards the centre of the stage, the ship started to roll. Undeterred, Mickey placed his notes on the wooden lectern, adjusted the microphone, and began to address the audience.

'The first question most people ask me is, "Where did the idea for *Angel Dwellings* come from?" To answer that I will have to try and take you back to the Manchester of my youth. Theatreland was Oxford Street, and on top of an office building, next to the Odeon Cinema, there used to be an illuminated advertisement for Bovril. It was a real old-fashioned electrical sign made out of hundreds of light bulbs and . . .'

Down in the stalls, the former Dinah Nelson recalled her own youth, recollected that same sign, and remembered that it had sat on top of the building which had also housed Boots Cash Chemist's.

This took her straight back to 1965, to the day she was dragged back from her honeymoon to dance attendance on Edna Tench. Dinah was no longer sitting on a rose velvet seat in the QE2 Theatre; instead she was, once again, cramped up inside the toffee-paper-strewn interior of Bud Turnock's Mini. And the car was making the U-turn which would reveal the sight that was to wreck her life.

Three figures, that's what she saw on the opposite side of the road: a man, a boy and a dog.

The boy was Tyrone, the dog his new pup. The broad-shouldered man, shepherding them along, was sun-tanned. One dark eyebrow was deeply divided by a jagged scar. If anything, it made Rory Brogan look even more desirable than he had done on the day he set sail for Cyprus.

And yesterday I got married to somebody else, thought Dinah. That was the moment when she had let out the sharp cry which caused Bud Turnock to ask her whether she was all right.

'Just drive on,' she said desperately. Even twenty-four hours ago I could have *run* to him, she thought. She actually wondered whether she had started hallucinating: 'You did see a man and a boy and a dog?' she asked Bud.

'Sure. A sort of greyhound with yellow eyes. Want me to turn back?' They were already passing the Midland Hotel.

'No.' Inside her mind she was already constructing a conversation. '*Rory, I waited for you. I did wait. All those years seemed long enough to be sure. And there wasn't one second of them that I wasn't missing you and loving you . . .*' But now she'd gone and committed herself to another man 'in the sight of God and this congregation here present'. And Rory had always been very strict about anything to do with churches.

Inside the little white car they continued their journey down Peter Street. The next landmark they passed was the Free Trade Hall. Its Victorian sandstone facade had been recently cleaned: above the Italianate colonnade, the front of the building was hung with a pair of purple and lemon banners. One read 'DEATH? DON'T MAKE ME SMILE.' The other said 'Personal Appearance of June Gee – TV Psychic'.

In the middle of the Atlantic the *QE2* gave another lurch, and this same soothsayer rose to her feet, and, adjusting her acupressure bands, began to head for the exit.

Dinah watched her go with a hatred that had been on the brew for thirty years. This was the woman who had pronounced Rory 'dead'. How often had Dinah thought of seeking her out and killing her?

Too often for it to be left unaccomplished. Other people

281

might think of 'When I come into money', Dinah had always kept herself going with dreams of revenge. And recent events in her life had distilled these dark ambitions to a point where they could only be satisfied by action.

But over the years she had developed a sharp business brain. One which understood the importance of timing, of the correct location for the right event. In short, she knew exactly how to close a deal.

The basis of her plans for June's imminent demise were already in place. Once Dinah's husband had started exhibiting his 'tendencies' on this voyage, she had gone straight to the purser and had him moved into a separate stateroom.

His snoring had been her public excuse. Privately she had said to him, 'Every time these obsessions of yours rise to the surface, life becomes impossible. It's like living with a packet of itching powder.' For whole years of their married life she had tried to be understanding. These days, they were more than rich enough for her to be able to afford to have him shunted out of her sight. But not out of mind: he was too scandal-prone for that.

The ocean liner had plainly decided to do a bit of shunting of its own. The sensations it produced within Dinah made her feel as though she had suddenly grown to enormous proportions, and that somebody was systematically rolling her over in a big feather bed.

Up on the stage, because he was on his feet, the effects of the heavy swell were having a completely different effect upon Mickey Grimshaw. As the ship described another languorous plummet, the lectern started to sway to starboard, he seemed to be being pulled to port, and his trousers chose that moment to remind him that he had forgotten to put on a belt.

As he clutched at his waistband, Mickey felt he was being granted some small understanding of how Sorrel must have felt at Buckingham Palace. In an attempt to regain control over the situation he called out, 'Any questions?'

But quite a few of his now unsettled audience were

following June's earlier example and heading for the exits. 'Somebody must want to know something?' he cried out hopefully.

It took little Polly Fiddler, the pools winner, to save the situation. The stage lights reflected down onto her National Health glasses as, above the sudden noise of the storm, she shouted, 'Will you have lunch with me, Mick?'

He was so glad of a response – any response – from that disrupted audience that he bawled back 'Yes'. And then he added, 'When I've finished signing.'

Book-signings were always held one deck down, outside the Ocean Bookshop. Authors were expected to sit at an antique desk – all Queen Anne legs and gilded ormolu mounting – whilst Mrs Marazion spread copies of their books open at the title page, ready for personalised dedication.

And people asked for the oddest things. 'Would you please put "Maybe this will bring you to heel, Marvin"?'

'What's your name?' he asked the woman.

'Doris, but it's not for me.'

Nevertheless, Mickey wrote, 'Doris has asked me to say "Maybe this will bring . . ."' He always lived in mild fear of being called upon to defend one of these dedications in open court.

The next person in the queue was Jack Lawless. 'What would you like me to put?' asked Mickey automatically.

'What would you like to put?' came back in those deep and bantering tones.

Without a moment's hesitation Mickey wrote 'Go away' in big bold letters. As he scrawled his signature he was already having second thoughts.

But Jack had read what he'd written. And now he treated the author of the cold message to the most hurt-filled look that Mickey had ever received. Nevertheless, the younger man picked up the copy of *A Town To Remember*, turned on his heel and walked unhappily away.

'He just paid for that privilege,' said Mrs Marazion quietly.

If there was one thing Mickey hated feeling it was unprofessional. Nevertheless, there wasn't time to dwell upon his private life because he had just noticed another 'author aboard' patrolling past the table – presumably to see how many copies her rival was moving.

Ten minutes later Mrs Marazion said, 'I think we shifted fifty. Not bad in this weather. Before you give me the pen back, would you sign me some stock for the shop?'

Polly Fiddler, in her own signature royal blue (blouse and skirt this time) had chosen to wait for Mickey further up the glassed-in corridor, on one of the sofas which faced the sea.

'Look how the spray's hitting the window,' she said. 'It's beginning to look like a mucky windscreen. And that sea could be dark grey gloss paint that some giant had heated up.'

The sky was a paler grey and the horizon seemed to be leading a life of its own. One minute it was a normal horizontal line, the next it had tilted to near-enough vertical.

'Magic!' cried Mickey as the great ship took another dive. 'Though God alone knows how the Radio City Rockettes are going to be able to perform tonight.'

'Much more of this and I'll be back on the tablets,' observed Polly.

'Does that mean lunch is out?'

'I didn't need food, I needed to talk to you.'

That was the moment the midday whistle blew and the First Officer delivered a little homily over the Tannoy which ended 'in this weather we normally say to the crew "One hand for yourselves and one for the ship". To you, our most valued passengers, we can only say "Two hands for yourselves".'

'Cunard would probably hand out mink coats for getting in the lifeboats,' said Polly wryly. A companionable silence fell. She broke it with, 'I've decided I don't much like rich people. Give me our Rita every time.'

'Is that the sister you're going to visit in the States?'

'Rita's a red setter. I thought of phoning her but hearing me voice might just unsettle her: we're very close.' Silence fell again until she said, 'Paid smiles.'

'What?'

'All the staff are forever smiling but sooner or later they'll expect us to pay for it.'

Did she want him to explain the tipping system to her, he wondered. Was that what she wanted to talk about?

'I've done bar-work all me life,' she said. 'I bought my little house with sixpenny tips that went in a glass behind the bar. Sixpence for a smile: there's more ways of being a prostitute than taking five pounds at the bedroom door.'

Mickey was in complete agreement with her. 'I've done much worse than hire out my body. All my life I've earned money by letting people inside my mind. Even in the middle of making love I've reached for a pencil to write down some word I could use to describe it in a story.'

'I've seen his bankbook.'

'I beg our pardon?'

'Jack's bankbook, he showed it to me. Most boys on the game are very easy come, easy go. Not that lad!'

'But why should he want to show you something as private as that?'

'To prove how serious he is about you. To show me he's not after anything. He's bobbins about you, absolutely bobbins!'

This was not an expression with which Mickey was familiar so he filed it away for future use.

Polly had not finished. 'You don't get many chances like Jack Lawless in one lifetime. I don't care who you are, you don't.'

All Mickey's objections to the idea boiled up like the raging seas. And then they boiled down. Having already trotted them out to Sorrel he did not want to put them on parade again.

But Mrs Fiddler, it seemed, was ahead of him. 'He likes your age – a bit of distinction's an added attraction. He doesn't mind the fact that your body's past its best but he knows you mind . . .'

'All this instant fancying is madness.' He was telling himself this as much as he was talking to Polly Fiddler.

'He said you already auditioned for him.'

'I did what!' It was definitely more of an exclamation than a question.

'He said he read one of your books when it first came out. And all he wanted to do was write to you, there and then. But he didn't think he'd got the proper words.'

'Which book?' Don't let it be *A Town To Remember*, he prayed inwardly. And Mickey Grimshaw was not much given to asking favours of Heaven. Just don't let it be the one I wrote 'Go away' in. 'What was the title?' he asked Polly.

'Don't know. But he said it was about the feeling you get when you think of home.'

'Oh my God!' Mickey was remembering those hurt-filled eyes. And then he remembered the months he had spent slaving over that long manuscript. Remembered thinking, 'Somebody out there will know what I mean, they'll understand and they will come and find me.'

'You've gone very quiet,' said Polly. Her tone suggested deepest satisfaction. 'Why don't you go and look for him?'

Jack was not in the Britannia Grill at lunch time. The two tables were apart again and Mickey ate on his own. Sorrel was lying down in their cabin and Mrs Fiddler had announced her intention of doing the same thing. 'But, if it calms down, I'll get up for the captain's cocktail party,' was what she had said.

After lunch Mickey made his way to the Lido and asked one of the camp waiters – a fan – whether Jack had eaten there.

'No but he came through and went out on deck.'

Mickey decided to follow this example. By now the swell was so intense that the outdoor swimming pool had had to be drained. Of Jack there was no sign, and a passing ship's officer said to Mickey, 'I really wouldn't advise you to be out here this afternoon, Sir. If you got washed over the side we wouldn't want to have to turn back for you.'

Not in the bars, not in the souvenir shops, not amongst the group of men deliberating over novelty evening ties in Harrods. Could he be listening to Miriam Brickman giving her piano recital in the theatre?

Not there either. Mickey had already tried ringing Jack's cabin and now he retired to his own.

Sorrel was lying on her bed in one of the white towelling robes from the bathroom. 'You can buy these, you know. They're cut really generously, I think I'm going to get one.'

'How are you?'

How was she? Filled with thoughts of that little bit of her body that they'd taken away: the one that they were trying to grow on a glass culture dish, in some Frankenstein laboratory. 'Okay.'

He was not kidded. Nevertheless he was on the wrong track. 'Seasick again?'

'No. Not really. I'll make tonight's party. I'm going to wear that antique Fortuni dress, the one Ruby gave me.' Only now did she half slip up: 'I've left it to the Museum of Costume in Platt Fields.'

Half was enough for Mickey. 'We'll be in New York in three days,' he said.

'Three?' The cocoon of the voyage was erasing all the edges of the usual shape of time.

'Move across. It's ages since we had a cuddle. Do I feel very fat?'

'You feel all I need.' And it was no less than the truth. Not like Barney had felt, not in any way erotic – just gloriously close and comfortable. They could have been seventeen again. 'All those dreams . . .'

And he knew exactly what she meant. The ship was ploughing its way through the ocean he loved and Sorrel was close and smelling of Moment Supreme. 'I never felt so *there* in my whole life,' he murmured. 'And Polly Fiddler says he likes me for me.'

'What did I tell you?'

'Don't get me thinking about Jack or I'll have to roll the other way.' He kissed the back of her neck and allowed the distant thrum of the ship's engines to lull him into deep sleep.

This left Sorrel with a new worry. Just what was Mickey expecting of Jack Lawless? Sexual high jinks would be the logical answer. And the porn star's revelations in AA meetings had led her to suspect that even one kiss – one which had genuine meaning to it – would be capable of throwing him into a stat of frantic confusion.

The delicately hypnotic drone of the engines was working its magic on her too, and it was not long before she found herself being rocked to sleep in the cradle of all sailors.

Mickey awoke to find that dusk had fallen and that Sorrel was already in the bathroom. As he yawned and stretched she emerged in the valuable Fortuni frock.

'You don't move in that dress,' he said lazily, 'you undulate.' The rare garment, in palest, shimmering, apricot silk, was pinch-pleated from shoulder to hem. It fitted where it touched, and this was how the near-kaftan was meant to fit. The only fastenings were tiny silken thread-covered toggles. 'You can see bits of flesh between the gaps, Sorrel. Have you got anything on underneath?' She had transformed herself into ageless, and the dark red hair – piled up on top – looked to be of the same quality of silk as the clinging evening robe. 'Fortuni was a genius.' In his mind's eye he had already donned a white dinner jacket to add to the picture she presented.

But other thoughts had been bubbling away beneath these fashion notes: Jack, Jack, what of Jack? 'I'll just make a telephone call.'

He let the number ring twenty times to allow for Jack being in the shower, but there was still no answer.

No sooner had Mickey replaced the receiver than the telephone bell began to purr. 'It's me,' said Polly Fiddler. 'Not having that injection was false economy; I'm feeling dog-rough. The captain will just have to do without me. Did you find lover boy?'

'No.'

'Me neither. I got bothered about him. I even braved it down to the gym. Oh well, p'raps he'll show up at the do.'

There is a special atmosphere to captain's cocktail party evenings. The guests at tonight's gathering would all be blue chip passengers from the Grill Rooms and the Caronia Restaurant. The large party for the common herd of the Mauretania dining room would not take place for another twenty-four hours.

'Have you noticed how everybody's walking more slowly, for swank?' asked Mickey as he and his leading lady promenaded along the long corridor of their own Two Deck. 'All the big frocks are out and the men look as though they've shaved twice.' This was said out of the corner of a serenely smiling mouth; it was as though the pair of them were back on the stage. 'What the fuck *have* you got on underneath that dress?'

'Tiny pants and one of those old-fashioned half-cup bras; the kind that used to go over the bed-end with a thump.' She had reverted to her normal voice.

'Shh,' reproved Mickey. 'Not in front of the Holy Family!' A cabin door was open to reveal a dressing table covered in jewelled icons and dominated by a gilded crucifix, swathed in rosaries. 'My God! I wonder whether they've also got somebody from Securicor in there?'

'It will all belong to one of the holy ladies,' said Sorrel. 'They're enjoying the ultimate Catholic luxury, they're travelling with their own private chaplain.'

'How on earth did you learn all this? Lift or stairs?'

'Let's walk. You learn all the best gossip in the launderette. One deck down, next to the synagogue. They discuss everything from the size of Jack's dick to the woman of seventy who spends the whole day wrapped in bandages.

She only takes them off in the evening, and she's supposed to look twenty-five then.'

The cocktail party was in the Queen's Room. As they queued to get in, flashbulbs were exploding at regular intervals at the head of the line. And in the distance a harpist was playing 'Don't Cry For Me Argentina'.

'I wouldn't cry for anybody in this pampered gathering,' observed Mickey. 'Not unless it be poor John and Rosemary.'

Captain and Mrs Burton-Hall were positioned just inside the doorway. That was where the official photographer's flashbulbs were going off.

He's handsome and she's beautiful, decided Sorrel. They were both a mite on the short side, like British royalty. And they were even nodding and smiling like puppets out on parade. If Sorrel was aware of this, it was because she often had to hide behind a similar act herself. They're very good at it, she decided. And the woman's evening dress is every bit as antique and valuable as my own.

Mickey must have spotted it too because he came straight in with, 'Where did you get that, Rosemary?'

'Los Angeles. A film studio auction. It's one that Adrian designed for Norma Shearer.' She had the very faintest hint of a Northern Irish accent and eyes which brimmed with fun. 'Have you been being very wicked, Mick?'

'I'm sorry we didn't get to have the pleasure of your company at our table,' the captain was talking to Sorrel. His white mess jacket made the suntan and the good teeth and the beard look like something else out of a film. 'Mind you,' he nodded towards his wife and the author who were both busy laughing, 'Those two together can be a bit of a handful.'

Sorrel was startled to find herself feeling the faintest stab of jealousy. Mick was her own private unicorn, not somebody else's.

'That's the most beautiful Fortuni dress I've ever seen,' said Rosemary Burton-Hall. Her tone betokened genuine admiration for great craftsmanship so Sorrel decided to like her.

Flash! The photographer had chosen the moment when they were all smiling.

'There's one thing about them that isn't traditionally British at all,' said Mickey, as he and Sorrel moved into the primped and scented throng. 'They're absolutely mad about one another and they're not afraid to show it.' His eyes were already raking the chattering crowd for Jack. 'Did you know that a sailor only has three pairs of underpants? One on, one clean, and one in the wash. Rosemary once told me that.'

'Only three? Even the captain of the *QE2*?'

'Oh I expect he's lashed out on a few more by now, but that's how they're trained at naval college. And they wash them by trampling on them, in the shower. I find it rather Chinese.'

Sorrel was still watching the captain's wife. 'They *are* just like us,' she said. 'Permanently on display.'

'Would you have it any different?' he asked her sternly. 'We can't complain, it's what we chose. And look at the perks it brings us.' His spirits were rising audibly. 'I love this Transatlantic run – love it! See that woman in the black satin halo hat? She's Puerto Rican. I've been on with her before, she even wears hats at breakfast. And as we get towards New York they'll get bigger and bigger. The woman next to her, the one in the silver cake-frill dress, has a whole cabin full of dolls; she gives cocktail parties for them.'

Registering the expression on his companion's face, he said, 'No it *hasn't* got anything to do with real life, Sorrel. Quite frankly you can have enough of worthy causes – in my experience they only write back and ask for more. Shelter must have spent more on postage than I ever sent them in the first place!' This diatribe was interrupted by a white-jacketed waiter, offering glasses of champagne from a silver tray. 'Such a pity you haven't got old ale in a sweaty clog for Miss Starkey,' murmured Mickey.

She decided to speak up for herself. 'Actually, do you have anything non-alcoholic?' This first waiter lifted an eyebrow at another one who hurried across with a similar tray of orange juice.

Helene Kramer, the American psychic, emerged from the crowd to take a glass. 'Vitamin C is supposed to be good for *mal de mer*,' she said. 'At least the sea's settled down a little. Art,' she called out to her husband, 'get me one of those little lobster patties, get two while you're at it.'

Above the delicate strains of the harp and the polite hubbub of conversation, voices were beginning to rise up in something which sounded suspiciously close to exasperation. Women's voices. The more restrained one belonged to the social secretary who was saying, 'The thing is, tonight's party is for Grill Room passengers.'

'That doesn't apply to me.' This other female voice was as slurred as it was strident. 'I am above class distinctions. I always eat in my cabin.'

Through a gap in the throng Mickey saw somebody he had not seen in years.

June Gee.

Not black-wigged Stella Artemis. No, that bad nylon wig had been cast aside to reveal terrible old June in freshly peroxided glory. She had even tucked white gardenias into the piled-up blonde hair, and trussed herself into a gold-sequined sheath.

'Dear God,' breathed Mickey, 'it's an old silver one of Shirley Bassey's, gone rusty. She looks for all the world like bad drag.'

The social secretary was attempting to placate the attempted intruder with, 'These mistakes do happen. If you look at your card you'll see that your invitation is for tomorrow night.'

June's voice turned into a self-pitying whine. 'Not wanted, eh? Not good enough. It's come to that, has it?'

Speaking quietly Sorrel said, 'I never thought the day would dawn when I'd actually feel sorry for her.'

But Helene Kramer, was having none of this. 'I'm much more sorry for the people she said she'd cured of cancer. For my money, selling false hope has to be the ultimate sin.'

'Yes but look where it's got her,' said Mickey. 'God knows I hold no brief for June but this is just like Buttons being thrown out of the ballroom in *Cinderella*.'

'The zip fastener on that frock is under terrible strain.' Sorrel had been watching June as she turned her back on the gathering. Now she began to move away – defeated. 'Oh look, somebody's taken pity and followed. It's that white streak woman, from the Height.'

'Oh her,' said Mickey dismissively. 'I tried being polite and she snooted me.'

But the sight of June had reminded Sorrel of her own programme of recovery. 'Yes but we can never really see inside anybody else's head, so we can't know what motivates them.'

Dinah had no doubts whatsoever about her motives: she wanted revenge for the horrors that the spiritualist's announcement of Rory's 'death' had brought about in her own life. 'Miss Gee,' she called out quietly. 'It is Miss Gee, isn't it?'

June turned. 'Travelling incognito,' she mumbled. 'But I thought I'd let my public catch a glimpse of the real me. Thought it might boost the attendances at my lectures. It's that cruise director,' she added in paranoid tones. 'He sneaks in at the back and counts heads. I wouldn't be surprised if he radios reports to New York.'

Dinah would have liked to have kept June moving but the flabby clairvoyant was having none of that. 'Did you see Sorrel Starkey in there? I knew her when she was still called Sheila.'

If I don't urge her out, thought Dinah, people will remember that we were together and that won't do at all.

But June hadn't finished. 'I knew Mickey Grimshaw was queer before he knew it himself. A tuppenny poof from Irlams o' th' Height!'

'How would you like to come to my cabin and have a nice quiet drink?'

'Now you're talking!' June finally allowed herself to be steered out of earshot of the harp music.

Still listening to 'Can't You Feel The Love Tonight' the 'tuppenny poof' had stopped thinking about June Gee. Instead, his eyes were searching the chattering throng for a glimpse of Jack Lawless. They did not find him. Eventually they came to rest upon the bulky man with the failed hair-transplant, the one Jack had gone off with the previous evening. He appeared to be somebody with eyes on a detective hunt of their own.

Mickey decided to make a conscious effort to engage Helene's husband in conversation. 'Have you got a new book out?'

'No, I haven't published anything since *You Can Have What You Want*. What became of that friend of yours who was so impressed by it?'

'They split up,' said Helene dryly.

I've barely thought about Joe since I got on board, thought Mickey. At least Jack Lawless has done that much for me. I should be grateful to him; I should be doing something in return.

The hair-transplant man began moving towards him. Once again he was in a brocade smoking jacket – this time in peach. It did nothing for his flaking pink complexion. And a pair of watery, little, blue eyes was attempting to attract Mickey's attention.

In an effort to avoid him, Mick turned to Sorrel and said, 'We should really invite Rosemary and John to dinner. The captain's table is in the Caronia and they're not allowed in the grills unless they're invited.'

Helene Kramer said, 'Did you hear about that woman from one of the penthouses? They invited her to dinner at their table and she sent a message back saying that she didn't eat with the crew.'

By now the hulk of a man in peach brocade was at Mickey's elbow. 'Could I have a word?' he asked.

Mickey, waiting for him to say more, found himself being edged away from the others.

The American cleared his throat and then whispered in

the Englishman's ear, 'Have you seen anything of "Mr Eleven Inches"?'

'Jack?'

'It's only ten and a half, actually. A friend of mine measured it.'

Why do I want to thump him? wondered Mickey. Jack's private parts are distributed worldwide on video, so why am I feeling as though somebody's just insulted my little brother? 'No I haven't seen him.'

'He's one mighty jumpy young animal.' The man had a cocaine-user's persistent sniffle. 'Mighty jumpy. Of course the stewards are fascinated by him – absolutely riveted. They watch his every move. Nobody's seen him since he went up on the top deck in that big storm.'

And my words sent him there, thought Mickey.

'If you look closely on the videos you can see scars on both wrists. It's only to be hoped . . .'

'Yes it is,' said Mickey too loudly. 'It *is* only to be hoped.' I wrote 'Go Away', he thought desperately; I wrote it inside a book he really cares about. But surely that couldn't be enough to . . .

The man cut across all of this with, 'He's not himself these days. He's quit his habit; I know that for a fact. And when I asked him to name his price – hardly an insult in that world – he told me to get lost.'

'He did?' Is joy, he wondered, shining out of me?

'Mick!' Sorrel was calling him, calling urgently.

'Excuse me.' He headed back to her side. 'Thanks. I really needed rescuing there.' And then he saw her face. 'What's wrong?'

'Nothing.'

It was his turn to steer her a little apart. 'Come on, what's up?'

'I might be imagining it.'

'Imagining what?'

'A pain.'

'Where?'

'Here.' One hand went to an armpit.

'Has it ever hurt before?'

She shook her head.

'Okay,' he said decisively. 'We get the doctor.'

'We don't. Honestly, Mick, I'd rather not. What could he do? And, anyway, I could be imagining it.' But she wasn't; the pain felt like a harsh pink circle with a dark red centre. 'In fact it's gone now.' A lie. 'Quite disappeared. I suppose I concentrate too much on that area, I'll just go and take a pain-killer.'

He was too quick for her. 'Why, if it's gone?'

'To make sure it doesn't come back. Promise me you won't fuss. Are you about ready for dinner?'

'I never seem to stop eating on this ship, and I'm supposed to be watching my weight. I'd even thought of waiting for the midnight buffet.'

'Why don't we both do that together? I don't need walking back, come and find me later.' The actress ever-present within, was already looking for the route of her exit – and now she saw a convenient gap in the crowd. 'Pick me up about eleven.'

She's gone, thought Mickey, and she's left me with two worries for company – her health and Jack's whereabouts.

'I just saw Mel Tormé in the corridor,' said Helene Kramer. 'He says the sea's calmed down enough for him to be able to come down the big staircase. He thought he was going to have to sneak on from the side.'

Mickey Grimshaw's own shipboard celebrity status had risen since that morning's lecture appearance. It was as though this had freed the curious to ask the same questions that haunted his life on dry land. 'Did you ever imagine it would be the success it has become?' 'Where's the real Angel Dwellings?' (At least he could now say that the Queen asked the same thing.) And 'Was Mamie Hamilton-Gerrard as big a cow off the screen as she was on?'

They always said 'cow' and almost invariably used an inflection to indicate that they did not generally employ the word.

It was a point of honour with him to answer each

question as though it was being asked for the first time. Actually, it was the only thing which kept him sane. Thirty years I've had of this, he thought; and in two seconds this woman's going to say, 'You must be sick to death of being asked the same questions.'

Having done his duty he always took that statement as his cue to ease himself out. Except where was he going? He had already searched the ship from end to end for Jack. And having made a big show of doing without dinner, what else was there to do?

I'll allow myself one gin and French, he thought, and then I'll go and have a sweat in the steam room.

By the time he got down to the gymnasium, all thoughts of 'floating five-star hotel' had vanished. Here the throb of the engines sounded much more persistent, the ceilings were low, the floors were made of riveted steel. You were definitely on a ship. And here again the swimming pool had been emptied against rough weather.

The whole place appeared deserted. Mickey climbed out of his evening clothes and hung them in a locker. Taking a crested white towel from a pile he tied it around his middle.

Deserted or shut? There was no steam left in the steam-room. *No Steam in the Steam-room*: it sounded like the title of a play about Aids. Mickey was remembering the Everard Baths from his earliest days in New York, and Dave's on Broadway in San Francisco. Establishments which had specialised in sex for exercise. You bought your ticket and you took your choice of the other ticket-holders – instant rapture in cubicles a single-mattress wide.

Most women had been horrified at the thought. Mickey's straight men friends had often voiced envy of the lack of complication: 'You mean you just say: "That was great, thank you and good-bye"?' But nobody had known about the virus.

These days it took Mickey Grimshaw fully five minutes to count his dead, and still the stragglers would come drifting in from distant reaches of the graveyard. Even now he was remembering Eek, the boy who'd had to travel all the way from Manchester to San Francisco before he'd dared to allow himself to believe he was truly queer. Eek had been taken off in the first dramatic cull; the doctors were handling things better these days.

Mickey tried the door of the sauna cabin marked 'Men'. No, it was not locked. The interior was in darkness As he stepped inside, and spread his towel on the lowest wooden bench, the slats beneath his feet were still baking hot.

Flat on his back and quite naked, Mickey Grimshaw considered gay life today. The men of his own generation, the ones who had survived the health crisis, were, for the most part, more paired-off and 'married' than straights. Instead of two-point-four children they had two-point-four dogs.

Come to think of it, they weren't his own generation. He had been around so long that the majority of these friends were at least ten years younger than himself. In some instances, twenty. Dinner parties had replaced the orgies of the bath-house era. Nowadays it was all grilled polenta and shaved parmesan and 'a particularly good Chardonnay'.

I'm not even in on that any more, he thought. Not with Joe gone. Back in the Sixties there had been a song about having stayed too long at the fair. Mickey Grimshaw let out a deep sigh.

Through the hot darkness, as if in response, somebody cleared their throat.

Mickey sat bolt upright in naked shock.

A deep voice, one which just missed being truly hillbilly, a voice which had thrilled millions by whispering out erotic instructions on the soundtrack of *Lawless Explosion*, this icon of a voice said to him and him alone: 'I'm afraid I removed the electric light bulb.'

12

A hundred yards down from the Free Trade Hall, Bud Turnock's Mini was brought to halt by the traffic lights. 'Want to tell me what's wrong?' he asked.

Dinah shook her head. 'Just take me home.'

They didn't speak again until they were passing Salford Hippodrome, where Bud said, 'We're seeing the other twins tonight, Heidi and Trudi. Heidi's mine, she's got a gold front tooth.'

He obviously wanted her to encourage him to talk about this new romantic attachment, just as she would once have talked about Rory Brogan to anybody she could get to listen. If the memory was painful, anything had to be better than the thing she'd been thinking since she'd glimpsed Rory on Oxford Road – that the idea of a corpse had been easier, much easier to handle than the reality of enduringly attractive flesh and blood. It was like one of those old films they used to show at the Gaiety, *The Return of the Living Dead*.

Why hadn't she just got out of the car and run to him? By Pendleton Church she must have asked herself this same question ten times over. And always found herself coming back with the same answers: Rory was strict, Rory was upright, Rory had rules. His family would have been certain to have told him that she had stopped being his fiancée, that she was somebody else's wife. 'Where are you going?' she asked Bud, startled.

'Eccles. You said to take you home.'

'That's not home.' The words were out before she could put a brake on them. 'Take me to my mother's.'

Saracen Street had its own Sabbath rituals. It was after two o'clock so most of the Protestant children would already have been despatched to Sunday school. And this was always the cue for cheap brocade curtains to be drawn across front bedroom windows. Sunday afternoons were regarded as permissible baby-making time.

As Bud drew his car to a halt, Dinah handed him the Boots' package. 'Can you take these back to Ellesmere Park?'

'Where shall I say you are?'

'I don't know.' There was no plan of action in her mind, just the urgent need to find out more. 'Say I nipped to my mother's. I'll phone. Tell them that.'

She had not got her front door key on her so she had to knock. All-seeing Mrs Jelly of the piggy eyes was already out on her front doorstep.

'You're soon back,' she called out hungrily. 'Married life not suiting you?'

Just open the door, Dad, prayed Dinah.

'Have you heard who's landed in?' Lily Jelly was making a stabbing gesture in the direction of the Brogans'. 'That must have knocked the sawdust out of your dolly!'

Dinah had not even thought about gossip but it was obvious there could be no stopping it. Poor John! It was the first time she had given him so much as a thought in his own right.

It wasn't her father who opened the door, it was Eva. 'You here? I don't believe what I'm seeing,' she said. 'And that makes the second time today. Dear God, I've not even worked out how to break some news to you.'

'Rory? You don't have to.' As they creaked their way down the lobby Dinah brought her mother up to date.

'Edna Tench behaved shockingly at that reception,' said Eva. 'Shocking wasn't the word! She fell on the floor, kicking, and you could see all her grey underclothes.'

By now they were in the kitchen. 'Where's me dad?'

'Having forty winks, though I should think he'll need a hundred. The Brogans were singing in the street till half-past five this morning.'

'Oh God,' Dinah flung herself into one of the unyielding fireside chairs. 'Why wasn't I singing with them?' And only now did she begin to cry.

Eva was made of sterner stuff. 'Because you weren't told.'

'You mean they knew?'

'Everybody but Tyrone. They were scared he'd talk. They'd been expecting him since Thursday. At least that's what they're saying in the paper shop. It's the talk of the Height!'

'They kept it from me on purpose? Nobody could be that cruel, nobody. Has Rory been over to see you?'

'He's been carried aloft on an old kitchen chair,' snapped Eva. 'He's been serenaded with accordions and cheered heavens hard. But no, he's not had the grace to show his face here.'

By now Dinah was sobbing helplessly, and when words did come tumbling out they were full of pain. 'He looked so beautiful, Mother. He's got a new mark that splits up his eyebrow, but it didn't stop him looking beautiful. I love him, Mother. All I know is that I love him.'

'Do you want hot sweet tea or a little drop of brandy?'

'Tea. I wouldn't want my breath to smell of booze when I'm talking to him.'

'Talking to him? What's to be said?'

'God knows.'

The tea was brewed in virtual silence. The most Eva came out with was, 'And Edna Tench is going to be a dead weight around your neck.' Then after a bit, 'I'm giving it you in a pot mug. You're in too much of a state to be trusted with china.'

Dinah took the mug from her mother and trailed off into the front parlour. For the first time in years she took up the position that had once occupied a large part of her adolescence, she waited behind the cream Nottingham lace curtain for a glimpse of Rory Brogan.

But when I see him, I know I'll run to him, she thought. And what will I say? 'Could you send Tyrone inside, please?' were the only words which sprang to mind. Beyond that, all her ideas were about as useless as screwed up sheets of paper. She tried to remember the prayer which went with the green scapular but it came out all muddled.

'Just help me, Holy Virgin, who once gave him to me outside a pub on Deansgate. Just help me.'

'What you doing talking to yourself?' Eva had stolen into the room. 'I'm not going to wake your father up. It's not as though he could do anything to help.'

'Nobody can.'

'Have you eaten anything?'

'Yes,' said Dinah. And then she wondered whether the lie could have done away with her recent prayer. 'No, I haven't. But I don't want anything.'

'They could have gone off to see that other tribe of Brogans in Levenshulme.'

'It's the first time I've ever realised what an awful hum that electric clock's got.' Levenshulme was one possibility. The other was an afternoon Mass at the Holy Name. 'Did they miss going to St Luke's this morning?'

'I wouldn't know; we weren't up ourselves. How was the honeymoon?'

'All right, I suppose.' Except I thought a ghost came and made love to me, she thought. And now he turns out to be alive and tramping the streets of Manchester. 'It was certainly different,' she observed wildly.

'Dinah . . .' It was unusual to see Eva looking embarrassed. 'Stop picking at that good curtain. Did you . . . er . . . get round to the intimate side?'

'Don't be so bloody dirty-minded,' snapped Dinah.

Eva flared up to join her with, 'And don't you speak to your mother like that! I've a good reason for asking. Not that I'm very well-versed in these matters, but if you didn't do it . . .'

'We did.'

'Bang goes your chances of an annulment then.'

'That's Catholics,' said Dinah wearily.

'I think you'll find you're wrong there.'

'We did it. I'm stuck.'

'I was only trying to be helpful,' said Eva primly. 'It wasn't an easy thing to mention. Could you fancy a play on the wireless? It's got Gladys Young in it.'

'No thanks.' And still her mother lingered. 'Why don't you go and listen to it?'

'You *are* my daughter.' This was said quietly. 'I know you was always more your dad's little girl but I do feel for you.'

This was so unexpected that the tears began again. 'What can I do, Mum?'

'Not a lot that I can see. It's been such an upset sort of a day that we're having our Sunday dinner at teatime. I'd better go and see to that joint.'

Soon the eerie hum of the clock was accompanied by distant noises of the oven door. And the sickly smell of roasting breast of lamb began to permeate its way into the front parlour.

Dinah continued to gaze through the cream lace. Eventually she saw two sets of bedroom curtains being drawn back on the other side of the street – not at the Brogans' though. Children started returning from Sunday school just as Mr Noonan's ice-cream cart pulled up. It was still horse-drawn and he only had a handbell.

Either the sound of this or the excited babble of children released had lured Josie Brogan – the spiteful sister – out onto the pavement. She was carrying a white basin. When her turn came, the ice-cream man measured nine scoops of vanilla into it. So a lot of people must have stayed the night and the ice-cream would be accompanying tinned fruit salad. Dinah had once been privy to every detail of the Brogans' routine. But they had deliberately kept her in the dark about their most important event in years.

I must be awful, she thought wretchedly. There must be something about me that's very nasty. And then she said aloud, 'But Macushla wouldn't have done this to me. She'd have wheeled herself over and told me, difficult kerbs or no difficult kerbs.' This was as good an excuse as any for more tears.

Even as she was drying them a dog began to bark fiercely. Then another barked back in answer.

And here were Rory and Tyrone marching down the street with the lurcher on its bit of clothes line. For a moment they were hidden from view by Noonan's departing horse and cart. And that brief obliteration was enough to remind Dinah of all the empty years, and to send her flying for the front door.

She flung it open and ran as fast as she could across the cobbles. 'Rory!' she called out joyously.

He froze. Tyrone and the dog continued moving but Rory stayed stock still. 'Go in,' he said to his brother. 'I'll be with you directly.'

Directly? How short did he intend their conversation to be? 'Rory,' her arms had gone right around him and all she could do was repeat his name, 'Rory, Rory . . .' Dinah might just as well have been embracing a tall cast-iron pillar-box, for all the response she was evoking. Eventually she managed, 'Could you say something, please?' And it sounded curiously formal.

'I hear you made "other arrangements".'

She could hear his mother's cold Irish tones in those last two words. 'They knew, Rory. They knew and they didn't tell me.'

She could tell that this must have worried him too, tell it by the way he said, 'Only on Friday night: they didn't know till Friday night.'

'Friday would have been plenty of time to call it off.' His body was so resistant that she felt obliged to let go of him.

'I'm told he's a man with plenty of money. They'd seen the way you kissed him on doorsteps.'

The pain in his eyes echoed the pain she was feeling inside. 'Where have you been, Rory? All these years, where have you been?'

'Wandering. I was given up for dead. The last thing I remember is being hurled into a wall with Greek writing on it.'

Just as June Gee had said! Even in this most dreadful of moments Dinah marvelled at that.

'And nowadays Greek's easier for me than English.'

'You couldn't just wander for nine years,' she protested.

'Greek Cypriots are good. I was taken in, off the roadside. I didn't know who I was. I didn't even know what I was. Dogs made more sense than me.' Only now did he look at her, really look at her. 'But I always remembered your beautiful face. I didn't know why I remembered it but it was my one treasure.' His own face was older than the one she remembered, and the lines etched into the dark tan seemed to have added a new sensitivity. 'Now I come back and find you're somebody else's.'

'Only by one night,' she pleaded. 'And even when I was doing it, I pretended it was you.'

'Then all I can say is he's got himself a bad bargain.'

That scar in his eyebrow is the one part of him my lips have never touched, she thought. But any loving ambitions were wiped out by a sudden surge of anger. 'You got in touch with them but not with me.'

'The authorities did the getting in touch. I was sure Stasia'd tell you.'

'Well now you know better. And how did you suddenly get your memory back? It all sounds a bit convenient to me, if you don't mind me saying so.'

'I do mind. Not that it's any of your business now.'

'I didn't mean to be sarky,' she said hastily. 'I'm sorry, I'm really sorry. Tell me. I need to know.'

'Over the years I got a lot of little jobs going. I was deep sea diving, down into an old wreck, and the air supply ran out. They hauled me up and put me in a decompression chamber and that's when the memory started coming back. And a pretty bloody pantomime that led me into. All the borders had altered. The red-caps weren't half surprised when I handed myself in.'

'You're not trying to tell me you managed to stay vanished for nine years?'

'That's what I *am* telling you. I've got Greek brothers now who are as good as Paddy and Tyrone. You'd have to have been in the war to understand.' His tone was distinctly dismissive.

But she couldn't leave it at that. 'Archbishop Makarios is practically in the history books by now.'

'So are you, Dinah. So are you.' He was already heading for his mother's front door.

'Rory! No.' She held on to one of his sleeves. 'Let me tell you what it was like for me. You didn't come back. There was no real word, and then this spiritualist at Pendleton told me you were dead.'

'What were you doing trusting one of those?'

'I waited for ever,' she said quietly. 'And then I settled for second-best. He's a good man but I'd divorce him tomorrow.'

'Not for me, you wouldn't. I don't want a divorced woman. She'll have waited, that's what I thought. The minute I got my memory back it was the first thing I thought of. I'll go straight home and I'll get Dinah.'

'I'm here,' she cried.

'No.' Again he moved towards the house.

This time she dodged ahead of him and risked two restraining hands upon his sleeves. 'Answer me one question. Do you still love me?'

He did not push her away. Neither did he make any move towards her. 'I'll always love you.' He said it quietly. And as he looked right into her she saw that his eyes were bright with unshed tears. 'You're mine.' His next words made it obvious that he had been giving the whole matter a great deal of recent thought. 'I know it was a long time, and I know you weren't getting any younger. But you've done it. You messed about with another man and you've married him. I'll never want anybody else, Dinah, but we can't change the fact that you've got a husband.' He spaced his next words out very carefully: 'And I would like to kill him.'

There was only one more thing she could think to ask. 'Would you have me back if he was dead? I'm not thinking of doing him in,' she added hastily. 'He's all right, you'd like him. But, if he was out of the picture, would you marry me then?'

'Let's just say I'm going back to Cyprus to be a con-firmed bachelor. Let's leave it at that. There's nothing to keep me round here. Did you know that my mother and father are going back to Ireland?' Rory let out a deep sigh. 'We've both had a raw deal, that much I will say. If they'd told you on Friday, would you really have called the other off?'

'Like a shot.'

His arms went right around her. She suddenly realised he was weeping. 'It's not fucking fair,' he sobbed. 'Life just isn't fair.' Detaching himself from her, Rory Brogan turned and walked into his parents' house without so much as one backwards glance.

And all I'm left with is a closed door, thought Dinah. And if I knock on it and demand more, where's it going to get us? Nowhere.

'Come in,' hissed a voice from across the street. It belonged to her mother. 'Come in, everybody's watching. We could have sold tickets,' she added, in more natural tones, as Dinah reached their own pavement. 'Out tele-recording, are you?' This was aimed at Mrs Jelly who 'just happened' to be brushing her front flag-stones. 'You bad old bat,' Eva muttered as she nudged her daughter into the lobby and closed the front door. 'Well?'

The only answer Dinah had to offer was a flood of tears. Tears and sobs. And when Eva tried to hold her close she pushed her away because she wanted to remain in the state where the last person to have touched her was Rory. It wasn't much but that was what she wanted, and Eva had gone and ruined it by laying a hand on her arm.

The sobbing mounted into uncontrollable hysteria. 'He's turning right round and going back where he came from.'

'Lower your voice,' said her mother. 'Think of the connecting wall.'

'Never mind the bloody connecting wall, think of your father!' It was Tommy, at the top of the stairs, in a singlet and trousers. 'Your wedding's left me with a hangover as long as it's broad, and now you're back here wreaking more havoc.' By this time he had lumbered, barefoot, to the bottom of the stairs. 'Get in that kitchen,' he commanded.

The simplest thing to do was oblige him. Dinah wondered whatever had become of the Tommy of her childhood: the father who used to ease difficult moments by playing a quick medley on the piano.

In four short sharp sentences Eva brought her husband up to date. '. . . so now all that's left for her to do is go back to Ellesmere Park.'

'No.' Even Dinah was startled by the ferocity of her own response. 'I'm not going back there. It'd be a mockery.'

'Oh yes you are,' said her father. 'You go back there even if it means me taking my belt to you.'

'Well, well, well,' scoffed his wife. 'Never laid a finger on her when she was little, left me to make myself unpopular then. It seems it took a kidney stone to turn you into Mr Big! Mr Downright Nasty too.'

'We're talking here about a girl who wanted to step out of her own class – determined to join the upper ten. You stood up in that church, yesterday, Dinah Nelson, and you promised all sorts. All sorts, in front of half the Height! Anyway, you've stopped being Dinah Nelson, you're Dinah Tench. And much luck it seems to be bringing you.'

'I told him,' said her mother mock-patiently. 'I warned him that Worthingtons on top of table wine would only aggravate his condition. But would he have it?'

'I'm not going back,' repeated Dinah.

'Well you're certainly not stopping here.' Her father cleared his throat and spat phlegm onto the fire.

'Where am I meant to go then?' pleaded Dinah.

Tommy reached into the hearth and snatched up the iron coal shovel. 'You can take this into Light Oaks Park and dig yourself a hole, for all I care. And stop looking at me like that, Eva. Wives belong with their husbands. She's going back.'

*   *   *

There being no buses on a Sunday, Dinah walked to Eccles. As she passed by The Place she didn't even think to stop. Dinah associated it with things which ran in harmony and, today, her whole life felt atonal and discordant. Neither did she spare the Catholic church more than a glance. Well, not beyond throwing the silent message 'You certainly weren't a lot of help', to the life-sized Virgin Mary in the concrete cave in the garden. Incredibly, she found herself adding, 'But don't just dump me, don't just dump me.'

The descent into Eccles was accompanied by more of the automated ice-cream bells. Never again would she be able to hear the Merry Widow Waltz nor the song 'Wooden Heart' without remembering the desolation of that afternoon. And ice-cream would be ruined for her, for ever.

Ice-cream? 'I scream' more like! Only what good would that do? And what was she going to tell John?

When Dinah eventually found herself face to face with him, in the kitchenette at Comfrey, she settled for the truth. 'Rory came back but he's going away again.' Honesty forced her to admit, 'He doesn't want me now.' And then she closed down the revelations with, 'I never want to discuss it again.'

'But you did come back,' said John gratefully. And she was reminded of a boy she had once seen being a dormouse in an infants' school concert.

Tinkle-tinkle.

Surely not more bells? This one was ringing within the house – coming from upstairs. 'Whatever's that?'

'I put it on Mother's bedside table. It's that brass souvenir with a Cornish piskie on it; we got it in Bude.'

Bought in Bude but surely cast in Hell, this insinuating tinkle-tinkle was to be the tune to which they would be expected to dance for many months to come.

No nurse lasted longer than three days. Cleaners generally left immediately after their first summons to the upstairs front bedroom. Edna Tench might have been bedfast but this did not mean that she was about to relinquish the reins of her household. The pixie hood was back in place, her blue lips were set in a straight line, her whole mind was bent on control.

In her new role of nurse-cum-maid-of-all-work Dinah hardly ever went down to Tyrell and Tench. When she did manage to snatch a little time off, her understudy, Eugene Gannon, would take over.

'Peplum Street is the Land of Love, these days,' he would tell her as he donned a printed pinny. This was a continuing saga of the Turncock twins' obsession with Heidi and Trudi ('two domineering bints in the making, if you ask my opinion'). And of Eugene's view of Avril's passion for Alistair Seddon of Aquarius Galactica: 'The man sports enough hair to make you want to hand him a violin. And there's a nasty barnyard gleam in them little orange eyes.'

Edna Tench's greatest delight came in criticising Dinah. The way she spoke, the way she walked, absolutely nothing about her new daughter-in-law was right for her.

'Mind you, I don't talk proper and I do tend to slouch,' said Dinah to John. 'But I'm going to do something about it. Lessons: I need lessons. It's months since I had a farthing in wages. You can get some cash off her and send me to elocution and deportment.'

John had worries of his own. At long last he had keys to the Peplum Street safe. But something was missing, something important – the formula of the Gentlemen's Remedy. For years this had always lain on the bottom shelf in a brown manila envelope with a red wax seal.

'I could tell him what happened to that,' said Eugene. 'On the morning of the day you got married she came down early, took it out, ripped it up, and flushed all the bits down the Dolly Varden. That red seal was bobbing on the water for days!'

When John broached this accusation in the upstairs bedchamber, all Edna would say was, 'I've committed the formula to memory. There's enough stock made up for two years. I'd say it would be in your own interests to keep me well and happy. If I drop off my perch, bang goes your guaranteed pension for life.'

In the privacy of their own bedroom John said, 'I wouldn't care but, when the new laws come in, we'll be obliged to print the contents on the side of the boxes. And your friend Daisy Carver won't be able to dive into chemists for things that have got tincture of opium in them – they're going to be made to change their formulae.'

Dinah's own changes were effected in Manchester. The deportment lessons came from Lucy Clayton's in King Street, a model agency which also offered time-killers to bored housewives. Instruction was given by a Chinese-looking girl who was said to have worked for Jacques Fath in Paris. 'Tuck your tail in, Dinah. Now then: ball, heel, ball, heel . . . measured steps.' There wasn't that much to learn so they threw in make-up lessons for good measure. Eight trips up that staircase, off Manchester's smartest shopping street, did wonders for Dinah's confidence.

Acquiring a new accent was an altogether lengthier process. Mrs Mottershead deplored the word 'elocution'. Instead she taught 'speech and drama'. Her lessons were given in a rented studio, one of the warren of little rooms which led off the galleried walkways above the ground floor of Forsyth's, the piano shop.

Mrs Mottershead's biggest claim to fame was that she had herself been taught by the woman who discovered Robert Donat. She was tall and bony with eyes that looked as though they'd been put in with a sooty finger, and she smelt of bottled lilies of the valley. 'Had it not been for clinical stage-fright, Dinah, I was destined to have been the next, great, white hope.' If Mrs Mottershead's voice was over-mellifluous, her pupil nevertheless realised that there was much to be carried away from this bare room, with its upright piano, two shabby armchairs, and a silent metronome. But she suspected that everything she was being taught would need toning down before she dared risk introducing it into everyday life.

'Repeat after me: "He called for madder music and for stronger wine",' intoned her teacher.

Dinah could not see this being a lot of use at Comfrey, where the last dregs of the sherry had been consumed by a Scottish nurse who also stole a Habitat pepper mill before departing.

Dinah and John had been relegated to the smallest bedroom in the house. There was space enough for a double bed and not much more. It was a case of creep around and climb in. They could have had the room next to Edna's, but Dinah refused point-blank to fulfil her marital duties with her mother-in-law on the other side of the wall.

She was bitterly ashamed of the fact that she fulfilled them at all. So why did she do it? Her reasons were akin to the Catholic Mass: she did it to conjure up Rory Brogan. Sometimes she even arched her back to the thought of the sacred words 'Do this in remembrance of me'. And afterwards she would wonder whether she had compounded her other sins with blasphemy.

But, at night, in that little back bedroom, she could make believe that Rory came to her. And every time these couplings were over she would look at her husband and remember Rory's words: 'He's got a bad bargain.'

She didn't like herself. She didn't like herself at all. Still, at least elocution was giving her more confidence in her own abilities. And the food she cooked for John was much more adventurous than most of the dishes which landed upon the Royal Worcester and Spode dinner plates of Axminster Road. *The Alice B. Toklas Cookbook* had joined the complete collection of Elizabeth David's on the shelf next to the cooker. And she and Avril were going to special classes with an ex-chef from the Midland – in the gas board showrooms in town.

'Monsieur Genoux is almost as excitable as Alistair,' said Avril. They had just learned how to cook *Les Tripes à la Mode de Caen*, and had moved from the gas premises in the town hall extension to the Mokarlo, a bland coffee bar off Albert Square. But all of Avril's roads inevitably led back to Alistair Seddon who lived on a barge. 'He's hugely sexual,' she boasted.

'Avril! It doesn't take much to put me off cappuccino.'

'Last Saturday night he woke me up five separate times. Talk about rocking the boat! Don't think I'm knocking it,' she said wistfully, 'but just sometimes I wish he'd leave me alone long enough to cook one of these recipes we're learning.'

'I'm not at all sure about that tripe in white wine with black peppercorns.' Dinah was eager to get the subject away from sex.

The years had not rendered Avril any less nasal. 'Is it very wrong of me to want to settle down and have kids? I'm thirty-one, Dinah. Thirty-one and well-handled. And if the truth be known, I've only ever allowed liberties because I wanted more out of life.'

'Well you certainly weren't going to get it from all those commercial travellers. Fancy a brioche?' The mention of kids had left Dinah feeling uneasy.

'I'm on a diet – again. Anyway there were only two commercial travellers. What I want is what you've got. And what do I end up with? A man who's doing Gillette out of business, somebody who drives down to Moss Side to buy cannabis off black men.'

'What I've got?' Dinah was scandalised. 'A life of carrying trays upstairs to a woman on a commode?'

'Axminster Road, I'm talking about. Respectability. Coffee mornings and cross-stitch embroidery. You weren't brought up as rough as me, Dinah.'

Nevertheless, Dinah had a long memory. 'There were a lot more than two commercial travellers. And what about the milkman who wanted you to meet him at Warrington and bring four silk scarves?'

'All of it was in the hope of a home and a family.'

Uneasiness rose up again. Dinah wiped it away with, 'Does Alistair talk much about Aquarius Galactica?'

'They're nothing like Tyrell and Tench. It's all aimed at the youth market. Everything's packaged psychedelically; their biggest advertising is in horoscope magazines.'

'What can they sell to kids?'

'Love potions. Aphrodisiacs. Paul Snowden would kill to get his hands on our firm's remedy.'

313

Out it finally came. 'Would you say that seven weeks was a long time to be missing a period?'

She did not rush to visit Dr Blakeney. It took her fully three weeks to decide which empty bottle to use for the urine sample.

'Is it true they inject the sample into female toads?' she asked the doctor as he washed his hands.

'That will be all, thank you,' he said to his woman receptionist. By now Dinah was fully dressed again. 'We'll run the test as a formality but there's really no need. You're due for a Christmas baby.'

As she looked out of the consulting-room window she could see dog roses in bloom in the formal garden of his Edwardian house. And she realised that she could expect to remain pregnant until time had stretched itself to a point where that drab holly bush would be bright with winter berries.

'Was this baby planned, Dinah?' He had come to know her well in the many months he had attended upon Mrs Tench. He would often make old Edna his last call of the morning and then he would allow Dinah to give him a cup of coffee, something which had raised the newcomer's social standing on Axminster Road. Today, on his own premises, he moved back behind the good quality fake-Sheraton desk, sat down, and invited her to do the same.

'It certainly wasn't planned,' Dinah said from the patient's winged armchair. 'I'm not asking you for a abortion,' she added hastily.

'You wouldn't get one.' This was not the man who was generally pleased to accept 'a little milk and one sugar, please'. He was regarding her thoughtfully. 'Oh well,' he said eventually. 'You're young. You're strong.'

'Meaning?'

'It's hardly the ideal environment for a first pregnancy. It could be a lot worse,' he added hastily. 'You could be a single mother on a council estate.'

At least that single mother would be in charge of her own life, she thought as she walked home. In charge and not answerable to every whim of 'the dowager-bitch upstairs'. This was Eugene Gannon's latest description of Edna. He had agreed to come round and answer her every tinkle-tinkle whilst Dinah was at the doctor's.

'So how's your back?' he cried as Dinah let herself into the house.

'What back?' An ill-considered response. Only now did she remember that she had covered her visit to the surgery with some vague reference to a pulled muscle.

But an unwary reaction had been enough to set Eugene's snake eyes dancing. 'Well, well, well,' he enthused breathily. 'Is it to be elasticated waistbands and a voluminous smock?' A white finger flew to his narrow lips, just like a ballet dancer miming the words, 'I have said too much.' Pointing towards the lounge he whispered 'She's come downstairs. It's the first step towards the motor car outing the doctor was talking about.'

'Dinah,' called an imperious voice from the front lounge. If it made a change from the brass bell, Dinah wasn't sure it was one for the better.

Edna was sitting on the settee, surrounded by glossy brochures. 'I wrote to Blake's Motors,' she said. 'John can get rid of that disgraceful old Jeep; I'm buying us all a new Hillman Minx.'

'No, please no.' Dinah had always seen John's Jeep as his one stab at personal liberty.

'I should have known better than to expect gratitude. It's time I went out, Dinah. Doctor's orders. I can't bounce around in a truck. Not with my condition. So how's the mysterious back?'

'I'll survive.'

'Anybody fancy a little sardine sandwich?' asked Eugene quickly.

'I fancy you should walk out of this room, close the

door behind you, and abandon all thoughts of listening from outside.'

'"God bless you and keep you, Mother Machree,"' muttered her employee as he reluctantly obeyed her.

'Back ache!' Edna spat out the words contemptuously. 'Did you tell him about last month's morning sickness as well? Did you mention all the extra trips to the toilet? You must think I've just come over! Anyway, where do we stand? Did he agree to shift it for you?'

'No.' For the first time Dinah caught herself feeling hugely protective towards the new life within her. 'Why should he?'

'Because this isn't a house,' said Edna icily sweetly, 'it's a nursing home. A nursing home for one person. Me. You little fool,' she snapped. 'If you'd just come to me within the first month I could have dispensed you a purge that would have got it away within the hour. As things stand, you've gone and brought medical science in.' She made it sound as though Dinah had been consulting black magicians.

'I'm only having a baby.'

'Only? *Only*?'

'If you already knew so much and you felt so strongly about it, why didn't you say something?'

The mauve lips tightened.

'Why?' persisted Dinah.

'He *is* my son you know,' said Edna, in tones that sounded curiously near to ashamed. 'To say something would have been to admit that John was no better than dogs in the street.'

'And how did John get here?' roared Dinah. She was as angry as she had ever been in her whole life.

Edna was shaking her head from side to side, like somebody double-denying something. 'Aren't I ill enough as it is, without having to admit to myself that he's done the same animal thing his father did to me. At least you had the excuse of a mother-in-law. At least you could have said, "No, John, not with Mother in the house; it wouldn't be nice." But *no* . . .' the voice continued to rise. 'You let him *invade* you.' Without pausing she shouted at the door, 'And you can take your ear away from that panel, Eugene Gannon – this is no conversation for virgins.' After a moment she hissed at her daughter-in-law, 'Go and see whether he's gone.'

'No.'

'All right then, if you want dirty washing in public we'll have it. Blakeney's not the only doctor. There are men in London who make a fortune out of illegal operations. John will just have to make discreet enquiries at the cricket club.'

'At the . . .' Dinah began to laugh wildly. 'Did you hear that, Eugene?' she called out. 'You're a vile old bitch,' she said to Edna. And just the saying of it made her feel better than she had felt for weeks. 'You don't deserve to be a grandma. But you'll be one. I'll make sure of that.'

'Do you *want* to kill me?'

'That's a very tempting question.' But the truthful answer was that Dinah Nelson had only ever wanted to kill one person. And that person was still June Gee.

By the time John's Jeep pulled up the drive, his mother had turned back into a series of padding footsteps and protesting bedsprings – heard through the ceiling above Dinah's head. She had been watching out for her husband in the bay window of the lounge, determined that the news of the baby would be broken by herself and not by his mother.

Tinkle-tinkle. Edna had timed her summons to coincide with his foot reaching the inside doormat.

'Let her ring.' Dinah was already out in the hall.

'But it drives you mad,' he protested mildly.

Tinkle-tinkle-tinkle-tinkle.

'John, come into the front room.' With a nervous glance upwards he did as Dinah asked. Light nights were back and he looked tired in the evening sunlight which was streaming through the leaded panes. Tired and good. She could already visualise him leading a little boy by the hand. Or will it be a girl? She only just missed wondering this aloud. This day had fatigued her, too.

'She's up and creaking about,' said John. 'Has there been another bust-up?'

'We're having a baby.'

In one moment he shed ten years. As he moved towards her his whole being seemed energised with happiness. No this was more than happiness, it was joy – pure joy. The faintly crumpled suit was still exactly the same as it had been before, but the man inside it was totally transfigured.

'She's said terrible things,' sighed Dinah as she got lost in a grey flannel embrace. 'She wants us to get rid of it.'

'I'll get rid of her first. A baby . . .' He was still shining with rapture. 'A bloody baby! Should I be hugging you as hard as this?'

'She thinks we're filth.'

'Filth? I never believed in God as much as I do at this moment.' His excitement continued unabated. 'Will what you've got for dinner keep? Let's go out. Let's go right back to where we started. Let's go to Prestbury. When's it due?'

'Listen! She's coming downstairs. This is the latest trick in her repertoire.' Through the open door Dinah could hear that the sound of old Edna's descent was accompanied by the sort of heavy breathing which Mrs Mottershead would have dismissed as 'over-acting'.

The Edna Tench who came cautiously into the room was infinitely frail. The strings of her pixie hood were hanging down, a blue-veined and skeletal hand held onto a glossy brochure, the feet looked too small for her late husband's indestructible brogues. 'I understand that congratulations are in order,' she ventured hesitantly.

John flashed Dinah half of a puzzled glance and merely offered his mother, 'Yes.'

'Well that's the way of the world,' she said quietly. 'That's how the line continues.'

Dinah felt as though she was being painted into a

corner; one where she could only be perceived as a liar. 'Just a minute,' she said truculently.

'Have five minutes, take ten if you like,' replied her mother-in-law calmly. 'You're going to find that there's a lot of hanging around to pregnancy. Now sit down, John. I've been thinking. You can't risk bouncing her around in her condition in that old Jeep.'

'But we love the Jeep,' he protested. Nevertheless, Dinah could see that seeds of doubt had sown themselves quickly.

'You might love it,' said Edna, 'but it could cause her to miscarry. An older woman knows these things.' The frail claw raised the glossy brochure. 'You can put your Jeep in the *Evening News*. I'm going to buy us a nice Hillman Minx.'

'Sometimes I think we underestimate you, Mother,' he said gratefully. 'Thank you very much.'

'My pleasure.' And darting Dinah the tiniest glance of triumph she marched out of the room – another Tench who could knock ten years off her own age in as many seconds.

'You fell right into it,' said Dinah. 'Right into it.'

'I don't want to be critical, Dinah, but she only seemed to want to please.'

'To please herself! Now she'll even own the wheels beneath you. I'm not kidding, she's got us stuck on fly-paper.'

'The thing is,' said John, 'you're bound to take a distorted view because your hormones will be doing funny things.'

'I give up. I just give up. And don't patronise me.'

Obviously attempting to change the subject John said, 'Do you remember the world's oldest drug fiend?'

'Daisy Carver? Considering I saw her around Salford for all of my working life, I'm hardly likely to have forgotten her. That mother of yours robbed me of my job and now we're even going to need permission to drive out of Axminster Road. I think we should get a couple of bikes!'

'A brand-new Hillman Minx isn't to be sniffed at, Dinah. You're talking a bob or two, there. Your friend Daisy's got herself in a mess – a real mess. She's keeping very iffy company. And we're the ones who promised ourselves we'd help her.'

13

The sauna cabin smelt like Northern California, it smelt of eucalyptus. As Jack's voice cut through the darkness Mickey had hastily repositioned Cunard's towel around his midriff. Now the light flashed on and Mickey said, 'You could give yourself a nasty shock, messing about with the bulb like that. Do you often remove them?'

'Always, if I get in first.' The porn star, seated on the wooden slats of the upper level, was also sporting a towel around his famous loins. 'People get very curious about the merchandise.'

Well don't think I'm looking, thought Mickey, who was already going to lengths to gaze in the opposite direction. As he stared at a knot in the unvarnished pine panelling, he said, 'Now I know how people must feel when they try to avoid mentioning *Angel Dwellings*.'

'I was just going to,' said Jack unconcernedly. 'I grew up on it.'

Which made Mickey feel about a hundred and four. And his worst fears had been realised: he had been copped semi-naked with all his dilapidations on view.

Jack was ahead of him. 'You're good for your age, except for the gut. And sit-ups would soon take care of that.'

This helped, but only a little.

Jack's next line was altogether more reassuring. 'I'd give anything for a mind that works like yours. Given half a chance, I could write a book.'

'Then why don't you just sit down and do it? That's all it takes.' It was his standard reply to this all too familiar assertion.

'I couldn't because my thoughts won't connect with the pencil. That's where you win over me.'

Mickey Grimshaw finally allowed himself to look at

Jack Lawless – really look. Dark hair, gleaming-smooth skin, deep chest muscles with nipples like Egyptian cat's eyes . . .

'You like?' asked Jack.

But it was only in the same way that Mickey would have been polite to any admirer of his television serial.

'Very much. You've not made the mistake of staying too long in the gym.'

'Actually, I won't bore you by asking you about the programme.'

'Good. I won't ask you to take your towel off.'

For a long moment Jack looked Mickey straight in the eye. Long enough to leave him wondering what was coming next. What he got was, 'Do you mind if I talk about your books?'

And he's as at ease with his own body as a cat is, too, marvelled Mickey. 'Sure I'll talk about them. Anybody who's read the longest one has to have given me at least forty hours of their life.'

'Was *A Town To Remember* the longest? That book was such a friend to me.'

I'd be a friend to you, thought Mickey eagerly. I'd be a much better friend than any of my books. But he was always fascinated by the idea of his own words establishing complete relationships with total strangers. 'Where did you read it?'

'On a night flight from Atlanta to LA.'

'It's never been published in America.'

'I just found it with the in-flight publications, in that net thing, in front of my seat. Somebody must have left it behind.'

'And here we are,' said Mickey in wonder.

'Yes, here we are.'

Silence fell. It was Jack who broke it with, 'Tell me what you're thinking.'

The truth? Why not. 'That any talent I've got has brought me some amazing experiences.'

Without so much as a heartbeat's pause Jack Lawless asked, 'Do you have a lover?'

'I did. He went. And you, have you got a lover?'

'No, no lover. I'm not saying there haven't been special relationships . . .' His voice tailed away. And then it came back with '. . . it would have been easier to talk with the light out.'

'So remove it.'

Eucalyptus blackness was restored.

'Am I really in the dark with the star of *This Man is Lawless*?'

'Yep.' Jack sounded quietly contented. 'Do you mind that I already feel very close to you? All of your childhood had to be in that book.'

'No, I don't mind. It was.' Mind? Mind! 'Tell me about your own childhood.'

'Not a pretty story.'

'Tell me anyway.' Did that faint creaking sound mean that under cover of darkness Jack was moving closer? Mickey could not be sure.

'I'd had three fathers by the age of nine. The rest was just British juvenile courts and approved schools. Only, after a bit, they changed the name to special schools – didn't change the nightmares. I was supposed to have suffered from what they chose to call "behavioural difficulties". Boiled down, it meant that I was a runaway street kid at fifteen.'

He's articulate too. Mickey was, once again, marvelling.

'What would you like from me?' asked Jack quietly.

Mickey Grimshaw had never been somebody who was short of an answer. 'I'd like to go away and think about it.' The situation felt much altered: life was suddenly filled with gloriously wild possibilities. 'Yes, I'd like to go away and make up my mind.'

'Good.'

'Is it? Good, I mean.'

'Oh yes. A punter would have known straight away.'

*   *   *

As Dinah steered June along the upper landing, the one which led to her own stateroom, she suppressed an insane urge to recite an old nursery rhyme.

> *Won't you walk into my parlour?*
> *Said the Spider to the Fly,*

But it was you who turned me into that spider, June Gee, she thought. You who changed the course of everything.

'Oh God, I'm coming unravelled,' said the psychic. 'Look, I'm shedding sequins!'

Dinah peered down at the corridor carpet, navy blue edged with a design of nautical ropes. 'No, that spangle's mauve, you're in gold tonight.'

'My confidence has taken some terrible knocks recently,' moaned June. 'It's no wonder I get confused. *And* the blood pressure's not what it should be.'

Dinah slipped her key into the lock. 'Here we are.'

'Just fancy, a chandelier at sea!' enthused June. Dinah had conducted her into the living area.

'Yes but it never tinkles. It's wired to stay rigid.' She motioned towards one of the white leather sofas. 'Do sit down.'

June stayed on her feet. 'I'm not dressed for sitting. Under this gown I'm trussed into a bit of engineering from Rose Lewis on Knightsbridge.' She edged one sequined buttock onto a cocktail stool instead, and settled a slightly soiled, white, kid-gloved elbow on the curve of the Art Deco bar. 'Did you ever encounter Rose? Most brilliant corsetière in the world. Hungarian originally. Dead now.' Maudlin self-pity took over as she added, 'I was once a fucking elegant woman.'

'Brandy?'

'Yes. And no ice.'

I won't doctor the first drink, thought Dinah. When I've got her a bit more sozzled she'll never notice what she's swallowing.

Nevertheless, Dinah's mind was already card-indexing through the possible whereabouts of the valium tablets –

the ones she normally doled out to her husband. Left to himself he would have eaten them like dolly mixtures so she was forever having to change their hiding place.

'I practically *made* Zandra Rhodes,' said June. ' "Put me in sky-blue-pink, Zandra," I used to say. In those days I didn't give a bugger! Ta.'

As Dinah handed over the brandy balloon she wondered whatever had become of the girly-girly dolly of yesteryear. It was amazing to realise that the June who had once been so awake and aware had bloated herself into this garrulous old wreck.

'Ever been to Mustique?' it asked. 'There was more to Roddy Llewellyn than met the eye. But Princess Margaret?' June's voice had suddenly gone very high society indeed. 'An amateur crooner one minute and Catherine of Russia the next. Just as you thought she was going to ask you for a safety pin, you realised she was expecting a deep curtsy.'

Does she do this in pubs? wondered Dinah. Does she spend her life renting out these tarnished memories in return for free drinks?

'Margaret never actually sat with me,' confided June. 'Sat, in the psychic sense. Mind you, I was once smuggled into Buck House, and the *Daily Mirror* had a photographer up a ladder, against a wall, outside.' Without a moment's pause she added, 'And, yes, I did go to prison.'

She does use telepathy, decided Dinah, her own mind having just leapt from Buckingham Palace to Holloway Jail. It was as though June was linking in with her.

'I don't know how my gift works, never have done.'

I'll ask her for a reading, thought Dinah.

Was it a coincidence that June immediately assumed a smugly pleased expression and held out her empty glass? If she was going to be one jump ahead the whole time, Dinah's half-formed murderous plan could be very far from foolproof.

*   *   *

Sorrel was waiting in the cabin for the ship's doctor to arrive. The pain was no better and no worse than it had been at the party. Half of her wanted to undress, to see whether her lump had grown; this was also the half which set her thinking that ordinary people were so lucky – they could have a brandy to calm themselves down.

But years of AA meetings had handed her a fatalistic attitude towards problems: she had been taught to hand them over to 'a power greater than herself'. And it worked, it really worked.

Against cancer?

This thought was so all-embracing that she didn't quite register the doctor's first knock. By the time she heard that it had definitely come again she was already on her way to the bathroom, which meant that she was handy for the door.

Dressed in mess whites, the doctor reminded her of an old-fashioned cigarette advertisement, the kind where greying temples were meant to add glamour and distinction.

'Mrs Shapiro?'

'Please come in.'

'You're on the passenger list as Miss Starkey.'

'I'm Mrs Shapiro for anything serious. And I've a feeling this is.' She offered him the concise explanation she had been rehearsing for the past twenty minutes.

'I think we'd better take a look.' As Sorrel undressed he said, 'I've written a treatment for a television series.'

Was there anybody who hadn't, she wondered.

'Sold it to London Weekend.'

This caused him to shoot up quite considerably in her estimation. And five minutes later she was ready to rank him with the doctor who discovered penicillin.

'Didn't it occur to you that the pain could have been caused by this antediluvian brassiere?' he asked.

'No. All I could think was "carcinoma". I wish I'd never heard them say that word.'

'There used to be a waxworks at Blackpool,' he said.

'It's still there.'

'Has it still got that Victorian girl in the coffin? The one who was supposed to have died from the effects of tight lacing.' The twinkling stopped. 'Are you on any kind of sedative?'

'No, I can't have them. Supervised, I suppose I could,' she corrected herself. 'But please don't offer them because they fill me with healthy fear; I'm an alcoholic.'

'Three more nights on board,' he said reassuringly. 'And then you'll have your test results. Throw that bra away.'

'I'll burn it if you like.'

'Not on board ship, please. Our greatest fear is fire.'

The ease with which he got himself out of the cabin was something else that was as polished as an old cigarette commercial.

Smoking probably bred my lump, she thought. And even when I wanted to stop, Lettie Bly was forever having to drag away on a fag, in the show. Sorrel carried the Fortuni dress into the walk-in wardrobe area and hung it on a hanger. Once again she was dressed in the oh-so-useful white towelling robe.

'Naked!' yelled a triumphant voice from the sleeping quarters. 'I met him stark bollock naked.' Mickey had returned. 'Where are you?'

'Here. But I'm coming out.'

'Actually it was a bit more decorous than I made it sound. We both kept our parts covered.'

It reminded her of the days when he had first discovered the gay scene in London. All those years ago, when such activities had been highly illegal. Which had never stopped him from haring back to Cornucopia Mews to retail his adventures to Sorrel. And now he was reliving the more recent escapade in the sauna cabin.

'He's got a thing about me,' he said in a voice of joyful near-disbelief.

'I keep trying to tell you, you're an attractive man.'

'Maybe in your world, not in mine. He loves the books. Shall I tell you something? I laid bait in *A Town To Remember*. It was as though I said, "If you're out there, come and find me." And he's here. What did the doctor say?'

It only took a minute to tell, and then Sorrel returned to the subject of bait in Mickey's plot. 'Did nobody else ever apply?'

Just for a moment Mickey looked embarrassed. 'A man with home-permed red hair once followed me around, for a whole weekend, with the book in his hand and a hopeful expression. And I had a couple of raunchy letters with Polaroids, sent care of my publishers. Sorrel, I hope you don't mind but I'm going to open one of those little bottles of champagne.'

She didn't mind – genuinely. In fact she was thrilled that Mickey felt he had something to celebrate.

He was already at the refrigerator. 'When I was sixteen I would have walked all the way to town to meet a man like Jack. A glass. Where do I find a glass?'

'On the tray.'

'At thirty I would have seriously considered sacrificing a month of my life for one night with him.'

Warning bells began to go off inside Sorrel's head. She was remembering the Jack Lawless she had heard talking in recovery meetings, the man who could sell sex without thinking about it but 'only yearn' when it came to the real thing. 'Of course, you wouldn't mind if it wasn't very sexual,' she ventured.

'Who wouldn't?' snapped Mickey as the champagne cork popped.

'I mean there *is* more to life than that.'

'He's amazing at it. I can't pretend I haven't seen the videos because I have.' Mickey raised his glass in a silent toast to the future. 'And he's that tiny bit older now, which makes him less pre-packed and air-brushed. That was the part I never fancied.' He was already savouring both the taste of the Bollinger and the idea of delights to come.

She was really worried. 'Wouldn't you settle for something platonic?'

'Why the fuck should I? He's so nice, Sorrel. Surprisingly gentle inside. But that won't stop him being wild at the other.'

Don't let him look at me, she thought. He's always

been able to read me like one of his own scripts – don't let him look.

He looked. 'You know something, don't you?'

'No, I'm just theorising.' Would he swallow that?

For a moment it seemed that Mickey would because he said, 'God preserve me from women who've been around gay men so long that they think they know everything. The one thing you always fail to accept is that we're dick-driven.'

'You have no romantic ideas about him at all?'

This sip of champagne was more thoughtful. 'Okay, I'll level with you. I've waited all my life for this man. If he hadn't turned up I would still have had a great time looking. But there would always have been something missing.'

'So the years with Joe were nothing?'

Another sip. 'They were comfortable, convenient: something we both just fell into. But Jack's the one, Jack's the real thing. And he's taken the trouble to come and find me so you can forget the word platonic.'

But she couldn't.

14

Oh that Hillman Minx! Cambridge blue, four doors, hell on wheels. This was not the fault of the manufacturers. No, all the troubles came from the woman who sat in the front passenger seat.

'I am managing director of the firm,' Edna would say. 'It would ill-become me to sit in the back. Besides, there's more room there for Dinah to spread herself out.'

By this time Dinah was six months pregnant and much changed in outline. But she had rarely felt so well in her whole life, though she did not ascribe this to the copious quantities of Slippery Elm Food that her mother-in-law obliged her to ingest on a daily basis.

'I'm sure it makes me go more than I need to,' she said to Avril. Not that talking to Avril was easy these days. She had found her first white hairs and this had heightened her craving for a wedding ring.

'I've bought a bottle of Clairol and I'm rationing my favours,' was how she expressed it. Dinah's pregnancy had rendered Avril broody. 'God knows I've always had child-bearing hips, but if my waist has got to go I'd like it to be in the cause of a baby and not just the passing years.' The Cult of Youth had dominated the Sixties. 'These days any teenager with two legs and a little bust is a dolly-bird. Me, I'm beginning to feel like an old doll. One of those on the top shelf at the fairground; the kind that never gets won.'

She looks like one too, thought Dinah. And she still looks as though she ought to be in Ukrainian national dress. 'You want to try and attract Alistair with more than sex,' she suggested.

'Nobody could take more interest in Alistair's work, nobody. Of course Aquarius Galactica has got its own Edna Tench – Mr Paul Snowden. Not that I see a lot of him but he haunts everything. Sometimes I feel as though he's even with us in bed – Alistair is very jealous of his charisma.'

These same charms had much impressed Mrs Mottershead, the drama teacher. Having mastered the basics of standard English speech, Dinah had now graduated to reciting extracts from plays. She would haul her ever-increasing weight up the stairs of Forsyth's to deliver scenes from *Time and the Conways* and *She Stoops to Conquer*. The drama teacher's famous 'clinical stage-fright' precluded any personal appearance on the boards, but it did not stop her directing productions for the Nameless Amateur Dramatic Society.

'They are more or less semi-professional,' she would say. 'And Paul Snowden would send Peter O'Toole back to the dressing room with very serious doubts about his own abilities. Dark hair always looks better on the stage than blond. And Paul Snowden's nose was not made with a surgeon's chisel, it is naturally aquiline.' Thoughts of this paragon of all the theatrical virtues had caused her to grow more expansive. 'Once baby's here, Dinah, we might prepare you for an audition.' She could have been talking about a pilgrimage to the Holy Land.

One person seemed to have ceased her everlasting trail around the streets of Salford – Daisy Carver. It took the sight of her, on Deansgate, in Manchester, to make Dinah realise this. And to remind her that John had said something about Daisy having fallen into bad company. Pregnancy, Dinah had discovered, was somewhat akin to ink eradicator or an indiarubber: the woman had simply vanished from her mind for months.

By now it was September and little Daisy was already wearing an ankle-length musquash coat, made of pelts the size of hot-water bottle covers. The brown eyes beneath the veil of an Edwardian straw boater looked so wildly dazed that Daisy could still have been dressed for last winter.

'Hello,' said Dinah as she emerged from Forsyth's shallow arcade.

'Hello ... yes ... hello.' In the months since their last meeting, the tiny creature had grown thinner, more scuttering.

Dinah, who still filled at least one painted diary a year, noted that the skin of Daisy's neck had started to hang in vertical folds, and that she had bound these together with a black velvet band around the middle. 'How are you doing?' Dinah ventured, as she registered that Daisy Carver absolutely reeked of a smell which she associated with childhood visits to the dentist's.

Not that Daisy was staying any too close. It was as though she was aware of the twitching nostril and anxious to be off. 'I'm fine,' she said, 'absolutely splendid.'

She didn't look it. And having just emerged from one of Mrs Mottershead's lessons, Dinah was very aware of the vagaries of speech: for the first time, she realised that Daisy must once have fallen under the influence of somebody with a distinctly middle-class accent.

'Never better,' cried Daisy. And then a Pickford's van just missed her as she scuttled across the road whilst the lights were still on red.

Dinah chose to cross further up Deansgate. She was on her way to Lewis's, the department store. She needed more emulsion paint from their basement.

In the early days of her pregnancy she had repainted the box room at Comfrey in primrose yellow, and replaced the picture rail with a roll of broad 'Yellow Submarine' bordering. This first attempt at home-decorating had filled her with such deep satisfaction that she had gone on to totally revamp the kitchenette. Few things in life had brought her as much simple pleasure as her own paint-roller, and then the more ambitious hack-saw and chisel.

They had also brought her father back into her life. He seemed to take a real pride in the fact that she was turning herself into a craftswoman. But he never wore his increasingly uncomfortable false teeth to visit Ellesmere Park; it was as though this was his last gesture against 'the boss class'.

'We could all be struck down with painter's colic,' said Edna Tench. But she didn't say much more than that because she was very keen on anything that saved money. In fact it was she who had chosen the 'silver birch' shade of emulsion for the staircase, the paint that Dinah was buying at Lewis's.

She generally carried it home herself, one half-gallon can at a time. John was always a little dubious about this strenuous exercise. But it got Dinah out of the house. And in her opinion, it could be no more harmful than the ante-natal clinic's own routines, which included passing giant pompoms around a roomful of other expectant mothers – with your feet. Anyway, she always stopped half a dozen times and rested the paint can, on her way to Victoria Bus Station. That was how she came to spot Daisy Carver for the second time in one afternoon.

Manchester Cathedral could not be said to stand in a close. Instead, the building was surrounded by small shops and 'family and commercial' hotels and the subterranean warehouses of wholesale cheese and bacon merchants. The savoury aroma of their produce hung on the air in the passageway that ran between the cathedral and the Mitre Hotel.

Outside a shop that bought old gold, stood an iron lamp-post with a Manchester Corporation rubbish can attached to it. It wasn't so much the ancient fur coat and the eye-veil which caught Dinah's attention this time. It was the fact that Daisy was rooting amongst the rubbish.

For food? That was Dinah's first thought. But now she observed the situation more closely, and realised that the old lady was trying to bury something beneath the discarded newspapers and half-eaten hamburgers.

'Caught you!' The words were out before Dinah had time to consider their possible effect.

It was a startling one. Before her eyes Daisy turned into a dithering wreck. 'I knew the extra empty would lead to trouble, I knew it.' The brown eyes were glittering like those glass stones set into Highland game-bird

333

claw brooches – glittering wildly. A cotton-gloved hand grabbed hold of Dinah's arm. 'You won't say anything?'

'Of course I won't. And anyway to whom?' The voice trained by Mrs Mottershead was finally confident enough to use the grammar she had been taught at the High School.

'To anybody. You see, if he found out he could cut me off. Ask me no questions and I'll tell you no lies.'

'Come into this snack bar and have a cup of tea.' No response. 'Coffee then?' But Daisy just shook her head. 'Well I'm going to have one. Why don't you just come in and sit down and talk?'

'No.' Daisy was like a tightly wound spring. And her eyes kept going back to the rubbish container, as though she was having second thoughts about the deposit she had just made. 'Except it would only draw further attention . . .' She was talking to herself again. 'Dear God, what's it come to? Whatever's it come to?'

'You tell me,' Dinah tried gently.

'"You are never to tell,"' Daisy was obviously quoting some memorably stern injunction. '"Never. Or that will be the end."'

'The end of what? Is it something to do with your "stuff"?' hazarded Dinah.

'What time is it?' Daisy's eyes went to the cathedral clock. 'Five to three.' Now she began calculating on the darned cotton fingers: 'Five minutes to the bus station, ten minutes till the bus . . . I've got to go. I've got a date with the Devil.' Again the hand seized Dinah's arm. 'You wouldn't tell anybody I call him that, would you?'

'Who are you talking about?'

'Wouldn't do to say.' Giving the rubbish can one last fearful glance, she began to rush towards the main road.

What could she have been hiding? Everything about Daisy had been so crazily frenzied that Dinah hesitated to look immediately – the old woman was quite capable of scuttering back and catching her in the act of snooping. But whatever was hidden wasn't going to waltz off of its own accord. I might just as well have that cup of tea before I investigate, thought Dinah.

The snack bar proved to be little more than a lunch counter with high stools. And one of these stools was already occupied by a woman who must have bought one of the hairdressing gadgets that were perpetually demonstrated in Lewis's basement – the gadget which left a kirby-grip anchored inside a tight sausage curl. The woman had her back to Dinah so that all the curls looked like a magistrate's wig, except for the fact that her hair was black – glossy black.

Natural not dyed, decided Dinah, just as the woman swivelled round on the high stool and treated her to a look that was worthy of a judge at the Old Bailey.

It was Josie Brogan, Rory's spiteful sister. The passing years had caused her mouth to turn down at the corners; a tipped cigarette was hanging towards the beginnings of a double chin. 'I see you're in pig,' she said, nodding towards Dinah's stomach. 'That should clip your wings a bit.'

'How's the family?'

'All gone home, all over the water.'

It had to be asked. 'And Rory?'

'You'll get no address from me.'

'I never asked for one.' But she would have done. Given half a chance – even a quarter of one – that was precisely what she would have done.

Josie leant down, picked up a string bag full of tins of cheap marrowfat peas, and then headed for the door without so much as a nod of farewell.

As she watched Rory's sister pass the lamp-post with the rubbish bin which still held Daisy's secret, Dinah contemplated her own inner madness. She wanted that address because . . . it was ridiculous. She needed Rory to know about the baby. Every fibre of common sense told her that it could not be his, but common sense and reality were something she had always abandoned in the arms of her real-life husband. 'It's John's,' she told herself out loud. 'You're barmy.'

'What can I get you?' The man behind the counter had finally deigned to notice her.

Dinah just shook her head and carried her half-gallon paint tin towards the door. It would be easier to try to discover the nature of Daisy's insanity than it would be sensible to dwell upon her own. With this in mind, she began to make her way towards the corporation trash can.

That night John arrived home with a silver rattle in the shape of a teddy-bear. It was the same one Dinah had admired in the jeweller's arcade, on the night John offered to buy her an engagement ring.

Getting a room ready for a baby and making sure that it had basic clothing were one thing, but the mother-to-be couldn't help feeling that actually buying an unborn baby a present could be tempting Providence.

However, she did not dwell upon this thought because she was anxious to tell her husband about Daisy Carver's odd behaviour.

'But what was she hiding?' he asked, after she had given him the bare bones of the story.

'John?' came a voice from the top landing. They were down in the hall. 'Is he there, Dinah?'

It was his mother. These days Edna was much more mobile. Now revealed in all her pixie-hooded glory at the top of the stairs, she much resembled their most recent nickname for her – the Inspector. 'John, there's bird-dirt on the bonnet of the Minx.'

'I'll see to it later.'

'Do it now. It could eat its way into the paintwork.' She was very proprietorial about the new car, in fact she often referred to it as 'my little motor'.

'The rattle's lovely,' said Dinah to John. 'Thanks.' She gave him a quick peck of appreciation. 'Get a window leather and I'll come outside and tell you about Daisy.'

But Edna insisted upon more than a quick rub with a

chamois leather: the whole bonnet had to be washed with Fling Car Shampoo. 'To reinforce the Simonize polish,' she said knowledgeably. These days the retired herbalist was much given to watching a television programme called *Drive In*.

It was a beautiful September evening and dogs were barking their farewells to the summer. As John attacked the car with a bubbling sponge, he said, 'Right, tell me about Daisy.'

Dinah began to recount her search in the trash can, in the shadow of the cathedral. '. . . the only thing that wasn't stale food and old toffee wrappers was an empty medicine bottle. No label, nothing.'

'So?'

'I unscrewed the top and sniffed.' Dinah recalled the moment with distaste. 'It smelt of exactly the same heavy chloroform as she did. Not like when she used to get those little bottles – much stronger. You'd have been scared to light a match!'

John straightened up. 'She's got in with an iffy chemist, down by the Freedom Hall, near to the docks. Not that there's much freedom left for the poor souls he takes advantage of!'

'How do you know?'

'I've seen them waiting in doorways for him to open. Alistair Seddon told me the rest of the tale; this pharmacist buys odd bits from Aquarius Galactica.'

Children's voices were ringing through the barking, and somewhere up Axminster Road a rubber ball could be heard bouncing on gravel. 'You mean to say that Daisy's swallowing those things in psychedelic packets?'

'Them? They're nothing.' John wrung out the sponge. 'Just old remedies in new packaging. No, this man obliges the waifs and strays of Salford with sinister concoctions of his own.'

Edna came out of the house and began to walk across the crazy-paving. 'We might go for a little run after supper,' she said, 'take our last look at the sheep for the autumn.'

'Not tonight, Mother,' said John. 'Dinah and I might have to go off on an errand of mercy.'

'Using my car presumably. And what "errand of mercy"?'

'At Sunday School,' said John, 'I was always taught that you shouldn't tell your good deeds or they didn't count.'

'Did they also mention anything about honouring thy father and thy mother?' But Edna could not have been very keen on the idea of an outing because she began to drift towards the garage. She had recently invested in a new battery charger and a foot-pump, and she was much given to checking that Mods and Rockers had not made off with them.

'You really stood up to her,' said Dinah in surprised admiration.

'You mean my guilty conscience did. I've known about Daisy and that chemist for ages. I didn't want to worry you while you were expecting.'

'Well I am worried,' admitted Dinah. 'The poor little soul was just like an over-wound-up clockwork mouse. Whatever she's on has driven her gaga, John. Absolutely gaga. But what can we do?' It was only now that she recalled his once having told her about getting some colonial Empire-builder off morphine.

'Come on.' John began to carry the bucket back into the house. 'The first thing we've got to do is talk to her.'

'But is it any of our business?' Trudging behind him had made her feel her weight and induced the beginnings of apathy.

'It's certainly *my* business. On our own wedding day I marched into a chemist's shop and almost certainly helped her down the road to ruin.' He emptied the mucky suds down the kitchen sink. 'I do feel part-responsible. And you weren't above getting her medicine, either.'

'Let's go and see my mother.'

'Why her?'

'She knows where Daisy lives.'

The Inspector, still outside in the garden, rapped on the

kitchen window. 'Dirty water should go down the grid,' she shouted.

'There are two junk shops on Broad Street,' said Eva. They were in her back kitchen. Unlike Josie Brogan, she had taken to dying her hair. The original white streak at the front was encased in a piece of the new metallic kitchen foil. She was colouring the rest back to black; an inky preparation oozed round the bottom of a soup plate and she was applying this to her roots with a paintbrush.

'You can snigger, Dinah, I used to snigger at your gran'ma, but you'll be doing this yourself before long. When you get to Broad Street you don't want to go to the first junk shop, you want the second one. It's got "We Do Not Buy Stolen Goods" on the window – probably a lie. And you've got to go down the grubby ginnel at the side, and round the back. Phew, this arm's aching!' She rested the brush back on the plate. 'What do you want with Dirty Daisy, anyway?'

Dinah exchanged a quick glance with her husband. 'I'd rather not tell you.'

Eva also shot John a glance. 'The pair of you aren't up to anything daft, are you?'

'I don't think so.'

'All right, *make* a mystery of it. The woman dwells in a shed. It sticks out from the back of the building. And even bin-men would think twice before they went down that alleyway!'

It only took them five minutes to drive to Pendleton. John was a bit nervous of leaving the Minx on the main road because there were gangs of children about. Here the noises of dogs barking, and of laughter, sounded more sinister than they had done in safe Ellesmere Park.

The ginnel proved to be a narrow passageway between two tall buildings. 'The only way down it is to push sideways,' said Dinah, 'it's just to be hoped that it will accommodate my bump.'

The alley opened out into a dank courtyard, flanked

339

on three sides by the peeling whitewashed backs of dingy terraced houses. The fourth side was dominated by a ramshackle wooden building with the word 'Bethesda' carved over the skeletal remains of a rustic porch.

'It must once have been a little gospel hall,' breathed John. The air in the gloomy quadrangle stank of chemical works and of cats, and the paving stones were littered with rusting milk crates and old accumulator batteries and sections of ancient bed-spring. 'Somebody's even left a mangle out to rot.'

'Well go on then, knock.'

He stepped towards the door but, before he could raise so much as a hand, it was flung wide open.

Daisy Carver, in the tattered remains of what must once have been a Japanese kimono, barred their way. She was holding a yard brush menacingly, and the silken sleeves of the oriental garment had fallen back to reveal arms that were little more than withered flesh around sticks of bone. 'Yes?' she snapped.

Dinah said the first thing that came into her head. 'I've never seen you without a hat before.' Daisy had a full head of luxuriant grey hair. Had the old woman answered the door of the mission in a bishop's mitre, the younger one could not have been more surprised. 'Your hair is absolutely beautiful.'

'What y'after?' Daisy was staring hard at them. 'Three times in one day is too much. What y'after, what do you want?'

'We want to help you.' John Tench's gentleness was his greatest charm.

Daisy reacted to it with, 'Nobody can. My light went out in 1917.' She was away in one of her dreams. 'It was your dad who used to sell me poppy syrup.' Her voice hardened. 'They get you used to things and then they call you names for wanting more.' Her mad old eyes flickered nervously towards the backs of the houses opposite. 'Shh,' she said to herself. 'Not on your own doorstep.'

'If we could just come inside,' ventured John.

'Nobody's been inside for years. That's why I cook over

a little Kelly lamp – the electric failed. Doesn't do to let people in. They don't just read the meters, they see what you've got.'

'You've got a problem,' persisted John. 'Those bottles have turned round and bitten you.'

'Be quiet,' she said, panicked. The sound of somebody's back door rattling open was added to the cries of distant children and the thwack-thwack of their rubber ball. 'Go away, Mr Tench. Leave me in peace.'

'You need help.'

'You're not a bad lad,' she said in grudging admiration. 'You did go into Bairstow's for me, in striped trousers and a swallow-tail coat . . .' Her eyes travelled over to Dinah: 'And you shouldn't be standing around in your condition.'

'So why don't you let us in?'

But the way was still barred with an upraised yard brush. 'That would make you the first people over the doorstep since I threatened to shoot the sanitary inspector. I've got a gun you know. Oh yes,' she called out to invisible neighbours, 'it's well known round here that I've got a gun!' She nodded towards Dinah's bump. 'When's it due?'

'Christmas.'

'I suppose I could stretch a point,' she said. 'All right then, come in.'

Daisy Carver did not just have grimy lace curtains at her windows, she also boasted double layers of chicken wire as well. The whole of the interior of the building was lined with varnished pitch-pine panelling, the vaulted ceiling was held in place by fretwork beams. It was like being inside a small-scale Sunday school. There were even wooden boards for hymn and psalm numbers.

All of the pews had been removed and . . . Dinah's powers of observation began to boggle as she tried not to inhale the combined odours of wood-resin and decay.

Everything she was seeing would eventually be committed to the pages of the painted diary. But what should she start remembering first? Furniture: a brass bedstead covered in old coats, a three-piece suite piled high with yellowing newspapers, four, no *five* big wardrobes, and sundry chests of drawers. All of these stood on bare boards.

And even that wasn't accurate: the wooden boards may have been uncarpeted but they were far from devoid of clutter. In some places the floor was almost ankle-deep in everything from egg cartons to discarded Littlewood's circulars.

After Dinah's eyes had darted through all of this she realised that John had been looking at something else. He was standing in front of a set of vast library-sized bookshelves and gazing at their contents in astonishment.

Medicine bottles: hundreds upon hundreds, nay, thousands of empty medicine bottles glistened in the dying light of the evening sun. There were tiny blue and green ones with labels that had faded into little more than brown curls, and then there were more rows of much more familiar bottles labelled 'Boots Kaolin and Morphine' and 'Abercrombie's Chlorodyne Compound'. They represented the only tidy area in Daisy Carver's temple of chaos. 'And look,' cried John, 'Here's a whole section of our own poppy syrup. I've only ever seen that label in the old sample books.'

Dinah simply had to ask Daisy, 'Why do you keep them?'

'To remind me of what I'm doing to myself.'

'So you do realise it's harmful?' She only hoped that this did not sound judgmental.

'Anyway, I *stopped* keeping them,' said Daisy defiantly. 'And that's what led to the trouble. Mr Pettinger wanted to know what I did with my empties.'

Before Dinah could ask, her husband muttered, 'He's that pernicious chemist.'

'Cup of tea anybody?' Daisy must have been recalling her manners.

'Not for me' and 'I've just had one' chorused John and Dinah, almost too quickly. It really was a very dirty shed.

But Daisy was too busy recalling the chemist to be offended. 'When I told him I had a collection of empties, Mr Pettinger said, "You're to bring all of mine back – pronto. And, in future, you can hand over one bottle empty and I'll give you another one full." And that was when he stopped putting labels on them.'

'Have you any idea what he's giving you?' asked John.

'One of the other ladies – you get to know one another when you're standing waiting for him to open – she's a struck-off nurse. And she said they were his own version of Brompton cocktails.'

Once again John treated Dinah to an aside: 'It's what they give to terminal cancer patients.'

But Daisy must have overheard him. 'There's no *giving* to it,' she snapped. 'That man's had a mint of my money.' Her voice drifted into one of its hazes: 'It all started because he hadn't got the patent diarrhoea mixture. "We can mix you a little something of our own," he said. You could tell the woman assistant didn't want anything to do with it, she moved right down the counter and acted as though she was otherwise engaged.

'But he said he was very happy to oblige. And he didn't make me sign the poisons register. So I went back. And I kept on going back. Only, one day, he didn't have any. And that morning, nothing I could get from any other shop seemed to touch the spot. "Come back tomorrow," he said, "I'll have put some more up by then."

'Sweat? I was running in it! That was the first night I knew what it was to sweat like a damp cellar.'

John interrupted her with, 'And could I suggest that when you went back the next day the price had gone up? A friend of mine told me about this carry-on. It's bloody disgraceful.'

'The price has gone up twice since last Whitsun and I've started to get scared of the stuff. That's the only reason I'm telling you. Do sit down.' Every now and then the woman she must once have been reasserted itself. 'Shift the newspapers onto the floor. Whoops . . . you've walked into the cat's dinner,' she said to Dinah. 'Never mind, it's only boiled pluck. Scared I am, really scared. Sometimes I find meself in the middle of traffic with no memory of having left the kerb. And dreams and what's real get very mixed up. You *are* here, aren't you?' she asked not without humour.

But all frivolity fell away as she cried out, 'I've turned into a zombie and I know I must smell of the stuff because people make cracks about somebody having left the gas on.' Her voice dropped to ashamed. 'I nod off on buses. Inspectors and conductors have to wake me up at the terminal.' Tears began to roll down the seamed old chamois leather cheeks. 'I'm lost,' she wept. 'Fogged up and lost.'

'Yes you are,' said John. 'But we've come to bring you back to yourself.'

In the years to come, that October, the month of Daisy's recovery, would always be how Dinah chose to remember John. For his firmness and kindness, and for an authority which his mother had never allowed him to exert in Ellesmere Park. 'We'll need people we can trust,' was what he'd said. 'What we're going to do is strictly illegal.'

'What *are* we going to do?' asked Dinah.

'The less you know the more innocent you'll sound if you're ever questioned. Who do you trust?'

Dinah answered unhesitatingly, 'Avril and Eugene.' By this time she and John had already begun the mammoth task of cleansing and tidying up the interior of Daisy Carver's Bethesda shed.

'But not too much,' begged the addict, who had already panicked at the idea of being asked to decide which of the forty bedraggled remains of hats she wanted to keep.

'All of them,' she said in the end. And it was the same with battered shoes and gloves and with a mountain of old handbags. 'Those that weren't my Jessie's were her mother's and her sister's. I often think they're watching,' she explained. 'If they are looking down on us, they must be horrified at the state I've let their things get into. You must see that I can't just chuck their good things out.'

Empty photo frames with cracked glass, unfinished needlework abandoned half a century earlier, cards of perished elastic, all of these were also judged to be valuable.

But at least the windows of the shed got cleaned, and the floor was brushed into view again, and the shiny brown leatherette-covered armchairs were divested of their piles of newspapers – even though this was done to cries of, 'You're chucking out Mr Churchill's rise to power and the whole of the Abdication!'

John maintained that Daisy was 'doing anything and everything to put off the evil moment when we start to detoxify her'.

But the woman they were trying to help had overheard him. 'Let me tell you why I want to keep me collection of empty bottles. I want them there till it's all over. I might be daft but I had had this dream of the three of us taking them down to the public tip. It was beautiful, we was like people on a picnic.'

John smiled encouragement at her but his mind was plainly on other things. 'Your whole problem started with our poppy syrup,' he said. 'I've made some up to the original formula. What we're going to do is reduce the dose on a regular basis.'

'I've tried cutting down on my own before,' protested Daisy.

'You didn't have help then,' John reminded her.

'I'm still scared I'll slip down to Pettinger's when nobody's looking.'

'No you won't because I've just been and spoken to him: at home, in front of his wife.' This *was* a different John. 'You've had your last bottle, Daisy. Mrs Pettinger's threatened to shop him if he sells you one drop more. She's a big woman and she reduced that little weasel to bitter tears.'

But Daisy had not finished. 'After you've gone home, I could still slip down to Boots All-Night Chemists. It's years since they warned me off. I bet I could still wangle meself a drop of something or other, to keep me going. It's not as though you can go and see Mr Boots! I'm only telling you because I know what I'm capable of.'

'Do you remember that photograph we took of you?' asked John.

Here we go, thought Dinah. Here's where the balloon goes up. John at least had the grace to look embarrassed as he said, 'We've taken the liberty of sending the all-night branch a copy, with an anonymous note asking them not to sell you anything morphine-based.'

'There's another late-night chemists at Bolton,' said Daisy defiantly. 'Open till nine, I know all the dodges.' And then: 'If you've any sense you'll send them a photo too.' It was as though she was blocking off her own final escape route. 'I want to manage it,' she said to herself, 'but I'll never do it, never.'

'You will,' said John. 'You're going to be able to walk past Pettinger's shop with your head held high.'

'I don't think he saw it as wrong,' mused Daisy. 'I think he was on something himself; you get to know the look in the eye.' Her voice filled with awe. 'When I first touched that stuff of his, it was a bit like being kissed by God.' Awe vanished. 'It didn't take me long to realise that the Devil himself lives near the docks, and he's got himself up in a white coat.'

The following morning, detoxification began in earnest. John had some holidays owing to him so he was able to be on hand to supervise the early stages of withdrawal. Dinah was there to make endless pots of tea and to feel generally helpless.

Only Daisy Carver could know the true realities of the situation, and for the first three days she was in no position to explain them coherently. As she lay sweating and twisting and turning, inside freshly laundered sheets, she spoke of hearing invisible brass bands, and she recoiled from the words of some phantom hell-fire and brimstone preacher. She claimed he was telling her, over and over again, that she had brought this damnation upon herself.

'He says he's going to make every minute last an hour,' she gasped. 'And, by God, he's as good as his word! I've got knives in the shanks of me legs and they're twisting and turning. I could draw you a map of all the muscles in my body. They're all at war with one another.' These revelations were punctuated by sudden cries of 'Bucket!' and vomited rushes of black bile.

Dinah opened the main door of the miniature Sunday school to let in some fresh air, and motioned to John to join her in a courtyard. 'You do realise we could be killing her?'

'No. So far she's bang on target. I didn't just go into this blindly: I rang a Drug Help Line in New York.' This new John was full of surprises. 'I got it out of one of Alistair's hippie magazines. And you're only privy to half a story.'

'Tell me the whole one,' begged Dinah. 'She's got me worried to death. 'The way she screams for those little glasses of that stuff of yours is awful.'

'Somebody should stay with her tonight.'

'What's the whole story?'

'For her own good you're better off not knowing. Do you think Avril would come and stop over?'

'I'll stay myself. You can tell your mother I'm with mine at Saracen Street. Don't invent an illness though, I'm too superstitious for that.'

This was the night when Dinah Nelson learned that it is truly darkest before the dawn. Through the wire-netting at one of Daisy's windows she spent what seemed like for ever watching the sky turn to solid black velvet before a pale glimmer of light began to twitch in the darkness, and then it magnified itself – until all of morning had broken over the broken chimney-pots across the courtyard. And she finally understood what Macushla had meant about getting up to see the day break with somebody you love because she found herself wishing that John had been there to share the wonder of the newness of it all.

John not Rory. That had come as a surprise. Of course, in the greater scheme of things Rory Brogan would always be her one real passion. But John was her reality. And love had managed to find its way in.

The night in the shed had offered Dinah no possibility of sleep. 'Just hold my hand,' Daisy had begged. 'I'm full of terrible fear.' Every now and then the old woman had dozed off but fear must also have haunted her dreams because she kept on letting out distressed cries of 'Help me, Jessie', and 'I hurt again'. Mumbled ravings too: 'I'm sorry, Jess. I'm truly sorry. I only started doing it because I didn't want you to be on your own in that cold grave.'

Now she was turning the pillow over with her eyes closed and muttering, 'Which shop shall I start at today?'

'It's morning,' announced Dinah loudly. 'We've just been given Pendleton back, and it's all brand-new.' Daisy opened her eyes. 'How are you feeling?'

'I think I could eat some salty porridge. And I've not woken up with an appetite in years.' But within minutes she was wondering aloud as to when John would arrive to administer her measured dose of his liquid.

And when he did come, the contents of the little medicine glass were a shade paler than they had been the day before. Daisy did not fail to notice this and by lunchtime she was watching the clock for her next infusion.

Dinah took her husband on one side. 'How can you be sure you're not swapping one bad habit for another?'

'Because I'm not. Here you are, Daisy. Can you hold the fort a bit longer, Dinah? I'm needed at the office.'

By four o'clock she was becoming only too aware of her own advancing pregnancy. Her back was aching and both her swelling ankles and the baby, kicking out restlessly from within the womb, seemed to be protesting that they had been too long denied of sleep.

Just as *Children's Hour* was starting on the Home Service, relief arrived in the shape of Eugene Gannon – the first person to make any fuss of the cat in days. Both he and Avril had already been systematically introduced to Daisy, and after he put on the kettle he gazed around in wonder at the changes which John and Dinah had wrought in the Bethesda shed.

The wide-eyed Irishman brought a great rush of new energy onto the premises. 'Don't you resent all this cleaning up that's gone on around you?' he asked the woman in bed. 'Myself, I like a bit of clutter: we always used to have a tame hen that lived in the kitchen at home.' With that he took off his crow-black raincoat and brewed the first of what would eventually be many, many pots of tea.

As the autumn days grew shorter, the contents of John Tench's medicine glasses of special herbal 'cure' gradually turned from deep gold to pale straw-coloured. And the shadowy interior of the shed took on the atmosphere of a private club, a setting which could have been designed for the exchange of confidences. The process of tidying up continued, and the revealed contents of Daisy's wardrobes, her drawers and her ottoman trunks made ideal cues for conversations of deepest intimacy.

'Mother of God but this dance frock is purest Lily Elsie,' cried Eugene, late in the afternoon of the same day the gas was reconnected. 'It could have come straight out of *The Dollar Princess*.' The dress, draped across his black front, looked as though it had been woven from gentian violet cobwebs.

'Jessie's sister's, originally.' Daisy herself was in a grey afternoon dress (circa 1911). And if she glistened with unaccustomed cleanliness, it was probably because she had been dragged off to Ladies Night at the steam baths – to sweat the last of the toxins from her system.

Eugene was still fingering violet lace over watered silk. Looking at his own reflection in the long mirror which lined the wardrobe, he said quietly, 'It would have been lovely – lovely.'

'To have worn women's clothes?' asked Daisy cannily. There was no criticism in the question. In the past few days they had all been through too much together for there to be any question of that.

Nor was there heavy concern within the answer. 'No, no, no,' piped Eugene melodiously, 'the clothes would have been merely incidental. I would just like to have been a lady so I could have loved a man.'

'I'm jumpy,' said Daisy. 'Quarter of an hour to me next glass.' She shifted her attention back to Eugene. 'What's to stop you loving a man anyway?'

'Just the Church, just the Pope, just nineteen hundred and sixty-odd years of Christianity. And if I so much as *think* about it I have to confess to Impure Thoughts.'

'That means I must have done impure deeds,' said the woman in the antique afternoon frock. 'And they were done for love so they were wonderful!' Even without the aid of morphine she was still capable of floating off into reverie. 'The very first time was at Simpson's Hotel in Scarborough. We went there especially for romantic purposes. I was still being passed off as Jessie's maid at the time.'

'But that's awful.' Dinah moved across the room to put the kettle on. 'Why did she have to pass you off as a servant?'

'Because I talked rough and, even when she gave me money to buy clothes, I'd no idea of style. But she soon got me sorted. By the time we went down to Torquay she had me absolutely covered in buttons and bows. Of course Jessie always favoured a collar and tie herself. And away from her mother she sported a monocle. That was why she used to sing "The Piccadilly Johnny With The Little Eye-Glass". But she did like me dressed nicely.'

Dinah suddenly realised that this must have been why she had never seen Daisy out twice in the same outfit. That her elderly friend must have spent many decades, on park benches, dressed in anticipation of visits from a dead girlfriend – someone she had been constantly attempting to sip back from the past. And now Dinah came to think about it, this was no odder than her own bedtime adventures with the phantom Rory.

Eugene must also have been dwelling inwardly upon himself because he said to Daisy, 'I suppose it was all right for you and your friend because you had no religion.'

If this was a statement that was tinged with mild resentment, Daisy's reaction blazed with fury. 'No religion? I'll show you no religion!'

By now she had rushed at a tall chest of varnished wooden drawers and was pulling the middle one open. 'What do you think these are?' In her hand she had a triptych of icons: enamelled and jewelled portraits of the Holy Family, each one sitting inside a golden archway. 'That's how much "no religion" she had.'

'It must be worth a king's ransom,' gasped Dinah.

'I've got seven: all sizes, all different.'

The next words burst out of Dinah before she'd had time to consider them: 'And you live in a shed?'

'I never meant to roll downhill, it just happened. But I'm not having him say that Jessie was godless. First she was very High Church – used to go all the way to St Benedict's Ardwick. And then she gave up Christianity in favour of the Order. They were a gang of sacred fanooks who used to meet just round the corner from you,' she nodded at Dinah. 'Magi House, Ellesmere Park; it all went up in flames. But I've still got souvenirs of them.' From the same open drawer she produced a handful of turquoises carved in the shape of beetles. 'Egyptian scarabs. I can hardly credit, now, that we used to queue up to kiss 'em. Veneration, it was called.' Daisy's eyes went back to Eugene. 'If you're that way inclined, I do think you should try loving a man, before it's too late.'

Eugene did not reply, he just hung the violet dress back in the wardrobe regretfully. And before long it was his turn to be replaced by Avril. It was never a matter of one coming and one going: the party just swelled for a bit and then diminished as somebody was lured away by the distant sound of home-going buses.

'And it does feel like a tea-party, too,' said Avril. 'It's much less of a sick room than when we started. Daisy doesn't have the cramps any more, doesn't do that imitation of a caged lion . . .'

'No but I am missing something,' insisted the centre of all their attention. 'It's the smell of chemists' shops. I still keep imagining myself walking past those rows of tins of baby powder, with fear in my heart.'

'Of what?' asked Dinah.

'Of the dispenser. For years dispensers have had the power to make or break my day. I've often been as far afield as Wigan. So that walk from the shop door, a strict thirty seconds after opening time, was always filled with hope and terror.' She treated them to a haunted smile. 'I'm giving that up as much as anything else.' Now she began peering at one of her keepers. 'Avril, have you gone deformed?'

'Me? No, why?'

'You keep holding your wrist at a funny angle.'

This was the moment Dinah noticed the engagement ring. 'Insanitary Alistair has never proposed?' She asked the question with joy.

But Avril chose to answer with considerable hauteur. 'What was that you just called him?'

The nickname 'Insanitary Alistair' was a private joke which had grown up between Dinah and John. 'It's just that he has all that raggy beard and hair,' she explained lamely.

Avril was plainly in a forgiving mood: 'If you saw him in his Y-fronts he's just like the Yeti.'

Through that wall is a junk shop, thought Dinah. And beyond that is Bolton Road with 57s and 77s and number 8s going to the Height. And would anybody sitting on top of one of those buses ever realise that they were within twenty yards of an old woman coming off patent medicines, and a man who can't have the love of another, and a girl who's just got engaged to somebody with more hair than the Missing Link? Or was all of life like that? Were there bits of the extraordinary going on along every single bus route?

It was later than the usual time of day when John generally came in after shutting up Peplum Street. 'But he went off early, to harvest some late marigold seed at the Growing Grounds,' said Avril.

Daisy looked perturbed, 'Tonight's the night he should be bringing me a fresh bottle of my special stuff.' There were only dregs of John's replacement elixir left at the bottom of the clear glass bottle.

'It's all made very secretly,' said Avril. And then she reverted to a previous subject: 'Alistair may be hairy but he's absolutely scrupulous about personal hygiene: I'd like that to be properly understood.'

'Absolutely,' said Dinah, only hoping that it hadn't come out too quickly. There were no two ways about it, Alistair Seddon's aura was distinctly gamy.

'John goes upstairs to the little lab off the top consulting room and brews it there,' said Avril. 'I should think it's the first thing that's been made up there in years. Let's have a sniff at that bottle,' she said to Daisy. 'Have you any idea what goes into it?' she demanded of Dinah.

'None.'

Daisy could have been handing over the crown jewels. Avril removed the cork and sniffed.

'Please put that down.' Unobserved, John Tench had stolen quietly over the threshold of the shed. 'Before you ask, I *have* brought you some more,' he smiled at Daisy.

And for a moment – just a fraction of a disloyal moment – Dinah was left wondering whether her husband could be turning into a new breed of Pettinger. It could not be denied that Daisy's whole life seemed to revolve around the morphine substitute.

These thoughts which had rubbed Dinah with guilt, seized her again in the car on Eccles Old Road, and they were still lingering around her brain as she and her husband walked into the lounge at Comfrey.

Edna Tench had recently developed a new trick. It started when she unearthed an old photograph of John, aged three, with Little Lord Fauntleroy curls and a huge satin collar. John would willingly have despatched this chromium-framed portrait into the bin but Edna had a use for it.

It had become her new friend. Anything she couldn't face saying to John and Dinah was addressed to the child in the picture. Some of the things she said were downright manipulative ('How nice it would be, John, if you were to stop wearing workmen's blue overall bottoms and pretending they were trousers'). But today her growing jealousy of the attentions being paid to Daisy Craven manifested itself in a new way. She regarded her grown-up son coldly, pointed towards the framed photograph, said, '*That* is the little boy I love,' and left the room.

'John . . . ?' As he handed her a drink, Dinah simply had to ask him something. 'Thanks. How dangerous is that stuff you're giving Daisy?'

'Not dangerous at all.' These days the sherry bottle and the glasses were openly displayed on top of a set of Habitat bookshelves, one of several items of new furniture bought against the day when they would have a home of their own.

'You mean you've reduced the strength?'

'I mean it never had any in the first place. Cheers!'

Dinah did not even think to take a sip from her glass. 'So why did you pretend it did? All the rest of us have been treating that stuff like Communion wine.'

'That's exactly how you were meant to treat it.'

'Did you know that there's a pompous streak in you? It needs watching.'

He refused to rise to the bait. 'Come here, let me hug both of you.'

'I doubt you've got long enough arms,' she said gloomily. 'Why have you kidded her?'

'I never meant to.' He was holding her as close as her bump permitted. 'When I phoned that Help Line in New York they said that reducing the doses wouldn't work. That the only thing to do was cold turkey her – stop the drug altogether. She's clean, Dinah. The last vestiges of that muck was sweated out of her in the Turkish bath. She's absolutely clean.'

'The only dependence now is psychological.' The conversation of the previous evening had begun again over the Kellogg's boxes. Edna Tench thoroughly approved of Corn Flakes, she considered that Dr Kellogg had invented

354

them in a good cause: he had been seeking a cure for masturbation in men.

But she was not sure she approved of the idea of getting a woman addicted to a solution of water, harmlessly coloured with saffron and flavoured with brown molasses. By now John had seen fit to make Edna privy to the whole story. 'Strangely enough,' she said, 'quite by chance you've hit upon the same route your grandfather used with laudanum-fiends. His name for that opiate was "the tuppenny ticket to madness".' When talking upon her own subject Edna regained all the authority that had once dominated Peplum Street: she became somebody worth listening to. 'But he always said that you couldn't just reveal that you've deceived them; you have to make an event of it.'

'How?' asked John.

'Cases vary,' she said grandly. And making the most of her brief return to power she swept out of the room.

Except she has tremendous power over us really, thought Dinah. Otherwise we wouldn't be here. 'How can we give Daisy an event?' she asked her husband. 'Am I meant to order a cake or what?'

John must have been thinking deeply because he didn't answer immediately. When he did speak he said, 'I'm going to bunk off work for a few hours. It's beautiful outside. Let's go down to Pendleton and give old Daisy a morning to remember.'

It was one of those late October days when the light was so golden and hopeful that it seemed almost impossible to believe in the idea of the coming winter. Daisy's striped cat was sitting cleaning itself on the top step, and for the first time ever the door of the former Bethesda Mission was standing open.

Inside her shed, Daisy Craven was listening to Peter Dawson singing 'The Floral Dance'. The sound was coming from the horn of a wind-up gramophone; wonder of wonders, Daisy had one of the new yellow dusters in her own hand, and she was using it to polish a small green jade Buddha.

'Another of Jessie's phases,' she said. 'Jess bowed down to idols for a bit. But this one always felt lovely to the touch. Have a feel.'

As Dinah took the statuette from Daisy she caught sight of the golden icons, lying in a drawer which had been left half-open. Could it have been the sight of them or the feel of the Buddha which was filling her with this unexpected sensation of well-ordered contentment? She was inclined to believe that it had something to do with both.

Madness? All Dinah knew was that this feeling was as impossible to define as the special atmosphere which always seemed to hang over The Place at Irlams o' th' Height, that these unexpected charges of gently serene energy did more for her than any organised religion had ever managed. All this on a Wednesday morning at half-past nine!

Daisy's mind must also have been running on the time; she was, after all, a woman whose thoughts had never been far from her next swig of escapist syrup. 'Did you bring the key?' she asked Dinah. John's special elixir always spent the night locked up in a wooden medicine cabinet, which hung on the wall.

'You don't need the key today,' he said. 'You don't need the medicine.'

Daisy cried out, 'You're never cutting me off? I thought it was all meant to be gradual.' She looked really frightened. 'I'll pay whatever it costs.' For just a moment panic gave way to hurt surprise. 'I thought you were different from the rest – getting you used to stuff and then saying "All gone". But you can charge me what you like for having said that. *I need to have it*!'

'No you don't.' Quietly and happily he began to reveal the hidden details of the story, ending with the words 'saffron and cinnamon and sugar and water.'

'So I'm truly free of it all?' asked Daisy in wonder.

'You're truly free. John's taken the morning off for you,' smiled Dinah. 'We're going to have a bit of a ceremony.'

'Truly free.' This time she sounded as though she was begining to believe it.

'Yes,' smiled John. 'It's time we took your empties and dumped them on the tip.'

'Have you brought a van?'

'I beg your pardon?' He was busy sizing up the display of bottles on the library shelves.

'I said, have you brought a van? 1917 was a long time ago!' Daisy bent down and seized hold of an iron ring, set in a trap-door in the floorboards. 'Hand me that boudoir candlestick. Reach for those matches.' Dusty wooden stairs led down into a cellar.

Flaming candle held aloft, Daisy led the way down into a bone-dry undercroft. Leaning drunkenly against one wall was a small Sunday School banner, embroidered with the words 'Come To The Mercy Seat'. But that was not the only noticeable thing in this brick-lined pit.

More medicine bottles: candlelight winked upon shelf after shelf after shelf of them. And those that weren't on shelves had been piled into tea chests and buckets and other improvised containers. 'You could say I'd started a tip of my own,' said Daisy modestly to John.

'We need to get it all to the public one.'

'You do see what I meant about a van?'

One of the Turnock twins arrived with a Bedford, borrowed from a contact of his own at Aquarius Galactica. The woman traffic warden on Broad Street was not keen on the idea of it lingering at the kerb, but John acted blond and shy for her. And once she saw the boxes and crates and old tin baths – all of them full of bottles – being brought out into the daylight, she just stood there as mesmerised as the rest of the small crowd which had gathered to witness the little event.

As Ham Turnock carried the final load down the very narrow ginnel, between the tall buildings, he said, over his shoulder to Dinah: 'Babies must feel like this when they're being born. You know, pushing their way down a tunnel to the light.'

It was half-term so some of the observers were children.

And one of them was heard to wonder whether Dirty Daisy was one of those people who went round, on a cart, exchanging empty bottles for paper windmills.

'But you're Clean Daisy now,' said Dinah placatingly.

'Thanks to you and my hero.' The two women were on the bench seat of the van. John was following in the Minx.

'Quite a little procession, aren't we?' said Daisy. 'We should have hung the truck with bunting. I'm free – free. I can hardly believe it.' She began to sing a bit of 'The Floral Dance', the part about dancing to the band with the curious tone. 'I danced to a most curious tone for donkey's years, *that* much I *do* know.'

Brindle Heath gave way to the area known as 'the new shops' and Daisy said 'Cuttiford's' under her breath as they passed a chemist's. And when they turned the corner of Bank Lane for the tip, she pointed back and said, 'I always used to avoid Gledhill's because Mr Molyneux, behind the counter, said he didn't like what I was doing to meself. Mind you, he was an expert on too much of a good thing: married a woman with enough tits to keep a regiment occupied. Just listen to the wicked clanking of all those bottles of mine.'

'Never mind, it's over. All over. And you've no idea of how brave you've been. You've been really brave.'

'I most certainly have.' If there was one thing Daisy had never lacked it was spirit. 'The worst part was lying in me degradation on that marble slab in the Turkish baths. But wasn't that naked black woman beautiful? You shouldn't be listening to any of this,' she said sternly to Ham Turnock.

He just grinned across at her and said, 'We're here.' The van came to a halt on a dirt road. 'Any further and they might have to send a search party out to find us.' On either side, dark mountains of household rubbish rose up to meet the Delft-blue October sky. The dirt track ended at the edge of an escarpment which looked down into another valley of household wreckage, where decaying mattresses appeared to be kings.

John's car had also drawn to a halt. Now he got out, and with the assistance of Ham he began to struggle with the padlock which secured the back doors of the Bedford. Together they carried the first load of bottles – in an old wicker laundry basket – to the edge of the man-made cliff.

'Stop,' called Daisy as she picked her way over to join them. 'You've got to be in on this too, Dinah,' she shouted over her shoulder. 'But I want to be the one to throw the first one,' she said to John. 'Just as a gesture.'

'Feel free. You must have spent thousands and thousands.'

'To say nothing of the constipation! I suppose I'd better just pick any bottle, like drawing a raffle ticket.' The one she settled on was labelled 'Dootson's Cure-All'. 'I bet you'd no idea that a little old woman could bowl over-arm,' she said to Ham Turnock.

'Just don't take a run up to the edge,' he enjoined her. 'You might go over.'

Daisy weighed the bottle in her hand. More to herself than anybody else she said, 'How many times must I have downed another slug and told meself "When it's gone it's gone"? Well now it *has* gone.' Instead of apeing a bowler at Old Trafford she simply walked to the edge and let the bottle slip from her fingers. It landed with a tinkle amongst some rusting jerry cans down below. The thunderous applause which followed was provided by the released contents of John and Ham's laundry basket. 'Thank you,' said Daisy quietly. 'Thank you very much indeed.' And she began to laugh wildly.

Fearing hysteria, Dinah asked, 'Are you okay?'

'Very okay. Never better. I was just thinking about you two – you and John. You think you've surprised me. Well it's nothing like the surprise I'm going to give you.'

The last days of Dinah's pregnancy were haunted by two things: her hatred of that pair of smocked and washed-out cotton maternity dresses, and by the sound of workmen's drills.

'To think I actually chose this frock,' she bellowed at Dr Blakeney. You had to shout because, outside, Axminster Road was being dug up to an extent which had practically turned it into a building site – the workmen even had their own huts. 'We're no longer "unadopted",' she explained.

'Yes and we've had to pay for the privilege, too.' Edna Tench never left her daughter-in-law alone with the doctor for long. Having spent a lifetime avoiding the medical profession, Edna's lately developed hypochondria meant that she viewed the general practitioner as her own body-servant. 'Six hundred pounds for the corporation to take over the responsibility, and I wouldn't care but common tarmac is going to ruin the rural aspect.'

'Count yourself lucky you don't live at the Height.' The doctor accepted a piece of shop-bought cake from Dinah. She had now ballooned to a size which precluded any thoughts of bending down to the oven. 'Caraway seed, how nice. Yes, the Height soon won't be there.'

Preparations for a massive new road scheme had already obliterated one side of the village, and some bland modern building development had begun to erase the character from the other.

'The noise is terrible,' Eva had said, the last time Dinah visited Saracen Street. 'But at least we're going to get a flat out of it.' These flats, for pensioners, were being built on an area which had always been known as the cobbles. 'They've pulled all those quaint little cottages down. People stood there crying.' This thought did not prevent Edna from sniggering as she said, 'Your father's only getting in on my merits. I'm the OAP. Did you know that there's going to be a roundabout, bigger than Piccadilly Circus, near the Pack Horse?'

What would happen to The Place? 'Listen, Mother, I've got to go.' It was odd to think that, in all these years, Daisy Carver was the only person who had ever known Dinah's true feelings about that strangely haunted croft.

'You're never thinking of walking in your condition?' Eva was viewing Dinah's tightly straining coat with alarm. 'Let me go to the corner and phone for Mr Baldwin.'

'No, I just want to have a last look at everything – before it goes under the bulldozers. I'll go into the Pack and ring for a taxi from there.'

'You'll have a job,' snorted her mother. 'The Pack Horse has gone, there's a picture of the hole in this week's *Reporter*. Do you remember the photo that caused all the fuss? The one taken of you, out tennising. You'd have a job leaping round Light Oaks Park today!'

As Dinah let herself out she noticed that somebody had put a new front door on the Brogans' old house. That wouldn't be there for long: not if the plans for the new shopping centre, currently on display in the public library, were approved.

Bolton Road was clanging mayhem; half-demolished shops, with fireplaces still hanging on the upstairs bedroom walls, brought back memories of the blitz. And when she finally picked her way over to The Place, Dinah could hardly believe her eyes.

It wasn't there.

It was even hard to tell where it had once been. The pub, the croft, the gentlemen's conveniences, everything as far as the Congregational Sunday School had been churned up into a plateau of clay, cross-hatched with big cruel tyre-marks. Even the stone thunderbolt had vanished. But the worst thing was that the *extra* feeling no longer lingered on the air. And its absence made Dinah realise precisely why she had come here. She had come to pray for a safe journey through childbirth.

'It's a compulsory purchase order, Mother.' John had come back to Comfrey at lunchtime, brandishing the letter. 'They want Peplum Street.'

'We can appeal,' said Edna. They were all in the kitchenette, where Dinah had been attempting to cut sandwiches at arm's length. Her mother-in-law was still

361

talking. 'Salford Hippodrome appealed, it was in the paper.'

'Appealed and lost.' John had brought back to suburban Ellesmere Park all the energy of somebody who had been interrupted in the middle of a busy working day. 'And if they won't spare a theatre, why should they spare us?'

'Don't ask me, John.' His mother spoke patiently, much too patiently. 'I'm nobody these days, I'm just a back number.'

But we can't do a single thing without your signature, thought Dinah, as she buttered two extra rounds for her husband.

'And John,' said his mother, 'would you please oblige me by cutting that harrying tone out of your voice; we don't want me having another stroke.'

All this did was cause John to become even more agitated. 'You've never had a stroke,' he said. 'Whatever else you've had, a stroke was never on the agenda.'

'I've had an episode,' she said defensively. 'That's what Doctor Blakeney called last Tuesday's business – an episode.'

Dinah recalled it as a tantrum brought on by boredom. In fact she was beginning to wonder whether Mrs Tench had developed a crush on Clifford Blakeney – it was any excuse to get him over the doorstep.

'Tyrell and Tench will soon be out on the street, Mother,' fumed her son. 'And you were the one who saw fit to sell off all the other premises.'

'Where did you park my good Minx, John? Axminster Road is nothing but Irish labourers, sweating their spades up and down. If I was taken poorly, no ambulance could get to the door. Public highway? It's more like a battlefield!'

'I'm on my way to an appointment at the account's.' Anxiety had not affected John's appetite, he was already eating the sandwich meant for his mother. 'We're going to review all the firm's assets.'

'Why?' demanded Edna.

'Because bricks and mortar are at a premium. Half the businesses in Salford have found themselves on the move; that's the ones who haven't gone under.'

'Which will not happen to us,' said Edna. 'Could you put a little drop of non-brewed condiment on that tuna, Dinah? We'll never go bust while we've got the Gentlemen's Remedy.'

For months now, the very mention of this product had acted as an inflammatory upon John. Today was no exception. 'If you'd just let me auction the formula,' he said, 'all our problems would be over. Beecham's have been after it, so have the London Rubber Company: they wanted to rechristen it "Something Else for the Weekend".'

'You can be very distasteful,' snapped his mother. 'The formula stops where it is. Inside my head.'

These days John was capable of putting up a struggle. 'All we have to do is get them both to put in bids. It's the only safe aphrodisiac that really works. We could even retain an interest; we're sitting on a potential gold mine.'

'You're full of very big ideas,' said his mother disparagingly. 'Personally, I'm more interested in the fate of that car. Where did you park it?'

'Right out by the old Clarendon Nursing Home, I couldn't get it any nearer. Did I lock it?' he wondered aloud.

She knows exactly how to pull his strings, thought Dinah as John headed for the front door. 'Bye,' he called back.

Preoccupied with an unexpected tickle, she barely answered him.

'Sell the formula,' snorted Edna. 'He wants to learn to change the record.'

'I've just had a sort of internal tickle. Oh my God!' Now she felt as though she'd wet herself in a big way. 'Look!' The insides of her legs were dripping.

'Your waters have broken,' said Edna in a voice which suggested that she was back in the white coat she had always worn to see patients.

'John,' called out Dinah urgently. 'John.' The only answer was the sound of workmen's drills. 'How in God's name are they going to get the ambulance to the front door? Christ!' she cried.

And then Dinah bit upon the word because she suddenly felt as though she had been lifted up by a giant hand, one that was squeezing and shaking her at the same moment. Mindful of the lectures at the ante-natal clinic she gasped out, 'I'm sure this much shouldn't be happening this soon. Something's wrong. Will you phone Doctor Blakeney?'

'And how's he meant to get his car up?' scoffed Edna. 'Beyond the junction of Axminster and Rydal it's all trenches.'

'Surely he can walk?' This was through gritted teeth because more pain was rushing towards her.

'My Doctor Blakeney, walk? To dance attendance on you? You must have a very exaggerated idea of your own importance.'

As Dinah collapsed onto a wooden chair, Edna went into the top drawer of the kitchen cabinet and produced a brand-new clothes line, still banded with a blue and white paper wrapper. From where Dinah sat, the older woman appeared to have taken on new height, become even more angular – with hands that had fingers like ten spatulas. 'The old ways are still the best,' she said. 'We'll get you upstairs and loop this rope round the bed-end. I shall be the one to deliver my grandchild.'

15

The noise of the ship's engines seemed to have changed. At his cocktail party the captain had said that passengers might soon notice this happening because he was putting on 'some extra spins' in an attempt to make up the time lost in circumnavigating icebergs.

'If ever there was a ship called the *Lusitanic*,' slurred the woman who had tried to gatecrash the party, 'it would be packed from prow to stern.' June was slumped in her sequins on one of the white leather sofas in Dinah's stateroom. 'The public has a great appetite for the macabre.'

And you are somebody who has built a whole career on that bit of knowledge, thought Dinah, as she took hold of the glass held out by June, and treated it to another generous shot of brandy.

How many did that make? And how many had she doctored with crushed up valium tablets, below the counter of the cocktail bar? Four? Five?

I would never have believed I could be so premeditated about killing her, reflected Dinah. I still quite liked myself, all those years ago, when I first thought of doing it.

In those days she had hated June for deceiving her into thinking that Rory was dead, had seen her as the woman whose fabrications had wiped out any chance of happiness. And that single event, in the Co-op Hall, had led to another, which had caused a third, and then a fourth. By which time, counting was becoming more than painful. Nevertheless, in the ensuing years, Dinah had seen herself as June Gee's judge and jury.

But was she really capable of playing the part of public hangman? Not public, private, she corrected herself: she was pretty sure that nobody had seen her steer June up the stairway. At just that moment, a discreet knock sounded on the door from the corridor, and before Dinah had so much as got to her feet the door opened to reveal Anna, the maid. Her dark Middle-European eyes were already taking in the sight of the spangled psychic on the sofa.

'I came to turn down bed, Madam. I come back later.'

Dinah judged that she had seen too much already, that it needed nipping in the bud – now. 'Just a minute, Anna, I want your help with something. I'll only be a moment,' she told June, as she indicated that the maid should follow her into the marble-lined bathroom.

'Close the door.'

At the best of times Anna looked frightened, tonight she looked terrified. 'What is?' She had a faint moustache.

'That lady in there – that person. You have not seen her.'

'But I have,' protested Anna. 'She big blonde, like bad girl gone old.'

English having proved to be of no use, Dinah decided to try the language of the rustle of money. 'Do you want the other passengers to know you come from Bosnia?'

'No, they no tip.'

Dinah still found this hard to believe. After all, Albania had been much more in the headlines recently. But the woman was plainly obsessed with the idea so Dinah said, 'Me no want to tell.' Where was this pidgin English coming from? 'Me want to give you big tip. When we get to New York,' she added hastily. The poor little soul must not be allowed to think that this was any kind of invitation to daily blackmail.

But she had misjudged her woman. 'I have children,' said Anna quietly. 'Since war everything costs. You no tell?'

I'll give her a very big tip anyway, thought Dinah – ashamed. Nevertheless she said, 'You just didn't see her.'

'Okay. Do I turn down bed?'

Might this return their relationship to normal? 'Yes please.' Allowing the stewardess to leave the bathroom, Dinah checked her own appearance in the mirror and remembered when she too had worried about a child.

Remembered Edna Tench urging her upstairs with prods from that clothes line – still in its brand-new wrapper. Remembered hearing herself screaming and shouting, and recalled the fact that these great cries of involuntary noise had afforded her not one scrap of relief from those waves of pain.

Oh those pains! 'Of course, it's a conspiracy of silence,' Edna had said. 'If older women told the younger genera-tion what it was like, the world would be depopulated.' That was just when another great shuddering sear of agony took over. And the awful thing was, right at the very core, at its heart – if this relentless torment could be said to have a heart – there was the weird revelation that the agony was second cousin to the pleasure-pain of sexual rapture.

The moment Dinah was granted this grim knowledge was the same instant in which she started to haem-orrhage.

'That good counterpane came from Affleck and Brown,' screeched Edna.

'Fuck Affleck and Brown!' roared Dinah. 'Get Blakeney. Get him,' she sobbed helplessly. '*Please*,' she whimpered. And then she heard herself shouting incoherently again as great claws seemed to rip at her innards.

The doctor's arrival – on foot with his bag in his hand – took the longest twenty minutes Dinah had ever known.

'Well this *is* a blood bath and no mistake,' he said cheerfully. He was barely through the bedroom door before Mrs Tench began wittering on about John having been nine pounds ten ounces 'with an abnormal amount of afterbirth'.

'You need more than a bit of help. And immediately,' he said to Dinah. 'There's no way we could get an ambulance anywhere near the house.' Opening his black case he produced a pair of big, gleaming, silver scissors. 'Needs must when the devil drives,' he said brightly.

These many years later Dinah had to steady herself against the wash basin as she remembered what had happened next. But she wasn't given the chance to think about it for long because the ship described a sudden roll and June called out, 'Have you gone down the plug hole?'

As Dinah walked back into the living area, the maid was emerging from the bedroom. 'I done just one bed. Right?'

'Pushed your hubby overboard?' June asked Dinah cosily. She appeared, if anything, brighter than she had been all evening.

Those people who tried to kill Rasputin must have felt like I do, thought Dinah. And then she recalled that he too had been some sort of mystic. Heavy-duty sleeping tablets, that's what would have to go into the next brandy. 'My husband has his own quarters.' And God alone knows what outrageous mischief he's planning in them, she thought.

As Anna left the cabin, June said, 'I've never liked a man around in the morning since I got false teeth. And then again it takes two slimming tablets to bring me round.'

Had June, somehow, used telepathy to pick up on the word 'tablets'? 'Do you go in for a lot of that sort of thing?'

'My dear, if you shook me I'd rattle. Pills to wake me up, pills to level me out. I'm a bit naughty,' she confided tipsily. 'I have prescriptions off several different doctors.'

Just like my dear husband, thought Dinah wearily, just like him. She had often wondered what would happen in the event of his ever really needing a general anaesthetic. And not for the first time, she reflected that so many of her own age group – the ones who spoke scathingly about the younger generation and drugs – were in no position to criticise. Even further back into the past there had been people like poor little Daisy.

And, oddly enough, it had been events in the later life of Daisy Carver which had redoubled Dinah's hatred of June Gee. The sequined psychic on the sofa was feeding cashew nuts from one paw into the other, and then into her mouth.

My God but you are evil, thought Dinah. People think of wickedness as dark and dramatic and sharply cut, like the man in the cloak on the Sandeman's Port advertisement. But they're wrong. Real evil is slack and messy and unprincipled.

'Got any kids?' asked June.

Only the one the doctor took away in a bucket. That was the most Dinah remembered of the climax of all that blood and shouting at Comfrey – a white enamel bucket with a wire handle and a wooden grip. It was the last she ever saw of that workaday item from the wash-house, the last she ever saw of her little boy.

His only epitaph was the words 'umbilical cord around the windpipe', and soon the ambulance men were carrying her along Axminster Road on a sacking stretcher. The ambulance itself was waiting at the corner of Rydal Crescent – white like the bucket.

And for months afterwards, years even, the sight of anything enamelled white, or of chromium-plated scissors, was enough to conjure up images which were so appalling that Dinah had to stop herself from emitting cries of remembered pain and of robbed despair. Even to this day she sometimes wanted to cry out 'Aaaah' when she thought of how little she had known about how much she had really wanted that child.

On the afternoon they lifted her up into the ambulance there was rain in the air. And curious schoolchildren, in maroon Barton Grammar School uniforms, were trying to pretend that they were too well-mannered to stare.

By the time she had been conveyed into Hope Hospital, dusk had fallen so that the maternity ward was full of bright electric light. Relentless light and visitors. And new mothers in beds, their babies by their sides in cots. Doctor Blakeney was still with her, as much in the role of 'accompanying family friend' as he was there as her GP.

'Where's John?' she asked. 'Why has nobody got hold of John?'

'All in good time,' he reassured her. 'We needed to get

you in here to get you tidied up. They will almost certainly take you down to theatre.'

Instead they took her to a delivery room. What happened next was not dignified and it hurt – really hurt. When the porters wheeled her back into the ward, she was suddenly aware that the room was almost ritualistically dotted with new fathers. And still there was no sign of John.

'You're written up for something to keep you comfortable for the night,' said the ward sister. To Dinah she looked little more than a girl.

I'm old for a first-time mother, she thought. Except I'm not a mother, I'm a failure. There was a name for women who had lost their husbands. Why wasn't there a name for a woman who'd lost her baby? And why did her arms keep wanting to make cradling shapes? Dinah suddenly felt as weak and as tired as somebody who had been deprived of food. 'Where's John?' she asked. Except they wouldn't know who he was. 'He's my . . .'

'We know. Oh look, you've got a visitor.' Avril had arrived at the foot of the bed, bearing bronze chrysanthemums in Cellophane wrapping.

'Watch what you're saying,' Dinah warned her. 'I'm liable to weep.' Why were the sister and Avril exchanging that little glance? And why was the woman in uniform murmuring 'Only if you have to'. Dinah came right out and asked, 'Only if she has to *what*?'

'I told you she was very intelligent,' said Avril nasally.

'Intelligent enough to know that something's being kept from me. Where's John? Why isn't he here?' Most unexpectedly, the young sister sat down on the edge of the bed and took hold of Dinah's hand.

How many years ago was that? And how odd to think, now, that even in those days she had already started thinking of herself as old. Well, she'd certainly needed a bit of sophistication to cope with what had happened in the years between!

Here, tonight, on the *QE2*, June Gee belched lightly,

said, 'Pardon me,' and then announced that, much as she hated to go, she had a lecture to prepare.

How am I meant to kill you? shrilled Dinah's mind. Do I have to take you to the crossroads and drive a wooden stake through your heart? It did not take the throb of the ship's engines to remind her that there were no crossroads on the high seas.

'It's an astrology lecture I'm giving, tomorrow.'

Dinah remembered Professor Petrulengo's book, the idiotic publication which had promised that her 'banquet' with Rory would eventually serve up its own dessert. 'I'm afraid I'm not much struck on astrology.'

'Me neither. But they're not keen on my discussing my real gift.' June suddenly became groggily businesslike: 'We haven't sorted out an appointment for that sitting I'm going to give you.'

Here at least would be a chance to try again. Dinah recalled that they'd had to resort to driving Rasputin out onto the ice in the end. Memories of this tale of Prince Yusopov and his friends were wiped away by the sound of a discreet knock at the cabin door.

'Yes, who is it?' Not that it really mattered now, though it would be as well not to emphasise to the world that she was well-acquainted with her intended victim.

It was only Anna again. 'I forget to leave chocolate mint on pillow.'

'It's all right, I don't want one.'

'Okay, if you sure. Goodnight, Mrs Snowden.'

'Goodnight.'

Today it was Sorrel's turn to be the one who woke early. In the other bed, Mickey was still asleep with one hand on a paperback edition of *A Town To Remember*.

It did not take her long to realise why he had been reading one of his own books. She remembered that Jack Lawless had bought a copy at the previous day's signing: Mickey must have been trying to judge the effect of its contents upon his new admirer. Although, Mick's account of the conversation in the sauna had suggested that Jack's infatuation went back some time.

Was I *ever* shocked by the idea of two men in love? she wondered. The man sleeping so contentedly must have been about thirteen when June had first suggested that he might be a 'homo'. If June Gee's normal then good luck to all the gay guys on earth, she decided. So far, on this voyage, she had avoided direct contact with her childhood neighbour. Sorrel couldn't believe she would reach New York unscathed.

Thoughts of that town caused her to check the size of her lump. In an attempt to take her mind off the subject of cancer she bent down and picked up the Daily Programme, which had been pushed under the door in the night. Turning the pages, she thought, I don't know why I'm dwelling on operating theatres and my own memorial service (Manchester Cathedral?) when there's so much on offer in here.

The one thing the programme did not list was any kind of coded message about the altered location of today's AA meeting. The bar they generally used was needed for some travel agent's private party. Maybe Jack would know.

Rather than telephone she decided to walk along the corridor and knock on his door. She was only slightly disconcerted by the fact that he opened it stripped to the waist, with that muscular chest covered in soapy lather.

'Just shaving my pecs,' he explained. She had never heard of anybody doing this before. Her slight bewilderment must have shown because Jack saw fit to reassure her with, 'It's all in the line of business. I did my first movie smooth and people have come to expect it.'

What people, and for what? The beginning of the answer came back to her as 'Mickey', and it really didn't do to dwell upon the rest.

Jack's cabin was not a twin to their own restrained and distinguished quarters. 'Could have been designed for Debbie Reynolds,' he said. 'Mind if I just finish shining up the muscles?' By now he was at the bathroom mirror and calling through the open door.

'I left just before the end yesterday. All I wanted to know is, where's today's meeting?'

'The equivalent bar on the starboard side. You sure that's all you want to know?' Foam was being scraped away and amazingly smooth amber skin was coming into view. 'I don't have to zip off all that much,' he grinned. His teeth were as good as Barney's had been at that age. 'You and Mickey are very close, aren't you?'

'The closest,' she assured him without hesitation.

'So what did he tell?'

After a moment of wondering how to answer she came right out with, 'Look, this is awful. Everything you said was under the seal of the meeting, Mick and I have never split on one another in a lifetime . . . I feel just like piggy in the middle.'

'"It's An Honest Programme."' Jack was quoting one of AA's best-known maxims.

'Yes, and last night he was the one sparkling away, just like you're doing now. I'm not kidding, you could float either of you out to sea as flashing beacons!'

'So?'

'So I thought you didn't go in for love affairs.' She hated herself for saying this but it was Mick she was defending, which meant that polite rules got thrown out. 'You said you simply couldn't cope with them.'

'And you were the one who said, in a meeting, that through all your bad years you had always clung on to hope.'

My God but he's attractive, she thought as Jack rinsed his chest and then reached for a towel to mop up the water which had splashed onto his blue jeans. There's a tenacity to his tone of voice that I could nearly go for myself.

'Tell me what you're thinking,' he said quietly as he towelled his chest.

'No.'

'I've said too much in those meetings.'

'That's what they're for – unloading.'

'And learning.' He began to pull a white tee shirt over his head. His temporarily muffled voice said, 'You clung

373

on to hope, why shouldn't I?' As his head came through the neckband, Sorrel reflected that he had done well to leave the shaggy eyebrows untouched, that they kept the over-classical face real. 'All I can do is try.' Sexy and bewildered, that's what he looked. 'I'm supposed to be one numero uno stud, but there are emotions involved here, Sorrel. The chances are I'm about to come spectacularly unstuck.'

16

So how did Dinah Tench (née Nelson) turn into Mrs Paul Snowden? John Tench was dead: that much Dinah took in as Avril and the nursing sister sat at either side of the bed in the maternity ward, each of them holding one of her hands. He had died in the cause of speeding towards the hospital to be with her; his car had gone into the deepest of the roadworkers' trenches, the one they'd dug for the new drains at the corner of Rydal Crescent.

No baby, no John, no hope of going back to Saracen Street because her mother had already moved into her pensioner's flat. Dinah was practically comatose with misery.

'It's just postnatal depression,' said Dr Blakeney. He had brought a potted plant onto the ward for her.

'I've plenty to be depressed about.'

'And in the night she rambles on and on about somebody called Old Edna,' said the Sister, to the GP, in the kind of guarded tone of voice which people normally reserve for speaking in front of a clever child who might or might not understand. 'We're going to have to turn her out soon, Doctor. We're worried she might become institutionalised.'

Didn't they realise that it was *safe* in Hope Hospital? That once she was outside, her emotional amputations would all be on public view? She wanted John and she wanted her dead baby. And after that, all her turgidly revolving mind could concentrate upon was what she didn't want. She didn't want to go back to cheerless Comfrey – to Edna Tench.

But that was where she was heading now: a wife who had not been well enough to attend her own husband's funeral, a mother who had never even held her own child. And, oh God, would Avril ever shut up?

'Edna kept shouting down into the grave, Dinah. Sobbing and shouting, and she even struck out at the undertaker when he tried to lead her away.'

Avril's fiancé, hairy Alistair Seddon, was driving them home from the hospital. The detour he made, to avoid the fatal corner of Rydal Crescent, took them halfway round frost-laden Ellesmere Park. He used this time to repeat his arguments as to why Dinah should stay in close contact with her mother-in-law.

Boiled down, he was saying that John's actual will had left her badly provided for. But that she would eventually benefit from his late uncle's shares in Tyrell and Tench. As she tried to take all this in, Dinah reflected that, whatever happened, the Growing Grounds were hers and hers alone.

'If you're not there whilst the merger's going on,' said Avril, 'she could rook you.'

'What merger?' Dinah's mind seemed to be operating at two levels. An echoing version of her own voice was perpetually keening inside her own head ('*John, who I'd just started to love*' and '*My baby . . . my poor little baby*') but there was also a kind of listening tube, which went up to the surface and caught words like this one – 'merger'. ('*Did God take the baby away because I pretended to myself that Rory helped me make it?*')

'We've told you,' said Avril. 'We keep on telling you. Aquarius Galactica wants to acquire Tyrell and Tench. We'll all benefit.'

'When did you say your wedding is?' Dinah was only making conversation, attempting to gain a foothold on reality.

This was not how Avril chose to see it. 'If you think we're being grabby . . .'

'I don't.' It was the truth. 'I'm just dreading seeing Edna again. I dunno . . .' She let out a deep sigh as she gazed out at the snow, which had just started to swirl around the black silhouettes of suburban conifers. 'I suppose we've both lost children. That might finally give us something in common.'

It didn't.

The gates of Comfrey were deceptively – almost hospitably – wide open. Alistair drove the car right up to the front door. As Dinah, still uncomfortable in the nether regions, lowered her feet onto the concrete, Edna appeared on the top step – looking more than ever like a grey gargoyle.

'I suppose you realise you killed my son?' she said to Dinah.

'I've lost a son too,' she protested weakly.

'You lost a lump of bleeding gristle. You never raised it. You never chose all its clothes and saw it as your future.'

Which makes two mothers who've thought that about me, reflected the alleged villainess.

Avril reacted much more hastily. 'Right, that does it! We're not leaving you here with this; you're coming home with us, Dinah.'

'No. I'll stay.' The snow was making her long for her own bed, and the word 'future' had caused her to think of finances. And if men's mothers chose to see her as wicked, she would bide her time and show them what wicked really meant. But for the moment she just hauled herself upstairs and looked around the chilly bedroom that would never see her husband again.

The first thing her eyes rested upon was a little silver cup inscribed 'Awarded To John Tench For Consistent Endeavour'. And that was when she allowed herself to give way to noisy grief.

This was what Dinah was remembering as she sat in the Grand Lounge of the QE2. A bound sketch pad sat on the glass-topped table in front of her, together with the water-colour pencils she always used to colour her illustrations, in the painted diaries, when travelling.

Another of the morning rehearsals was going on, on the stage. Although these were never advertised in the Daily Programme small knots of cruise passengers often gathered to watch other people working.

Of course, rehearsals had come into the early days of

her relationship with Paul. It was Mrs Mottershead, the elocution teacher, who had first taken Dinah along for an audition for the Nameless Society's production of George Bernard Shaw's *Candida*. And Dinah had been surprised to find herself cast in the role of Prossy – the vicar's secretary. At first she was convinced she had been given the part out of sheer charity. But it had not taken her long to realise that, when it came to taking their turn in the spotlight, the members of the amateur dramatic society had elbows as sharp as any West End actor.

Paul Snowden was playing the part of Marchbanks, the young poet who was supposed to be in love with the vicar's wife. Strictly speaking, he was too old for the role. 'But wherever he goes, people are always mesmerised by that face,' said Avril bitterly. She had, of course, long known him as Alistair's partner. 'He looks just like beautiful Georgie Best crossed with Lord Hunkum-Dunkum.'

Instead of drawing the ship's cabaret rehearsal, Dinah began to sketch Paul as she had first known him. She used briskly stabbing strokes because, in those days, he had always seemed made of energy. The whole of that dramatic society had practically hurled the couple at one another.

But what was a tall and attractive man of thirty-seven doing so very unattached? And was he after her at a personal level, or had Aquarius Galactica – still in the midst of their never-ending takeover negotiations – had they also set their sights on the Growing Ground?

'I think they're drug peddlers,' was Edna Tench's opinion. 'Look at the length of their hair. And why should that Alistair Seddon want to sail all the way to Amsterdam on a boat?'

'Because he likes boats, he lives on a boat.' Dinah and her mother-in-law did not have many conversations these days so she always tried to do her best with any little bit that was going. 'Are you really going to sell out to them?'

They were in Comfrey's anaemic lounge. Edna adjusted a blurred photograph of her father in a chip-carved wooden frame, and said, 'The great days of the firm are over. There'll soon be no premises, just stock and goodwill.'

'And experienced staff.' Jobs had ceased to be so easy to get and Dinah was thinking of the Turnocks and Eugene. 'Paul says he'll take them on.'

'Oh it's *Paul*, is it?'

'Nobody says Mister any more.'

'I do. And he calls me Mrs Tench, up hill and down dale, whenever the subject of the Gent's Remedy is mentioned. And they only want that because it's sex.'

If she dies tonight, thought Dinah, the formula will go to the grave with her. But that day Dinah had been giving much more thought to the idea of letting Rory Brogan know that she was a widow.

These many years later, she only had to think of his name for her hand to reach for her softest 4B pencil, for love to guide the hand which drew the outline of the well-remembered profile. And she drew it much larger than the jerky little sketch of Paul Snowden.

By the early seventies Rory's family were solidly back in Ireland, leaving nobody in the Height with a forwarding address. The generally held view was that they had dodged off with cash raised from unsuspecting Salford moneylenders.

Dinah was pinning her hopes on getting Rory's address from Father Paddy. She knew that he had left his old parish, so using her best Mrs Mottershead voice she rang the Bishop of Salford's palace and said, 'I'm looking for a priest.'

The man who answered the telephone only allowed her a cold little Irish, 'Yes.'

'I used to know the man in question well. Very well indeed.'

Many years later, in the light of lurid newspaper revelations about girls and priests, Dinah would come to see that this had been a somewhat naive approach. As it was, the man at the other end merely measured out, 'We don't reveal information of that sort,' and left her listening to the dialling tone.

The sudden blast of the ship's midday whistle brought Dinah into the present with such a jolt that she broke the point of her expensive Venus pencil. This page of the diary looked a bitty mess. But, right back to the days when she drew her experiences into fourpenny books from the bottom shop, it had always been a point of honour not to rip out any entry. Today, the odd thing was that she had neglected to draw the one thing which was really dominating her thoughts: June, June, June.

Wasn't that part of a song, from a musical? The amplified rehearsal tape was belting out the opening bars of another. The troupe of entertainers were heavy on nostalgia, and the leading woman singer began to lip-synch to the words of 'Lover Come Back To Me'.

No song on earth was more calculated to conjure up memories of her fruitless search for Rory's whereabouts during those final months – those bone-dry final months – with Edna Tench.

The old herbalist's crush on portly Doctor Blakeney must have cost the National Health Service a fortune. 'Ring him and say the blood pressure's down again,' she urged Dinah.

'You'd explain better yourself.'

'I *am* feeding you, you know. Feeding you and watering you and keeping a roof over your head.'

Even when the division of the spoils from the sale of the business was settled, Dinah knew she would be left wondering whether she had the heart to abandon this wicked woman. Edna might stage performances for the doctor but it had to be admitted that she seemed to be showing real signs of getting weaker by the day. 'I feel like the last dead leaf hanging on a tree,' she would sigh as she chewed on one of her eternal dry Ryvita biscuits. Crunch, crunch, crunch: the only time Dinah got away from the sounds of mastication and the eternal sighing was when she went off to rehearsals for *Candida*.

That bloody awful 'Lover Come Back To Me' had always been a turgid lament, she really didn't want reminding of the day she finally conceded that she was not going to find Rory. Early summer: even on unhappy Axminster Road everything was suddenly blazing forth in aggressive newness. And Rory Brogan was nothing more than decreasingly hopeless drawings in sad sepia.

The day she finally accepted this was the first time she took Paul Snowden up on one of his frequent offers to buy her a drink, on the way home from the Nameless Society's rehearsal room.

It was June the twenty-first – the longest day. As they emerged from the dark little theatre into the streets of rackety Rusholme, the late evening sunlight seemed to be inviting Dinah to linger. So she accepted his invitation with, 'Is there anywhere we can sit outside?'

'I think they're trying a few chairs, on the pavement, outside the Nun's Prayer.' This was a theatrical pub in the city centre, near to the Opera House.

'I was speaking to Aberdeenshire this morning,' he said as he came back outside with their drinks in his hand. 'They said they'd never seen the Northern Lights as clearly as they did last night.'

And Dinah had never looked at him as closely as she was doing now. In the past she had seen him as Marchbanks in the play, or as Alistair's partner – a distant business colleague. Now she was looking at Paul in his own right.

'You're almost too good-looking,' she said. Her artist's eye had gained a voice, and it must have been dispassionate enough to give him the confidence to reply 'I'm not gay'.

'I didn't think you were.' This was the truth; though John, she remembered, had always said, 'There's just something about him you can't put your finger on.' And he'd said that before men's clothes turned Byronic. Nowadays, Paul's black curls tumbled onto black velvet shoulders and his trouser bottoms were even wider than her own. 'Why have you never been married?'

'Perhaps I was looking for a wife who'd bring me the Gent's Remedy as a dowry.' The smile was teasing and it revealed his only physical imperfection – one white front tooth grew very slightly over the other.

Yet she knew he wasn't joking. In this strangely drawn-out sunlight she was seeing him for what he was: calculatedly businesslike, generous and quite kind.

That night she drew Paul Snowden into the diary, standing at the far side of a sign which said 'Emergency Exit'. If Dinah had become calculated, it was because Edna Tench was driving her to desperation.

As the weeks went on, the same woman who had spent a lifetime avoiding doctors surrendered to the deepest embraces of imaginary illness. She would, it seemed, do anything to catch a glimpse of her beloved Blakeney. Edna even spoke, in front of her own son's widow, of changing her will in the doctor's favour.

Dinah began to wonder whether the old woman's mind was controlling that increasingly sickly body. Stabbing pains, swellings, inexplicable skin eruptions – Edna seemed able to summon them up in moments.

Far worse were the lassitudes, the days when it was all she could do to put one foot in front of the other, when she seemed to tire the very air around her.

And, oh, how she exhausted Dinah! Lassitude turned her mother-in-law into a mist of sighs and a skeletal hand extending an empty glass; her craving for barley water seemed to have grown perpetual. 'I won't trouble Blakeney,' she would whisper faintly. But Dinah recognised these sighs and mews for what they were – foreplay. The equivalent of intercourse came in the shape of a personal consultation with the increasingly abashed doctor.

It could not be denied that Dinah often thought of just packing her bags and leaving the old malingerer. But she stayed for the same reasons she had once stayed on at Tyrell and Tench: she had no intention of quitting until she could carry away something of value. However, Edna's bouts of cultivated exhaustion often sent Dinah off to the Nameless Society drained of everything but just enough energy to get her through the evening's rehearsals.

Paul Snowden proved himself to be somebody who was capable of solid support. He too was in the middle of a waiting game with the old harridan. 'And even half an hour's meeting with her leaves me feeling as though I've had lead injected into my veins.'

The final dress rehearsal was in September. That evening Edna did her best to prevent Dinah leaving the house. She half-sat and half-lay on an upholstered armchair in the lounge, saying that her own mother had 'simply faded out as dusk fell'.

'I've still got to go,' said Dinah. 'All the others are depending on me.'

But thoughts of Edna controlled a lot of her evening. On the stage, Dinah just about managed to turn herself into the character of Prossy. Off it, all she could do was fret about that frail and listless figure. Once the final curtain had fallen, and her costume had been handed over to the wardrobe mistress for alteration, she prevailed upon Paul to give her a lift home.

He dropped her off at the gates of cheerless Comfrey. She had always been discouraged from adding colour to the flower beds. They were still dotted with sporadic clumps of dusty ornamental heathers and little bursts of that miniature bracken known as 'dragon's fumes'. Dinah's own mother had been right when she said that Edna had 'not got a lot in her garden'.

But, tonight, there was plenty going on in Edna Tench's lounge. In fact there was enough activity to change the course of the rest of Dinah's life.

Mickey carried his mid-morning coffee out into the open air. Sunlight was dancing off the sea, the weather was altogether calmer. And looking one deck downwards he could see that people were sunbathing around the edge of the pool, which was in the process of being refilled with ultramarine water.

No Jack.

But Mickey knew that he would come across him

sooner or later. He just hoped it was before he delivered his second lecture. For the moment he was luxuriating in the thought that he was not making too much of an idiot of himself by being just a little bit in love with Jack Lawless. Cunard were absolutely right in describing their transatlantic crossings as 'The Only Way To Go'.

A little bit in love or wildly, blindly, hopelessly infatuated? Did it matter? He knew now that these feelings were, to some extent, returned. All he had to do was tell Jack what he wanted from him.

These romantic thoughts were disturbed by some chattering woman's voice saying, 'This afternoon her lecture's on astrology.'

The woman's female companion joined in with, 'I can never have my horoscope done properly because you've got to know the exact hour of your birth.'

'I know mine because Mummy's always saying that, just as I popped out, the *Angel Dwellings* theme music was just starting.'

Mickey had never known for sure whether he really believed in God, but he felt himself suffused with gratitude towards whatever force it was that had invested him with his talent. Without Jack's passion for *Angel Dwellings* the chances were that he would never have bothered to open that abandoned copy of *A Town To Remember*.

The heady smell of sea air was suddenly erased by a great gale of perfume. Not only was it much too early in the day for all that French scent, it was emanating from every perspiring pore of June Gee. Dressed in straining royal blue and white sateen she looked a bit like an old-fashioned seaside pierrot – trying to be a sailor.

'God but I slept well last night,' she said, sucking fervently on a cigarette which was already tipped with shocking-pink lipstick. 'Went out like a light.' She seemed distinctly cock-a-hoop and the explanation was not long in coming. 'I've pulled a rich client,' she bragged. 'One stateroom for herself and another for hubby. Dying for a sitting, she is. Up on her back legs and begging for it. Of course I don't have to tell you that I daren't

384

risk doing it on board.' June treated herself to a good scratch under the bust. 'I'll just have to string her along till we get to New York. They're going to be at the Hotel Pierre.' Flagrantly defying ship's regulations, June flung her cigarette overboard. 'And what have you been up to?'

Just don't start the telepathy bit, thought Mickey. I don't want you spoiling something special. The fact of the matter was that he had startled even himself by the answer he was going to deliver to Jack Lawless's romantic question.

Sit reading on a ship and people will make every effort to skirt around you. Sit sketching, and if you're not careful you'll find yourself gathering a crowd. Well, three women anyway – the ancient and holy ones who generally had a priest in tow.

In the Grand Lounge Dinah had turned over the page. But instead of drawing the dance rehearsal, her sepia-brown pencil was outlining a scene from the past. Sepia for memory: she was drawing the sight she had seen through the window at Comfrey. These days, the present often being too painful to contemplate, the painted diary was frequently filled with a lot of memories.

Dinah had decorated the borders of this particular sheet of hand-made paper with a whole selection of angry musical notes. That was because, on the other side of the leaded glass, the old wind-up gramophone had been blaring out 'The Ritual Fire Dance'. And an almost disbelieving Dinah had found herself taking in the sight of her mother-in-law – shoes kicked into a far corner – energetically conducting some imaginary symphony orchestra with a steel knitting needle.

The woman who had claimed she was dying had made a quite remarkable recovery. In fact she appeared to be filled with manic energy. But her daughter-in-law was suffused with deepest rage.

As Dinah opened the front door, and then slammed

it behind her, the music ceased abruptly. By the time she got into the lounge Edna had reverted into a living shipwreck, beached upon the sofa. 'You're back,' she breathed weakly.

'It won't wash. I saw.'

'Saw what?'

'What you were doing. Poorly? You're fit to turn out for Manchester United. You had me nicely kidded!'

Edna had the grace to look a little shamefaced. 'Conducting's a hobby I've always kept to myself.' She was trying to slide the knitting needle down the side of a cushion.

'I could be having a nice night out,' stormed Dinah. 'Everybody else has gone to the Koh-i-Noor for a curry.'

'I'm not sure I approve of your going to Indian restaurants. You might get food poisoning, and then who would there be to look after me?'

'It strikes me you're more than capable of looking after yourself. And stop making yourself quiver. It's not ninety seconds since you had more zip than John Barbirolli.'

But the quivering was turning into convulsive tremors. 'I'm having an episode,' breathed Edna in the kind of awed tones that most people would have reserved for their first sight of an erupting volcano. And now the voice could have belonged to somebody who wanted to run. It began to rise in horror as she cried out, 'I am, I'm having an episode, and this time it could get my brain. Make it stop, Dinah.' She was actually begging and pleading. 'Please make it stop.'

'I can't.'

The frightened voice changed again. This time it sounded as though it had grown too big for Edna's mouth. 'All we've got left is the formula.'

'Rubbish.' Even as she snapped this out, Dinah realised that the older woman was genuinely panicked.

'If it gets to my brain the Gent's Remedy's not written down anywhere. Listen . . .' Her speech had really thickened. 'Five parts damiana, three of ground kava kava, one part false unicorn root . . .' Her voice was definitely losing clarity now and she had to beckon Dinah to her side so that she could mouth the final ingredient.

'But that's not even herbal,' protested John Tench's widow in amazement.

'It still works!' This final attempt at indignation was too much for Edna and she collapsed back into the embrace of the armchair, her bottom false teeth falling out of her mouth.

That was what Dinah was drawing now, on the *QE2*, on the finest paper that money could buy.

'Everybody should have a hobby.' It was one of the holy ladies, the women in expensively dowdy cotton frocks, who had been watching her drawing. By now the other two had drifted away. This one must have been about seventy. She had dark eyes that were both intelligent and interested. 'May I have a proper look?'

'Not at that page, it's a rambling mess.' Dinah turned back to a lightning-fast sketch she had made of the band playing on the dock at Southampton.

'It's wonderful,' said the woman appreciatively. 'And the thing that's so nice is the fact that, on dry land, I would never have dreamed of striking up a conversation. Being on ocean liners always reminds me of the kind of very good private hotels we always stayed at in my youth. The ones where it was perfectly permissible to introduce oneself to other guests.'

Dinah recalled her own childhood: Blackpool boarding houses where the landladies always wanted you out, straight after breakfast. The Nelsons had always been supposed to have been going to Middleton Towers Holiday Camp, but somehow they had never got there.

The woman with the skinny shanks, the one who had known a more genteel upbringing, was still talking. 'I too have a hobby. I collect religious artefacts.' She snapped open her handbag and produced a miniature Russian icon, a jewelled and enamelled Angel of the Lord and a kneeling Virgin – in a mount which had every appearance of having been fashioned in solid gold.

Dinah let out a little gasp.

'I don't expect you've ever seen anything like that before?'

'But I have,' said Dinah in wonder. 'If I could go back about twenty-five volumes in this diary I could show you drawings of a whole row of the same things.' They had been the foundation of her present fortune, they and the formula for the Gentlemen's Remedy.

'How fascinating. This beats anything in a palm court at Eastbourne. I am Miss Meech. Let us trade reminiscences.'

Still no sign of Jack. There comes a point in a sea voyage, one shore left far behind, the other still a distant and invisible prospect, when time blurs to nothingness. But, on this particular crossing, the days were marked by the ever-increasing size of the Puerto Rican woman's hats. She might just as easily have been Chilean: small, dark, bright-eyed, beautifully groomed and always dressed in the near-black shades of a raven's wing. As she patrolled the sun deck in her tiny, high-heeled shoes, Mickey observed today's hat, a close-fitting skull-cap surmounted by a huge asymmetrical halo of deepest turquoise stretched silk.

This elegant vision had obviously decided that the sea miles between here and Southampton constituted an introduction because she nodded as they passed one another, and when their route-marches crossed again she paused and she spoke.

'I suspect we are both looking for the same man, Mr Grimshaw.' Her slight foreign accent was elegantly clipped and she was plainly not given to waiting for confirmation or denial of her statements. 'I am trying to prevent a friend of mine from committing a very grave foolishness with him.' Now she had started it seemed there could be no stopping her. 'I feel safe in talking to you. I attended your lecture, admire your honesty. Diverse sexualities are as shades of the rainbow to me. But I have seen you with this man and he is gigolo.'

The newly unleashed romantic side of Mickey wanted

to rush to Jack's defence. But it was the strong dose of caution within his makeup which determined him to hear the woman out.

'Your shipmate cannot go back to the Negresco at Nice. The police showed him the road out of Monte Carlo; he had to go and skulk in Villefranche where there is nothing but a quay full of seafood restaurants and the ghost of Jean Cocteau.'

That reference meant that she had to be older than she looked. Mickey's eyes went in search of tell-tale signs behind the ears, but the skull-cap concealed all.

Anyway she was ahead of him. 'Forty-seven,' she announced matter-of-factly. 'But Assumpta is only nineteen. And rich? My God is she rich in her own right! She offered him ten thousand dollars in whatever currency he chooses.'

Worldly as he was, Mickey could hardly credit what he was hearing. 'Ten thousand for sex?'

'For a baby. She wants him to give her a baby and his signature on a piece of paper. Take my advice and detach yourself from him, Mr Grimshaw. He is bad.'

Dinah's new friend, Miss Meech, had revealed that she was on Two Deck, but in one of the more luxurious cabins, which entitled her to a table in the same restaurant as herself – the Queen's Grill. So that was where they went for lunch.

'We've rather graduated,' said Dinah, 'my husband and I. In our early days we were always in the Mauretania and we've worked ourselves right up to here.' It wasn't so much the wall-carvings, nor the gilt and white porcelain place settings, that she found impressive. No, it was more the sound of obsequious waiters murmuring the name of one of the great Italian motor manufacturers, and dancing attendance upon the descendants of the original purveyors of American canned soups and breakfast cereals.

'Shall your husband be joining us?' enquired Miss

Meech as she broke an onion bagel and contemplated a soup cup of smoked ham and champagne broth.

She really is magnificently dowdy, thought Dinah. As to her own husband: 'He's given to disappearing acts.' Today, Paul had not so much as knocked at her own door to be given his morning supply of tranquillisers – which had left her wondering where on earth he was getting them from. 'I think I glimpsed him near the Casino.'

'Is that the old Duchess of Argyle over there, or is she dead?' whispered Miss Meech. 'Now that really *was* a divorce case. I should explain that, before I converted to Catholicism, I used to be what is known as a top-flight divorce lawyer. Tell me about your husband.'

For years now, Dinah had a speech rehearsed and ready – a speech designed to test the skills of just such an expert. 'You were quite right about the ship causing people to loosen up; I'm almost tempted to tell you the story of my life.'

'Actually, it's my face,' said Miss Meech confidently. 'When I was first articled to Prothero, Belling and Cohen, old Sir Giles Belling said to me: "That bird-like interest of yours will be the making of your career." Why don't you tell me whatever it is? You are obviously dying to unload something.'

Dinah spread her crayfish paté onto a wafer-thin rice and sesame cracker. Telling Miss Meech about the days of her youth – those years with Rory and then John – recounting these could have taken for ever. But whole decades with Paul Snowden could be reduced into a few bizarre milestones of stories.

'Of course,' wheedled Miss Meech, 'if I'm being intrusive . . .'

'No, you aren't. And that man was quite right about your face.' Dinah paused and considered the situation. How many times had she set up appointments with lawyers and then cancelled them? Too many times.

But Miss Meech was another woman. A woman and a lawyer, and plainly a successful one if she could afford to eat in the same restaurant as a Kellogg and a Campbell.

Somebody whose opinion might well be worth having. 'This is lovely but I'm suddenly not hungry,' Dinah said, pushing aside her plate. 'And this must be about the thousandth time Paul has evaporated on me.' She took a deep breath and came straight out with the opening line she had so often practised inside her own head. 'I entered into a marriage of convenience. And my husband never had the courage to tell me that he was not as other men.'

'Homosexual?'

'If only!' said Dinah, and she said it fervently. 'That I could have coped with. No, this was something much more unexpected.'

The Chart Room was a long narrow bar, with an illuminated ground-glass map of the world on the wall behind the counter. Mickey Grimshaw was sitting in front of it, on a high stool, thinking of doing something he had not done for a long time: he was thinking of getting drunk.

'Vodka Martini?' asked the barman, who had been on the ship for as long as Mickey could remember.

'A large one.'

So Jack's busy flirting with me and fathering children in one and the same breath, thought Mickey. I am, of course, mad. Everything about that young man is for sale – everything.

'I'm buying you that drink,' said a deep voice.

'Oh no you are not.' The man he'd been thinking about had materialised behind his shoulder.

Jack held up his hands like a surrendering Red Indian. 'What did I do?'

'I hear you make babies for money.' Mickey didn't care if the barman did hear.

'I'll have an orange juice,' Jack called across the counter. 'You been talking to that crazy young feminist?' he asked Mickey.

This seemed an unlikely description of the woman in the ever-enlarging hats. 'No, to a friend of hers.'

Jack let out a deep sigh and settled himself on the

next stool along, which brought a lot of black denim-covered thigh muscle into play. 'The feminist had seen the soft-core version of *Lawless Abandon*. The director got famous so it was screened at some Grade Z art-movie house.'

Furious as Mickey was, there could be no denying that Jack wore tight, white, tee shirts better than any other man on board. The taut, little, embroidered logo proclaimed that the simple garment must have cost a good hundred and fifty dollars. And we all know how you got that sort of money, thought Mickey grimly.

'Look,' said Jack, 'she saw me as bloodstock. She's one of those cookie girls who reserve the right to give themselves a baby. It would just have been me and a paper cup.'

'Thanks.' The barman had placed Mickey's vodka Martini on the counter. This time he did lower his voice: 'Are you telling me that you turned down ten thousand bucks?'

There was tiny silence, and then Jack said, in embarrassed tones, 'I only do safe sex.'

'I don't get you.' Mickey had not started on the drink. Instead, he was twiddling a toothpick which speared the green cocktail olive.

'The movies are condoms, condoms, condoms. I've had eleven HIV tests, all of them – thank God – negative.' Jack's shaggy eyebrows had all but met in embarrassment. 'There's just a short period where the virus can fail to show up: I couldn't saddle some unborn kid with the risk of that.'

And Mickey loved him again.

'So what are we going to do about us?' Jack accepted his orange juice from the bartender.

'Is there really an us?' asked Mickey quietly. The proposal he had intended to make was suddenly striking him as rather less than honourable. 'You think?'

'Yes I do think.' In one decisive movement Jack had reached across the bar and placed a hand on top of Mickey's.

But the way he did it – the hand was still lying there – doesn't look cissified, thought Mickey. It just has that American look of two men who are really close. And I want him closer – much closer.

But the hand had been withdrawn. And now Jack said, 'Don't think I'm on the make. One way and another I'm probably as well off as you are.'

'Okay, what is it *you* want?'

'How about dinner tonight? Just the two of us. We could try and get into the Princess Grill. The head waiters never mind trying to find somebody else who wants to swap restaurants for just one meal.'

'Would that be fair on Sorrel and Mrs Fiddler?' Oh blow Sorrel! he thought. Wasn't she the one who said that this was not going to be a physical affair?

'Polly and Sorrel will be just fine.' Jack had stopped sounding real, he'd gone halfway American again. 'They only want to remember Manchester in the old days; all they can do is talk about the Cromford Club and Clifton's Film Star Fashion shop.'

'Okay.' Mickey raised his glass in a toast. 'To us.'

'Us.' Jack downed his orange juice in one gulp and said 'I'm going down below. Need to catch up on some sleep. Pick you up at nine.' Every female eye in the bar followed him as he strode towards the exit.

Why does he need to catch up on sleep? wondered Mickey. What was he up to last night? And do I have the right to think thoughts like that? Maybe I do. Wowee, maybe I really do! The rest of the Martini went down his throat like glorious quicksilver. Mickey gazed at the ground-glass map of the world and felt as though he owned the whole planet. That chest, those arms . . . but shining above all of Jack's more obvious attractions was the fact that he had refused to compromise an unborn child.

'Better?' asked the barman, nodding towards the empty glass.

'So much better!' Mickey strolled out of the bar. On the long corridor outside he gazed through a porthole at his friend the ocean. Wasn't it gypsies who always showed their true loves to the moon and to the sea? In his imagination he was already inventing dialogue, ready for the Princess Grill.

His wave-washed reveries must have kept him occupied for fully ten minutes. That was when he registered a solitary figure, standing by the huge oval table, at the far end of the covered walkway. A half-completed jigsaw puzzle always sat on the green baize-covered top of this Regency antique. The forlorn female silhouette turned towards the light, and he realised that it was Sorrel.

Mickey hurried over to join her. 'Are you okay?'

'Fine,' she lied. 'No, not really.' He had looked so happily enraptured, gazing out to sea, that she had not wanted to burden him with her own misery. 'Things keep going round in my head, that's all.'

'What things?'

'That doctor in London.' She wasn't sure she could tell the rest. She hadn't even mentioned it in AA meetings.

'What about him?'

'I could be mad . . .'

'Everybody knows you're mad.' It was said with the same uncomplicated love that had held them together since they were eight years old. 'Tell me. You've got to.'

'When he'd finished examining me, he asked me to wait a minute.' She didn't want to go on.

'And?'

'He excused himself for a minute, and he went across the corridor and got another man; he said he was a big fan of mine.' Again she paused and this time Mickey allowed her to continue in her own time. 'He said he was his radiographer.' Now she let out the thought which had haunted her ever since. 'It felt as though he was measuring me up, for size, with his eyes. And they were muttering something about "cell cultures". Mick, what are they going to *do* to me?'

The same promenading passengers who had observed Mickey with Jack Lawless, through the big windows of the Chart Room, were now treated to the sight of the author embracing his red-haired leading lady like there was no tomorrow.

And there might not be many more tomorrows, he reminded himself. 'We'll get through it,' he promised her. 'We always have done.'

'This could be one scene that you *can't* rewrite for me.'

'How dare you? I never had to rewrite a word of your dialogue in my life!' But I can't just dump you for dinner tonight, he thought. Not when you're in this state. 'Go and sit down for a minute. I've got to make a phone call.'

He dived for a public telephone within sight of the big staircase, the one flanked by huge full-length portraits of the Royal Family. The purser's office connected him with Jack's cabin. 'About tonight: I've got to chuck. Please believe there's no rejection in this, in fact we can all have dinner together. Sorrel's in a state. She needs me.'

Strangely enough, Jack seemed to understand: 'Calm down, it's okay. Will she still need you at midnight?'

'Midnight should be my own.'

'No, it's going to belong to both of us. Meet me in the jacuzzi on the open deck. I'll find you in the hot-tub on the stroke of twelve.'

Dinah and Miss Meech were the last passengers left, lingering over coffee, in the Queen's Grill. The frumpish lady lawyer was also enjoying a Turkish cigarette. Pointing to a painting of the upper decks of the ship, she said, 'Did you know that they can still use the yardarm as a gibbet? And that the captain is still allowed to hang people?'

'No, I didn't know that.' But it led Dinah to wonder why she was bothering to seek divorce advice when she was still hell-bent on doing away with June Gee. Dinah's murderous intentions were of such long standing that her sense of humour had lost its power to diffuse them. And anyway, with any luck, she would get away with her crime – leaving Paul Snowden as the only shadow across an altogether more satisfactory future.

'Let us recapitulate,' said Miss Meech. Half an hour earlier, once the pair of them had fallen to dissecting Dover soles, she had agreed to abandon Catholic scruples by giving Dinah the benefit of her experience. 'But only in the abstract, my dear. And even then I suppose I could be deemed to be assisting in the commission of a Mortal Sin. Yes, let us recap: the doctor placed your mother-in-law from your first marriage in a nursing home, where she subsequently died.'

'Yes, but not before I'd married Paul. She kept screaming she was going to change her will. But, fortunately, she'd got too gaga.'

'So your present husband married a potentially rich woman?'

'Richish, for those days. Nothing by our later standards. It was the formula that was the real attraction.'

'And from the start he offered you a marriage of, let us say, "companionship"?'

'He just said: "You won't mind if it's not very sexy, will you?"'

'He definitely used the word *very*. Think carefully, this is important.'

'Definitely.' But even as she said this, Dinah began to squirm inside because she had some idea of what would be coming next. And, quite frankly, she wouldn't know how to answer.

It came. 'Was this marriage ever consummated?'

'I don't know.'

Miss Meech fixed her with a thrush's eye. 'Did sexual intercourse take place?'

Dinah was sure that the squirming must now be showing on the outside. 'Well, *something* happened. But not for quite a few years and I can never be sure whether it counted.'

'You are going to have to allow me to be the judge of that.'

A small procession began to wend its way into the

396

restaurant. It was headed by a rotund and mature Catholic priest, closely followed by Miss Meech's women friends and a thin young man on a walking stick, who looked almost too poorly to be on his feet.

'I have been gathering together the faithful,' boomed the priest in the tones of someone who always assumed command. 'We took lunch in the Lido and now we're going to say the rosary in your cabin, Muriel.'

'Which gives you my Christian name,' said Miss Meech to Dinah as she picked up her handbag and rose to her feet, all skinny arms and legs. 'Decide what you want to tell me, and then give me a call.'

'Come along, Muriel,' chivvied the priest, 'we don't want to keep Our Lady waiting.'

Miss Meech, however, had not finished with Dinah. 'But do be sure to telephone. It strikes me that you've got too much locked up inside for your own good.'

17

How much should she tell Muriel Meech? That was what Dinah was wondering as she sat in an armchair in the ship's library, pretending to be immersed in the memoirs of Lauren Bacall.

Her mind went back to the early days of that second marriage. Much of her inheritance had gone into developing Aquarius Galactica – already a thoroughly healthy concern. But her cash infusion nudged the company into the big export market, and plaited her own financial fortunes with those of Paul Snowden. Though the returns were enormous it did not take her long to feel thoroughly trapped.

They never lived up to their whole income, but soon after the wedding Paul decided that they ought to buy a late Victorian house in Didsbury, a South Manchester suburb with a high opinion of itself.

The weight of this large quantity of bricks and mortar made her feel trapped even more deeply into an alien way of life with her chilly bridegroom. Dinah came from the easy-going north of the city; in fact, strictly speaking, the Height was in Salford. Even Eccles had been a place of childhood visits to the market, and trips to the pantomimes at the Broadway Theatre. Every corner had held a memory for her. She thought of every bit of local history as part of her own makeup.

The tree-lined streets of solid West Didsbury were exactly how she imagined the South of England. Not neighbourly, too far up driveways. No, upon reflection, halfway like the Southern counties. The whole hog would have been different enough for her to have embraced it with ease. As it was, Dinah felt she was in a semi-foreign land just a five-shilling taxi ride from the centre of Manchester.

But five shillings had already turned into twenty-five new pence. And life warmed up a little when Alistair and Avril bought a house with a back garden which bordered on to her own.

'I see what you mean about this place,' said Avril. 'The woman next door to me goes on about "our wonderful little Didsbury fishmonger" as though she'd given birth to him herself.'

By this time Avril had two children of her own – both boys. Two more mouths to feed when Paul seemed intent upon edging Alistair further and further away from the centre of their business interests.

'I know it's not you,' she would say to Dinah. 'But Paul's attitude even leaves me scared of the size of our new mortgage.'

The name of Dinah's house was already chiselled into both of the stone gateposts when they took possession – Arlington. Detached and tall and thin, it rose up on one side to a narrow slate-roofed tower, just like a child's money box.

Paul described the exterior plasterwork as the worst fake Tudor on earth. 'But there's not a lot we can do about it,' he said. The interior was a different matter. All the reception rooms had been half-panelled in what the estate agent from Reeds Rains had described as 'a wealth of old oak'.

On Paul's instructions, it all disappeared under three coats of best white emulsion. Likewise the three floors of oaken staircase were treated with snowy gloss paint, and the stairs themselves were covered with fitted coconut matting. Out went the elaborate stained glass, and all the curtains in the house were made of lavish quantities of plain unbleached calico.

This pristine background achieved, he then proceeded to furnish Arlington with a combination of both Habitat and severe late-Georgian furniture, which could still be bought relatively cheaply at auction. And Paul had been collecting paintings by Manchester artists since he was a schoolboy, so the walls were hung with canvases by

Alan Lowndes and Harold Riley – all with their frames removed.

'None of it has anything to do with me,' said Dinah to Avril. 'It's not a house, it's a stage set. All he needs to do now is hire somebody to come down the staircase singing a miserable song by Stephen Sondheim.'

And then there were the attics. The one in the tower had proper windows but the rest were simply lofts with glass skylights. 'Better left,' was Paul's decision. 'If we ever fall on bad times – and we're not going to – they can be converted into a self-contained flat. For the moment I'll just have my darkroom up there and the rest can be locked off.' His dark and moody photographs were of near-professional standard.

And he was moody himself. There were times when he got himself wound into states of great tension until something – Dinah never knew what – brought him downstairs full of easy charm and flooded with release.

As his obsession with money-making increased, amateur dramatics became a thing of the past. Yes, trapped, that's what she was. Trapped in low-lying West Didsbury.

'I've heard of "fur coat and no knickers",' said Avril, 'but this is the first place I ever knew where they pinch the washing off the line.'

'You're joking!'

'Underwear keeps on going,' maintained Avril stoutly.

'Do you think we're suffering from inferiority complexes?' suggested Dinah.

'All I know is that I love it when the car goes back over the Salford border.'

Dinah herself headed north of the city quite often, to visit her mother and to call upon Daisy Carver. John had always maintained that the old shed-dweller might replace the addiction she had conquered with another one. Drink had been his fear.

'I go all over to Spiritualist meetings,' boasted Daisy, gleaming clean these days. 'Mind you, I'm used to buses from the days when I used to traipse off after me stuff. I've been put in contact with Jessie more times than I can tell you: she's got two of her horses with her on the Other Side. How's life in a double bed?'

'How much are you spending on this Spiritualism?' countered Dinah. In reality the Snowdens had a pair of twin beds, and the fitted haircord between them was in no danger of getting worn out.

As they prospered, the utilitarian floor-covering was ripped up and two workmen spent a whole weekend sanding the bedroom floorboards. One of the men had looked like Rory Brogan had once looked, which depressed Dinah. What was worse, he had not given her so much as a second glance: she was getting old, heading for forty. Why, once or twice she'd even caught herself defending Didsbury. In truth she had come to see it as comfortable and intelligent and civilised, to realise that even its petty snobberies were often self-mocking.

'But somebody's still pinching underwear,' maintained Avril. 'It stops and then starts again; I'm trying to work out whether it goes with the full moon.'

Dinah sometimes felt that something similar had happened to her own sex-drive. It was not that it had vanished, more slunk away into a corner in unwanted embarrassment. There could be no denying that she sometimes pleasured herself, when Paul was out. And then wondered whether the Ice Prince did the same thing when she was off the premises?

But where would he do it? Feeling guilty about even imagining this, she went off to hide her nasty battery vibrator; even before she'd closed her handkerchief drawer she had decided that Paul must sneak up into the locked attic.

Why not the bathroom? Not mysterious enough for him, she decided. The former amateur actor had designed the whole house as a production in the round, so even masturbation would call for an appropriate setting. Yes, definitely that locked attic.

And what would he fantasise about? She had absolutely no idea. They shared that bedroom, he wasn't shy about her seeing him naked, yet she had no idea of what went

401

on in his head. Those people who said they looked like brother and sister were nearer the truth than they realised!

The thing that really worried her was that she had concurred in a lie. In the very early days of the marriage he had said, 'We're not the kind of people who think sex is important, are we?'

And in the throes of a heavy period it had seemed easier to agree with him. But that agreement would appear to have been taken as a licence for a life of perpetual chastity. Money, that's what the Ice Prince was interested in – making lots and lots of money. She had once caught him sniffing a wad of new five-pound notes and the expression on his face had been precious close to rapture.

As the Seventies turned into the Thatcher Years, Aquarius Galactica was transformed into AG (International) Limited. The psychedelic packaging became a thing of the past. Everything was given a new, sharply geometrical look; even Paul's hair was cropped like an astronaut's. One product alone retained its Sixties look: the Gentlemen's Remedy had been renamed 'Vesuvius', the tablets were now volcano shaped, and the label described it as 'formulated in the Summer of Love'.

'Vesuvius – The Only Genuine Aphrodisiac!' said the show cards. These were on view, in New Age health stores, halfway round the world. But a small disclaimer on a leaflet wound round the neck of the bottle, inside the box, covered them against legal action by 'men of low libido'. It was all very cunning. Nearly as cunning as Paul Snowden himself.

Of course she hadn't known about that streak, not until he slipped up.

These days Avril wouldn't set foot in gleaming Arlington, such was the estrangement between Alistair and Paul. If Dinah wanted to see her, she had to nip through the gap in the hawthorn hedging.

Avril's house was all bicycles in the hall and roller skates underfoot and never-finished mountains of ironing. But there was always a good smell of some cheaper cut of meat cooking slowly in the oven, and she had given up Co-op coffee in favour of real Colombian beans.

Above the clatter of the coffee grinder, Dinah said, 'Just look at that bit of guttering hanging down off the back off our house. I'm surprised the Ice Prince hasn't noticed it.'

No comment from Avril. The grinding noise had given way to silence: highly embarrassed silence.

'Has there been another bust-up with Alistair?' ventured Dinah.

'No, but there's likely to be one with me. That underwear of mine's started going missing again. And it's your antiseptic husband who's stealing it.'

Sorrel was in bed by half-past eleven, trying to pretend that she hadn't noticed Mickey stuffing a pair of bathing trunks into the pocket of the silk evening trousers he was wearing with his blue velvet smoking jacket. 'Do you know who you've started to look like, Mick? Rod Steiger. Be sure and keep things safe tonight. Sex I'm talking about.'

'You're not supposed to know,' he retorted indignantly.

'Not supposed to know?' She threw away all pretence of being sleepy. 'It was like having dinner with two tomcats. Did you know that men stretch a lot when they're anticipating making love? I doubt that poor waitress will ever get the gravy stains off her uniform.'

'I do not look like Rod Steiger,' he said, checking his face in the mirror.

'Oh go on, get off on your date.'

Once he had gone she gave way to perplexity. Hadn't Jack Lawless said over and over again, in AA meetings, that he was incapable of celebrating affection. ('Sex for exercise, yes. Even the thought of the other freezes me up.') His reasons, when eventually revealed, had left her wanting to put her arms around him – filled her with pity. Yet tonight, at dinner, Jack had been practically shining with fondness for Mickey. Now the pair of them were sneaking off together. And in the distance she thought she could hear thunder.

Outside, on the corridor, Mickey had almost reached the short staircase which led up to Deck One. He too was thinking about the mechanics of lovemaking. He was remembering the early days of what had been called the Gay Men's Health Crisis, recalled seeing the first packets of Trojans for sale on Castro Street in San Francisco – the last place on earth to be in need of birth control.

That was the day he had decided he would never place his own life on a latex trampoline. He just hoped that Jack would understand that screwing – in either role – was definitely out. You could still do plenty without that.

At the top of the stairs he could hear some distant cocktail pianist playing nostalgic strains of Cole Porter. The *QE2* at midnight has to be about as glamorous as this world gets, he thought. As he walked out onto the open deck the night sky was like a star-cloth in the finale of an old edition of the Ziegfeld Follies – complete with cut-out circular moon.

And if my similes are cheap and theatrical, he thought, I don't give a fuck! They brought me to this point in my life. The early years of my career might have been hard going, but tonight I feel blessed.

There were no lights left on in the little Pavilion Restaurant which dispensed hamburgers during the day. The pool was empty of people but completely filled with water again. And at the far end, on a raised level, more water was slapping and lapping inside a pair of deserted Jacuzzis.

Changing rooms? Ah yes, over there. And there was a light shining under the door of the one marked 'Men'.

As he stepped inside Mickey recalled Sorrel saying that there was no sexier sight on earth than a man in a white evening shirt and black trousers. That's what an already bare-foot Jack Lawless was wearing at this moment.

'Hi,' said Mickey, trying not to stare as Jack removed the black bow tie, and then began to undo the buttons concealed behind the plain pleating of the shirt.

If I carry on staring like this, he thought in a panic, I'll be in no state to take off my own pants. And Jack knows the exact erotic value of silence.

The sex star was filling the silence with a direct gaze from those oh-so-green eyes. When he finally spoke he said, 'Why don't you undress?'

How many times have I thought about renewing my gym membership? wondered Mickey. How many sit-ups would it have taken to equip me for this moment? 'I'm very conscious of that fact that I won't look as good as you do.'

'Aren't you forgetting I already saw you once?'

Yes, and the sauna had a flattering, tan-coloured, electric light bulb, thought Mickey.

But Jack was not to be deflected. 'Want me to help you take them off?'

When his body had still been in good shape, that might have been nice. 'No, I'll manage.' He could not help noticing that Jack was down to a jock strap.

That firm gaze was straight out of one of the porn star's own videos. He had almost managed to make himself look as though the eyes were in close-up. Mesmerised, Mickey removed every stitch of his own clothing. Now he was wearing less than the other man.

'Okay,' sighed Jack. 'Let's get it over with.' Down came the constricting athletic support. Lightly massaging his parts back to comfort, he said, 'The Chinese maintain that this quantity ain't gentlemanly. You're allowed a good hard look. Everybody wants one. I'm used to it.'

'Why downgrade yourself? You must know you're more than just a big dick.'

If these words had broken the erotic spell they also seemed to have charged Jack with real pleasure. Reaching towards a pile of clean white towels he said, 'When I can, I try not to bother with trunks: they make me look grotesque.'

Mickey climbed into his own. They were black with a cord at the waistband, which needed adjusting.

'Let me do that.' As Jack tightened the cord he said in

tones of grateful wonder, 'I actually touched you. I did, I touched.'

Suddenly I feel ageless, thought Mickey, as the pair of them padded across the open deck. He has managed to wipe out all the years.

The water in the raised Jacuzzi was pleasantly warm to the skin. It was swirling round and around. And the moonlit waves of the sea were rolling in almost straight lines, towards the far horizon. 'If there are better moments than this,' said Mickey, 'I've never had one.'

Jack slipped an arm around his shoulder. 'And again I touched you!'

Why was he making it sound as though this was some sort of miracle? Doubts returned. 'Is it that I'm so ancient?'

'I *like* your age. All those years that went into *A Town To Remember*. Any guy can lift weights and get what I've got. Most of what I've got,' he corrected himself. 'Do I bring the cock into conversation too much? It made my life a nightmare at school.'

'Tell me about when you were little.'

'That part of me was never little.' Jack let out a groan. 'There I go again! I am *so* cheap.'

'I expect it haunts everything. Like *Angel Dwellings* does with me.' Bubble, bubble, bubble, went the swirling waters, lap, slap, lap.

Yes, perfection, thought Mickey. And suddenly he did not want this important new influence in his life to start recounting tales of Borstal to the streets of London, Piccadilly meat-rack to West Hollywood. He just wanted him to be there. To *be*.

But Jack must have felt that something more spectacular than that was required because he said, 'What's a nice boy like me doing with a life-style like mine?' And then chose to answer himself in wry tones: 'I guess I'm just lucky.'

This line was the first real evidence of anything shop-soiled that Mickey had encountered in the man. Anxious to divert it, he asked, 'How did you get into those movies anyway?' That was debatably show-business. The kind of story that would have interested him under any circumstances.

Jack's answer was drowned out by a flash of lightning and a clap of thunder that both seemed married into one moment. As Mickey clambered out of the tub he yelled, 'That wasn't just near, it's here!'

'Chicken,' teased Jack, still in the water and making lazy swimming movements with his arms.

'For God's sake, you're surrounded by metal,' cried Mickey in alarm.

'And?' The smile was still wonderfully relaxed.

But Mickey was getting even more wound-up. 'You could get struck by lightning, you dumbo!'

'And would you care?' Flash-crash. Another zigzag danced above the outline of the ship's funnel. 'Would you care?'

'I'd care, I'd care, I'd care.' Mickey had literally seized him by the hand and pulled him out of the Jacuzzi.

In the changing cabin, as they dried themselves off, Jack said, 'Just listen to that rain, hammering on the deck outside. God, I love rain. That sound is so beautiful.'

They were obliged to wait in the doorway, for it to slacken off. Am I meant to make a move, wondered Mickey. Or does he see himself as the one who's setting the pace? At one time I wouldn't have wondered, I'd just have made a pass. So what was stopping him now: fear of rejection, fear of failure? Once again he found himself wondering *Just what is he after*?

'Okay, it's stopped coming down heavily enough to mark that velvet jacket,' announced Jack. 'Let's go down below.' They crossed the deck and began to descend the short stairway. 'Did you notice that fat fortune-woman up there?'

'June? No. What was she doing?'

'Just gazing out to sea. And another woman was standing spying at her, from the shadows. It was kind of spooky.'

So June's stalker was still at it. This revelation left

407

Mickey feeling unsettled. 'Noticing things is supposed to be part of my job,' he said uneasily.

'Nobody notices things like somebody who's hustled on Santa Monica Boulevard.'

This was not the top end of the call boy trade. 'You did that?'

'Even after I was supposed to be famous.' They were on their own corridor. 'But in dark glasses.'

'Why?' Now they were outside Jack's door.

'To see whether I was really attractive. I thought maybe I was just photogenic. I guess I wanted more than the camera to like me.'

This time it was Mickey Grimshaw who tried to put everything into a long look. But it couldn't have worked because Jack simply placed his key in the door and said, 'I need sleep.'

'And that's that?' The words were out before Mickey could suppress them.

'On a first date? Yeah, that's that. Goodnight.'

He was gone. Ditched by a porno star who'd put himself on offer on Santa Monica Boulevard to any passing motorist. Yet over-riding this was the thought that Jack had refused to get out of the water until Mickey admitted that it really mattered. It was all too Rock Hudson and Doris Day to be true. But at least his powers of observation were back because Mickey was certain that he had just caught sight of two tall men, in deepest drag, disappearing hurriedly around the corner. Stewards, he decided: stewards who had sneaked up from their own bar – the Pig and Whistle.

But he was wrong.

Dinah did not have far to go to get out of the thunderstorm and back to her cabin. Once she'd towelled her hair dry, she unlocked the wall-safe and took out her bound diary. Dinah had never left the illustrated journal lying around since . . . how many years would it be?

They were still living in Didsbury. It was the same week

408

Avril had told her about the missing washing. The news that her husband was stealing women's underclothes had a strange effect upon Dinah: she felt as though life had dealt her an actual physical blow. She'd actually had to sit down. And, metaphorically, she had not got up again for several days.

She seemed to spend her whole time considering how to broach the subject. *'By the way, isn't it about time you gave Avril her bra and pants back?'* But it wasn't funny, it was too bizarre for that. And though she and Paul had used the years of their marriage to evolve a dashing, dodging way of life, at least it had been one which had allowed for frigid privacy. She was not sure that she had the right to invade that.

And then he invaded hers.

Dinah had been entertaining an American buyer, had driven him off to lunch at the Admiral Rodney at Prestbury, and then brought him back to see the garden at Arlington. This copy of an eighteenth-century herb garden was something of a showpiece for the company, which rendered its upkeep tax-deductible. Neither Dinah nor Paul ever laid so much as a finger on a trowel themselves. Instead, the garden was tended by green-fingered Eugene Gannon: the job constituted his semi-retirement pension. Whilst he was a figure who had faded into the background of their lives, the Turnock twins had matured into area reps of considerable acumen.

The garden was looking good that afternoon. The Elizabethan-style pyramids of scarlet runner beans added just the right amount of colour to its more sombre mysteries. Dinah dispensed tea in the rustic summer house, and then sent the client back to his hotel in a hired limousine – the driver was always instructed not to let on that he didn't really belong to AG (International) Limited. Even the bees had exceeded their duty by swarming at just the right moment. Afternoons of this nature were very carefully thought out.

But today's visitor, the owner of a chain of health stores in the Mid-West, had been a man of considerable charm and of striking near-cowboy appearance, so Dinah had determined to make a quick sketch of him whilst he was still fresh in her memory.

The bound book was lying where it always lay in those days, on her writing desk in the airy white entrance hall, which was almost a room in itself.

Dinah made it a point of honour never to look back on one of her drawings until it was at least a week old. That way she could view her own work dispassionately. The one she turned back to, now, was a black-and-white drawing of a cocktail party. But somebody had seen fit to 'improve' it in red ball-point. Beneath the sketch of Paul, in his own handwriting, were written the words 'Not very flattering, darling'. And he had taken it upon himself to colour the lips in the same offensive scarlet.

Never before, in her whole life, had anybody added so much as a pencil stroke to her pages. 'And least of all a fucking knicker-thief!' She shouted the words out loud and they were caught up by the parquet-floored hall's own echo. '*Knicker-thief, knicker-thief!*'

If he could invade her privacy, she could invade his. Half-formulated thoughts took on an instant shape. Something often brought Paul down from the attic with a smile on his face: something secret and hidden. The stolen underwear was something else which smacked of furtive mystery – it all had to be part of a whole. And the answer had to lie on that locked top floor.

The only key lived on his key chain. But the house was half hers, which meant that the locked door was half her own too. And there was a coal hammer in the cellar.

The next few minutes were all stairs. Down to the cellar, up to the darkroom. The locked door lay behind Paul's big Kodak enlarger.

Raising the hammer, Dinah smashed it open with five angry blows. And then she reached inside and felt for the light switch.

'I don't often drink brandy,' said Dinah to Miss Meech, 'but when I came downstairs, from that attic, I downed half a tumbler of the stuff. And I still couldn't stop shaking.'

It was the morning of the fifth day at sea, and she had met up with Miss Meech, by appointment, in the relative quiet of the Queen's Room: the only sounds were the tinkle of coffee spoons and a faint hum of conversation.

'But what did you *find* up there?' demanded the lawyer who was all in black today. This was, presumably, to set off an enamelled and jewelled brooch. It featured the head of John the Baptist, rubies represented his dripping blood. 'What had your husband got hidden?'

'A woman's bedroom.'

'What?' They were false teeth and they narrowly missed flying out.

'And in the most fussy taste you ever saw. Pink light bulbs, a Marie Antoinette dressing table, and great big gilded mirrors. At first I found it impossible to believe that it had anything to do with Paul.'

'There was, presumably, a bed?'

Dinah shook her head. 'Just a chaise-longue. But there were wardrobes. They must have been got in whilst I was out because they were absolutely enormous: white with gold metal trimming.'

'Empty?'

'Crammed full of the most expensive clothes. I was already buying designer labels by then, but some of these were by the big Italian names. Not just dresses: coats, furs, everything. That was in the first wardrobe. The second was even odder.'

'Am I ready for this?' enquired Miss Meech, who very plainly was.

'It was more a fitted cupboard. Shelves and shoe-racks.' Dinah was remembering her own amazement. 'All the high-heeled shoes were absolutely enormous. And the shelves were full of wigs on polystyrene heads. Blonde ones, black ones, everything from great big Hollywood styles to one that looked like Victoria Wood's own hair.'

'How on earth did you confront him with all of this?'

'I didn't. Not directly. Oh look, that bloody harpist is lugging her instrument into the middle of the floor again! No, I decided to answer Paul in the same way he'd annoyed me.'

Dinah could almost taste that cloying medicinal brandy again as she remembered herself – downstairs at Arlington – opening the diary at a blank double-page. Remembered herself beginning to make a drawing of what she had seen in the attic.

'In the foreground I had an open dressing table drawer,' she recalled for Miss Meech's benefit. 'And it was full of stolen underwear – in every size known to woman. It was rather a striking sketch, though I say it myself. I really overstated the pastel shades. And once the colours were dry, I put the diary back on the writing desk in the hall. And I left it wide open.'

What had the packets of Polycell been for, and the rubber balloons? That was what Dinah wanted to know as she sat waiting for the sound of Paul's car coming up the drive. He wouldn't be needing dinner tonight, that much she already knew via a message from his secretary. Apparently he and the other American client had enjoyed a late and massive luncheon at the Midland.

By now it was eight o'clock, so the painted diary had been sitting on the Regency writing desk for a good two hours. Dinah had even watched an episode of *Angel Dwellings*, a programme she generally had no time for at all. Its closing theme music must have drowned out the purr of the Bentley because, the next thing she knew, Paul was calling out from somewhere inside the house: 'Any messages?'

'On the hall desk.'

Silence.

Too long a silence. Dinah considered getting to her feet and going out to see what was happening. No, it was up to him to make the first move. Mentally, she was rehearsing her opening line: 'You should not have drawn in my book.' But she never got the chance to deliver it because, diary in hand, Paul marched into the room saying, 'None of these things are mine.' It was just like one of those board meetings where he started off with a high-vitality attack.

She tried to reconcile the handsome clipped-haired figure, in the casual grey flannel suit from Brooks Brothers in New York, with the rows of flashily feminine clothes upstairs. 'If they're not yours, whose are they?'

'They belong to Pamela,' he said defensively.

'And who's she?'

'The other side of the coin.'

This was the very first time she had ever heard that puzzling phrase which was soon to haunt her whole life. 'I don't understand.'

'I know you don't.' He suddenly seemed short of breath. 'She's somebody I always wanted you to meet.'

'Explain.'

His lightning-fast answer was another bit of boardroom technique. 'I'd rather demonstrate.'

I'm not going to let him manipulate me like this, she thought. It's not as though I'm short of ammunition. 'Avril's knickers,' she said accusingly.

'I beg your pardon.'

She could tell he was playing for time. 'It's Avril's pardon you should be begging, not mine. Why have you been pinching things off clothes lines? Stop pacing up and down like that, I want some answers.'

And he did stop. 'Okay, I'll spell it out. I'm a cross-dresser.'

'You should have told me that before we got married.'

'I thought I could control it, Di.' He only called her that when he wanted something. 'And for a while I did. Fix me a gin and tonic.'

'Fix your own.'

He went over to the silver drinks tray and began to clank around with a decanter and a glass. 'Before the honeymoon, I burned everything: clothes, wigs, the lot.'

'What honeymoon? We were just two people who went on holiday together.'

He came back across the room and settled himself down, with his drink, on the opposite white leather sofa to the one she was sitting upon. 'Taking things off lines has always been the equivalent of a wank.'

'Would you mind telling me what full sex is?'

'Turning myself into Pamela. Except she's always there, inside me. She's just the other side of the coin. Look at me.'

She didn't want to. She was trying to imagine what face powder would look like on top of that five o'clock shadow. Except it was eight o'clock, and they had lived in this loveless marriage for thirteen years, and now was too late to find out something as big as this. 'If you'd just given me a bit of choice in the matter, I might feel differently.' Suddenly she didn't want to carry on with the conversation. 'I'm going to boil myself an egg.'

'I was always scared you'd be off like a frightened rabbit,' he said gratefully.

'I don't scare easily.' She was already at the door.

'Meet Pamela in the flesh. Judge her for yourself.'

That scares me, she thought. Even the idea makes me want to get into my own car and drive till the petrol runs out. It makes me want a whole new life. The present one, which had always seemed so sterile, now struck her as being as bizarre as newsagents' topshelf pornography. There had been magazines like that on the French dressing table in the attic – *Tranz Monthly* and *Men Into Women*.

'Meet her,' he persisted.

All their finances were as complicatedly entwined as a piece of jacquard weaving. Extracting herself from that could lose her a fortune. The fun had gone out of their lives years ago: there was no novelty left in boarding Concorde, her luggage had already seen the inside of enough smart hotels for a lifetime.

I couldn't expect anybody to pity me, she thought. But I've never really been Mrs Paul Snowden: just a counter-signature on a company cheque. 'All right, I'll meet her,' she said. 'But that doesn't mean I've got to like her.'

Dinah didn't bother with the egg. She was still thinking about how enviable her life must appear on the surface, and the emptiness of the reality. And it was all the fault of one woman. June Gee. That begetter of bogus messages from the dead.

Had it not been for that big blonde I'd be married to Rory, and not sitting here worrying about what I've just seen in an attic with a pink fitted carpet – something else that must have been achieved whilst I was out of the house. Paul's life must have been one long smuggling exercise. Not just clothes and shoes, but proper women's wrist watches and umbrellas, and two pairs of upswept reading glasses. And Dinah still couldn't understand that Polycell because the weird room had no wallpaper – it was painted lilac. He even had a white telephone extension up there.

And Pamela didn't just read dubious magazines, she subscribed to Italian *Vogue* and read novels by Jackie Collins. The Paul that Dinah knew would not have been caught dead on a train with one of those. And what was he doing to himself that was taking this long?

She didn't want to think about that huge satin basque with its cruelly elasticated gusset. That was a garment which could only have been made-to-measure. Just for something to do, Dinah crossed the room and placed the first record that came to hand upon the turntable of Paul's new sound system. The room was flooded with the metallically sinister voice of Eartha Kitt singing 'Lilac Wine'. All about making love under the lilac tree, and putting your heart in its recipe, and about it making you see what you wanted to see, and dream what you wanted to dream.

'Hello, darling.' Whilst Dinah's back had been turned, Pamela had made her entrance.

'She' was a caricature of Jackie Collins's sister, Joan. A tall version of the film star, made even taller by almost impossibly high-heeled shoes. People had often said that Paul was 'too pretty' for a man, but as a woman he looked as long-jawed as a pantomime horse. Thick false eyelashes added to this illusion and the angular and highly painted face was framed by a big black *Dynasty* hair-do. 'Hurry up and change. We're going out.'

'Where on earth can you go dressed like that?' gasped Dinah.

'Somewhere I've been going for years. Wear something a bit spectacular. Wednesday night is Tranny Night in Manchester.'

Pamela even had her own driving shoes.

And her own way of speaking, too. The content, rather than the tone, was reminiscent of a screaming pansy in a music-hall sketch. In fact, in Dinah's limited experience, even queers had stopped saying things like 'Get you, Ada!' Not Pamela.

'Darling, Manchester's alive with people "dressed" on a Wednesday night. The pavements are ringing to the sound of size ten stilettos.'

Though Paul was busy being Alexis Carrington, Dinah had not been foolish enough to attempt to go into competition. In fact, as she sat in the passenger seat wondering whether they were liable to get themselves arrested, she had some understanding of what it must be like to be a peahen.

'We're expected, darling. I phoned ahead.' Paul could have been rehearsing this kind of conversation for years.

'So who are we going to meet?' asked Dinah dully. They were already beyond the university and heading towards the city centre. For the moment her mind was just going with the flow, hoping to make some sort of sense of any clues that might be offered along the way. 'Are we going to meet your boyfriend?'

'Get one thing straight,' Paul's everyday voice was back with a bang, 'I am not gay.' The tone returned halfway to Pamela's as he said, 'I'm a heterosexual transvestite.'

Dinah's own voice remained neutral. 'I've never known you be any kind of sexual.'

But Pamela's got coyly syrupy. 'Now you're in on my secret, things could be different.' The big Bentley suddenly swerved to avoid an Indian in a turban. 'Oh look, I think he read me,' said Pam delightedly. 'That means he sussed,' she explained kindly.

But the creature driving the car was not really kind, decided Dinah. It was as though Paul had stopped being a person and turned into a weird collage: a penny-for-the-guy mask of a face, power-dressed shoulders, too much Giorgio perfume. A false fingernail tapped the steering wheel impatiently: 'You might at least pretend to be enjoying yourself.'

'Look, Paul, this isn't easy for me. In fact I think I'm being very broad-minded in just trying to understand. And you've still to apologise for scrawling in my diary.'

'Sorry, darling.' But it was Pam who had answered and Dinah was not yet prepared to allow that to count.

They parked the car in the rag trade district, at the back of Piccadilly. In the guise of a woman, Paul had a new way of walking through the darkening side streets: very fake-assured, with a lot of nervous, giveaway, sideways glances. And his strides were too long for a pencil skirt.

'We're here.' It looked like a mass-produced furniture store with a billiard hall above it. 'The club's on the top floor.' He pressed a bell, said 'Pamela' into a wall-microphone, and the door buzzed open.

His big heels made a terrible clatter on the bare wooden stairs. As she panted up behind him, Dinah registered that he was also wearing real, black, silk stockings, with seams. 'I still haven't had anything to eat,' she realised aloud.

'They do hot dogs, and you can generally get them to microwave a curry.'

Could this be the same fastidious man who had thought nothing of driving all the way to Yorkshire to try out the food of some restaurant's guest chef?

The upwards climb finally came to an end. A bouncer, a Greek-looking weightlifter in a dinner jacket and a black tee shirt, was standing beside a grubby white melamine desk, which brought home-improvements warehouses to mind. 'Evening, Pamela, you'll have to sign her in.'

'My wife,' said Paul. It was the first time Dinah had ever heard him say these words with any show of pride. 'Elaine here?'

The Greek nodded. 'With her Missus.'

A small bar, decked out with coloured picture postcards and cheap Spanish holiday souvenirs, led into a room that was trying to be a disco. The first bar had been deserted, save for a couple of mannish-looking women, downing pints. But the four spotlights in the bigger room were flashing down on a scene straight out of *The Muppet Show*. There were more of the 'Guy Fawkes' ladies, and Miss Piggy herself was already bearing down upon them, in the shape of a blonde roly-poly of a transvestite, wearing a black frock with a patent leather belt that was almost a corselette.

'Take a deep breath,' a quite an ordinary-looking woman advised Dinah. 'That's what I had to do the first time I came in here.' She was the real thing, no two ways about that. And she obviously belonged to Miss Piggy, who was now being introduced as 'Elaine'.

'And I'm Bea,' said the genuine woman, as Elaine and Pamela clomped off to the cloakroom together. 'Bea Palmer.'

'Paul's just ditched me without so much as ordering a drink,' said Dinah in surprise.

'You're with Pam tonight,' Bea reminded her. She and Dinah were the only people in the room in top-coats. With her dyed brown hair and her good tortoiseshell-framed glasses, Bea Palmer could have been an infants' school teacher, approaching retirement. 'What are you having?' she asked Dinah. 'Sit down on one of the settees and try and come to terms with things.'

The plastic-upholstered seats looked as though they could have started life in somebody's living room. For the second time that day Dinah settled for brandy. And then she wondered if this request had been a bit lavish;

but even if the woman's coat was dowdy, it was a good one.

The bar in this room was surrounded by men in inexplicable overalls. And two more of the masculine women were having an argument, by a pool table, with a couple of rough lads with good bodies – their shirts were open almost to the waist.

'Half-hearted rent boys,' explained Bea, returning from the counter with their drinks; her own was a tomato juice. 'They're only here for the queers. But the men round the bar are straight – night-workers from the post office. And most of the TVs are straight, except for that big girl with the brand-new bust – she used to be a drag queen but now she's well on the way to surgery.'

'I see,' said Dinah, who didn't.

'You're not the only wife who's had to walk in here for the first time.'

'I only found out today.'

'I know. Pam phoned Ellie. Here, have your brandy. Cheers.'

Was it the burned sugar taste of the drink, or just the place itself, which was suddenly making Dinah feel nauseous? Half rising to her feet, she said, 'I think I want to go.'

'You'd do yourself a bigger favour by staying.' The resemblance to an infants' teacher had, if anything, grown. Any minute now, Mrs Palmer looked as though she could be handing out Plasticine. 'Stay and learn. At least you've got me to explain things to you.'

'Is that why they waltzed off to the cloakroom? To leave us together?'

'They'll be comparing new eye-liners and swapping tranquillisers.'

Now Dinah *was* shocked. 'Paul doesn't believe in anything like that.'

'I only know what Pam likes.' Bea Palmer relented. 'Let me tell you how it was for me. We had one pub then, we've got two now. And two children, and one grandson but he came later. At the time I'm talking about we were what you might call young marrieds. He had his gun club and I was learning pottery, in the afternoons, at the Adult Education.

'It was winter, a Thursday afternoon, late on. There was a power cut at the Education Institute so they sent us all home. Even the street lights were out. And when I got outside the pub I could just see one candle glimmering in the upstairs living room.

'I still smoked in those days so I used my lighter to find my way upstairs. And, my God, when I got there I let it drop with a bang!

'There he was, dressed in my clothes, with a black beret on the side of his head, standing at the mirror, putting on that very pale Brigitte Bardot lipstick.' Bea was watching Dinah closely. 'Two children, a good little business, a good little life. So what did I do? I coped.'

Silence fell for a moment. That is to say that conversation stopped. Some recorded voice in the background was still singing about 'the naughty lady from Shady Lane'. Eventually Dinah asked, 'Do you love him?'

'Yes, Eric's still my man. But I've got quite fond of Elaine, too. You wouldn't believe some of the things she sends me shopping for!'

It was still hard to visualise Bea as a pub landlady. And it could have been Mrs Palmer, the imaginary infants' school teacher, who moved a little closer to Dinah, to murmur, 'It's brought a whole new dimension to the intimate side of life.'

Now Dinah did want to run. But the song 'YMCA' had taken control of the amplifiers, and Pamela and Elaine had danced their way back from the Ladies and into the centre of the floor.

By this time, Bea Palmer's lips were right up against Dinah's ear. 'See how the room is surrounded with mirrors? They're not dancing with each other, they're dancing with their own reflections. And, believe you me, they don't see knobbly knees and big hands, they only concentrate on the bits that look feminine.' Dinah could actually feel the woman's lips touching her own ears. 'Do yourself a favour, Dinah. Sooner or later he's going to ask you to zip him into a frock. And if you've any sense you'll give it a go.'

Dinah needed to think of something, anything, to put a stop to these attempts to get her in deeper. 'Could you just explain something?' She preferred honest shouting to that mouth-to-ear technique. 'Could you tell me what the Polycell and the balloons are for?'

'They mix one and pour it into the others. Falsies – liquid Polycell gives a lovely natural bounce.'

'I don't think I'll be getting involved,' said Dinah firmly. But, from out on the dance floor, Pamela was eyeing her up and down in a way that Paul had never thought of trying.

Why was that scratched recording of 'YMCA' turning into genteel harp music? Because more than fifteen years had rolled on and Dinah was recounting the tale, the story which had stayed for so long unreleased, to her new-found friend, Miss Meech. 'I couldn't even tell Avril because Paul and Alistair had reached the stage of litigation, and they were already throwing everything but the kitchen sink at one another.'

The tale had left Miss Meech's mouth hanging as wide open as the mouth on the enamelled face of John the Baptist, on the Russian icon-brooch, in her lapel.

'I've got a brooch like that,' said Dinah matter-of-factly.

Miss Meech stiffened. 'Whilst I am quite prepared to believe your revelations of sexual irregularities, this item of jewellery is one of a kind.'

'A lot of people would ask you whether it was made by Fabergé. I can tell you, for a fact, that it was the work of another crown jeweller to the Czar – a man called Beriosova.'

'You are absolutely right,' gasped Miss Meech. 'But wherever did you get yours?'

'It was handed to me in a lawyer's office, in a suburb of Manchester called Swinton – which is just about as far from the Imperial Crown Court as you can get.'

'Tell me more,' begged Miss Leech. 'Please tell me more.'

The letter from Adcock, Little and Carr had been forwarded on to Dinah by the most recent owners of Comfrey, who had got her address from the people to whom she sold the house, when Edna Tench died.

'If we hadn't found you soon,' said Bertram Adcock, senior partner in the law firm and the man who had actually written to her, 'we were going to be reduced to advertising in the *Evening News*.' He was a plumply pink and balding man in a black jacket and striped trousers.

Dinah judged him to be well into his seventies. 'So am I one of those people who are going to hear something to my advantage?' The letter had not been specific. She was used to lawyers' offices in modern purpose-built buildings. This one was just the first floor of a converted Edwardian villa, on the main Manchester Road, with a good view of bird-droppings on the tops of passing buses.

'I'm more or less retired,' admitted Mr Adcock, after he had failed to find himself an ashtray. 'I don't come in very often these days. But the will in question terminates a family connection which went back many years. Not with the deceased,' he added hastily. 'I fear the deceased died in Ladywell Hospital, which was once the workhouse. Our connection lay with the source of the original fortune.' He had finally decided to stub out his cigarette in a saucer, under a cactus, on top of the desk. 'It would be my grandfather who was originally retained to act for the Gilmour family. Their money came from biscuits. Of course I can just about recall Miss Jessica Gilmour . . .'

Goodness but he's pompous, thought Dinah. And I wish he'd stop looking at my legs.

'She smoked a little clay pipe, you know. And it was always said that she went into Worsley Woods, every morning, to shoot her own breakfast.' Adcock transferred his eyes from Dinah's legs to her bust and lowered his voice to murmur, 'I believe that Miss Gilmour and Miss Daisy Carver had rather an unconventional *arrangement*.'

'No, they were just lesbians.' And after some of the things I've seen in the last couple of years, the weird places I've allowed Paul to lead me into, I can't get worked up about something as uncomplicated as that, she thought. 'What have I come into? What's Daisy left me?'

'The capital assets alone are in excess of half a million pounds. And then there are these.' He extracted a key from his watch-chain and began to walk across the linoleum-covered floor, towards a massive iron safe, in the corner of the room. 'This is something I have *not* forgotten how to do.'

The first thing to come out of the safe was a brown envelope, from which he produced a glossy theatrical photograph of a naked woman peering over the top of a wonderfully luxuriant feather fan. 'Old client of mine,' he said, twinkling roguishly. 'Vanda Bell, originally a Swinton girl. She's made a mint. But even Vanda wouldn't sniff at the contents of this old leather bag.'

The portmanteau he pulled from the depths of the safe brought Mary Poppins to mind. 'All yours,' he said, handing it to Dinah.

The rusted lock looked as though it had been broken for years. As Dinah pulled the two sides of the bag apart, it came open with a sigh. And she answered it with a gasp. Abanazar, she thought, must have felt like this when he first looked into Aladdin's cave.

Icons: Daisy's Russian icons jumbled one on top of the other, not even wrapped. 'I've not seen those since we cleared out her shed.' And she realised, with a great deal of guilt, that she had not seen their former owner since they had exchanged strong words about that replacement obsession. 'Are they studded with real jewels or are they just brilliants?' she wondered aloud.

'Real. Very real,' Adcock assured her. 'Worth rather more than the capital assets. As executors, we've already had them valued for probate.' Bertram Adcock hesitated for a moment. He was obviously embarrassed by the thought of what was coming next. 'I expect you know that Miss Carver owned large stretches of Irlams o' th' Height?'

'Streets of houses was the rumour.'

'An exaggeration, but the road redevelopment scheme left her even wealthier than before. Lest you should imagine there has been any *irregularity*,' he seemed very fond of this word, 'I should point out that these sums were made straight over to a religious organisation.'

'She couldn't stand churches.'

'Spiritualism,' he mouthed the word in the same way that Pendleton people mouth the word 'cancer'. 'A hundred and ten thousand pounds went straight to the June Gee Foundation.'

So Dinah's fears had been well grounded: Daisy had indeed swapped one addiction for another. And it sounded as though dabbling with the dead had cost her even more money than morphine.

That's another nail in your coffin, June Gee, thought Dinah. My own life is utterly valueless; one day I'll have yours.

But the icons and the holy brooches (St George and the dragon, and the head of John the Baptist) did have value. 'Do you have some old newspapers or something, to stop them banging against one another?'

The old lawyer looked round the office helplessly. 'I don't come in very often these days,' he said again, this time helplessly. He suddenly looked like a little boy whose holiday was coming to an end.

'They'll just have to bang.'

He saw her downstairs and they parted company on the main road, outside his office. 'You should really have brought a bodyguard with you.' Mr Adcock was nodding towards the old portmanteau. 'This marks the end of a very long connection, a very long connection indeed. My goodness, Swinton's changed,' he sighed.

The next little town up from the Height certainly had changed, reflected Dinah, as she made her way back to her car, which was parked beneath a concrete shopping precinct. Might it boast a fishmonger's, she wondered. Of course it couldn't be as good as our own little Didsbury fishmonger. My God, I've *joined* them, she thought. And just as we're leaving South Manchester for London – Belgravia no less! All her thoughts could have continued to take her into the future, had not the sight of a face brought back the past.

Rory's face.

Except it wasn't Rory because a priest's collar sat under that firm jaw – it was Holy Paddy.

'Wherever have they kept you hidden?' she cried in delight.

'I've been out of the diocese since you last saw me but I'm back now.' He seemed genuinely pleased to see her. 'We were going to have a beautiful new parish church.'

Memory had dimmed the blue of the eyes, the whiteness of the teeth. Except it's only the brother, she reminded herself sternly.

'It was going to be grand,' he enthused. 'We'd chosen it from a building catalogue. And then some flamin' Victorian Society stepped in, and now we've got to keep the old one. I'm just off to see the Vicar General. You're getting the speech intended for him. I've got to find money for a new roof in the original 1850s tiles. And disappointed people just won't give cash for that.'

'Paddy, I went to enormous lengths to try and find you. I think the bishop's palace thought I'd got a crush on you,' she laughed. It was just so good to see him again!

'How's John?'

'Dead. I'm married again.'

'Ah well, the years roll on.'

'Paddy?' She could hear herself assuming a false and wheedling Irish tone. 'Would you ever give me Rory's address?'

His own tones were the genuine item. 'I would not. Better left, love. Better left.'

'Is he married?' One glance at Paddy's face was enough to tell her that this was not the case. 'Paddy, do you remember that night at the Broadway Ballroom? When you and Gervase thingy-me-jig dressed in his brother's clothes – so you could meet girls.'

'Ah, the sins of youth.'

It had to be admitted that Paddy had grown a mite condescending but perhaps that went with the job. 'I never told anybody about that night,' said Dinah. 'Never. Give me Rory's address, Paddy. Please give it to me.' She was begging and she knew it. 'I only want to write and wish him well.' Was that a lie? She was not sure. But she wanted that address, she was sure of that.

And she got it.

After a moment's Christian consideration, Paddy fished in an inner pocket, pulled out a tiny flip-back notebook and a pen, and began to write. 'I just hope this doesn't get me in bad with the Boss.' Jocular eyes rose up to heaven.

'It won't, it won't,' she assured him fervently, and only just resisting the temptation to ask who it was that 'loved not wisely but too well'. 'All I'll do is drop him a note.'

Paddy handed over the scrap of paper. 'You look like Sherlock Holmes with that owd bag.'

'I think that boss of yours just spoke to me,' said Dinah. 'Just a minute.' She opened the portmanteau and handed him the first icon that came to hand. 'There's your new roof.'

By the time Father Paddy had ceased his paean of thanks, the bag was beginning to grow heavy in Dinah's hand. What was more she was hungry. Instead of going straight to the car she went into a pub called The Bull's Head and ordered a sandwich.

She had just thrust the gold-framed icon blindly at the priest, without looking which one she had given him. She only hoped it was not her favourite – St Anthony of Egypt. No, here he was, still sitting on top of his stone column in the middle of the desert – the sand was pictured in tiny canary diamonds. And here were the brooches.

'Are you with the pantomime at the Civic Hall?' The waitress had arrived with her ham sandwich.

'No, why?'

'I just thought that piece of costume jewellery was a bit garish for real life.'

It had been the ruby-studded John the Baptist brooch, still in its original Beriosova box. The only item she eventually kept for herself and never sent to Sotheby's. And this most unusual holy ornament was virtually identical to the one Miss Meech was wearing, here in the Queen's Room, today.

'Fascinating, my dear.' Miss Meech had been drinking in the whole story. Now, it seemed, she was after another one. 'When you sought my advice yesterday, you mentioned *eventual* sexual activity with your husband.'

'Yes but I wasn't sure whether it counted.'

Dinah suddenly saw the old woman in a new light. Saw her as pruriently curious. 'Miss Meech,' she said. 'With what I've told you already, have I got grounds for divorce?'

The lawyer looked gravely unhappy. 'This is precisely the dilemma I spoke of when we first met. This is why I gave up my divorce work. Holy Mother Church is much keener on the idea of two people trying to make a go of things.'

'Then you've had your last cheap thrill out of me!' Dinah was more annoyed with herself than with Miss Meech; years in business had led her to believe that she was an excellent judge of character.

And I was wrong, she thought, as she went to look for a staircase that would bring her out at the level of her stateroom.

'Dinah, hang on a minute.' A woman's voice was calling up the stairwell from the landing below.

It was a voice with which she had grown increasingly familiar in recent years, and it still reminded her of an infants' school teacher. And even here, on the *QE2*, Bea Palmer looked as though she should be supervising finger painting.

'Four days, flat on our backs,' she panted. 'I've not had so much as one meal in the Caronia Restaurant. We should have had the injections. Eric's done better

427

than me; at least he's managed to trot out and about a bit.'

So that's where Paul's been getting his tranquillisers, thought Dinah. 'Why didn't you tell us you were going to be on board, Bea?'

'Paul told us to keep it as a surprise for you.'

Paul would have known full well that she would have never boarded the ship had she known that they would be on the passenger list. When cross-dressing urges were upon them, Paul Snowden and Eric Palmer were a pair who could cause trouble in an empty house. And now they were loose on a crowded liner.

'I don't think our restaurant's going to be as posh as yours,' said Bea, 'but it's all wonderfully glamorous. I can't quite believe it, Sorrel Starkey's just walked past me as though she was an ordinary human being.'

The 'ordinary human being' was now sitting, alone, at one of the tables on the covered walkway opposite to the Chart Room, perusing a guide book to New York.

At the next table, two hefty middle-aged women were playing a card game she recognised as 'honeymoon bridge'. The mid-ocean atmosphere, that super-protected feeling that this voyage would go on for ever and ever, had been erased by many small indications that – tomorrow morning – the ship would be docking in New York. Down on Sorrel's own landing, the stewards were already delivering freshly pressed city clothes. And, just as Mickey had said she would, the Puerto Rican woman was sporting a hat with a wider brim than yesterday's.

One of the women at the next table slapped down some cards and said, 'So they can do nothing for Jean?'

'Nothing at all.'

Sorrel carried on leafing through the pages of *Manhattan Unveiled* and pretended not to be eavesdropping. She was trying to discover the whereabouts of the New York actors' church – the famous 'little church around the corner'.

'Charlie's absolutely beside himself.'

And I mustn't listen in to other people's conversations, she thought. Listeners never hear any good of themselves. Not that these coffee lace American matrons would have any idea who I am.

'They opened poor Jean up and that let the air in. You can let air into the womb but not into the stomach, not if it's malignant. They don't give her three months.'

Old wives' tales, thought Sorrel. I'm not going to let myself be frightened by old wives' tales. But she was frightened, very frightened. The kind of frightened that calls for a pair of arms around you. But the man they belonged to was dead.

So why am I worried about joining him? I'm not. If there *is* an after-life, I can't wait to see him again. It's pain I'm scared of: pain and this inescapable feeling that something's trying to eat its way out of me.

'Are you all right, love?' Polly Fiddler with a new hairstyle from the Steiner salon, was peering through her spectacles with an expression of magnified concern. 'I've just left love's young dream – Jack. He's trying to find Mickey to make another date for tonight. Are you okay?'

Sorrel was beyond lying. 'No. But I honestly don't want to talk about it.'

But Polly continued to look so like Lily Gander, the nextdoor neighbour who had brought warmth to Sorrel's chilly childhood, that the actress within gave way to the real person. 'I've probably got malignant cancer. I'll know in New York.'

'Where?'

'At the Algonquin Hotel.'

'Where've you *got* it, you pie-can!'

Sorrel's fingers went to her breast. 'Here.'

Polly took hold of the same hand. 'Feel,' she commanded as she guided it to her own bosom. 'False as a glass eye! The other one's real enough but the one you're prodding was taken off ten years ago. I'm still here,' she beamed. 'I'm living. But I've been where you are and it's the worst place on earth. Does the idea of being alive suddenly seem very sweet?' she asked cannily.

'Never more beautiful,' admitted Sorrel. 'Frightening but amazingly sweet.'

'Well it is sweet. Always was, always will be. And all any of us have got is this second. So why not enjoy it? Good morning, girls.'

Sorrel could hardly believe her ears. Polly had just addressed these words to two men who were promenading past. Girls? They didn't look gay at all: one had the appearance of an international businessman, the other could have been a publican.

'TVs,' said Polly. 'Straight trannys. I used to do Sunday night's relief behind the bar of a club at the back of Piccadilly. I remember those two from the days when they used to arrive with all their gear in carrier bags, and change in the toilets. The law goes easier on them these days.'

Sorrel reflected that the QE2 had a great deal more than quails' eggs and caviar and lecture recitals by Broadway composers, to take your mind off your troubles.

'But I know that kind,' continued Polly. 'Born exhibitionists! It's not in their nature to let an opportunity like this one slide. You mark my words, Sorrel: before we get to New York you're going to see the Ugly Sisters in person.'

18

This being the last night of the voyage, the dress code was 'informal'. By eight o'clock, Dinah had all her clothes out of the closets, and Bosnian Anna was busy with hangers and new tissue paper and the many-drawered steamer trunk. 'I no see the lady the other night,' she said suddenly.

'Don't worry, you'll get your tip.'

'I no see her,' she repeated.

No but I've got to, thought Dinah, and tonight. Her stomach gave a nervous lurch; it had been doing this all day, ever since she conceived her plan. A plan that left her wondering whether all this careful packing was strictly necessary. Tomorrow morning she might be led off the ship in leg irons and taken straight to Sing-Sing.

'Here,' she handed Anna the sealed tip envelope. She knew the woman wouldn't open it in front of her, they never did.

'You dine in Grill, Madam?'

'I'm not sure.' She was still waiting for June Gee to return her call – she had left a message on the answering machine in the psychic's cabin.

'Somebody at door,' said Anna.

'Let them in and I'll see you later.' Maybe June had chosen to appear in person. But the voice conversing with the maid, in the little entrance hall, was distinctly masculine. And it was Paul who walked through the archway into the sitting area. The beauty of his early manhood had long been replaced by an appearance of haggard grandeur. He looked rich and bored, and he looked like a man who wanted something.

'Pills,' he said, without any preamble.

'Where've you been? It's been days, practically the whole voyage.'

'Does it matter? I'm here now.' He held out a hand. 'Pills.'

They were no longer part of her plan. 'In my toilet bag in the bathroom. Take the lot with you, Paul. I'm sick of trying to save you from yourself.'

As he passed her he paused to stroke the sleeve of her grey, wool-crepe, cocktail dress. 'Nice,' he said. 'I love that silver beading – it's absolutely encrusted.' He said this last word in the lascivious tones that men on building sites generally reserve for words like 'tits'. 'But you know me, Di. I prefer something *silky*.'

You mean Pamela does, she thought. She knew the signs, she could almost feel the buzz coming off him. Pamela wasn't just simmering under the surface, she was about to make a public appearance. 'Paul, you wouldn't be so stupid? Not on a ship.'

'Moi?'

She always hated it when he fluttered his eyelashes. 'This isn't Marrakesh,' she said. 'I can't hope to shut a ship's captain up with a handful of foreign currency.'

The only answer she got was the sight of his back, disappearing into the bathroom. He emerged rattling plastic pill bottles like a pair of tiny maracas, and the Carmen Miranda imitation took him as far as the door, which closed behind him with an expensive click.

I'll draw a picture of those jiggling hands, thought Dinah. She had not packed her diary, it was still in the wall-safe. The diary, the water-colour crayons and – most precious of all – every single one of Rory's letters from America.

These had started to arrive after she had written her own tentative first note to the address provided by Holy Paddy. She had not meant the letter to be manipulative . . . or had she? It was just that she had needed to be able to tell *somebody* the truth, the absolute truth, about her second marriage.

In her youth, Rory Brogan had always represented a lot of things: her lover, almost her brother, her best friend. And she had chosen to write to the brotherly aspect of the man.

432

His replies were less terse than the bald communications of his days in the army. But these answers caught precisely the protective tone she needed. And just occasionally, in a noun or in a treasured adjective, she thought she could feel his love shining through. No, she *knew* it was still alive. And that was only at the beginning.

'I have become more Greek than a real Greek-Cypriot,' he wrote from New York. 'They are great ones for doing a bit of this and a bit of that. Nowadays I have no less than five different business interests.' There was a light engineering workshop, and a half-share in two soup 'n' sandwich bars; he also owned a building in the borough of Queens, which housed a gymnasium and some Greek culture centre. 'I devote a lot of my time to running a boxing club.'

Dinah's most treasured possession on earth was a photograph of him surrounded by Greek-American youths who were wearing athletic vests and shorts and protective headgear. But silver-haired Rory was in a grey track suit and he looked . . . he looked a man. Oh God, he looked such a man: tired around the eyes but still glorious.

The tone of his letters stayed relatively impersonal until Dinah wrote to him describing an event she still thought of as 'that night with Pamela'.

By this time the Snowdens were living in London, in a big flat in South Eaton Place, overly interior-decorated in a style that was, by turns, both sumptuous and restrained. Cream and white and bronze, to show off Paul's new collection of real – but sinister – 1890s Arts and Crafts Movement furniture.

The drawing room had a huge overhead light-fitting which had been specially made out of copper – battlemented and designed to take real candles. These were only lit on special occasions. But, that particular evening, Dinah had returned from a meeting with the accountants in High Holborn to find enough candles blazing to stage a remake of *The Bride of Frankenstein*.

And sitting beneath their dancing light was raven-haired Pamela, in a white silk dress which brought both

Ancient Greece and Bo Derek to mind, though the long black wig could have been borrowed from the mother in *The Munsters*.

'Why champagne?' asked Dinah, dumping her briefcase on a Voysey side table.

'Why not?' said Pamela from the depths of a massive sofa – a valuable Arab carpet had been used to upholster it. 'Why not?'

As she took off her gloves, Dinah noticed more flames flickering above the pillaged High Altar candlesticks. 'My God,' she said, 'shares in Price's Wax Nightlights must have gone up tonight!'

'This isn't just any night.' He was looking up at her from underneath heavy false eyelashes.

'Paul,' she said wearily. 'You have great taste; why do you always fuck up when it comes to Pamela's clothes?'

'You're not talking to Paul. And if you don't like my clothes, why don't you suggest?'

'No.' He was always trying to get her to play these 'two girls at home' games and she wasn't about to give in tonight. 'It's your life but I don't want anything to do with that side of you.' If only he had told her before they entered into this sham of a marriage, she thought for the thousandth time. I never had any choice in the matter, that's what's so unfair.

'I've not just swallowed champagne,' said Pamela.

'If you've been doing cocaine again, I'm going to a hotel.'

'I've swallowed two Vesuvius tablets.'

My God, thought Dinah in alarm, I always knew that pinching the formula of the Gentlemen's Remedy would come back to haunt me.

The false eyelashes were fluttering again, they were so fake they could almost have been battery-operated. 'Did you know that Pamela has a lesbian side?'

'I'm going out.'

'You're not.' Pamela kicked off her high heels and headed for the door to the corridor, turned the key in the lock demanded by the insurance people, and dropped

434

it between her fake breasts. These days, liquid Polycell and balloons had been abandoned in favour of the silk-covered jelly breast-forms more usually worn by women who had had mastectomies. 'You're not going anywhere. I'm horny as hell inside these knickers.'

'You are disgusting,' she shouted.

'So dominate me,' he said happily. 'Most girls like me adore powerful women. We've even been known to pay for the privilege.'

'There isn't enough money on earth.'

'I'm talking about hookers,' said Paul, watching her closely. His lipstick was a cruel shade of cerise. 'Anyway, you're my wife, and I've never had my conjugal rights, and I want them now.'

She slapped him right across the face, and all he did was take the gold kid belt from around the waist of the wide silk frock, so that even without shoes he suddenly looked like a towering parody of pregnancy. 'Hurt me with this instead.'

'No.' She was frightened now.

'If I raped you, would you punish me?'

'You just try it! Just try it, that's all.' Tones of Saracen Street in the middle of Belgravia.

And he did try. Clawing and fumbling and losing false fingernails, he forced himself upon her.

'*Afterwards he cried because it was all such a dismal failure*' was what Dinah wrote to Rory. And he wrote back offering to put her in touch with some Greeks in London who would be happy to 'take care' of Paul.

His letter read: '*If you were just free, if only you hadn't married him in church . . .*' And the church had only been because Paul had wanted a wedding that was all silk and lace. In later years she had often wondered whether he had ever tried the wedding dress on himself.

The sound of a ringing telephone recalled her to the shipboard present. Dinah picked up the receiver and a slurred voice said, 'It's Stella Artemis here, returning your call.'

'Ah yes,' Dinah was trying to keep very calm, 'that sitting you're going to give me: how about tonight?'

'I'd thought of coming to your hotel in New York.'

'I fear that will be one long board meeting,' improvised Dinah. 'No, I will give you a thousand dollars, in cash, to do it tonight.' Now she came to the part she had already rehearsed: 'But Miss Artemis, or may I call you June? Can we do it out on the open deck, by the swimming pool?' Mrs Mottershead would have been proud of her next bit of coy acting. 'You see there's a sailor in my past. Gone now, long dead.'

'There is no death,' said June automatically.

'No, of course not. Twelve o'clock, out on deck?' Most people, she surmised, would be in bed early tonight, in order to be up again to see dawn break over the Statue of Liberty.

'Make it just after twelve,' said June. 'I've gone onto a shrimp diet, they're through you in no time, so I'll be filling up again at the midnight buffet. You did say cash?'

Got you, thought Dinah. Got you like a fat rat in a trap.

'Why don't they melt?' Polly Fiddler asked Sorrel. She was peering at one of the ice sculptures, which towered above the seafood and the cold cuts of the midnight buffet in the Lido.

'They're melting even as we speak,' said Sorrel. 'Melting by the second.'

'And every one of those seconds brings us closer to New York.' Polly sounded nervous. 'I can't think why I thought I wanted to see that sister of mine. When we were girls, my mother always said that she had to keep a chair handy to shove between us – like an animal trainer.'

The late feast was more crowded than usual. Sorrel had already heard people around her announcing that, rather than get up early, they were going to dispense with sleep altogether. 'Are we having a dessert?' The one thing she did not want to do was catch the eye of June Gee, whom she had observed piling a plate with enough shellfish to open a small fishmonger's; now she was carrying her catch towards one of the exits to the open Quarter Deck.

'I'm not very gateaux-minded,' said Polly. 'The thing I'd really like to do is see the Yacht Club in action. It's the one place I've not been.'

'We might even find the boys there.' Mickey and Jack had spent yet another meal flashing one another smiles that were worthy of lighthouses. 'Let's look for a staircase.' How odd it was to think that all these passengers, whose faces had become as familiar to her as those of the extras in *Angel Dwellings*, would vanish from her life tomorrow morning.

'One level up or one down?' asked Polly. 'Five days and I'm still confused.'

'Up.'

This short flight of steps took them to the foot of a much more spectacular staircase. And coming down it were two figures whose long evening skirts proclaimed the fact that they had failed to read the Daily Programme.

'My God,' breathed Polly. 'Bartlett and Ross, back from the dead.'

It was years since Sorrel had heard the names of these female impersonators, once the most famous Ugly Sisters in British pantomime. And the descending 'women', in deep conversation near the top of the crowded staircase, could indeed have been dressed for a grande finale. The chubby little blonde was in a pink ruffled frock, reminiscent of Princess Diana before she got the clothes right. The haggard one, in the blue-black dinner dress, was also wearing a dark wig which had been styled to resemble Medusa's writhing snakes.

'Hello, Pamela,' bawled Polly Fiddler.

The towering brunette, arrested in her progress by the unexpected sound of her name, turned away from her companion and . . .

'Dear God, she's caught her heel in her hem,' breathed Sorrel.

Everything went into slow motion. People on the steep

stairs actually seemed to move to the sides to allow the grotesque figure to fall unimpeded. Nobody – not one single person – made the slightest move to stop this tumbling, bouncing, descent. And at the bottom, as the body rolled to an inelegant halt, the black wig fell off and revealed a cropped grey head.

'Pamela!' screamed the Max Factor pancake-faced blonde, from the head of the staircase. 'Ooh, Pamela.'

'Did I say *back* from the dead?' asked Polly Fiddler quietly. And this time she was not joking.

This Jacuzzi has become 'our place' thought Mickey, the midnight whistle our serenade. This time Mickey, too, had not bothered with bathing trunks. Instead, he had just wrapped a towel around his waist in the changing room, and slipped it off to climb naked into the swirling waters.

Over to you, Jack, he thought. You started this, let's see where it's going to get us tonight.

Silence, save for the sounds of automated bubbling and the faint throbbing of the ship's engine; but no words – that kind of silence. Out of the corner of his eye Mickey observed a distant figure in flared slacks and a glittering cocktail top, emerging from inside the ship. Could it be? It was. June. June Gee carrying a plate of something and settling her weight into a deck chair, in the moonlight.

Still no conversation; just companionable quiet which managed to be erotic around the edges. And then: 'How much are you like the young writer in a *A Town To Remember*?'

'He's me. They're all me. Even Red Biddie was me.' Under the circumstances, was it sensible – attractive – to align himself with this famous female harridan?

But Jack returned to the hero of the first novel with: 'He didn't have time for love. Do you?'

'Are you offering?'

'Are you buying?'

'Depends on the price.' God in heaven above, thought

Mickey, this man's past turns every conversation into a minefield.

'That was below the belt,' said Jack quietly.

Mickey tried to mend the atmosphere with, 'You haven't got a belt on. Neither of us have. We've abandoned who we usually are.' And if that sounded high-flown, it was nothing like as extravagant as the line from *The Merchant of Venice* which he was having to restrain himself from quoting. *You see me, Lord Bassanio, where I stand, Such as I am.* His attention was deflected by moonlight flashing onto a glass door. Some woman had opened it, and now she was moving across to join June Gee.

Fancy June feeding her face out on deck, thought Dinah, as she approached the clairvoyant and her plate of jumbo prawns.

'I'm just tuning in,' explained June as she chomped. 'Getting in on the beam. Navarna has to be centred right in front of my middle eye for it to work.' She removed a brooch, but it soon became clear that this was not for any psychic reason when she began to use the pin as a toothpick. 'It's not true that you mind things less as you get older. Not in your case, anyway. That's what Navarna's telling me. Did you bring the money?'

'Yes.'

'I'm being given an Irish tenor now. I think it's John McCormack. He's singing "Macushla". Would that signify?'

Impressed, in spite of herself, Dinah blurted out, 'Yes.'

'Who's Roy?'

'You mean Rory.'

'That's right, Rory.'

This is exactly what happened, all those years ago, in the Co-op Hall, thought Dinah, amazed. It's almost word-for-word the same thing. 'Rory is somebody whose life you ruined. Just like you ruined mine.'

June immediately rose to her feet, wobbling with indignation. 'I beg your pardon!'

'Don't waste time begging my pardon,' said Dinah

439

firmly, 'because there's no way I could ever forgive you.' This attempt at control gave way to outraged fury. 'You wrecked my life and Rory's and you even blood-sucked a fortune out of poor little Daisy Carver.' She had edged the psychic, who was still holding onto her plate of prawns, right up against the ship's varnished rail. 'You're bad. You stink. You're going right over the side.'

'Are you mad?' gasped June as she swiped out at Dinah with the plate. But she lost her hold on it, and prawns and plate clattered to the deck.

Dinah pinned her up against the rail again. Though she could tell that the old circus elephant was terrified, she had not bargained for her putting up such a struggle. But Dinah Snowden was fuelled by anger. Years and years of frustration went into her attempt to punch June in the stomach.

If the spangled blonde was flabby, she was also made of cunning. She had diffused the impact of the blow by doubling herself up like a screeching folding bed. 'Help,' she screamed. 'Murder!'

Dinah tried to put a hand over June's mouth but the psychic retaliated with a savage bite. And still she was kicking out and screaming for somebody, anybody, to come to her assistance.

That was the moment when Dinah felt herself grabbed by the elbows, from behind. She wrenched her head around to discover that she was being restrained by a man with no clothes on. None at all. And June was being similarly restrained by another naked man – one who was spectacularly well hung.

'I had to stop you,' said Mickey to Dinah. 'She's not worth it. Nobody loathes her like I loathe her but she's already been dealt her punishment: she has to go through life as herself.'

Even more frustration than she had ever felt before, plus a terrible sense of anti-climax, had reduced Dinah to tears. 'I was going to do it,' she sobbed. 'I wasn't messing, I *was* going to do it.'

'I know.' As he stroked her dishevelled hair out of

her eyes, Mickey could have been soothing Sorrel. 'I do know.'

By now June had started to get her breath back. 'You saw what she did, Mickey – heard what she said. I'm going to sue that woman for every penny she's got. I'll have the roof from over your head,' she snarled at Dinah.

'No you won't,' said Mickey.

'I'll go to the police,' she yelled.

But he had already remembered the carpet bag full of research material, down in his cabin. 'If you go to the police, so will I. I've still got a tape-recording of you trying to get thirty thousand quid out of me. Fancy another trip to Holloway?'

June looked long and hard at Jack Lawless's nether regions. 'You ought to keep that thing on a reel,' she said. Now she turned her attention to Mickey. 'Remember the first day we met, in Rookswood Avenue, when we were eight? You said: "My name is Mickey Grimshaw and, no, you can't see my dick for sixpence." And I told you then that, one day, I'd see it for nothing.' She flashed him a look of boldest triumph. '*Now* try and tell me there's nothing in clairvoyance!'

High above them, the ship's Tannoy crackled into life and a disembodied voice said, 'Would passenger Dinah Snowden please report to the purser's office immediately. Dinah Snowden to the purser's office immediately please.'

Tonight the long corridor on Two Deck was something of an obstacle course. There were stacks of luggage outside the door to each cabin, and, once again, the red boiler-suited Filipinos were much in evidence.

'Coming in?' Jack asked Mickey, his key already in the lock.

'Why not?' Why, he wondered, were they both giving performances that were about as wooden as the straight acting parts in Jack's films?

It was the first time that Mickey had set foot in these pastel-shaded quarters, but his attention was immediately caught by the one item in primary colours. A boxed video entitled *Your Night With Lawless*.

'I talk to the camera,' explained Jack. 'Well, to begin with. But that's only the soft-core British version.' He flung himself down on one of the beds.

Mickey chose to flop onto the other. 'How many English guys are there doing your sort of work in Hollywood?'

Jack began to count them off. 'Aiden Shaw and Grant King and that other guy from Liverpool . . .' Suddenly sitting up again he looked Mickey straight in the eyes, just like the photograph on the front of the video. 'Do you want the private show?'

Mickey Grimshaw was surprised to find himself pausing and considering his answer. He was thinking of a gay cinema in San Francisco. An establishment in the Tenderloin District which featured live appearances by the same performers who starred in the triple X-rated films. 'You ever appear at the Trade Theatre?'

'Sure, when I was starting out. And collected dollar tips inside the top of my white gym socks.'

These were all the clothes that the handsome and sexually aroused performers had left on, by the time they descended into the auditorium. A loud speaker announcement always said: 'The laws of the State of California do not permit patrons to fondle the genitalia or buttocks of the performers. But tips are acceptable and indeed welcome.'

Though the theatre had a runway, which jutted through the middle of the stalls at eye-level, the strippers soon jumped right down amongst the audience. The place was rarely packed. The people present had reminded Mickey of teeth left inside a partially decayed mouth. And the nude performers would position themselves in the gaps, and encourage each member of the audience to touch them anywhere but the officially prohibited areas.

Those guys must have experienced every shade and shape of fingertip on earth! Here and now, what could Mickey hope to offer that was new? 'No,' he said quietly. 'I'm the one who doesn't want to see the private show.'

Jack let out a little sigh of purest contentment. Very politely he asked: 'Would you mind if I came and just lay down next to you?'

'It's your cabin.' Did that sound churlish? 'No, please do. It would be nice.'

'If a bit like John Wayne and Gary Cooper.' Having transferred from one bed to the other, Jack was now indicating the decorous space between them.

Something told Mickey not to move across it. And if we're not careful a grim silence is going to loom up, he thought. Sooner or later it always happens, when we're together. Borrowing one of Jack's own tricks, he said, 'Tell me what you're thinking.'

'I'm thinking about the school that fucked me up. Talk about Dotheboys Hall! Nicholas Nickleby didn't experience the half of it. Or if he did, Charles Dickens drew a veil over it. Is this boring you?'

And that's another of your social dodges, thought Mickey. 'No,' he replied, just as he was meant to do. 'Not a bit boring.' Why was Jack moving a couple of inches even further away from him?

'The child psychiatrist was the worst. He came in from outside. I was thirteen,' Jack remembered. 'He used to lock the door and inject me with pentathol. And then he'd get me to tell him my sexual fantasies.'

'Like what?'

Jack sat up, his whole body language had changed, turning him into somebody who was putting a brake on the desire to writhe. 'He got me to assume positions.' The words sounded curiously formal. They could have been an iron manhole-cover over thoughts that were too dark to reveal.

Mickey's immediate instinct was to reach out and put his arms around the man reliving torment. But, again, his instincts warned him that to touch might be to ally himself with Jack's inward recollections. That he could become part of the terrible darkness. Just for something to say, he asked: 'What did this bastard look like?'

'Rod Steiger and I think I loved him.'

I'm getting out of here, thought Mickey. And fast.

'Could we meet up in New York?' asked Jack quietly. 'Could we just go out and about a bit, like two guys who are getting to know one another. I *like* you. Oh I *do* like you.'

. There was longing in these words, and pain. And it's all too complex, thought Mickey. Hating himself, he said: 'I don't think we could do that.'

'Why?' The voice could have belonged to the boy in that locked room.

Mickey already had the line rehearsed, though he had not been expecting to deliver it under these circumstances. 'This was only ever going to be a little shipboard romance.'

'Have the private show anyway.' Jack rose to his feet, and started to unbutton his shirt.

The eyes which gazed into Mickey's had changed, they could have belonged to any sidewalk hustler. They took him straight back to other pairs of eyes, male strippers' in the Trade Theatre. 'Look,' he said awkwardly, 'I don't want this. Honestly, I don't want it.'

Jack's hands fell to his side. 'Then that means I've got nothing to offer you – nothing at all. I think you'd better go.'

Whatever else Dinah had been expecting to find in the purser's office, it was not a crowd. But that was what had assembled to receive her: the purser himself, the Anglican chaplain (who proved to be American), the social secretary, and Miss Meech and Father Ambrose.

'We actually witnessed your husband's demise,' explained the woman lawyer. 'I felt it beholden upon me to come because I was sure that you would be having to handle mixed emotions.'

This was no less than the truth. Dinah had been placed upon a typist's swivelling chair and everybody was circulating around her as though she was already wearing wide-skirted widow's weeds. Somebody had inadvertently let out the fact that Paul's body was 'on ice'. And she found herself wondering whether he was in the same cabinet as the ice sculptures from the midnight buffet. And whether it would be a last kindness to try to have him buried as a lady?

By now it was five past one in the morning, and there had been much talk of 'head office' and of the British Ambassador and of the New York Port Authority.

'Your poor head must be buzzing,' said Miss Meech. 'Is she free to go now?' she enquired of the purser.

'Yes, of course. Would you like somebody to look after you?' he asked Dinah.

'I shall do that,' said Miss Meech firmly. 'We had already struck up a degree of intimacy.' She paused for a moment, perhaps to give Dinah a chance to deny this. But the new widow was too dazed to react. 'Come along.' Miss Meech had seized the advantage again. 'I want you to just come and sit down quietly in my cabin.'

It was not far away, just one deck downstairs. Miss Meech got rid of the priest along the way; you could tell she had once been a member of the Church of England by the casual way in which she said, 'That will be all, Father, thank you.'

The lawyer's accommodation was only marginally less lavish than Dinah's. But it was much more Holy. The dressing table could have belonged to the last Czarina of Russia: it was piled with icons, and standing in their midst was a baroque crucifix hung with several sets of rosary beads. And – yes – the once-so-familiar tapes of an old green scapular.

'I'm going to leave you to sit here on your own for a little while,' said Miss Meech. 'You need to collect yourself, you need a little peace. And goodness only knows there are enough properly blessed objects in this room to grant you that. I shall only be next door with Mrs Hagan,' she reassured Dinah. 'She was with me at the moment of the er . . . tumble.'

Skinny Muriel Meech, with her tightly scraped-back hair, hesitated in the doorway. 'Could you find it in your heart to try to forgive your husband? It would be awful if this whole business was to turn your life rancid. Just next door – that direction.' She was already gone.

But what was there to forgive? He stole knickers off lines, he dressed up as a woman. So what? If anything was unfair it was that I married two people instead of one. And it took me years to find out. But we prospered. My goodness, we prospered. There's nothing on earth I haven't been able to have – except the one thing I always wanted. So, if you want forgiving, Paul, I forgive you.

Had the presence of all the sacred objects adjusted the atmosphere? All Dinah knew was that a strange feeling was beginning to steal across her mind. And yet it wasn't new: it was as old as her childhood, as inexplicable as the magic caught within the smell of incense at St Luke's, as familiar as the hopeful aura around the boulder at The Place. It was as though tonight and the past, and all of that and all of this, were one and the same thing.

As she gave herself up to this amazing idea, it dawned upon Dinah that – at long last – no lawful impediment stood between herself and Rory Brogan – that he was only one ship-to-shore telephone call away from her.

Raincoats were in evidence again for the first time since Southampton. Not that it was raining, just cold and shadowy, out on the Boat Deck, which could have been a stage – lit for a rehearsal. Mickey said to Sorrel, 'We're already in the Hudson River.' These words still had the power to strike excitement in the pit of his stomach.

And fear into Sorrel's heart. Somewhere out there in the darkness lay New York, where the results of those gruesome tests awaited her. 'Look, there's Jack, over by the rail,' she said.

'No Sorrel, I won't look.' Mickey spoke warningly and incisively. She had been asleep by the time he eventually got back from an unhappy nocturnal roam around the ship, and the story of the death of Paul Snowden had taken precedence this morning. 'Leave him be.'

Somebody else was doing the same thing. The Puerto Rican woman was steering her younger friend past Jack Lawless in the manner of a nun in charge of a whole procession of schoolgirls.

Mickey suddenly found himself filled with anger. 'I wish a wind would rise up, and get under that great black brim of hers, and *blow* her to Manhattan!'

'Why the fury?'

'It's probably with myself.' He was quieter now. 'It *is* with myself.'

'Why don't you just go over and say hello?'

'Because we already said good-bye. Don't look now, but there's the new widow, over there. And not in black, either.'

Ten yards away, Dinah was only too aware that a whole lot of people were trying not to stare. But what did she care? Her on-board bill was going to be enormous because she had spent half the night talking to Rory on the telephone. And even at this moment he was probably getting out of bed to come and meet her on the quayside.

This gloriously satisfying thought was suddenly interrupted by somebody crying out 'There she is!' just as they had done when the Manchester Italian Society carried the Madonna along Deansgate. But this time they were talking about the Statue of Liberty. Her upraised torch was casting a beam of phosphorescent green light onto the dark surface of the water. And tugboats were already edging sideways across the waves – like crabs.

From the boat deck of the QE2 an old woman's voice rose up in spontaneous song.

> *'How beautiful for spacious skies . . .'*

Others joined in. Some wept. Dinah heard a man saying, 'When my grandfather arrived from the Old Country they kept him on Ellis Island for three weeks.'

> '. . . America, America
> God shed his grace on thee
> And crown thy good with brotherhood
> From sea to shining sea.'

'When Noel Coward said "Strange how potent cheap music is" he certainly said a mouthful!' Mickey Grimshaw had moved across to join Dinah. 'Are you okay? Still going to the Pierre?'

'Not now.' She risked saying it aloud. 'When I was a little girl I fell in love with somebody and he's waited all these years for me.' And now dawn was truly breaking over New York. 'It really is an island, isn't it?' she exclaimed. 'I always forget how like a child's pop-up book it is.'

'A city in 3-D,' said Mickey happily, 'with stereophonic sound. And we don't even have to clear Customs and Immigration.' They had already done that, the previous evening, when Port Authority officials had come aboard by cutter.

'Is it wicked of me to be a happy woman?' asked Dinah. 'Because that's what I am, I'm finally happy.'

The luxury of Cunard's service becomes most apparent when it is over. One moment Mickey and Sorrel were still pampered guests of the shipping line, the next they were out on the clanging quayside, in the massively echoing boatshed, knowing only that their luggage would be in a section marked 21.

'Porter!' yelled the experienced voice of Mickey Grimshaw.

'Somebody's already got him,' said Sorrel.

'No, they can pile their barrows yards high. Over here, Porter. There's no rush now,' he said to Sorrel. 'We'll see him again in the taxi queue – outside.'

'Has the ship really brought us right into the heart of New York?' she asked in wonder.

'Right there. The Algonquin's just minutes away.' How

are the mighty fallen, eh? He was looking at the ant-like scurryings of passengers who had suddenly ceased to be little emperors and empresses. 'Watch that fucking bag,' yelled a woman whom he recalled as an elegant mid-Atlantic socialite. 'That bag's got a fuckin' computer in it!'

'Nice language, I *don't* think!' Polly Fiddler had materialised in a royal-blue gaberdine raincoat. Except, amazingly, there were two of her.

'Polly, you never told us you were a twin,' gasped Sorrel.

'I've spent most of my life trying to forget it. Forty years apart and she still turns up wearing near enough the same coat as me!'

'Mickey,' called out another woman's voice. It belonged to Dinah Snowden. 'Could you just come and meet somebody? Mickey's the man who saved me from going to the electric chair.' She was talking to a tall man who was holding on to her as though he had chained himself to a box of valuables.

A dish, thought Mickey. Knocking on a bit but a great smile and a body that must have lived in a gym.

'All mine,' said Dinah quietly.

'Would you please come to the wedding?' asked the man, with real gratitude.

'So there's going to be one?' asked Mickey.

'There is.' Suddenly sounding much more Irish, Rory Brogan said, 'I don't have to tell you that there's a bit of a funeral to sort out first. It doesn't do to speak ill of the dead but I'd willingly dig the bastard's grave myself.'

She's got somebody to look after her, thought Mickey, as they all moved outside, into the sunlight. I've spent the last few years making sure there was always a roof over Joe and me, I spent a lifetime making fortunes for other people: where's the somebody who's going to watch over me?

He found himself repeating an old mantra, all but saying it out loud: 'Negative thoughts and negative actions have no power to harm me at any level of consciousness.'

I've got myself, he thought. And I've always been bloody lucky to have me!

'Just think,' he said to Sorrel, 'we were only little kids when we met in that genteel boarding house in Blackpool, and here we are in beautiful, towering, million promises, New York.' Even the taxis were coming onto the rank at a high-energy pace. 'Come to think of it, we're going to another boarding house this morning – the poshest literary and theatrical one on earth.'

But the name 'Algonquin' held no magic for the driver. His identification details, in the back of the cab, proclaimed him to be Mohamet Mahmoud, his English was non-existent, and Mickey was obliged to write down the address of the hotel. 'Probably Iranian,' he said. 'They're the latest. If you look out of the window, Sorrel, you'll see that the streets go one way and the avenues the other.'

How he could patronise! 'I believe I learned that in the Olympia Cinema, Irlams o' th' Height, when I was five years old.' New York, she reflected, did not look as though it had changed a lot since those days. And then she wondered how much her own body had changed, altered, been eaten away, since the ship left Southampton. In her mind's eye she could already see the varnished wooden pigeonhole, behind a hotel reception desk – the tiny compartment which would contain her death sentence.

'Your first sight of a Broadway theatre.' Mickey was pointing through the smeared window again.

'But I didn't think we were on Broadway.'

'Neither are most of the theatres. Look, Sardi's!'

I'll never have a New York first night now, she thought. I'll never go to Sardi's Restaurant to wait for the reviews.

'Here,' bawled Mickey. 'Stop.' The driver obeyed so peremptorily that the whole of the back seat shot forward.

As they got out of the cab a woman walked straight up to Mickey and said, 'Pardon me, Sir, but have you just had a facial?'

He felt quite pleased. 'As a matter of fact I haven't.' It took him several seconds to register the McDonald's paper cup and the fact that she was begging.

Porters were already wresting the baggage from the trunk of the cab as Sorrel said, 'This hotel looks like those drab places that used to surround Russell Square in London, when we were young.' There was a cat lying on top of the radiator in the narrow entrance hall, and when they got into the real lobby everything seemed frozen in 1954. 'It's just like the set for *Separate Tables*, even down to the potted palms.'

'For God's sake lift your jewel case off that chair,' hissed Mickey. 'It's sacred, they keep it for some ghost. Good morning,' he beamed at the woman receptionist. 'I expect you're tired of being told that you look like the young Jackie Kennedy. My name is Grimshaw and this is Miss Starkey travelling as Mrs Shapiro. I believe you have a little suite for us.'

'And I believe we have a fax for Mrs Shapiro.'

Oh my God, it's a varnished wooden pigeonhole, thought Sorrel. Just like the one I saw inside my head. And here comes the sheet of white paper. I just can't bring myself to reach out for it, I can't. This could be my very last moment for holding on to any kind of hope.

'Want me to read it?' Mickey had already taken the fax from the receptionist.

Sorrel nodded and watched his face. For the second time that trip she thought she saw the suggestion of tears in his eyes. She closed her own.

'You're okay,' he said. 'Listen: "Tests proved negative. Call me when you get back. Give my love to the Big Apple." And it's signed Martin Schachter.'

Troubles of the world removed from their shoulders, the new arrivals gave themselves up to the pleasant business of signing in. And the two porters, a pair of Jewish cross-talk comics out of a 1940s film, must have decided they were definitely staying because they began moving the luggage towards a small lift. 'Shapiro, huh?' said one, without any attempt at lowering his voice. 'He musta married out.'

Upstairs, the door of the suite opened straight into a small sitting room. 'And look who's hanging on the wall,' cried Sorrel in delight. 'It's an original cartoon of Noel Coward and Gertrude Lawrence.'

'It's a photocopy,' Mickey corrected her. 'And I'll bet you anything that the frame's screwed down as far as the brickwork. Welcome to New York! What do you want to do first?'

'I think I'd like to go to a meeting,' she said quietly.

Mickey was all impatience: 'You're never craving for a drink?'

'No. But we're meant to share the good times as well as the bad.'

All of this was beyond him. In Mickey's mind, people either had a drink or said 'No thank you'. But presumably she knew what she was doing.

'There are dozens of meetings a day, here,' she said. 'I've already got a number to ring. Then all I have to do is get a taxi. But I should do it, Mick.'

He had things to do too. Just as in his childhood a visit to Blackpool had always involved checking that the Opera House and the Grand Theatre were still standing, here in Manhattan he liked to cast an eye over old stomping grounds.

As he crossed Times Square he realised that he was walking in an unaccustomedly butch manner. Mickey started to laugh. Five days at sea have given me a sailor's roll, he thought. That should stand me in good stead on 42nd Street. But he was in for a surprise.

Mary Poppins had taken over from the Midnight Cowboy: West 42nd Street, once the haunt of male hustlers, the home of porno cinemas, was busy being sanitised by the Disney Organisation.

Where did we all queue up to see John Holmes? he wondered. And which corner housed that battered dime museum, the freak show where Tiny Tim was once on exhibition as 'the human canary'? It must surely have been here: 42nd at 8th Avenue.

He was looking to the left and the right for the New York equivalents of the Trade Theatre in the Tenderloin. The Eros Cinema was still open for business, but the

Show Place (See The XXX Stars in Person) and Gay Male Follies had both vanished. So the stories which had reached England, the ones about the Mayor starting to clean everything up, were true.

It must all be going on *some*where, he reasoned. That sort of thing doesn't just go away. And where were all the video stores? Mickey finally admitted to himself that he had come out to buy a wistful souvenir.

He had already wandered past the Port Authority Bus Station when he saw the neon sign, House of Tomcats. And he remembered the store which lay behind two windows full of sun-bleached physique magazines and faded video covers.

It was about the size of a branch of W H Smith's in an English seaside resort. In its own way it was every bit as comprehensive. Magazines and sex toys took up the front half of the shop. The rear was filled with a rabbit warren of library shelves – stacked with many thousands of boxed videos.

There was nothing of the British 'under the counter' atmosphere to these sales proceedings. The stock was so wide-ranging that it would not have been unrealistic to demand the whereabouts of 'the older skinheads section'. As it was, Mickey browsed his way past the great pre-Aids classics, *The Boys Of Venice* and *Like a Horse,* and marvelled that he had ever been shocked by the photo-illustrations on the boxes.

Hitler's Germany must have desensitised people like this, he thought. The first time you saw something, you were staggered. The second time caught you thinking, Oh that again. By a third sighting it had become a case of So what?

Not that he was sitting in judgment. If radical women wanted to rant against heterosexual pornography, that was their business. The one thing they never seemed to understand was that gay men loved being sex-objects.

By now, he had reached a somewhat perverse section: one which involved tin baths and urine. And there were limits and Mickey Grimshaw had reached his. And yet, he reflected, in its own bizarre way, this world was curiously reminiscent of the worlds of television and publishing. And the performers, it seemed, were just like authors doing a bit of personal snooping in book shops.

'How am I doing?' asked a deep voice. 'How have my sales been while I was in Europe?'

Except, it wasn't just any deep voice – it belonged to Jack Lawless. Mickey froze in his tracks, which kept him screened behind a section labelled 'Tattooed'.

'You're selling good. How's your sobriety? You still doing the meetings?'

'Sure. You?'

'Yeah, yeah.'

Not for the first time, Mickey wondered whether the whole of the United States was on a Twelve Step Recovery Programme. And I shouldn't be listening like this, he thought. I should be finding the Solo section. But the one soloist he was seeking was still talking.

'I was already thinking about stopping doing clients, before I left. And now I'm going to give up all this video pigswill, too. Once you get past thirty, an orgasm in close-up adds ten years to your age.'

The other man's voice suggested agreement. 'Towards the end, the veins in poor old John Holmes's neck stood out like parachute chords.'

I could be here all morning, thought Mickey. Should he, he wondered, reveal himself?

'The real reason I'm quitting is that I found my way to my feelings again.'

'Congratulations.' There was no irony in the other man's voice.

'It was a guy on the ship – older. And he didn't give two fucks for me.'

'Wrong.' Mickey had stepped right out into the light. Self-doubt crept in again as he asked: 'You *were* talking about me?' Oh that smile, he thought. And there are great reserves of kindness behind those mocking green eyes.

'Yeah, I was talking about you.'

'Then come for a walk.'

Jack spread his hands as if to say 'What else is there to do?' and led the way out into the sunlight. 'So where we going?' he asked.

Viewed from the top of the Empire State Building, New York was even more like a pop-up book. 'It's for all the world like looking down on Gotham City,' said Mickey. He and Jack were outside on the observation deck, which was caged round with serious metal fencing, with inwards-curving spikes.

'Excuse me,' said a voice which could only have belonged to an old queen, 'but don't I know your face from Manchester?'

Not here, thought Mickey in near despair. Never *Angel Dwellings* up here!

The little man, addressing him, looked like Humpty Dumpty: bald head, bow tie, and all. 'Oh yes,' he continued, 'I would have recognised you anywhere. You're Rusty Taylor and you used to have a club in Pitt Street – the Troubadour.'

It would be easier to lie. 'Quite right.'

'Happy days,' beamed the man.

'And nights.' Mickey started nudging Jack towards one of the viewing machines (25 cents to zoom in on any bit of cityscape of your choice). It was the younger man who provided the coin, and Mickey chose to focus upon Pier 90, where the *QE2* was still drawn up.

'Don't let anybody tell you that's just a ship,' he said to Jack. 'She rights wrongs, she heals breaches, she brings people together. I love her, I really love her.'

'What if I was to say that I love you,' ventured Jack quietly. 'What if I asked you whether *we* were going to have happy days?'

'I'd feel obliged to ask about the nights.'

'I want to wake up and find you there. I want to be able to say "listen to the rain on the window".' He paused for a moment. 'As for the other: I'd like to start right out again, from the very beginning, and invent it as we go along.'

'And you'll never get a fairer offer than that, Rusty.' Humpty Dumpty had crept up on them again, from behind. 'What a lovely moment. God bless you my children! Do you know something,' he said cosily, 'I feel as though I've just performed a marriage ceremony.' And still he chattered on: 'What a coincidence, us meeting up here, like this.'

'There are no coincidences,' insisted both Mick and Jack. And, for the very first time, the pair of them could have been speaking in one confident voice.

Also available in Arrow:

☐ Behind Closed Doors	Tony Warren	£5.99
☐ Foot of the Rainbow	Tony Warren	£4.99
☐ The Lights of Manchester	Tony Warren	£4.99
☐ Lily-Josephine	Kate Saunders	£5.99
☐ Night Shall Overtake Us	Kate Saunders	£6.99
☐ Wild Young Bohemians	Kate Saunders	£5.99
☐ Breaking the Chain	Maggie Makepeace	£5.99
☐ Travelling Hopefully	Maggie Makepeace	£5.99
☐ The Would-Begetter	Maggie Makepeace	£5.99

ALL ARROW BOOKS ARE AVAILABLE THROUGH MAIL ORDER OR FROM YOUR LOCAL BOOKSHOP AND NEWSAGENT.

PLEASE SEND CHEQUE/EUROCHEQUE/POSTAL ORDER (STERLING ONLY) ACCESS, VISA, MASTERCARD, DINERS CARD, SWITCH OR AMEX.

☐☐☐☐☐☐☐☐☐☐☐☐☐☐☐☐☐

EXPIRY DATE.................. SIGNATURE...

PLEASE ALLOW 75 PENCE PER BOOK FOR POST AND PACKING U.K.

OVERSEAS CUSTOMERS PLEASE ALLOW £1.00 PER COPY FOR POST AND PACKING.

ALL ORDERS TO:
ARROW BOOKS, BOOK BY POST, TBS LIMITED, THE BOOK SERVICE, COLCHESTER ROAD, FRATING GREEN, COLCHESTER, ESSEX CO7 TDW.

NAME...

ADDRESS..

....

Please allow 28 days for delivery. Please tick box if you do not wish to receive any additional information. ☐

Prices and availability subject to change without notice.